BECOMING

THE TRUE STORY OF A PERFECT
LOVE GONE RIGHT

BOOK 4

—

*…come to these books with a willingness
to read beyond the expected.*

MICHAEL DEMERS

www.trafford.com
North America & international
toll-free: 1 888 232 4444 (USA & Canada)
fax: 812 355 4082

Introduction

"It matters not where my consciousness centers in this life or the next, or what anyone teaches differently, or however I may be challenged and criticized by others who see it differently and want to sway me to their way of seeing it, or who say my dream is impossible. As my soul roams the universe it will always be with the utmost thought and fixed determination that I am becoming or that I AM Adam!

Only in that manner can I create the reality I want for myself. Only with that strength can I attract the Woman to me who shares my dream exactly. That's what I want, that's what I am becoming regardless of any other soul who would tempt and beckon me into worlds of their own choosing. I am not theirs, they are not mine. The gods keep the timing, when the time is right for me, my well-beloved Eve will appear, and we will be ONE..." Michael Demers

Michael Demers retired comfortable, built a dream home in the Mojave Desert near Las Vegas, Nevada USA and settled in with Jen his beautiful wife. Baby boomers both they had worked hard, built a successful investment business and were about to enter their golden years. The marriage had been sweet except for a growing malaise in the last two years. No longer busy business partners they were spinning their wheels and not spinning them fast, Jen on mindless activities, Michael on the sofa reading.

Resentment was growing. Jen left his bed for another room and he didn't chase her, even when she beckoned from her bedroom door, bathrobe falling open, relaxed and ready, naked body steamy from a hot bath with candles. That was unusual for him, his sexual needs had always been strong and she had fulfilled, content with her man. They loved to spoon naked, mornings had always come with a smile as she did her makeup. Sometimes he stood behind her and brushed her hair, he was gentle, they were in love. But now with neglect she was growing distant, his mind was beginning to wander. Perhaps without knowing it they were preparing for what was to come, who knows how such things work…

Then for the third night in a row Michael alone in his bed had a recurring dream. He heard a voice telling him he'd become Adam and live forever if he could find Eve, the woman with a matching dream. It left a powerful waking impression, he felt that he could no longer ignore the voice, he had to do something.

Michael abandoned his retirement home, his enviable lifestyle and his wife. He bought a motor home and set out across America in search of adventure and Eve. Michael had always wanted to be a writer, his rational mind told him he was updating Steinbeck's *Travels with Charley* but he soon abandoned that too. There was something else driving him, pushing him hard, he was getting older, *he had to find Eve!* Along the way Michael kept a journal and made it public, it's a *delicious* read, I think you'll like it.

As we follow Michael we'll peek often into his private emails and we'll know in the end if he found Eve and became Adam, and what became of Jen left behind alone in her garden. Was Adam's Eve all along the woman growing roses, the acres of diamonds in Michael's back yard? Or is this story of a perfect love gone right the story of Michael and another woman he picked up along the way? We'll find out because this story is true, it really happened….

Let's dip into Michael's journal right here, a year after his adventure began. By now he has leased out the motor home and is living alone, a single man, divorced, renting a modest apartment by the sea in Victoria, British Columbia Canada. He's creating a series of books out of the million words he wrote into his journal as he traveled for a year. When an email begins with "M" it's a message Michael sent to someone. Here's how Michael wrote it himself.

M: (to Elaine) It was pleasant chatting with you over coffee today, I always appreciate your company and your time and counsel, you are dear to me. As we chatted I pretended you were my book editor, your every word needing to be preserved, in this case scribbled on a napkin.

I will enjoy making the changes you suggested, they are valuable to me, a woman's point of view on my male writing, most of my readers will be women. I think my readers will eventually come to like book character Michael, I mean once you get to know him what's there *not* to like? But in the beginning yes, he did buy a motor home and leave home with the intent to travel for a year and write a book, an unfulfilled dream he had for decades. His wife could have traveled with him had she wanted to, but she chose instead to be offended, rush to a lawyer and secretly file for divorce. He didn't find out he was being divorced until after he'd hit the road. His wife's regretting her choice to divorce now but it's done though they keep in touch. Like the plot? Michael

The story continues in Victoria Canada with Michael sending an email message to his former wife Jen.

Chapter 1

————◆◆————

M: (to Jen) I had a nagging feeling the last few days that I was missing something. And I was - *a whole book that I had already written!* So, now Book 3 has gone from 56 pages to 535 pages, it's ready to be polished after I do Book 2. Tonight I am starting Book 4 live.

Jen: You are just moving along. This is wonderful. Keep it up my magnificent writer.

Jen: Started to write but I just get sick and throw up. Really want to answer back. Love you sweetie.

M: I understand that you are ill from your surgery but when you are up to it it would be very interesting to know the how and why you seem to have changed so much the last few days. For the longest time your messages were almost always contentious, accusing, blaming, jealous, angry. And I fired right back in reaction. Quite frankly I didn't think you had it in you anymore to become the pleasant woman I once knew, the one who would give me hope of a perfect love in this lifetime, the one on the way to becoming my fantasy "Eve Mother of Nations." I thought often that it must be hope for another man that was motivating that and you were doing what you could to drive me away and blame me for it. But no more, you seem to have changed. I hope though that you don't lose your passion and just meekly praise me all the time and write only what you think I will like without telling me about your *real* struggles and desires and dreams. I do believe that you always loved me, you just had a very strange way of saying it.

Why did you change? Is it likely to last? What is your greatest desire, your dream?

M: (to Jen) Here is how I wrote the big cowboy story for Book 2. You may not like it but I think you'll have to admit that from a non-Mormon perspective it's good writing and my female readers are most likely going to love it. Get used to having a writer in the family darling, you don't have to agree with him or his book characters, just read the books as if you didn't know the author or in this case book character "Jen".

Jen: (responding to my "define vulgar" email) Inflicting pain, force, anything that takes dignity from a person or the sexes. I like playfulness and chasing each other. Scene's that involves both can hardly hold back the deep need for each other. Sex in unexpected locations that include risk. Scene's where he is at her apartment and after a morning jog he goes in to shower and she opens the door of the shower and he turns and all the good stuff begins and does not stop until all they ever wanted is complete. You could fill in the details.

Maybe a scene where they meet some romantic place that fits their personalities. I remember the big cowboy I dated years ago took me camping and he laid a blanket on the ground and then a double sleeping bag. We slept in our clothing but I made sure I was wearing something he would enjoy looking at, feeling and cuddling up to. But more than anything that outdoor sweet mountain air invited all his male sex hormones to rage. Of course he liked the woman standing in the moon light. It made him so hot that he just about went crazy. He got up walked around and came back got in bed and remained a good Mormon man. We were in our twenties. It could have been one of the best moments of his life.

Not for me. I'm not a cowgirl. I just kind of chuckled. Nothing in a whole year of dating brought that out in him or did it ever again. We did manage to go to sleep and woke up the next morning with cows all around us. He was a real cowboy and loved his horses and evidently cows to since then I wondered if it was the smell of cow paddies that got those hormones raging. This is a true experience I had. It could be made into quite a funny situation because I was unaware of his first choose of sleeping arrangements was under the stars. Maybe I will work on this more later.

We traveled on the next day and I remember trying to find a secluded place near a fast moving mountain stream to undress and clean my body but I felt his eyes were not just on outlook duty seeming I was concerned about a stranger coming upon us. Like I said he was a good Mormon boy that was not resisting taking a peek. When I have time I should spend some time thinking about what happened and write about it. It was funny when I think back. I did have a bit of fun with him.

M: (subject – the big cowboy – a night of stars and goddesses) Thanks for sharing that Jen, it's an idea that could be shaped into an interesting story. I'm more into intellectual analysis and philosophizing myself, that's why it's vital for me to add sex scenes and female points of view to my books or they'd never be read. Few people would want to read my dusty stuff except in anticipation of further scenes of pleasure along the way. Suzanne made this book *possible* to market and made it possible for me to be a writer, be grateful for her. When she climbed into Loa that night in San Antone and we embraced, her compelling woman sounds invited more, she was become my goddess. I went consenting into that hug, a man controlled by religion not expecting who would emerge. In that seemingly never-ending hug I experienced a renewal, a cleansing, a *baptism*, a writer and new man was born in the arms of Suzanne. I felt washing over me a spirit of absolute peace, a *knowing* that what she and I were about to do was wholesome and good. *It was right with us, it was right with God!*

Since that intense experience I have never again felt the religious demand for fear guilt repentance confession and forgiveness. There was no sin in what we did, the sin all along was in the cruel command of religion that we must deny that which is natural in ourselves to get to heaven. Ever read the Old Testament? There's not a lot of sexual denial there, they *lived* their lives, patriarchs sleeping with prostitutes, daughter with father, a man spilling his seed upon the ground rather than have sex with a woman he did not want, but spill he did. Did Jesus come to punish and control? Or did he come to love and free and it's men who twisted that message, well-intentioned or not. I do not hate them for it, there must be an opposition in all things or we could not know good from evil, light from darkness, pleasure from pain. It's just that so often evil is called good and good labelled evil.

Jesus taught to judge by the fruits they bear. As I see it the fruits of religion include fear, intolerance, guilt, denial, frustration, anger, hatred, self-righteousness, bombs exploding in the market place, crusades, war, bloodshed, the list could go on. And of course there are good fruits too, a lot of them, it's the *abuse* of religion that causes many of the faults of it. The fruits of nakedness and sex by consent, often forbidden by religion, can be pleasure and fun, contented afterglow, tenderness, connectedness, LOVE. And of course sex like fire can be abused, there must be moderation and consideration in all things. We're here to learn unconditional love. We must have evil to know good and which is our greatest desire. The universe is benevolent, love conquers all. That's my personal philosophizing this early a.m. To me sex and nakedness is beautiful, I see no virtue in denial for the sake of denial when there's consent. I love women because I feel free to look upon their lovely bodies with delight instead of taking only furtive guilty glances like I once did.

You Jen could have been Suzanne for your big frustrated cowboy, you had it in you. But you were young then, you didn't know your role. He could have made delicious love to you that night in the sleeping bag under the stars, the memory of what could have been could have been the memory of what was. You could have forever been in memory a lover, instead of just a lovely woman in the moonlight who never reached out hand or mouth to release his "raging male sex hormones." You did learn your role later though, I *know* you did, mmm, coming tonight?

Not only does sex sell but the thought of it flows life through an older man and gives him a reason for living. Your advice to remove the sex from my books so my children would be proud of me did not strike me as wisdom but did reveal how mired you are as was I in the mud of sexual self-denial. Being Mormon your big cowboy was forbidden to get naked in the night with the lovely woman on her back oozing pheromones into his sleeping bag. You *had* your "unexpected location", the male was there and the stars were calling. But that very scene in the mind of the strange and peculiar ones who control religion and its followers would twist it from romantic to *"the very appearance of evil."*

The best writing creates *images*, pictures in the reader's mind, preferably unforgettable ones. "Big cowboy" of course invokes a sexual image as does you wearing something he'd enjoy cuddling up to, and you standing siren silhouette in the moonlight. You naked bathing in the mountain stream with your raging man taking a peek is image provoking. I'm sure he liked what he saw, but it turned out to be only added cause for frustration, he couldn't touch your tits. (Was that last sentence vulgar to you?)

If the night scene on the mountain that you paint led to fulfilling sex and contented afterglow in each other's arms the next day, that big cowboy body having pounded away on your willing craving body lying perhaps on the sleeping bag under a tree, our readers would be satisfied, they got bang for their buck. But for most of them it's 'vulgar' unless they're into masochism to think of the frustration that cowboy must have felt and you his woman doing nothing about it. He took you to his paradise cow paddies and all because he *wanted* to have sex with you, and you never made it happen, he couldn't force himself upon you.

To most people there is nothing virtuous about denial of that which comes natural when both parties are consenting, as should be assumed with the two of you alone in the mountains overnight. Only to a deeply mired religious person could your story be satisfying, and even then I'm sure in the recesses of their mind it would be bittersweet. Even as a strict Mormon, when I read a fiction story where a man and a woman were falling in love I always looked forward to the time when they finally DID IT! It was a warm fulfilling feeling, a flowing of love and well-being, instead of one of frustration such as is your lonely cowboy story. You and I were Mormons when we first dated so we did not dare go 'all the way'. *But we sure didn't settle for frustration!* There was plenty more that we could and did do so when we went our separate ways late at night it was sweet dreams and hopes for more that we took to our less lonely beds that night.

You could have served your cowboy better. He would have loved you for it, and as I will always love Suzanne, he would have remembered with fondness lovely you and the special star-studded night given to you both on the mountain, the gift refused because you bought religion instead of yourselves and love.

That's what I get out of that promising story. It should properly have continued into the next day, the double sleeping bag drawing both your eager glances as you neared a secluded bluff of trees, his jeans shrinking with every step, no longer able to contain what was growing inside them. You're the woman Jen, tell me what *she* was feeling as she sneaked a peek at her big cowboy's jean-draped butt as the sheltering trees drew near.

Good foreplay, hugely unsatisfying sex, poor cowboy, lovely woman but a cruel one when she knew the man's raging struggle and didn't help him burst into a new world, a world of delight and contentment, a world filled with deeply satisfying memories for when he rocked himself to his final sleep. His goddess failed him on the mountain that night. But she learned her lesson I know, she's *my* goddess now and I am near content. Maybe your cowboy didn't fail *himself* when he walked around, you innocent on your back in his sleeping bag not knowing that a man sometimes *must* pleasure himself when his woman won't do it. Perhaps the flowers were extra bright in that spilled spot when Spring arrived. But as you say in recompense, your cowboy remained *"a good Mormon man."* Huh?

If a woman wants to keep a contented man at her side, *give him all the sex he needs...*

If a man wants to keep a loving woman at his side...

You're on sweetheart, your cue's been called. Write me about it will you.

See what a rampage you have evoked with that short story of yours? That's what I mean by playing "Suzanne". She's a counterpoint so I can point. She sends short messages and I the writer respond with longer ones. That's my job, I've already written millions of words, I'm better prepared to write the dissertations. Point counterpoint works well for me. And you Jen do not have to get into sex, we already have the taste and scent of *first* Suzanne, we'd follow her anywhere now. In the beginning during the troubles you would not allow me to print your words. But now you have become a major player in my books. You rank right up there with Suzanne and DeLeon, and newly emerging Elaine should she continue to play with me. Just play "Jen" from now on, I'd like that, she's the one in real life whose bed I sleep in at night. Or *will* that is when she's gets her lovely butt over to my place and plays naked with me, I could get into that.

Jen: Sweet heart, I guess I am on vacation from writing emails to you. If I look at the computer screen I get sick to my stomach. So it is hard for me to be on the computer at this time. I'll have family arriving Sunday and now that my meds have worn off. I don't feel so hot. I will stay in bed most of the time when they are here. I want this surgery to go right. I sure can feel the difference down there. I use to have so much pressure pushing down and I don't feel that way anymore. It feels good that way. You are going to have a new woman. I will call you soon. My daughter invited her dad up to see all his grandchildren and all his kids. It probably has been more than 30 years that he saw all together. I am standing for a few minutes while I write this email. Need to go and lay back down.

M: Thank-you so much for writing, I surely understand your need to be in bed. Hopefully your daughter drops in now and then to check on you, wish I could do that myself, I love you and miss your presence so much.

Last Christmas I was in Phoenix with my son and his family, motor home parked nearby. I'll almost certainly be on my own this year but that's not the tragedy you may think, I'm so used to being on my own now. Elaine seems to have dumped me and I'm not inclined to find another friend, especially with my health.

I'm intensely involved in getting Books 2 and 3 ready to submit for publishing. I work long hours from well before light each day on that project. It's possible that I can have both books done in less than two months.

Shortness of breath continues but I am able to walk as long as I walk slowly, I'm grateful for that. Today I slow walked to the beginning of the breakwater but didn't go on it. On the way back I sat on a bench near Dallas and Menzies. As I looked out over the ocean with hundreds of logs having floated in from some storm somewhere, the sun peeked out from the clouds and shone so warmly that I took off my jacket and basked in a short sleeve summer shirt. It was heavenly, my beautiful city on the sea telling me she loves me still. From here will be born three novels that have the potential to teach millions a new way of thinking if they're ever discovered. I love the books, they are wonderful.

I thank Elaine for the ten or so sentences she spoke that showed me how to reorganize and rewrite my manuscripts. Elaine is my angel with a message from God. I hope the books will be published traditionally but if not I will self-publish and trust that they will become known in social media.

Thanks so much for being so pleasant lately. That too is what I need to focus on as I undertake the huge work that is presented to me right now, the hope of you is life sustaining. All is well, life is flowing as it should. Sleep well my darling, your arrival in Victoria from Utah is approaching, maybe I'll have Book 2 ready by then. Life's good...

M: Be certain that nobody gets access to your computer, my emails are private and confidential, thanks.

Jen: Not a problem and I don't want them to read anything we email about.

M: Morning sweetie, hope you are getting better.

M: Feeling better tonight? I hadn't been outside today (raining) but tonight in the dark grabbed an umbrella and walked around the block. I tried to go slow but guess it wasn't slow enough. When I got home I was breathless and my heart was pounding explosively. I walked further yesterday though, just took it much slower, need to learn that lesson. (And take the elevator instead of the stairs.)

I'm well into polishing Book 2 now, nothing else to do, no emails except yours. I hope to hear from the literary agent soon even it's a rejection so I can search further and get another query in the works. I love my books, sure hope they are acceptable for the traditional book publishing world. I'd love to walk into Barnes & Noble and see them on the shelves, better yet see them being checked out at the cash register. What a rush that would be! Wish it upon me...

Sure, I no sooner write that nobody emails me anymore except (rarely) Jen and Law of Attraction takes that for desire and fulfills. Oresha hasn't written for weeks until now. Not sure that I want to answer but I guess because we *were* friends I'd better.

Oresha: Where in the world is Michael????? .... lol How are You my friend? What have you been up to lately? Long time no see... Are you back in the USA? Hope all is well.... Hugsssss....

Jen: I can't set to long at my desk. I did have the lap top by my bed but it made me sicker watching the screening. These pain meds sure mess with you. My daughter took me to the store today. I ask her if I was walking funny. She said yes you are. I could feel I was a bit dizzy and did not seem to be able to walk straight. Went home and she put the food in fridge and I went to bed. I told her today how much we enjoy getting together and will again.

Did you send a email asking Elaine to go to Messiah with you? If she does not answer then she was looking for a future long term dating partner and does not want to waste much time with casual friends. She probably feel she has enough of those. That's my take on it.

What do you mean inviting Kris? Where does she live or will you invite her to stay with you. I though you were not attracted to her. It sounds more like you want someone to interact more as a writing buddy. Keep going with book two. I am glade you enjoy writing. If you ever get tired of it. Take a brake. I think that's your plan when we get together next. Standing back for a while will clear you mind to see more avenue's for your characters.

I guess you never know who will be inspiring you next. I would like you to change my name. Is that possible? I would like to be called Jeanette. Would that be to much work. Maybe you already gave me a different name. Have you? Positive belief is the first step of what is right. MY sweet magnificent writer.

How are you feeling? I think we should find a Geriatric doctor for both of us. I know you're a dual citizens, did you apply for foreign medical insurance? If you did maybe both will take care of the bill. I am looking forward to us getting together. Love you Jenny

M: I did invite Elaine to go to Messiah with me but she had previously committed to visit her other daughter in Vancouver this weekend. She was nice about it, said she'd like to have gone. But I'll most likely not be the first to send the next email, I need to give her an out if that's what's she's wanting. I'm ok with that.

Kris lives in Victoria so when Elaine said she couldn't go I toyed with the idea of inviting Kris to Messiah instead, but I decided not to. Having you seemingly solid in my life combined with my health problem has changed my perspective on being with other women, I can get more work done on my books that way too. But strangely, five minutes ago I heard from Oresha, first time in many weeks. I'd sooner not respond and open that up again but since we used to be friends I guess I owe her an email. I'll not invite her to Messiah though, right now I don't think I'd even make it there. I'll be better in the a.m. just overdid it again, wish you were here.

It's easy to change your name from the way it is now to Jen, I'll do that tonight in all my manuscripts.

Jen: (re the cowboy story) I don't feel good enough to think about this right now. It could be an interesting story but rereading it. I realize my thoughts at the time were exciting to me but my writing leave much to be desired and the story is not developed enough to be interesting to the reader. Good thing you create some interesting thoughts. Love you sweetie.

Jen: I think we should order two wheel chairs for the cruse or request to have someone else handle our luggage and not stand in line. What do you think? I don't want you to be having a heart attack or end up in the hospital. If you need me to go back to Canada so you can get for sure medical help then I will do that. I just had a thought those long hours at the computer maybe contributing to your illness. Maybe use a timer and get up and starch every 30 minutes for 5 minutes. What do you think. I hope you hear from that literary agent also.

M: If it's a heart problem I'd have to have someone push the chair all the time, or an electric one. I don't think I'm that far gone. I get up and pace my apartment often, can't sit for long. I want to check if USA government health insurance is still working for me and if so will see a doc when we get to your city. That's a good base for me and you can continue with your business while keeping an eye on me and running me around if need be. Hopefully this will turn out to not be much at all and I'll be on my way with a few pills.

Jen: Ok sweetie, I love you, Please take care of your health. I do understand when you have these other women around you have to play the hostess and that takes more energy than you feel you have. did you get your package from your daughter. I have not sent a package even though I thought about it. But will plan a small different night for us when we get to a hotel or back to Utah. I love you.

M: How did you know my daughter was sending me a package?

Jen: You told me she said she was sending you a package. Just wanted to make sure you to a present on your coffee table to open.

M: Got it, thx and will open it later.

M: (to Oresha cc Jen) My ex Jen was here for a week and although reconciliation is not yet a done deal there's enough writing on the wall that I shut down my profiles and consider myself 'not available' on the singles scene. I'll be spending most of the month with her, wish us well. And I wish you well too my friend.

Jen: I thought you could change my name in your books to something close to Jeanette like a nick name possibly Jana. What do you think?

M: How about Jen instead of Jeanette?

Jen: That sounds real good to me. Thanks sweetie. I am going to bed but if I can not sleep I will check my email later.

M: You shall be known in all my books as "Jen". You're in time to make the change in Book 1 too, it's easy for me to do. Sleep well, sweet dreams.

Oresha: Hi Michael I DO wish You The Very Best with Jen! Does that mean you'll be leaving us... and moving back to Utah? Nice that you'll be spending time together Thank you for the kind wishes as well... I'll pass along your kind sentiments to Kathy. Please keep me posted... Big Friendly Hugs to You!... PS... would you mind if I borrow some of your Abraham DVD's while you're gone to the US? Guess I'd better get caught up on them before you move... lol Take care... ttyl.....

Jen: "The grass isn't green on the other side. It's greener where YOU water it." I just saw this quote and realized I must keep this and keep it in mind and remember to work on what is most important to me.

M: I agree, winning attitude. I've made changes in all the books, you are now Jen.

M: (to Jen) As I continue to edit my books it seems amazing at how 'lost' I really was and how unreal the women were who I interacted with via the internet. Even the women I physically met were very different than the ideal image I had created of them in my desperate need. My only consolation this morning as I continue to relive the last 14 months is the thought that there is someone REAL waiting to be with me. I NEED you honey, I want you, I love you.

Plus of course, I have written three books during those 'lost' months when I was not lying comfortably on the sofa at home reading someone else's adventures. I'll never regret what I did, I LIVED my life for a while, I am deeply enriched. But now I want to be with you in goodly circumstances, *that's* the reality I'm searching for more than fantasy.

You wrote last night: *"The grass isn't green on the other side. It's greener where YOU water it. I just saw this quote and realized I must keep this and keep it in mind and remember to work on what is most important to me."*

As always with words there are many ways to interpret them. Please assure me that "what is most important" to you includes me. Otherwise what you wrote could be taken as you having chosen family or business or a Mormon man or whatever as being your priority and you have decided to dump me. See how things can be interpreted so differently than the way the writer intended? At least I hope it's different in this case, that message could signal you moving away from me to somebody or something more important. It could also signal you moving closer to me, making ME your priority. Which was it your intention to convey?

From my point of view ALL the negativity I experienced from you right from the beginning resulted from your misinterpretation of things I wrote. I never *intended* to hurt you, but I can see how you took it that way. It's easy enough to do and to roar off believing that your own interpretation is right even as the writer denies that *your* story is his. It's all a matter of communication. That's why I stress the enormous importance of our being together physically and refraining from emotional contention beyond explaining the way we see it and asking if that is true - then putting our arms around each other and sharing a deep abiding endless love.

Assure me that I am "most important" to you?

M: (to myself) She just had female surgery and will be disabled in some ways for six weeks or more and she has family arriving today and she is expecting me to be with her for three weeks so there is no way that she will be approaching another man right now as I see it. However my question is valid and I am waiting for her response. She still hasn't taken down her singles profile and she has changed back and forth many times before, in fact although it is hugely pleasing to me in a way it's baffling that she suddenly changed to non-contention and pleasantness a few days ago. She never responded to my asking her for an explanation for that. So sure, I'm still concerned and a bit suspicious, especially if she doesn't respond to this message too.

M: (to Jen) You didn't respond to my message. I'd appreciate if you would sweetie. I'm not wanting contention, I'm wanting understanding. Enjoy family today, wish I was there too...

Jen: I think my change has to do more with the fact you settled to the fact you would be happy with one woman, me. You stopped expressing strong needs to be looking and being with other women "Eve's". I think getting ill has caused you to settled down and take a look at yourself and where you are at this time of your life. I sure don't want you sick sweetie. Like you said the past is the past and you can not change it.

I do believe we can learn from our mistakes of the past, that is, if we are capable of recognizing them. What is important for us is to not repeat what will not give us what we really want. I should have been strong enough to walk away instead of email fighting you on the subject of a life style I did not want to live. I guess I did not want to let go and was fighting for us and this method did not make me happy. I just don't want to fight.

I stopped fighting because you made changes and I followed. The past is the past. I know your life style has changed a bit this last year but not sure how long you had this attitude of multiple women in your bed happening in your head. Please tell me, will one day your life style once again change to wanting more than one woman in this life? Is it a need that will crepe up from time to time and will you wonder in search to satisfy those needs.

M: You 'blame' me again rather than searching inside yourself and telling me the truth about YOU. That has always been your pattern, I ask about you and you tell me about *me* as if I didn't know myself, only you could. You say you changed because I changed. I don't think that's true, I haven't changed, what most likely changed is your *attitude* towards me and I'm wondering why?

And as usual you confuse fantasy (the stuff of fiction novels) with reality. My track record is monogamy within marriage, it has been for decades. Do you honestly think I could throw that away in a few months? Your fears as usual are unrealistic (especially given my age.) I could just as validly ask you if you will be again searching for a *Mormon* man. Would that be more important to you than being with me? Please respond to my other email also, thanks.

You say that you were "fighting for us" when you were telling me you were making out with Al, on singles sites, talking with strange men on the phone, meeting up with at least one of them, and secretly trying to get on Mormon sites to find a Mormon man? What you say is not convincing except perhaps to yourself as you create a new story you can live with.

But then, we can choose to put the past behind us and move forward creating a new life for US. It's just that I was hoping to get a solid understanding of what *really* was happening between us. I know what was happening with me, I just don't know what was happening with you. Tell me about you? Enjoy the day, I do love you.

Jen: Ok, If that's how you feel. I have lots of company coming today.

M: (to Jen but not sent) You wrote this morning: *"I think it has to do more with the fact you settled to the fact you would be happy with one woman, me. You stopped expressing strong needs to be looking and being with other women "Eve's".*

But the truth is that I was looking for Eve for the last six months because you were unavailable to me while being available to strangers. Right now I'm at the part in Book 2 where I parked my motor home in your city six months ago with the intention of reconciling, yes, I wanted *you.* I can still vividly see in my mind the somewhat gleeful look on your face when you told me a few weeks ago that you "sure weren't" wanting to reconcile with me when I visited! (That was news to me.) *You were wanting sex, just not me!* That still troubles me. I felt when you told me that, that you had just used me while leading me along with the hope of reconciling and picking up our lives together again. At the time you thought we were still married so it would have been as simple as allowing me to move back into the home we built for us and putting my RV on consignment for sale. Done deal, we would both have had what I wanted and you were *saying* you wanted but obviously didn't.

Here's an extract from Book 2:

M: (to Ex) This entire parking lot is posted as a tow-away zone for RV's so I'm getting out of here. If you still want to visit me today I'll be at the overpass where trucks park at night. I'm feeling pressured now to get my RV on sale as soon as possible, so I'd like to get the paperwork you want done completed right away and be on my way to Montana.

I'm disappointed that you are no longer available. I thought you might be but your loyalty has been firmly transferred to others. I understand and don't fault you for it. My way seems clear before me now after pondering your continuing to make others your priority. That's a choice you could have made differently when I outlined what I saw as possible for a future together. I hope that we will continue to be friends, keep in touch, and maybe even see each other occasionally. I will most likely move to Victoria soon after my visit with family in Alberta. I may quite possibly settle there, maybe even get married should the right person come along.

Yes, I thought a lot about my future last night and my former ideas about us being together are not so compelling anymore. I have to face up to that, you are not available for me. My series of books may have reached a conclusion with Book 12 now completed. (The first series of small e-books since unpublished.) So my purpose for traveling and living on my own is done as I see it at this moment of writing. What will actually happen remains to be seen but I expect that what I have outlined above will prevail. Keep in touch, I do want to complete that paperwork but I now want to do it as soon as possible. Please make that a priority even if you have visitors, thanks.

Ex: It has been difficult today not seeing you. I wanted to see you. Rentals are a priority when my son is here. This is the first he has been here for a long time. I can't rent them with some of the problems I am having. Can't afford to hire someone else. Tomorrow, I have to rent a truck and buy items for the rentals and take it up and deliver them. Not sure how long it will take. Most likely will not be back until after 3:00 PM. If you are available I will come by if back early enough. We will get together for sure the next day OK. I will pick you up to come over to the house and we can work on your list of properties. I am sorry about all of this. I would of preferred spending time with you but responsibility is tugging at me.

M: Well written, thanks for explaining. My daughter is planning to pick me up in Great Falls. I need to get the RV sold and it may take some time, thus the rush. Sure, come over today if you can. I may do some walks so if no response when you knock on the door, call, I'll try to remember to take the phone with me. Enjoy the day.

(To myself) I'm a bit torn, she's a good woman and seems eager to see me. But she won't allow me to rejoin her in the marital home and take up life where we left off, so I *must* travel some more. And that means there will be other women in my life, though *right now I'd settle for one!* It's just that now that I'm back where I spent a lot of years and my ex is eager to have some time with me, even intimate time, all the old ways are knocking on the door. I did have an enviable life, our home is beautiful, I love our city, I left to write, *I wrote!!!*

End of extract from Book 2.

M: (to myself) So, there are valid grounds for my saying that I haven't changed with regards to you. Although I did waver back and forth over the next six months while you were unavailable for me my position today is the same as it was six months ago, *it was not me who changed, it was you.* My question is *why?*

But I won't send this message, just put it in my journal. I value too much the good will and the hope we've had for several days, and don't want to mess with the happy time you will have with your family. I love you darling, I hope you get to read this someday and are ready to better understand the difference between me and the "me" you created. Strangely, as I imaginatively created images of women at a distance they were positive and glowing, but the image you created of me at a distance is almost always negative and shoddy. Wonder why? That's the essence of why I thought over the last six months you have been trying to throw me away and get another man, *and blame me for it.*

I'm still suspicious and wanting to clear it up. How long will this pleasant new you last? Guess I'd better enjoy it while it's here, and that's another reason why I'm not sending this to you. I think after my visit that you still *won't* have a plan for us to get together permanently. And in your loneliness you *will* look for another man again, this time a *Mormon* man so you can better justify it to yourself. It would be simple and easily understood by those in your community that after loving me the whole time you finally dumped me because you concluded that I'd never again be a faithful Mormon. Done deal, you're in, I'm out, you walked away and got to blame me for it, perhaps your entire purpose all along, you got the power!

That's how I see it, that's my fear, and I think it's much more realistic than yours about a man my age leaving a marriage to go off in real life to get several women in his bed at the same time. Fantasy dear, just fantasy, most men have it even while they live with and are faithful to their wife. You yourself revealed your hidden wild side when you were here a few days ago. As we made love *you asked me to imagine ELAINE in bed with us* and to tell you what I was thinking and feeling! You knocked the socks off me for sure, I was pleasantly shocked. You are wild inside too like everyone else, it's just that I talk about it, you don't. Well my

17

dear, if you'll play along with me like that when we make love it's sure to be a successful experience each time, you know how to get me going that's for sure. But didn't having another woman in bed with us make you bisexual? Are you moving closer to my fantasy dream? I'd like that.

It's just too convenient right now for her, she's not available for other men until after my three week visit in addition to her recent female surgery. Then it would be easy for her to 'misinterpret' something I write and roar back into contention that drives us apart again and leaves me lost and looking for my Eve. If I am in poor health she may come to live with me for a month while I get that taken care of. There's a story in Mormon circles about a famous Mormon lady whose husband left her but she never remarried. Years later the man asked her to take care of him while he died of AIDS. She did, took him back into her home and served him daily. That's spoken and written of as a great example of womanhood: long-suffering, loving, forgiving, patient, kind, etc. etc. I'm sure any Mormon woman would love to have that story told at her funeral and left behind as a legacy of righteous living. Jen has often told me she'd take care of me if I got seriously ill. Is the story behind that motivation? Is she wanting to create that reality of me slowly dying and her taking care of me, demonstrating her great love and sacrifice for the man who abandoned her? Could be.

I bring to mind the very strong feelings I had not long ago that Jen and I were not to be. Of course that doesn't have to be a self-fulfilling prophecy, I do have the power to create my own life the way I want it to be. If an individual I want in my dream chooses not to be there, Law of Attraction will bring to me another who dreams my dream, like attracts like. Things seem to be fine with Jen right now, but as I wrote, it's convenient for her to be pleasant for the next few weeks, she can't go to another man anyway. I was strongly impressed today to get on the record what I wrote above. I need to be sure too that if I become disabled, control of my books does not get into Jen's hands to the point where she can alter my words to make her come out smelling like roses when thorns poke from her flower beds every step of the way.

I ask myself again, is this of interest to you dear reader? I guess if not you would not be reading. I love my books, I sure hope you do too. My experience getting my journal published as e-books (later unpublished) and those not selling was hard to take. But I've rewritten the manuscripts thanks to Elaine's suggestions and I think they are much better now. I hope so, I know what it cost me to live and write them, it wasn't easy. I surely hope other novelists don't have to hurt so much to give birth to their 'baby'. Perhaps because I actually *live* my books my struggle is self-inflicted and unique. Wish us well, what we do as novelists is for *you* our audience. We thank you for reading our creations, you are precious to us. Writers are sometimes ignored, please try to remember that behind every story you read and see on your screen there is a *writer* who worked long and hard to bring it to you.

As I lay in bed at midnight December 21 after working on Book 2 all day it came to mind that Oresha played a huge role in my life and my books and I should treat her well. So I wrote the following.

M: (to Oresha) You can come over and borrow whatever DVD's you want for yourself and Kathy, just let me know when you'll be coming. I won't need them until the end of the month. I'll trust you to keep track of them and get them back to me, there are still some I haven't watched myself.

M: (to myself) I should probably treat her to a meal or event now and then too, she was a good friend. But I can't walk with her like I used to do until my health is improved. I haven't said anything about that yet.

Nothing from Jen tonight, I think I'd be best to leave communication up to her to initiate. Hopefully she'll wish I was there with her family, but she may realize too that they are more important than I am and withdraw even more. I'll never be certain of her until we're living together full-time even though I still at times feel that we are married, it seems strange that we would not be, that divorce was not necessary.

M: (to Jen) I'm missing you sweetheart, I love you lots. I'm in work mode again and grinding away on Book 2, about half way there. Didn't even get out of the house yesterday but will today, if only for shopping. I hope your family visit is going super well and that your body is coping. Thinking of you.

Oh, I just came to the part in book two where you kind of invited me to go to Hawaii or somewhere on your companion ticket. Is that still on, or are there more important things for you now? (You didn't respond to my twice sent email about you going after the things that are "most important" to you, so I'm not even sure if I am among them or not?) I know you love me, but when do you think we can live together again? Any idea? Do you want to?

Please respond to those questions, I'm immersed in the past as I edit my books and again am filled with doubts about your commitment and availability for us. I need assuring, or informing if it has come to that and I need to plan my life again. Which is it? Most importantly, when do you think we'll be living together permanently? Enjoy the day

Oresha: Thanks for your kindness in letting me borrow your DVD's, yet again!... lol I'm not feeling too well right now... think maybe a bit of food poisoning.. UGH! I'll get back to you in the next couple of days about coming over to pick the DVD's up... When are you going to be away?.... I'll see how I feel tomorrow?.... and let you know, if that's OK?...

M: No rush, I'm planning to be in the area until the 6th. Be well...

M: (to Jen) It's interesting that you recently expressed a fear that I (at my age) would run away from you after we married so I could get two women in bed with me. But all my life I've been a one woman man and kept telling you that. (Fantasy is very different than real life as you know, you have fantasies too.) The only reason why I've been with more than one woman at times is that none of them was that one woman I wanted (or unavailable) and you yourself were not available to me until recently. (At least I think you are available to me, right now I'm not so sure, watching anxiously for a message from you, please write soon.)

Anyway, as I edit book 2 I came across the following in which you too affirm that I am a one woman man. This is a message you sent soon after I told you I'd lost Jackie. I'm impressed at how often you expressed love and caring for me. I think you love me baby.

Jen: *"Did I understand you when you once said your path is unfolding without a conscious direction. What is different now? A week later you are adding to the same series of book when I thought you were going to take it off line because no one was buying them. I would suggest you take the rest of the summer off and enjoy the delightful surroundings then settle into writing a personal journal in the fall if that's your desire. I think this course of searching for women is addicting, consuming, and cutting the life out of you. You are not cut out for this type of life. You are a one woman man."*

Should I stop sending messages like this? I don't want to bug you, I want to hug you.

Jen: Hi Sweetie, I think I meant, you might run off to be with another woman. I have no other man in my life except you and I do not plan on another man. I love only you. Been a busy day with 12 guest staying in the house. Wednesday I will have 14 guest but 22 for dinner. Hope you are doing better and feeling better. Love you

M: (to myself) I sent emails to Suzanne, DeLeon, Carrie, Karen, Kris, Jackie, the one I last called "Kira", and my first wife, in addition to of course children and siblings. I'm holding off on Elaine still hoping she'll make first contact, willing to give her the 'out' she may want. I have a gift here for her but won't mention it unless she comes over.

Jen: Hi Sweetie, I think I meant, you might run off to be with another woman. I have no other man in my life except you and I do not plan on another man. I love only you. Been a busy day with 12 guest staying in the house. Wednesday I will have 14 guest but 22 for dinner. Hope you are doing better and feeling better. Love you

M: I do not plan on another woman either so there, we're even.

You used to thrive on events like those you have coming up but with your surgery it is my hope that this time you'll be the conductor orchestrating everyone else so it all comes together. What a joy sweetheart to have all your kids under the same roof again! I used to like nothing better than that, just lying on the sofa watching my grown up kids have fun with each other, the great joys of parenthood. I do want to visit my kids and grandkids often in the future and renew our acquaintance, I won't feel so pressured to write once the first three books are in the process of being published. Hopefully we'll do those visits together, my kids all love you, wish yours loved me too. Maybe someday, speak well of me if it ever comes up, seeds need to be planted.

Sometimes lately when I think of you the pent up emotion of the past 14 months rises and I have to tamp it down or be destroyed, my body's too weak right now to indulge in anymore emotion, I'm way overdue for some warm beach time and nothing else. Surely we never ceased to love one another. Take care my darling, drop me a note whenever you can. I love you and look forward to a joyful life together, I'm your man. Your Michael

Jen: You asked me what changed in me. I have been thinking about it. Just like most things there are more than one answer to most questions. Most often the answer usually comes with out thinking to much. Meaning "what is at the for front of your thinking at the moment". The last couple of weeks I have felt a lot of peace and want to enjoy it. Because of that I don't want to engage in friction back and forth with our different view points. Maybe I don't want to sweat the small stuff. Love you Sweetie.

M: I'll go with that. I don't want any more contention either, I am totally burned out with it, just want the peace, and you within reach.

M: (to Kris) I hope all is well with you and your loved ones.

Kris: Hi Michael Yes all is awesome. Just had another trip to Africa. Much kindness

M: (to myself) I sometimes wonder how different my life would already be had I gone to see Kris as planned that day instead of backing out of an outing with her and rushing off for that foolish visit with Luchia and a stranger in Nanaimo. Kris and I exchanged a lot of promising messages before I came to Victoria with me backing away when she sent a photo showing that she was overweight at the time. Later we walked the breakwater and had tea at the café. When I put my arm around her she instantly wrapped hers around me. She's warm and affectionate and knows Abraham. She's pretty and didn't seem overweight at the time. (As if it should matter – my failing.) She gave me a copy of her book from which fell two little white doves and red hearts that I still have on display as I write this. Lynne the clairvoyant asked me who Kris was, I'd forgotten her. Anyway, I think I would have thrown myself into the charity work Kris does for children in Africa, it would have opened much newness of life for me. She was a flight attendant, we would have travelled a lot. I would have loved her. Should Jen fail me I will most likely visit Kris and see what comes of it, she's a writer and healer, a dear soul. I would have been good for her, God bless her.

I meditated a few minutes this morning and quickly got my groove back. I think my body is healing and I am becoming Adam again. Will Eve be Jen or Kris or another? Almost certainly not Elaine who knows I am on my own all these days and doesn't even message let alone visit and read to me, a fair weather friend it seems, she dumped me almost instantly.

Just a quick thought. Jen wrote once or twice expressing an interest in she and I getting involved in charity projects at a distance. Perhaps she and I will go to Africa with Kris some day and it will be Kris, not Elaine who becomes Jen's best friend in Victoria? Or is that just me imagining a threesome again? I wonder. I do think there is more substance for me with Kris than there would be with Elaine. But then, why should it matter? Who's Elaine? Oh, right, the angel who told me how to rewrite my books to give them a chance for commercial success. If you are reading this as a published book, it's likely because of Elaine. God bless Elaine. Yes, Jen too while you're at it…

M: (to Kris) You do get around. I hope your projects in Africa and your adopted children are doing well. Some day I might get involved with something hands on like that too instead of just financial donations from a distance. Sometimes I think responding to ads and donating for specific children in Africa and elsewhere is as much a donation to a church or NGO (non-governmental organization) as helping a child. The way you do it you actually meet the children - much better, you're a dear soul.

Hopefully we'll get together again sometime, I really enjoyed meeting you and our walk on the breakwater Kris. Take care, enjoy your family.

Kris: Thanks Michael. You as well. Yes our work in Africa is very gratifying and every cent we raise goes right to the Orphanage. It was a great trip and got a lot accomplished. Happy thoughts.

M: (to Jen) When I called my sister today and mentioned that you and I are still friends and would be getting together soon she asked me to give you her best wishes. Also, in an email to my brother and his wife I mentioned the same and they wrote back:

> *"How nice to hear from you and we are pleased that you and Jen are still friends. Please wish her our blessings when you see her."*

I think all of my family would be pleased to see us reconciled and living together. My guess is that all that is holding us back is your unrealistic fear of your youngest daughter. That's *her* problem not yours, I don't think she'd be anywhere near the challenge you think she will be if you'd only get some courage and face your fears. Face it Jen, it's YOU who is keeping us apart. Is that what you *really* want?

You still haven't responded to the message I sent to you twice. Am I among the "most important" things you are going to go all out to get? I know you love me, you know I love you. How long do you think it will be before we are living together permanently? Or are you content to just be occasional lovers? Please respond, this is important to me, thanks.

Suzanne: Hope you are with family as well. Do you have a wedding date set?

M: No wedding date and no plans to live together yet, just a pleasant truce right now, nothing's written in stone. We'll be getting together for a short cruise and a visit my new grandson. Then maybe ten days in the former marital home which she now owns. We'll see what comes of it. I've been trying to reconcile since a couple of weeks or so after you and I were in Las Vegas and I visited her. But she never commits, just leads me on with hope then gets contentious and walks away each time. Of course each time that happens I try to find another, think I have, then that falls apart too. I'm serious about marrying her, it makes so much sense, but I'll only believe it's true when we are actually living together with the expectation that it is permanent. She knows my home in Victoria is ready for her anytime and she is welcome to move in. She came to visit twice but didn't stay long, citing pressing family and business matters. (She's only four years younger than me by the way.)

So I don't know what will come of this Suzanne. And lately I'm starting to see in the mirror the aging man you saw in Las Vegas, much as I keep telling myself that can't be me, I *feel* so different. It's wearing tilting at windmills like Don Quixote. You never know what's going to come rushing out from them, fairy or dragon, heart in mouth each time you make the charge. I've been on an emotional roller coaster for 14 months and am about worn right out. I do want to get my three books finished at all costs before I try to relax, maybe find a warm beach somewhere and crash mindlessly for a few weeks. Book one is done, book two is better than half way there, and book three won't take more than a few weeks, so maybe three more months and the writing part is done. It's about time too, I'm getting real short of breath lately. Instead of the long brisk daily walks I did in the summer I'm down to six or so blocks a couple of times a week real slow. It's probably something I should take to a doc and may do so when I get home. Wish me well sweetie, I wish you well, still loving you.

Karen: I wish you the very best.

M: (to myself) That's disappointing, I'd love to have Karen for a pen pal, she's a really good writer. But then, right now it's not new stories I need, it's time to finish books two and three. Maybe when that's done and I've had a break I'll write her again and suggest being pen pals? But then if I'm married she may not go for that, and my wife (Jen) may not go for that either. Life's so fun when we pretend we don't remember what's coming.

Jackie sends me an e-card. I reply.

M: (to Jackie) Thank-you for the card Jackie, it was lovely. You are a beautiful soul. Be well sweetie.

M: (to myself) I'm wondering if Jen two thousand kilometers away is going to sense these exchanges of energy and question, maybe be jealous? With reference to the movie series "Star Wars", will Jen as she visits with her children and grandchildren somehow sense "a disturbance in the force"? That will be interesting to discover. Of course I'll let you know if something surfaces. If so, my guess is that because we're so closely connected, Jen will feel my love wandering if even only momentarily from her to Suzanne, and Jackie, and Kris, and Karen, and and... Yes, I am capable of loving more than one concurrently, it's just that it doesn't seem to be allowed by the women in western society who want their man exclusively for themselves. (Have I beat that drum enough? Ok, *but I love you too...*)

Jen: Yes Michael, You are very important to me. I don't know how long it will be before we marry? You say live together. We will work on that when the time comes. I think the most important thing now is to get you well. Love you sweetie

M: That was a bittersweet reply sweetie. I am encouraged that you finally responded to my question and tell me I am "very important". When someone doesn't reply to a question it usually means the response is negative, they just don't want to come out and say it. The longer the silence, the more that is confirmed.

But you know, six months ago we were at the point where I offered reconciliation but you would not discuss plans to get us living together. That troubled me all those months, it was as if you didn't really want to get us together. It still troubles me because that hasn't changed and you still don't see it as a priority, it remains a matter of "when the time comes." You will not commit!!! And that leaves me on shaky ground, exactly where I have been for months, nothing has changed in you.

The getting well part I can take care of myself. I think I am getting better now, I just need rest after those 14 months of turmoil. But the living under the same roof I cannot do by myself, that has to come from you. I have done everything I can, you continue to be invited to live in my home. Sure we could buy a piece of paper from the government that says we're married. What would change? *The only thing that will change for us is our living together.* Don't you realize that?

Do you have plans for us to live together? If not, why not and when will you actively plan and work it out? I've been asking that question for many months of uncertainty and loneliness, you haven't budged.

At least you know I still want you. Wish it was with you. This waiting is wearing real thin honey. I love you. Can you see it from my point of view? You haven't changed have you? It makes me wonder...

But I guess it's all in your hands, I've done what I can, I need to back away and take the 'pressure' off you again or you'll walk away, again. Except that we're getting together soon for a visit... Looking forward to it. Have fun with family, see you in a couple of weeks, should be a fun visit. But my heart desperately wants to rest in the right woman full-time. I'm still hoping it's you but I can never be sure until we're living together like normal couples do, you're very different that way, won't even make it a priority.

M: (to myself) As I think it through I realize that she hasn't really changed, she could very easily go looking for a Mormon man (her neighbor?) and dump me. I am becoming aware that I need to adjust my thinking and stop telling the universe that I am Jen's. *Maybe I'm not!* Maybe there's another woman waiting for me who would be much better for me and I for her? Anyway, I feel far less committed to Jen right now. I'm not ready to sign up on singles sites and start that again, but I am ready to open the door to the possibility that since getting together with Jen remains a rock strewn path with no end in sight, perhaps there *is* another waiting for me, desires are always addressed by Law of Attraction. My heart yearns desperately for the right woman. Jen continuing to drag it out makes me wonder... I'll withdraw into myself a bit more. Maybe I'll get together with Kris when she returns. That too though would be a long courtship I think, and I'd always wonder if Jen and I *should* be living together. Is she being fair to me? What is your counsel? What would *you* do?

M: (to Jen) There's an 18 day cruise to Hawaii return San Diego for $1200. It leaves in a few weeks. Just thought I'd let you know. Love you lots, enjoy your family. Sunny day today, will probably walk to the park. Maybe tonight I'll walk to Inner Harbor and people watch. I'm sure I could be with Oresha but don't want to, tomorrow will probably be a normal working day (writing) for me after opening two gifts from daughters. Enjoy the little ones, wish I was with you.

Oresha: Would it be convenient for me to drop over on Sat. or Sun. for a bit to pick up the DVD's?.... and say "Hi".....lol Have a grrreat day!... Cheers....

M: That should be ok Oresha, shoot me an email Sat or Sun morning to confirm. I hope you are recovered.

Oresha: Looking forward to seeing you on the weekend! I will email you ... and see what you're up to... Cheers!

M: (to myself) As I slow walked today a lady at the park wished me a cheerful day. It filled me with new peace and I thought maybe I should remove the explicitness from the sex scenes presently in my book. After all, if the ladies want to tell, let *them* tell what happened and what didn't. But first I must finish book 2 and book 3, then get to editing to family friendly if by then I still think I should. It might make for better books if readers apply imagination instead of eyesight when it comes to intimacy. But if I do that I won't tell Jen or my family, let them be surprised when they read my books and find that they are not the "sex books" that Jen seems to think they are. Yeah, I'd like that. And yes of course, I'd be proud to tell my children about my novels then.

M: (to Jen) Book 1 is the love story of Michael and Suzanne. Books 2 and 3 are the love story of Michael and Jen. Yes, really. Jen long ago took over from Suzanne and is the major of all players in my books, all eyes are on you Jen and what you will do. Please do not fail me now my dearest love, get us together permanently so we'll never again be apart. Do that and "Eve" the one Michael has been desperately searching for will be the woman he left behind tending the roses in his own back yard.

A true love story indeed, a most fulfilling one, everyone's cheering for us right now. *What will you do?*

At 6:45 p.m. I finished rewriting Book 2 of the Becoming Adam series. I may walk to Inner Harbor tonight but otherwise tonight and tomorrow will be routine, this time editing Book 3. I made my big meal of the week tonight, fried two eggs with one toast and some mild salsa. I thought of treating myself to a restaurant meal tomorrow but I know I couldn't eat even a third of the serving so I won't. Maybe a walk to the breakwater tomorrow. Elaine doesn't even know that she has a gift here waiting for her, maybe she'll never know, she has gone silent. It's probably just as well, it is my hope to focus on my Jen, if only she'll get us together permanently soon. If not, I don't know what will happen, Law of Attraction always offers choices... I love you Jen.

M: (to myself) I awoke at 2:30 a.m. and today finds me still at my computer working Book 3 at 5:30 a.m. though tired and will probably go back to bed. I'm enjoying reading how it was in the last few months and noticing how different real life was than I had remembered. My great hope remains to marry and live with Jen but I'm still far from certain of that. If by the end of my three week visit she is still not planning or talking about us living together then when I get home I will probably date again, maybe Kris. I think Elaine is gone for good. I don't think of her anymore, it's physical contact that is meaningful to me after all those months of virtual 'reality'.

I love Jen, but the only thing that will prove her love for me is making me a high enough priority in her life to arrange for us to live together. I won't marry until we are. She is still not planning us getting together so she has not changed from where she was six months ago. She won't even respond when I ask her about her long ago offer to use her companion ticket to take me to Hawaii. It seems that she is still holding out, possibly for another man, she is uncertain if she really wants me. She called last night and we spoke for a short while. It was nice to hear her voice, it was a pleasant conversation, but I still feel that I am being judged and perhaps found wanting. Let's see what the coming year brings, hopefully it will be Wealth, Immortality, and EVE...

Chapter 2

————◆◇◆————

DeLeon: Sharing with you my latest picture at the "formal" dance studio party - was a huge crowd - I didn't dance, just presented and enjoyed the hugs and love. Thank you for you wishes and blessings..... the same to you.. Thank you for an incredible time in 2014....

M: What a lovely photo Cleo. There's proof that you are "DeLeon" fountain of youth, getting younger every day. Enjoy the holidays, keep in touch.

Carrie: thanks for your latest note... a bit too much going on here, but i do want to wish you a happy day... and, will touch back in the next few days to hopefully connect... hugs, carrie

M: (to Jen) Did you find out if your sister will be visiting you for the month you thought she might? Are you thinking about when to get us together permanently or is that still something way off in the distance? I love you and miss you. I'm still counting on you coming through for us but until we're living together it will remain a distant dream that may or may never come. It's *you* I want.

Jen: To the Magnificent writer, Did you go to the Chinese doctor around the corner. Please do. I did call my sister but she was out. Haven't had time to think about when the time is right about us. My daughter will be here in a bit. Hope she does not pass the flue around. My son is very worried she will. I and little grandson are home alone at the moment. Interesting the oldest and the youngest. What does that say. Oh, he just walked in. I can smell a dirty dipper. I can't pick him up but we are managing. Love you sweetie

M: Well at least you know my name. I had a friend in Canada who used to call me "Magnificent Michael". Decades later he surfaced living in Las Vegas, still called me magnificent, guess it's appropriate.

M: This city is very relaxed, almost everything is closed today to give workers an extra long weekend. I'll try the Naturopathic Doc on Monday most likely. I went to the store to get something for chest congestion and the pharmacist directed me to a liquid product. I bought some but read the label at home and it warns not to use it if you have shortness of breath. I don't want to take a chance on getting worse (just hanging in there as it is) so I'll tough it out. Fish and chip shop opens in a half hour will go for takeout. Working on Book 3, I love my books, sure hope an agent picks them up and goes to bat for me.

Jen: Please do not be mad at me but I feel your children should know you are really sick. If something happened to you and I did not tell them you were sick then they might really be upset with me. I love you sweet heart and I want you to know family really cares.

She copies in a message she sent to my daughter today.

Jen: (to my daughter) I am not sure what to do. I think the family should at least be aware I think your dad is really sick. He most likely be upset I am telling you this. I visited your dad earlier this month and he has gone down two pant sizes and is really getting thin. He can hardy breath and his chest hurts him. When he goes for short slow walks his heart pounds really hard when he gets home and he has to lay down. I think this has been progressing for a very long time and is wearing him down. He said he will go to a homeopathic doctor Monday, when they open. He is coming to the states soon and if his US insurance is still in place he will go to a doctor here. He is concerned they will run a lot of test on him and if he still has it in place I will go with him. Love you all

M: I wish you had run this by me first, I didn't want to trouble them just yet. But I understand your motivation, I love you, wish you were here.

M: (to myself) Now I'm really in trouble! I'm huge on telling myself I am well and keeping on going. But now that my children are going to be thinking I am not well how can I remain in denial? My son sends me a draft of the will I requested from him and other papers.

M: (to my son) I'll look it over thanks. But gosh, there was a time when you could write your will in blood on the tractor that had rolled over on you! Guess it's a much more complicated world now. Take care son, I love you. Dad

Son: You can still do that. The blood on the tractor was a real case from Saskatchewan. If you want it simple you can handwrite it without witnesses. This is called a holograph will. Doing it formally like I sent will require 2 witnesses, none of which can be beneficiaries or spouses of beneficiaries.

M: Good, I thought so and just did it in writing, sealed it in an envelope near my computer desk. Very simple, I leave all my assets to be divided equally among my natural children. My handwriting, my signature.

Please don't be alarmed but I have been having some health issues lately, short of breath and irregular heart, will see a doc maybe Monday but want to avoid hospitals at all costs at least until I finish my third book which will take another two weeks, can't write on drugs and in bed. I didn't want to trouble anyone but Jen sent an email to your sister today without asking me for permission, so cat's out of the bag. I understand her motivation though, she knew about it and if something happened to me without her informing family ahead of time you would not think well of her. I'm not wanting anyone to rush to Victoria, it may not be much at all, it has been going on for a long time, just not getting better.

I have tickets to fly to Las Vegas for three weeks. I'll be with Jen most of the time and if my USA health insurance is still valid may wait to see a USA doc. That will give me time to finish my book. We'll see how it goes and meanwhile I'm resting a lot, walking very slowly only a few blocks now and then.

I'm happy, I've had the time of my life the last 14 months, wouldn't swap it for anything. And maybe my books will sell. On my laptop Book 1, Book 2, Book 3, passwords in a sealed envelope near my will. Please understand that although based on real life experiences and people, they are fiction, so don't judge me too harshly from the Mormon point of view, thanks. I love you all. Dad

Son: Thanks for the update. May I share this email with my siblings?

M: You may as well, I was going to wait but Jen told your sister today.

Son: Ok. I am sure she did it out of concern for you.

M: She did, I do not fault her at all. We have been seriously considering reconciliation.

M: If you and your sibs get concerned, please understand that I can't talk a lot on the phone. Brilliant conversation tends to take my breath away. So maybe just one or two of you call if you must and report to the others? But I'm always good with email, thx for understanding. Gosh, I wasn't ready for this. I'm real good at telling myself I am well but now that others are thinking I am not there's not much point in remaining in denial. Just want to get my third book finished mainly. I've already seen heaven, it's so beautiful there, who wouldn't want to go when they get the chance, you would too. We're all so incredibly beautiful in our white robes, the *real* part of us. This world's just illusion, don't sweat it too much...

Son: Have you included in or with your Will some instructions on where you would like to be buried, any particular special arrangements, funeral service program, message for a headstone etc.?

M: Your sister was on a roll some time ago and we went through all that. Those kinds of things are for the living, not for those who have awakened to themselves. I never did get established enough in any community outside of my family to make a difference to anyone, so no funeral at all would be my preference. Just get my kids together for a meal and happy conversation, I would delight in that and surely would be there unseen in your midst, leave me a comfy chair to sit in. Do what you will with ashes, scatter to the wind if you like, it should not cost anything to dispose of this wonderful body that has served me so well.

But you know son, this might not be anything at all. I still expect to live a lot of years, though it certainly is tempting to go when a possible chance presents itself. No heroic life-saving events, DNR would be my desire rather than be handicapped in any fashion or a burden on anyone, I am content with my life.

M: (titled Man on a Mission) While we're having this candid conversation maybe I'll insert a little story that you could share with your siblings. I've always felt that I was destined to do something unusual in life and I may have just done it with those books. I've felt that I had a "mission" to perform, maybe everyone does.

In 1984 when your mother and I were separated and I was living in Victoria I was spiritually 'initiated' into knowledge that most people don't receive. But it was decades too early for it to become well known, I knew that. So I kind of went 'underground' living a somewhat normal consensus reality life, doing my best to provide for a large family in the normal way of doing things, all the while wanting to be a writer but knowing I'd almost certainly never make enough money that way. But the story I want to tell is when I left Victoria and drove my old monster station wagon back to Alberta to try to reconcile with your mother and see my kids whom I missed so desperately.

Although your mother didn't want me to move in with her for a year she gradually began to soften and listen to her heart instead of harsh counsel from others who knew only one side of a story. I recall sitting outside the house with the police inside to 'protect' her from me! I think it was you my son who came out to the street and chatted briefly with me as I sat in my car, it warmed my heart so. (This may not have been the 1984 experience, she and I were separated several times.) But anyway, I began sleeping in my car in the driveway until your mother's bishop who lived nearby told her he didn't want me in the neighborhood at night. (I don't know what my crime was or what stories had been told about me, it's just that I was an outcast in that town.)

Anyway, I drove out of town to a coulee and slept there in my car. The cows would graze nearby and bump my car in the night awaking me. I cried a lot, I wanted to be understood and restored to my family instead of being a lone man in the wilderness. You know I was a strict Mormon almost all of my adult life. So it was not unusual perhaps for me to break from a bout of wailing impressed to face south and soul connect with Salt Lake City, headquarters of the Mormon Church. I was told then that my mission was not there, that it would be outside organized religion. Many years passed.

Fourteen months ago I was impressed to buy a motor home, travel, and write about my adventures. I didn't know when I left my comfortable home and enviable lifestyle that my wife would almost instantly file for divorce. There was no need for that, our continuing love for each other proves it, but it happened. Anyway, as time went on and I wrote a million words into my journal I realized that although I had a whole lot to teach and the time had arrived to do that, if I was going to reach a large audience I would have to write fiction instead of just another textbook type of book that would only be read by those already converted. I knew too that I would have to make my books entertaining or nobody would read them and be exposed to the real message between the lines. I knew that "sex sells" so I inserted that into my books, knowing that I'd be judged harshly for it, particularly by the religious ones in my family. But I did it, my mission was clear to me and how to do it, it was my time. Anyway, that's my little story, thought you might be interested, you were there.

M: (to myself) December 27ᵗʰ. I haven't heard from Jen since she informed me she told my daughter that I am sick. And this morning I feel zero connection with her. But then that's not abnormal, I'd often feel a connection with others at a distance but with Jen almost never except at peak moments. Wonder why? She may still be solid with me, I don't know, but I can easily surmise that now that she has spent several days with her entire family at her home she is feeling so close to them that I am insignificant and unreal in comparison? As I edit earlier parts of Book 3 I realize how often she deceived me about Al (Marty), telling me several times she would never see him again but she did in fact go back to him after that. I just can't trust what she writes except I do think she genuinely loves me, that's what's keeping me going regarding her. Is she any closer to planning on getting us together? My guess is that is far from her mind and will be at least until her company leaves. I'm still very uncertain where this is going for us. I think she struggles a lot with it and could easily give me up for another man. That seems a perfect solution for her, to marry a local Mormon man of means, her family would like that. Maybe she is just being pleasant because she wants to enjoy the time with her family? In writing that message to my daughter yesterday did she think I'd get mad at her and pull away, and that's what she's wanting? Anyway, as I've written before, the entire solution for us is to live together in harmony, nothing else is real.

Anyway, let's see what comes back from her. If it's contention I'll know she just wanted to enjoy her family and I'm just backup. But then, she's committed to three weeks with me so she'll most likely remain nice as that time approaches. What will come of that? Will it soon be boring for us to be together like it was last time? Maybe…

I've heard nothing from any of my kids. Are they not concerned about their dad? Or just so involved with holiday activities that they haven't checked email? Anyway, back to finishing Book 3, it will be a relief to have that done so I can get this health thing looked at and addressed without concern about being disabled in a hospital and/or on medications that could affect my functioning. Elaine sure has failed me, not a word from her, I can't trust what she writes either, she often doesn't follow through with what she says she'll do. Am I getting all too negative lately, betraying what I teach about Law of Attraction? Maybe, need to meditate, focus on becoming Adam regardless of the women I interact with. But first, I need to move Book 3 closer to being ready to submit to an agent or publisher, back at it, enjoy your day.

Jen: How are you feeling today? Love you

M: Lonely of course still wondering if you are real and mine like you once were. Otherwise, healthwise the same. Did my daughter get back to you? I hate talking about the health thing, it only makes it worse. Haven't heard from my kids. But hey, my daughter planned my funeral a few months ago anyway. Still thinking of living forever, though heaven sure can be tempting sometimes, we're all so beautiful in our white robes. Working long hours to rush Book 3, that's most important to me. Should I decide to move on, please do everything you can to get my three books published without changes whether you like them or not, thanks. Enjoy the day and your family. Your emails are important to me, please keep them coming.

Jen: I haven't heard from your daughter so I am not sure. Keep well my love. We have an appointment to have some good times together.

M: (to myself) I just happened to be standing looking out my window this afternoon when a young lady came out and checked under the hood of a car directly below me, just a few yards away. It was delightful to watch her, coat open, transparent white blouse and pink bra containing a lot of promise. She eventually looked up and noticed me smiling at her. As she got in her car to drive away she gave me a little wave of her hand and a smile. It warmed my heart.

I'm realizing the last couple of days that my focus has been on finding women about my age. But if I am becoming Immortal Adam with a rejuvenated body, it would be appropriate I think to be considering young ladies of child bearing age. (For my fantasy.) So I might start doing that. Today I'm thinking of Elaine a bit, wishing she'd come and read to me even as I continue to hope for Jen all the while knowing that she is capable of changing her face any moment and becoming contentious and undesirable again. Her history is filled with that though her own image is that she has always and continues to love me above any other.

Some of my kids have contacted me. I'm saying that I'm waiting to get to the USA to have my health problem looked at, though I might check with a nearby naturopathic doctor if open on Monday. I'm working long on Book 3 and could possibly have it done in just a few days. That's my biggest concern next to recruiting a literary agent to run with my three books and get all three into the agent's hands. Only then will I feel the pressure is off just in case something nasty comes along and I can't write anymore. This current paragraph is in Book 4, it now has 17,000 words where Book 1 has 340,000. A way to go yet but no feeling of urgency, I'm LIVING Book 4 real time right now December 27, 2014, life's great.

Oresha: Kathy cooked a scrumptialicious Birthday Dinner for me last night!... Today I'm moving kinda slowwww... lol I do have to get out and do a few things.... so how does tomorrow afternoon look for you for me dropping in for a bit.. and picking up your DVD's? Please let me know if that works for you? Have a great day! Cheers!..

M: Well, happy b-day to you, I don't remember if you told me, if so I forgot. I'll have a little bag of chocolates for you for a belated gift when you come, and perhaps a glass of Shiraz. Yes, I'll be home tomorrow. You mention walking "kinda slowww" so we'll get along well. That breathing concern I had has worsened and I'm not walking much anymore. Will have it checked out in soon when I get to USA. But I think I can still make it to my door to unlock it for you. See you tomorrow.

Oresha: Hey M.. Thanx! I'll try and get over closer to 2:00 if possible... lol Do ya want me to let you know before I leave my place?.... or should I just show up?... How sweet with the chocolates!... lol Yes... to a toast to US and to a GRRRRREAT Future for Us both!...YAY! I don't remember you mentioning anything about a "breathing challenge"..... sorry to hear about that! Let's visualize your "Perfect Wholeness"!... and walking up a Storm!.... Yeah!.... Looking forward to spending some time with you tomorrow! Take care....

M: I'll be home, just buzz. Shiraz it is, chilling.

M: (to myself) The thought came to mind today that in the dream I had of being in the same room watching Jen communicate with her spirit guide who seemed to be a much better man than I was, that the "guide" looked very much like me, even had the same first name as me. I thought he was my grandfather, that would explain the resemblance. Now I'm not so sure. I think it was a better part of ME!! All along my dear sweetheart Jen was having sex at a higher level with the man who would be her Adam, *me*. That new interpretation of the dream puts my and Jen's relationship on a different level, we are *destined* for each other. She is Eve, the perfect love gone right is OURS. Could this be so?

If so, why would Jen have been given the choice to die to be with her Adam? Or was the choice actually to live or die period, she was at the time thinking of taking her own life and of course had the power to do that. She would still have been with me when I followed her, or could have been reborn and come to me then with a different physical body. So many possibilities are presented that are logical. Do I like this new thought? *Yes, I love it!*

So, Jen and I are Adam and Eve. With us are ten beautiful young women who want to bear our physical children and populate new worlds. We, Jen and I are the forever stabilizing 'force' for our worlds, the stuff that holds them together. We for our children only are God the Father and Mother. The ten can leave when they have the experience they need to become Eve to another Adam, or stay with us forever, their choice, they will be replaced if they leave. Could it be then that Jen and I instead of being 'translated' made immortal, will resurrect and produce the *spirits* that will animate the physical bodies our ten bear? (Jen indicated that she and her Adam would do that. I thought at the time that her Adam was *another* man, one presently a spirit, but it could have been a higher part of me.) Our planets being a higher order than this one presently is, the children I father will be of a higher order too, it fits. But, I'm going beyond the mark here, it's just fantasy folks, relax, unwind, it's just a dream, you're waking now feeling much better than before… Welcome to the reality of unchained imagination and New Thought.

But then, I do want to have more children in *this* world too, so maybe we or at least I will be translated (made immortal) first before dying and being resurrected. However it shakes out, it's sure *exciting*! Still with me dear reader? Or have I lost you now with this heavy stuff? Hey, there's gotta be some good healthy SEX coming up, it has been a while. With Jen in Las Vegas maybe?

M: (to son after his message) I know it's simple to see a doctor, there's a walk-in clinic just a few yards from me. There are several reasons why I am delaying that. I do have B.C. gov health insurance. My thinking is that if I go to a medical doc they will put me in a wheelchair and rush me to emergency and/or for all kinds of tests like they did when I had pleurisy. I can't write if I'm in a hospital with tubes and meds, and I am within a few days now of finishing my third book of a series. I want to do that at all costs. If Jen or someone was here to run me around for those tests etc. I'd probably go except I have flights booked for a short cruise with Jen and don't want to miss that. Jen would come but she has her entire family with her, first time in a long time and they won't leave for a while yet. Also she just had female surgery and can't lift etc. for six weeks so we're both a bit of a basket case right now. So, just bad timing and a stubborn writer wanting to finish delivering his 'baby'. Thanks for the concern and advice.

I think I may have a collapsed lung because I am very short of breath, the slightest effort causes heavy breathing and when I lay on my left side it's painful and gets harder and harder to take a breath. Some days for periods of ten or so minutes at a time my heart pounds almost explosively as if it was trying to get out of my chest, it seems to shake my whole body. I think what started it all is several months ago while in a deep guided mediation with a breathing exercise I came out of it having lost my autonomic breathing. And I forget to breathe. That led to complications that eventually caused the heart problems that appeared two or so weeks ago but have now settled a bit. As per usual me I try to heal everything by ignoring symptoms and telling myself I'm just fine. Isn't working too well this time, yes I do need to see a doc, I admit. I thought I might try a naturopathic doc a block away tomorrow when they open. It's almost certainly a medical problem but at least a ND wouldn't be rushing me off to a hospital and keep me from writing. So I'll continue to work 20 or so hours a day to finish the third book before something happens, that finishing could happen by tomorrow I'm that close.

That's my story and I'm sticking to it son. I did listen to the phone message, thanks much very nice, got another from the fam in Montana, love to hear the children's voices, miss you all a lot. I love you all and yes I do expect to be around much longer just in a bit of a crisis right now. Hopefully the docs have a magic pill for it once I get to them as you say they might. Can't talk on the phone much because of short breath so email it will be. And back to work now at 4:30 a.m. getting real close to done the book, maybe even late tonight I'll have it completed well enough to submit to a literary agent once I get one. That's my destination, docs are just going to have to wait, anyway it's Sunday.

It's ok to forward this to sibs if it helps calm any situation caused by Jen's message to your sister which she told me about only after she had sent it, I didn't want to trouble anyone. I can't blame her, she thinks my situation is serious (it might be) and doesn't want to have sat on the news when she knew about it if something nasty happened. Enjoy the day and the warm isles, wish I was there. Dad

M: (to Jen) What a pleasant surprise! The last part of Book 3 was already formatted and ready to go. So today I finished the last of the three books in my series. Of course they could all use another go over but I am satisfied enough to submit all three to a publisher today if that was in the works. (It's not, I need to find a literary agent first.)

Just before I finished, Oresha came over to borrow eleven of my Abraham DVD's. It was nice to see her, it has been quite a while. I missed her recent birthday so gave her a small bag of chocolates. We talked for about an hour, I told her about my health problem. She said she immediately noticed that I had lost weight. As she went she gave me a hug and a sincere offer to come over anytime and keep me company. (We're strictly platonic.) I was almost overwhelmed to have such a friend as her, I've been alone so much over the last 15 months as my body wore down with the intense effort of writing three novels in a year.

Now, with that done and Michael's advice to get to a medical doctor "now" if I want to be able to keep writing, my plan is to go to the nearby walk-in clinic when it opens at 11 a.m. tomorrow. I wish you were here but I might send an email to my daughter and ask her to come. She hasn't contacted me at all, I'm disappointed, but she would be the one most likely able to come to me and take care of what needs to be taken care of. So if you don't hear from me for a while you'll know I'm most likely in hospital, I expect that to happen. I've about given up now with the books written, no longer fighting, accepting whatever comes, I'm good with it, it was a wonderful life. Please do what you can if need be to see that the three books are published, it's my message to the world, thanks. I love you sweetie.

M: (to daughter) Your brother advises me to get to a medical doctor right away so my plan is to go to the walk-in clinic a few yards from here when it opens at 11 a.m. tomorrow. My guess is that they are going to send me to hospital for tests and I may not be released? I don't know if that is what is going to happen but wanted to put you on standby as the one in my family most likely able to come and help with whatever needs to be done at a moment's notice, I'd very much appreciate that. I'll leave a note at the hospital for someone to call you if need be.

If they send me there, I will probably drive myself to the hospital. If you come, take a taxi there from the airport and get the keys to my car and apartment. There's a GPS in it. Either way, if I can I will send you an email or call (can't talk long, short of breath) tomorrow when I find out how this is likely going to play out.

I hate to trouble anyone but this has to run its course and that includes getting medical help and possibly a hospital stay with things that have to be taken care of that I can't get to. I'm sure Jen would come but she has family with her. I love my family. Dad

Jen: I am so glade you finished your books. Also glade Oresha came by and was company for a hour. I do miss you. Please call me if they send you to the hospital. I will keep my phone with me waiting to hear from you. Take your phone charger with you. I will catch a flight as soon as I can after the 2nd. Love you.

Daughter: Dad, Call me on my cell or send me an email. I will be skiing during the day, but there is wifi at the ski lodge. I will happily come if you need me. I will have to return home early to get ready for my cruise trip. I can have my sister come replace me after that if need be. Anyway, let me know how it goes.

M: (to daughter) Check with Jen before coming just in case she can get away, if so I won't need you to come but thanks ever so much anyway, I love you lots.

Jen: Of course I will come as soon as possible. Love you sweetie

M: (to Jen) I think the cruise is non-refundable but they might allow a different date if I'm in hospital? Wait though and let's first see what's happening with me.

Jen: That is my feeling also. I will do what needs to be done. Let me know as soon as possible what the doctor says.

M: I hate bothering people, except you of course, don't mind doing that at all. It still feels as though we are married, I'd marry you today if I could. I love you so much Jen. I feel as helpless as a little child right now as I start to unwind and relax into being sick without fighting it so I could get the books finished. This has got to run its course, I'd be pretty much useless on the cruise the way I am right now. Hopefully whatever they do it won't take long. If it's my heart apparently there's an easy fix. Yeah, saw that with DeLeon, major operation, though she only did one night in hospital so not too brutal.

Hope your family visit is still going well. Did all your kids arrive ok? What are your plans for New Year's eve? We used to watch the ball drop in Times Square at 10 pm. then go to bed. Not a very exciting life with me was it? Would you like to have been at a party?

Jen: I have no plans for New Years. I will stay home and watch the ball drop. Yes it may be a easy fix but I think all the travels should be canceled. I will come to you. My youngest daughter and her family did make it. She is in tremendous pain from her back. They left today. Kids had lots of fun. Love you

M: Would you like to have been at a party on those new year's eves?

M: Wait until tomorrow after we find out what the docs say before cancelling but I tend to agree with you, maybe it would be best if you plan to stay here for a while. My new grandson and family will understand if I postpone my visit to Phoenix.

Jen: No, Never thought to much about it. I was happy just being with you all those New years eve's.

M: You're so sweet, you tell me everything you know I'd like to hear. I've always known I'm boring so I often asked you questions about your former husbands and how much fun you had with them: dancing, conversing etc. Maybe we can make up for some of it yet.

Jen: Just get well my dear. We will have lots of fun together. We did take some wonderful trips together.

M: (to potential literary agent) Dear Agent, Further to my submission this will advise you that all three of the Becoming Adam books have been revised and all three are immediately available for submission. (See attached.) I am now requesting literary agent representation for the first three books in the contemporary "Becoming Adam" series. (850,000 words) I look forward to working closely with you to get these first three books published and marketed. I love them, I think others will too...

M: (to my children, Jen, siblings) 11:30 a.m. Family, As some of you know, my health has been poor lately. I just came from the clinic and was told I most likely have a collapsed lung, everything is "completely plugged" on one side. I am going to the hospital by taxi right away. I'll be at emergency for a while and will almost certainly be admitted. My affairs are in order so nobody needs to rush to help kind of thing. Jen will probably stay at my place. Hopefully by then I'll be home good as new. I love you all. Dad/Michael

Daughter: Thanks for the update dad. Keep us informed as best as you can. Luv you

Daughter 5: (let's number my seven children in order of birth, this one is "5") Siblings, I just called the hospital. Dad was just registered at Emergency so it will be another couple of hours before we know anything. I will call again later and keep you all updated.

2: (to siblings, tongue in cheek) More importantly, is the 3rd book done?

5: Siblings, I spoke with Dad. He is in the cast room in emerg. There are no open beds right now, but they will get him into one as soon as one opens up. He has a collapsed lung almost completely filled with fluid. They opened him up (while he was awake he said) to drain the fluid etc. He will be in the hospital for the next 3 days or so. Then he will be in Victoria for the next several months so they can monitor him. Dad sounded very shakey. He told me that everything is fine and not to worry. He is turning off his phone and won't have email until he gets home. When he does get home he will send out a mass email. I am his emergency contact and will call tomorrow. If there is any other news I will email again.

M: (to you) Much of what follows from now on are emails swapped between me and among my children and each other and a few from and with my siblings. This may be the story of my dying. Victoria, Womb of

Michael has perhaps become Victoria, Tomb of Michael. This is a true story, I'm *living* it.

7: Thanks for the update. Tell dad he is in our prayers and to actually follow the instructions for recovery.

1: (my oldest son, he's a medical doctor and very religious) Thanks be to God that Dad went to the doctor. Ditto to what 7 said! 5 to clarify was the collapsed lung also the one with fluid or where both lungs involved? Do they know why the problem(s) happened? Love to everyone.

My Brother: (to my siblings and 5) I'm forwarding this message from 5 to you and also letting 5 know of your e-mail address. 5 would have reached you herself but she did not have your e-mail addresses. Now she does ok? Michael was going to go on a cruise with Jen but I guess now he will have to stay put and take care of himself. Thanks for letting us know 5. We really are concerned and ask that you please let us know of any further news. We've been communicating with your dad through e-mail. We will be away for about 10 days on a trip to Cuba. However if you need to contact someone in the family, I also gave you your cousins e-mail address. We hope your dad will be better soon and will pray for his speedy recovery. It's also nice to know that Jen will be there soon. She will be able to keep us all updated via e-mail. Please get better soon Michael.

Oresha: Just a note to say "Hello"... and to wish You a Wonderful New Yr.! May it be filled with Love, Joy, Happiness, Good Health & Abundance! .... everything that Your Heart desires... and ...MORE! I've been trying to get in touch with you to see how you're doing... Please drop me a line or give me a call ? Take Good Care of Yourself My friend!...

M: (to family members – let's call this "List") Dear Family, I got home a few minutes ago after seven days in hospital with a tube inside my chest cavity to treat a collapsed lung. Jen is with me and will stay a few weeks most likely.

Two doctors spoke with me about three hours ago and went over the first results from the lung biopsy. It is not good news, I have inoperable lung cancer and it has spread to more than just two spots in my lung. It is of the "adneo" variety (spelling?.) They tell me even if I had gone to a doctor sooner it would not have made a difference, they do not know what causes such cancers, I have never been a smoker.

My next scheduled stop is a chest x-ray on Monday next week to see if the fluid is building again, and to a clinic to get sutures removed. Sometime possibly this week I will have to go to Vancouver for a "PET" scan I think they called it, they don't have such a machine in Victoria. When it gets to the point where I go to the cancer clinic I will be advised re radiation and chemo therapies to gain a bit of time maybe and will make choices and decisions then. At this point I'd sooner not prolong life much though I love you all and know this will be much harder on you than it is on me. I'm quite happy how this is going actually.

As for needs, I cannot fly for at least six weeks because I have had air in my chest cavity, so I will almost certainly remain in Victoria, we'll see how much time they eventually prognosticate and how often I need to be in for tests/treatment etc. Everyone is of course welcome to visit anytime (coordinate with Jen or whoever is here with me) but as for needs, Jen will take care of those until close for a while. I may then need someone to drive me around etc. we'll see how quickly this develops. Who knows maybe it will heal and I'll live a long life yet, I just don't want to be handicapped in any way, I'm accepting of whatever comes except that.

Sorry to have this news to tell you but that's what I was told a few hours ago, yes, it seems unreal to me too. My phone is on but please do not ask me to talk more than a few minutes, thanks for understanding. I love you all.

5: Dad, I will come when I get back home. I will stay as long as you need me.

M: Thanks 5, knew you would. Love you lots.

M: (to Oresha) You're such a good friend, I really appreciate your concern. I finally got the chest tube removed and went home tonight. Unfortunately the preliminary results of the lung biopsy are not good news, it seems that I have lung cancer. So I'll be very busy the next while, including a run to Vancouver to feed some new machine they have there. Jen is with me for a while and my daughter will come then so I won't be needing assistance. I wish you and Kathy the very best.

3: Love you Dad.

M: Thanks 3, kinda thought so.

Oresha: OMG Michael... I am so sorry to hear of your upcoming challenges... I am so glad that Jen is here with you!... and that your daughter is on her way! My thoughts and Prayers are with You!... Please let me know if there's anything I can do for you? I would like to get your DVD's back to you soon, in case Jen or You would like to watch them... if you'd like.. please let me know... When are you going to Vancouver for treatments? Please keep me posted..... I would very much like to meet Jen.. if/when she's up for it in the future... I feel like I would much rather talk with you on the phone/or in person... but I respect your choices.... and will try to express my feelings through email for now... even though how I feel is so beyond words... I believe that there is always HOPE!.... Much LOVE to You and Your Loved Ones! Your friend

M: Jen and I will invite you for a visit (and Kathy if she wants to come) in the near future. But first I need a few more days to heal from the hole they punched in my chest to drain fluid, and to get a schedule. I'll get back to you.

1: Dad we all love you here in this family. 2 and I would like to come so that you can have a Priesthood blessing one of the weekends this month. Please let us know about your schedule. I think that there's still a lot more for your doctors to learn besides the adenocarcinoma diagnosis. Presumably this is primary lung cancer (cancer can come into the lungs from other places and the would be secondary lung). The PET scan is meant to look for metastasis of the cancer, "Inoperable" only means they cannot operate. That can be for many reasons including tumour location. The doctors will likely be checking the biopsy samples further for more information such as further sub typing, tumour markets, etc.

Dad do you recall where they told you the masses are, their sizes, etc? Did they biopsy one or more than one of the masses? Usually most people don't recall much from these first preliminary meetings. Often people bring a loved one along to subsequent meetings with paper and pencil to take notes to aid in recall. I'm sure Jen would do that for you.

Right now I doubt that your doctors can give you a prognosis as they don't know enough yet. There are pretty good general statistics based on tumour staging that reflect how groups, but not necessarily how an individual, fare. These are numbers such as what percentage of persons with certain lung cancer characteristics are alive at one year, three years, five years.

As I understand it there is possible treatment at all states of lung cancer. There are new targeted treatments for certain tumour types as well as chemotherapy and radiation treatments. Palliative treatments can be very helpful at lengthening quality of life while perhaps not lengthening life itself. People often have productive, quality lives until close to the end of their life. I've seen that even be just days before the person dies. Treatments can be risky but then so is the alternative. Declining all life prolonging treatments doesn't have to mean declining all treatments. Most people want to be comfortable. That should be achievable.

Of course the hearts of all in this house are wrent. We want to respect your wishes Dad. My advice about treatment is that you and your doctors don't know enough yet to make decisions as you do not yet know your options (apart from no OR). Do what you need to in order to learn what can be learned, all of us turn more deeply to The God of Love Who Will Not Fail Nor Forsake. You have heard the Witness He has Given me. I again solemnly bear Witness of God and The Lamb. He Has Been so Kind to us through all the many medical and other struggles with my son. He Is Unchanging. Love 1 et al

M: (to list) Thank-you for that nice message 1, I appreciate the love you all have for me. Regarding prayers, as I mentioned to 7 last night during a phone call, I do welcome prayers on my behalf. But my hope is not for prayers of healing and intervention, my hope is only for prayers of "Thy will be done" because that is an unselfish and effective prayer and what I want. I have been prepared for this, for me it is a great gift given. I know where I am going, I have looked upon it, it is beautiful there, *we* are beautiful there in our glorious white robes and sociality. My soul longs for home, life has been wonderful, I am blessed beyond measure.

Our warrior 7 of course wants me to "fight" but I will not fight and disregard or cast away my wondrous gift for the pottage of a few more days on this planet. I accept, I embrace and love my gift, I open it gladly and breathe in of its fullness. The greatest experience of my life approaches, living out my dying. I long for it but want it comfortable and painless as you Dr. 1 and a hospice nurse friend of mine assure me it can be.

Our family lawyer 2 asked about the technical details of funeral etc. That of course is entirely for the living not for the one who has returned to Source, but the following would be my desire. Modify as you will, I won't haunt you if you do. At the following link during daylight hours you will see a live view of the Ogden Point Breakwater in Victoria. I loved walking that breakwater, just a ten minute walk from the apartment where I live. For several months I walked to the end of the breakwater then home every single day. There I saw much sea life even whales, dolphins, seals, sea lions, octopus etc. I was fascinated.

With that webcam you would have my memorial anytime you wanted to pause upon it and think of me fondly. Think not with yearning and desire to have me back but with the gift of happy memories, surely you can each find some of those in your long association with this soul who wants now only to be free. I don't want a traditional funeral or the expense of it, no headstone, just the cost of cremation, then gather at the end of breakwater and scatter the ashes remaining into the sea I loved so much. Picture the tiny creatures absorbing those remains, they going up the food chain to the dolphins and great whales, and symbolically a part of me in every sea on this planet, and washing up upon its shores, I will never be far away then.

But don't try to call me back, let me go I was born to be free, only be happy for me and our pleasant association. That's how I would have you remember me and tell my grandchildren in happy stories if any at all. I was always a shy quiet man, you couldn't have known me well, but I loved much and was mostly happy. Think upon that and release me, let me go forward where I want to go and be, I will always love you. You do not need my help or intervention or appearings or signs, just the happy memories. And I do not need your sorrow and sadness, let it go. Release

me please, let me go in peace and love and freedom and fullness of joy -
now *that's* what I want from you most...

Enjoy life, it was not meant to be lived in sorrow and sadness and
sacrifice, it was meant to be lived for joy and abundance. Savor each
moment, I call you as best I can to that. Should a present moment
disappoint then in your mind begin a new life in the moment to come,
and choose happiness in it. In your quiet moments of meditation and
reflection calm your scattered thoughts and focus on joy, you were
designed for a fullness of that. It's easily found by pretending that your
body is only vibration and you are speeding up that vibration, the joy
comes quickly in doing that. In *yourself* find love, for there you will find
God and you, and your light will be known, a beautiful city rising upon
a hill. I will see that light from my home among the stars from whence I
came and I will rejoice that I knew and still know and love you. I might
even twinkle a bit for you when you look up and wish upon a star for I
will be there. :-) The Sioux, some who say they came from the Pleiades,
have a saying that goes something like this: *"Taku Wakan scan scan"*
meaning *"something holy moving among the stars."* That would be us, it's
joyful there.

God be with you dear ones, surely I loved you all in my own quiet
way, and always will. Dad/Michael

M: (to literary agent) What an ending there will be for the four
book "Becoming Adam" series. In real life I the author found out
yesterday that I have inoperable lung cancer and am dying. That
could add a whole lot of weight to the philosophical musings found
in my books and would make Book 4 quite a looked forward to
event published after the author's death documenting conversations
exchanged as he lived out his dying. (See below.) Add that to Suzanne's
haunting real life hospice stories in the books and I think they will sell
very well if properly placed and marketed.

Anyway, I'm still holding the agent opportunity exclusive to you,
I haven't submitted a query to anyone else. I will provide all three of
the manuscripts (850,000 words) anytime you ask for them. Michael

Demers (my ex "Jen" in the books, is staying with me for a few weeks, you could talk with her if need be.)

Here's a hasty message I sent to my children early this a.m. It's a sample of what book 4 would contain as the next few weeks of my dying evolve. (insert message above)

Carrie: hi there... wanted to let you know there have been some pretty big changes in my life lately... first, the woman i was moving to sedona with has decided not to do her business for at least a while, as she has health issues to work on first... second, a man who's been in and out of my life for 40 years came back into my life in a very big way just before thanksgiving and i am leaving on thursday to spend some time with him in california... i have no idea how things will go, but it looks better than ever before that this might actually be our time, so we are going to see what we might create together... i will have access to my email, so we can keep in touch... i'm planning on being gone about a month, if all goes well... so...sending love and i'm off on an adventure...

M: I'm pleased for you and your prospects Carrie, thanks for the update, I wish you very well with your new adventure, please keep in touch. As for me it seems that I have now embarked on the greatest adventure we ever get to experience in life, living out our dying. Yes it's true, yesterday I was informed after a week in hospital that I have inoperable lung cancer. But I've been preparing for this, knew it somehow during the last few weeks and rushed to finish Book 3 a few hours before going to emergency with a collapsed lung. The next few weeks should be interesting indeed! My ex, Jen is with me for a few weeks and a daughter is on stand-by so I'll have loving care. Take care my good friend Carrie.

2: Dad, Thanks so much for the words. It is only natural for those that are left behind to feel some sorrow at the anticipated passing of a loved one but I agree that the focus should be on the joy of time already shared and I am satisfied that we will all be able to do that in time. I agree with 1 that you should continue to listen carefully to your doctors and care providers who are best positioned to assist you with the guidance necessary to be able to live out your final moments in peace and comfort.

1 and I had spoken of coming to see you in the next week or two. You indicate that perhaps it may be best to wait until you have a better indication of timelines. I would still like to come sooner rather than letter if you approve so that we can give you a priesthood blessing. My family is going to Orlando so if we do not come in the next two weeks then I would not be able to participate until likely later. I would prefer you not to have to wait that long and would be honored to be able to participate. We had thought of coming likely just for a couple of days. If this meets with your approval please let 1 and I know your anticipated schedule over these weekends and we will make arrangements to come. Could you also provide your address. Just so you have absolute certainty; those members of my family love you and wish you all the comforts and happiness you can find at this time. Love,

M: You are welcome to come anytime. At this point nothing is scheduled before Monday and as I think about it some of my treatments might require hospital stays so maybe sooner would be better. The16[th] would be my preference but come to Victoria anytime. We'll walk the breakwater together and I'll check out if your arm is strong enough to toss ashes into the sea.

1: Hey Dad could you spend your writing talents on memories of growing up, what you know about and stories about your parents and grandparents and further on, your recollections of your sisters and brother, memories of your children, and so on? Not just the "happy" memories but also the memories that bring the colour to what has sculpted our family. I often point to the photographs and pictures in the offices I use and tell my patients that without the dark tones we lose the perspective and the beauty of what we are seeing. I too am naturally shy. I would rather have you spend your considerable writing talents and resolve on memories than on any novels. I still fondly remember how you would rise so early and do family history work. Thank you for that. Love

5: Dad, I second 1's idea!!

M: (to list) It's obviously difficult for me to think of scheduling time for anything at this point. But I appreciate your interest. Keep in mind that I gave everyone (my children) a copy of my books of remembrance many years ago, some of you may still have them. I will of course respond to any *specific* questions I may be asked by email, that may be the best way to do this.

2: Perhaps you can record some memories on your laptop hard drive using the video or using a separate video camera.

M: (to Suzanne) Being Nurse, I think you detected in Las Vegas that my health was not optimum. But I functioned fully until about three weeks ago when I became so short of breath that I could hardly slow walk four or five blocks when I usually walked briskly for miles most days. I knew then that I needed to rush to finish Book 3 and I did. A few hours later I walked into a nearby medical clinic and was instantly sent to emergency. I was in hospital for seven days, getting home only last night while fluid was drained from a chest cavity to treat a totally collapsed lung. Along the way, CT scans revealed and I was told yesterday that I have inoperable lung cancer.

So now begins the most thrilling of adventures, one you are completely familiar with, living out my dying. It still seems unreal but it also feels like a great gift Suzanne, school let out for the summer unexpectedly early and I am glad of it. Jen is here with me for several weeks and a daughter is on standby so I will have constant loving care. Any words of advice you might have for one dying who loves the destination but is shy of pain along the way would be welcome. I want you to know that you have meant much to me dear one, I wish only the very best for you, take care sweetie.

Suzanne: My heart aches for you. Can you get onto a hospice program? What a blessing for book 3 to be complete. Share your thoughts with me, I'm here to listen if others are too afraid. Are you in any pain? I am holding your hand, I hope you can feel it.

M: You are so sweet Suzanne, thank-you for that lovely response. I read it to Jen and she responded, *"that was beautiful."*

I am not in pain that common pain killers will not address, just the tube wound healing, still leaking a tiny bit now and again. Sometime this week I expect a phone call to take the ferry to Vancouver for a PET scan. Once those and other tests are completed hopefully within a few days I will get to a cancer clinic and perhaps receive some notion of a time line. I will almost certainly refuse chemo and radiation, it is not my desire to swap this great gift offered me for the pottage of a few more days on this planet. Knowing myself, I jump all the way in and may not take a long time moving on to the destination that I have already peeked into and found desirable above all things this world has to offer, we are truly beautiful there, we will meet again.

I don't know about hospice programs but I do know that I will not tolerate pain and Canada's health insurance program is beneficial and abundant, I will look into it if need be. Of course I feel your hand in mine, how could it be any other way?

Suzanne: Once you are sure about refusing chemo and radiation, hospice should be offered. Please ask. You know you were interested in writing about the next life experiences, maybe you can share in your words the next days, weeks, and months. I want to read your story. Suzette is never too far.....

I communicate with her in her real name but yes, she did write "Suzette" instead of "Suzanne". Has Suzanne been so long gone then and only retained in my own imagination, and maybe yours?

M: I'll keep you posted sweetie. My story will be in Book 4 which I am now living/writing, to die for actually. Did you ever get your hospice stories published? I'd buy the book if you did.

M: (to list) When my two oldest sons arrive to lay their hands on their father's head and give him a blessing it is my hope that they will come prepared to be sort of a 'senior management team' having discussed matters with the others involved in a preliminary manner. Jen will be here and there are things to discuss with her such as what to do about my company which is still a going concern, how to manage it, and who and how to pay for that management. Disposal of my motor home, last will and testament or trust etc. complicated by the international location of my real estate assets and my RV.

I will need a certain amount of cash to take care of my personal needs for however long I live. Otherwise money, my car etc. is of little use to me if I am not given much time to live without handicap. This will be an excellent time to explore such things, I hope you will come prepared for a comprehensive discussion with Jen while I listen in and act as consultant, she knows my business and how to run it. I see this more of a fact-finding meeting than lawyer 2 actually executing documents, but it could be that as well. Your meeting with Jen would likely be followed by discussions with the Seven to hopefully reach consensus. But however you want to do it, you will find me cooperative and willing to help make the transition as easy as possible for everyone.

6: Thank you for the updates. I'm praying for you Dad and all my sibs. Please continue to keep me informed.

M: (to myself) I have not forgotten Elaine, it's just that Elaine has forgotten me. I have had no word from her for a long time. So that's where we'll leave dear Elaine except that of course I will let you know if she ever sends me a message. The same with Kris. I feel no desire at this moment to inform DeLeon either. That may come with time, possibly after I get a realistic timeline from the cancer experts as to how long I can expect to live in this physical body. It still seems unreal as if I am once again unrealistically happy about that which is fantasy. Hopefully this time it will be real, or this body will be chosen for immortality. It doesn't seem to matter tonight which way it goes, either way I am destined for a close and lasting encounter with God. Though I may rush back, this world is moving so fast and I think I yet have a role to play in bringing forth the Golden Age. And then too, *I am becoming Adam…*.

5: Dad, There has been some discussion among the women folk about you possibly coming to Alberta for treatment etc. It would be a lot easier for us as the great majority of us live in Alberta. Think about that.

M: With great respect for the women folk who make our meager male lives worth living, my health care insurance is B.C. specific and my chosen home is Victoria by the sea. If I'm still able I will drive to Alberta in the Spring for visits but it's highly unlikely that I would ever move to another province. Also, face it, all of you have a Victoria Secret wish to move here someday anyway, *so why not now?*

1+ (1's Wife): As far as I know, 1's only "Victoria Secret wish" is the one that involves his wife in some type of lingerie.

5: You are spectacular!!!!

M: That too, guys are like that, we can't help it... But Victoria might not be a good place for 1's shrink biz, Canadians are crazy who *don't* move to Victoria, we're all sane here.

M: (to Lynne the clairvoyant) It has been many weeks since I have seen you on Dallas Rd or anywhere so perhaps you have moved? But if you are still doing readings I think it's time for me to get a refresh and I would like to make an appointment with you. Please let me know, thanks.

M: (to list) I just got off the phone with the doctor. The final results from the biopsy are in. It is not "adenocarcinoma" as originally thought but is squamish cell cancer. There are multiple places in my lung and it has penetrated the lining. Doc reaffirmed that it would not be helpful to remove the lung. The PET scan will reveal where else it may be in my body, if I get an appointment in Vancouver for a PET scan that is. If the cancer clinic in Victoria gets to me first (it might be two weeks from now) they may decide they don't need the PET. Meanwhile, I'll go for an x-ray on Monday to keep tabs on the accumulation of fluid in the chest cavity so it doesn't collapse the lung again.

That leaves a few free days so I'll walk the park and seaside with Jen and tonight we'll see a movie at the Imax. I am feeling well, no pain except at the site where the tube was put in, it seems to be healing well. Jen is an enormous help and comfort, I'm very grateful for her, she doesn't *have* to be here. We'll do our weeping together that life on this planet has unexpectedly become so short. It still seems unreal, maybe that's the "denial" stage though I am not pushing off an early death, somehow it seems a reward, a sigh of relief after holding my breath so long, an eventual relaxing into it as it becomes more apparent to my awareness that this body that has served me so well is dying, as they tell me it is, I wouldn't otherwise know it.

I'll know more options when I speak with the cancer clinic people but maybe there's a hospice program at the appropriate time so I won't need to endure pain, that is the only thing I fear. It appears that death in the not distant future is inevitable and I'm ok with that even as I am of course cognizant that the greater pain is for those who remain behind. My greatest hope is that you never mourn, that you think only happy thoughts of me. You've had me for many years, be grateful for that as I am to have counted you among my loved ones. I love you all, you are each dear to me. Please forgive where forgiveness is felt needed, I don't think it was ever my conscious *intention* to hurt anyone though I'm sure I must at times have done so, it comes with living. This living out my dying may not take a long time, I feel as though it may pass swiftly. I am most content to move on to where I am going, I have caught glimpses, it's beautiful there and so are we. I'll never regret my life, it was wonderful, I loved much, I was mostly happy, I *am* happy. Somebody please check often to see that nobody has fallen from this list and that everyone who properly belongs on it is there.

7: I don't want Dad's son in laws to feel excluded or feel obligated to come for the Priesthood blessing or for that matter anyone else. Surely any family member is welcome as long as Dad is in agreement.

M: I'm wondering if an email may have gone out that did not have me copied into it?? I did happen to check an old email address and there was a message that my sons were coming to visit me. Is that true? It would warm my heart so.... Please send all messages to this list, that way nobody feels left out, thx.

2: (sent to an old email address) Dad, You may already be aware but in the event you are not me, 1 and 7 will be flying into Victoria on the16. We are all staying until Sunday evening. We have rented a car so no need to arrange transportation. I believe we will be staying at the Embassy Inn. Hopefully it is decent and within walking distance of your place. Could you please give us your address.

M: (to list) What a wonderful gift to have my sons visit me together. Everyone who wants to visit is of course welcome anytime. However, I can think of nothing more powerful than me and my four warriors walking together to the end of the breakwater and sitting there for a while with each other. Add anyone else to the mix at that time and it would be a conversation among several people. I think with just the five of us it would be all focused on us as one. Jen understands and offered to trail behind to take photos, maybe join us after a few minutes. *Such a great dream as that would be for me!!!* Anyone tipped off by cell phone could watch us from a distance on the webcam.

Let me know if anyone needs picking up at the airport and when. Jen and I will be pleased to do that, it's a 45 minute drive to James Bay from the airport, $60 by taxi, so don't hesitate to ask. Wow, all my sons together with me, just wow, life's worth living after all...

Jen's older daughter to Jen: Ohhh... This is sad news. Mom may you be blessed with the strength to help him through this.

Jen's sister to Jen: Soooo sorry to hear of Michael's illness.... My thoughts and prayers are with you both.... Keep in touch with his progress.... We just never know when it be might be time to go home. Love and Prayers

Luchia: (my artist friend) Hi Michael happy new year! I hope you are well. My guides are yelling at me to get a hold of you and invite you over. I'm not sure what that's all about but if you feel similarly nudged let's figure something out..... In any case I have thought of you often and will look forward to reconnecting in whatever way seems best for us.

M: Luchia, Well, I don't doubt that your guides are "yelling" at you because you are so connected and so uncanny with your spiritual abilities, I love that in you. It turns out that I got out of a seven day stay in hospital two days ago to treat a collapsed lung and drain the fluid. Along the way they did a couple of CT scans and a biopsy. I am diagnosed with inoperable lung cancer.

I am in no pain and if they hadn't told me this physical body that has served me so well is dying I would never have known. At this point in time it is undeniable, it's happening. The only thing I fear is pain and apparently they can control that very well. To me the news is a great and unexpected gift that I welcome and embrace fully, a chance to go home and refresh much sooner than I had expected. We'll eventually meet and play there, it's beautiful, I have caught glimpses.

And meanwhile my three books are finished and waiting to be submitted to a literary agent when the right one comes along. Book 4 is the story of living out my own dying, it will make an interesting read I'm sure. Of course lovely Luchia makes an appearance in the books.

Jen my ex is with me for a few weeks and I have a daughter on standby so I will receive all the loving care I need. As for healing and intervention, my preference is for the "Thy will be done" type because I am quite accepting of how this is playing out right now. I'm having fun playing a new unexpected role, the greatest adventure we ever get in this life, leaving it.

Take care my good friend Luchia, keep in touch if you like, I will always respond to your messages. I have fond memories of our interaction, we are surely family in some way. It is my hope that we were dear lovers in past lives, it just wasn't our time in this one. We'll be together again soon enough sweet one, I have some traveling to do first.

2: We have a rental car and all else covered so no need for any arrangements on your end.

Luchia: Oh my goodness. I'm a little bit stunned at the moment. The first words that come after that..... I'm sorry for you although you probably won't feel that way at all ..... And For me because I will miss you so!

I understand now how you felt when I chose to leave the island and you said you wished that we had been able to spend more time together. It is such a strange phenomena when we truly figure things out when someone is leaving in one way or another.

I love the way you see things and your courage is inspiring. I am glad your friend Jen is there with you. I don't get a sense of timing here and perhaps you don't know. I also couldn't find your phone number or I would certainly be calling rather than emailing right now. Would you like me to come and see you? I am fully available after Tuesday next week

What can I do to help and support you Michael? I am truly here with you and of course have to hear more about my book character.... This is my second time..... I am also a comic strip character..... Seems somehow quite appropriate.....

I remember our emails very well they are asked into my soul as you well know. I expect to be in Victoria very soon for our rendezvous let me know.

Luchia: (she attaches a small homily about taking life into your own hands) Hi Michael, was just told to send you this.... I just put this together today..... for myself I thought..... I am in the kitchen making quinoa porridge with grilled tomatos and garlic. I would like to come to you once your friend has left, and cook beautiful vegetarian meals for you for a week. Let me know when and how we can accomplish this. It turns out I am carrying around a portable cot-bed in the back of my car..... I had purchased it for my daughter's place when I visit, of course she decided I would sleep in luxury as she prefers to fall asleep with the tv on the couch. So with the perfection of universal timing, I have my bed already in the car and ready to go, and can make it over there anytime after Tuesday of next week. My number is, please send me yours. Take good care bello

M: You're so sweet Luchia. If Jen was not here I'd jump on your offer to visit and stay awhile but she's here most likely until the end of the month and then a daughter will be coming immediately. It's not scheduled yet but I may need to take the ferry to Vancouver for a PET scan, Jen will drive my car to and from. It's possible while we're there that she and I could take a hotel in your city for a night and visit with you. No commitment but I think that would be nice if you'd like it to happen.

I tire quickly on the phone and there's no privacy in my home (Jen is insecure and gets jealous of any expression of sentiment I give my female friends) so I'd much prefer that we communicate via email if that's ok with you. Enjoy the day Luchia

Carrie: well... that was quite an email... and, my heart is hurting for this news... i will say, however, that i have an amazing array of resources for cancer treatment that work! and there is no such thing as a terminal situation unless one chooses to believe in that, as i know you know... so the question is are you resigned to this fate, are you working with your LOA energetics to shift it and do you want help in any way? i fully respect whatever choice you make, but if you want to kick this thing in the ass, i'll do my best to get you all the information, connections and resources i have... and, if not, i will join you in your adventure as it progresses... sending you all my love and will stay in touch after i get to california... will be back online on friday... hugs and more hugs, carrie

M: It still seems unreal that my physical body is dying because if the docs hadn't told me it was I wouldn't have known. But the news struck me as beautiful, an unexpected furlough to go home for a while given a soldier too long on the battlefield. There I know I will find the rest and depth of love and acceptance that I need to regenerate, regroup, and fight again. But I'm in love with this planet and its people so I'll likely have more to do with helping prepare for the leap to a Golden Age, I want to see that safely home. Maybe my books will help with that, especially when the author is dead? Or will I die? Book 4 is not yet complete there are pages unwritten, so we'll see... Don't squeeze too tight when you hug sweetheart, it's a bit tender in places.

M: (to Marcy: healer, psychic surgeon, past life lover?, friend... cc DeLeon and Elaine) Marcy, I count you among my dearest friends so I thought it would be remiss to neglect sending you notice of a life-changing event in my journey.

About one month ago I became so short of breath that my daily brisk walk for miles along the sea had to be shortened to a slow walk of four or five blocks. I knew something was seriously wrong with my body but rushed to finish the third book in the series I am writing. A few hours after I closed the book I was in hospital emergency as a priority case. One of my lungs was totally collapsed. Over the next seven days in hospital my chest cavity was slowly drained by a tube inserted there and the lung became functional again. Along the way there were CT scans and other tests. Three days ago the tube was pulled and I was allowed to go home, but not before I was told that I have inoperable lung cancer and am headed to the cancer clinic and most likely hospice.

It still seems unreal but the news was beautiful, an unexpected early release from school for the summer. I do not wish to rage or fight, I will go gentle to the light. We are beautiful there Marcy! Wish me godspeed, it is a goodly journey to live out your dying already knowing where you are going.

My ex Jen is with me and will stay several weeks, then a daughter is on standby to come as long as I need her here. So I have and will continue to have the loving care and attention I will need for this change of circumstance. I am grateful for them and for my several friends including you who somehow seem to be family, "group soul" perhaps. You are doing well with your life, serving faithfully, we'll meet again somewhere I'm sure, God bless you and us.

Lynne: Hi Michael... nice to hear from you. It's true that I haven't been able to get out to the beach etc for a while but I am 'around'. I have been really busy for the past while and I am heading out for an appointment this morning. later today, I will have a better idea of whether I can be available on friday or next monday etc. I'll send you another message when I know for sure. Have a beautiful day!

Jen: (to her siblings) Hello family, I am in Canada to care for Michael. He had a collapsed lung and was hospitalized for a week. We now know from the biopsy it is Squamish cell cancer of the lungs. It is inoperable cancer. We believe it is in the late stage and waiting to find out what course he can take to make it as pain free as possible. I feel privileged to be hear with him. We both always loved and care about each other. Just sort of got lost for a short time.

This last eighteen months gave me a wonderful opportunity to be of service to my family made possible by my oldest daughter. I thank God for a daughter like her that is willing to make my life easier and take on my business burdens, so I can be free to follow the desires of my heart.

In August of 2013 I went to care full time for my new born (mostly motherless) grandson struggling the his first 21 days of life in intensive care. I spent about 9 months with him full time. He is doing wonderful now. After that I drove back once or twice a month to Calif. to check on him. I just could not stay away. He is a joy to his dad, even with the struggles of being a single father. He is amazing father. As you know my son owns his own company and has 5 employees working for him. So it is not easy. His oldest daughter decided to quite her second job to cares for the baby 3 days a week and my son cares for him the rest of the time. He takes him with him on the job when safe to do so..

Then I helped my youngest daughter through struggles along with her serious skiing accident. She is amazing, she works full time, going to school with only one class left to get her Bachelor degree, spent 9 months either in a wheel chair but mostly in leg braces. Her ex and her share child care equally and he is good help. I found 6 children under

12 is a bit challenging for me some times. Hard to keep up with 12 busy hands. Not used to picking up and taking kids to the places they need to be everyday. I found I can communicate well with the deaf one even though I know very little sign language. She seems to be in tune or is reading my lips.

As far as Michael goes. I am the only one that knew how sick he was for the last month. I waited while then with out his permission contacted his children and told them he was very sick. He did not want to effect their plans, even though they invited him to join them. He also had three books he wanted to finish. With their help he was finally convinced to go to the doctor and was sent to emergency with a total blocked collapsed lung. Now we know why and I am available to help and be with Michael during this time of passing on. He is very loving and kind to me. We really enjoy setting and talking. He was extremely thin so now I am feeding him lots of his favorite foods. With the help of hospital food and my cooking I am seeing a bit of weight coming back on him. His four sons will be here the 15th and help advice and bless his life. His daughters will come a bit later. They are very generous with kindness toward him. It could not be better one son is a lawyer and can do the paper work and one a medical doctor to advice him on treatments to make it as painless as possible. A third son a chiropractor. With those we love we never really loss that connection.

I had a wonderful time with 16 grandchildren and my 4 children with me. It had been at least 5 years since we were all together. We had a wonderful time eating way to much.

I want to thank those of you that sent Birthday and the get well cards. I am recovering well from my surgery. Had to wait for a two week appointment before I could go and be with Michael. It was good he was still in the hospital when I got here. I did not want him to go home alone. Here, is being on Vancouver Island in the beautiful city of Victoria on the Pacific ocean. The warmest place in Canada in the winter. I am doing well and exactly what I where I want to be. Please keep Michael in your prayers. It is my prayer that my family back east are all doing well. This time for us is a very special time of learning, loving, excepting and forgiving. I love you all.

Chapter 3

DeLeon: My Dearly Beloved - just last evening, I was sharing with roomy - as we had participated in the burning bowl celebration - of letting go. And you were all over my thoughts... and I finally shared with her after getting home, that I had fallen in love with you and still am... that my time with you was the most precious of any male in my life.. ever.. and I would have always welcomed you back on any level, as you were a part of my heart - forever,..... and at this moment I receive this email. I am, as you know in shock.. And eyes pouring with rain of saddness. I will email more today, Just wanted to respond immediately. If I had any kind of funds would be out there in a moment to be with you. You are so sacred to life, to all whom you've touched and to me. In Love to my Beloved Michael - Look what the Divine gave us, knowing what was to come. Omg, Omg, Omg. Your Beloved DeLeon..

Please provide me with the telephone numbers of those who will be with you in this journey, so that I can communicate with them. Also please give me the number of Jen and of your daughter.. And give them mine. and my email. More a bit later.

M: (to DeLeon) Another friend from our soul group writes to me this morning upon hearing the same news:

> *"I fully accept your journey into the light, and I also hold the space for a miraculous change in course for you to have a miraculous mind blowing healing. Both are beautiful options."*

Please accept my journey with joy and dry your tears dear one, I never intended to make you sad. I appreciate your reaching out but an exchange of emails (no telephone) would be most welcome sweetie. I have peeked into the place where we will be going and we are beautiful there. (Me first please, you haven't finished your books Lioness. I have written mine except this final one that I am living, it's to die for. :-)

There are grand balls in heaven DeLeon, I looked in on one. You're going to like it there maybe more than me. I might rush back for a better hunt. I have seen the game, it's gathering just over the next hill, should be fun... Be happy please.

Luchia: As you wish of course in all areas. If you and Jen would like I have space for you to stay here and of course it would be my great pleasure. My city however, is a bit of a ways from downtown and it would probably tire you to come. I understand that and do not wish in anyway to cause you discomfort meeting my needs. I am ready and available for any kind of service that you need my friend in fact I would love to express the sentiments to Jen.

I would like to tell her what a wonderful person you were to me in my dire and troubled hour of need after being abandoned hurt and literally physically broken and left for dead. I will never forget the kindness and compassion to which you responded to me then other and your friends all of you kindly strangers projecting positive healing energy towards me. I wish to be there in-kind for you and Jen in whatever Fashion that develops from that. Please share this with her if it feels right and appropriate.

Of course now my curiosity is piqued I must ensure that someday I get to read about myself through your eyes in your books. When you are feeling up to it please give me details about this. I have not told you that I also am writing a book the picture I showed you is going to be on the back cover. Yes it's true you will also be in my book in my section on kindly angels. The book is entitled 'the art of relationship: painting a new pattern.'

I will send you a copy they have done up for me of the new cover page it is awesome. Also please show Jen..... As I'm not going to be cooking for you in the near future I am going to with your permission send you an energetic transfer each time I produce magnificent awesome nurturing food.... If that is okay with you my friend. Day there are blue skies above and I wish you a beautiful day take good care. Your friend Luchia

M: Let's wait a bit to see about visiting, I don't have a timeline from the cancer people yet. But if I go to Vancouver there's a good possibility that Jen and I will visit, it's a good opportunity for that. I am not (yet) in a place of discomfort other than healing from the wound caused by the doctors to drain the fluid and expand my lung. But I hear you sweetie and your offer to come to me and be of whatever service you can, I hugely appreciate that, thank your (yelling) guides for alerting you.

I did not previously know that your wounds were caused by a man who beat you up, I thought you had fallen on the beach. No wonder you were in so much hurt Luchia, it was much more than physical wounds that challenged you.

The photos you mention were not attached, I would like to see them. I do look forward to the "energetic transfers" emanating from your city. It is not time yet to share my books with anyone but I will alert you when they are accepted for publication and if not before I am disabled, Jen just said she would let you know where to get them when they are on the market. I would buy your book when it is available, please let me know, thanks.

Elaine: ...what intense news! Are you in Victoria still? Can I come to see you? Would your family mind? I will respect their wishes, but we were never intimate, only friends, so perhaps they would OK it.... Do you want me to visit...? If you get this message, let me know... I understand everything you are saying still... Love and really kind thoughts to you.

M: Please visit Elaine, it would warm my heart so to see you again. It is still my hope that you and Jen will become friends, especially if you have some time and my work drags out, you two could do things together while I rest. Jen will be here until near the end of the month when my daughter will come until Jen returns. My sons will visit for the weekend, then my daughters towards the end of the month. You will always be welcome, my family will quickly see how you cheer me, I hope you will read to me again.

Elaine: I hope I will cheer you up. I didn't mean to be so distant... just overworked and overwhelmed and trying to cope. I am just starting to get my energy back, working 9 to 13 tomorrow, then 4:30 overnight till 8:30, same Saturday. Can I visit you on Sunday, when I won't nod off mid sentence? Can I bring you a kale smoothie? Yes, I will read to you, happy to do so. And happy to meet Jen... Let me know if Sunday OK... if not, any time Monday. Oodles of loving kindness,

   M: Sunday will be fine sweetie, let me know closer to the day about what time you are planning to arrive. It's most likely best if you don't mind to walk around to the front and buzz, I'll unlatch the portal for you. Yes, smoothie for sure, but I might not share. Jen is looking forward to meeting you, she knows we are good friends and have not been intimate. Gosh I'm looking forward to seeing you, it seems a long time since we last talked. I haven't shaved for a while so expect a new look, hopefully not too shabby...

   Elaine: Never mind the human shell... I only see the soul anyway. I'll email Saturday afternoon, after I catch up on sleep. Rest well until then and drink your white tea... sometimes things turn around....

   DeLeon: Michael, Have to share story about the turquoise ring you got me in Costa Rica - when we were on the ocean edge amongst all of the booths, etc.. First of all it's pretty much always on my hand. My cousin and her daughter and family flew me up to Pensacola Florida to be with them for a week over thanksgiving. Weather was much cooler down here - and the first day there, we went out to "early" dinner. At the end of our dinner - I shockingly noticed the turquoise ring was gone! I was horrified. (I did also note that, probably due to the cold, my pearlized ring - the big one that I always wore on my left hand, was VERY loose - probably due to cold.) Looked all over the restaurant, tables near us, asked the waitress to ask her "fellow" waiters, if anything had shown up. Then slowly, carefully searching...walked out to the car to see if it had fallen off - in the car, out of the car, on the way. I am soo upset. Sadly walked back into restaurant to join the family- Then on the way out - where the greeting person was, along with a manger.... mentioned it to the manager, described it to her and gave her my card and said if anyone turns it in, please, please call me. Then she said..'wait a minute" a gal who was just interviewing for a job here, brought a piece of jewelry in - that she had picked up in the parking lot - but looks like something off a necklace, not a ring.. She took me in the back, pulled out this box, where she had put it - and omg - there it was.....but....it had been run over and flattened, but all still in tact! It needs to be rounded again and the ring bands, stretched back out - for a jeweler to do, as I don't want to screw it up. How incredible that could have been anywhere in Florida - but it was destined to stay with me, and it has. I could actually turn it into a necklace, very easily.. However, I loved it as a ring. Anyway, Michael, it is still with me and so are you.

I know you don't like the phone - but I do want ability for connection with Jen and friends... okay? When are you going into the Cancer Center -what is the name of the Center and where is it - Please let me know, My Lord. So, strange, just yesterday I came across the card you made for me.. Cleo DeLeon, Writer

M: I'm glad you got your ring back. I am expecting to get a call for an interview at the cancer clinic within two weeks. The next step is an x-ray on Monday to see if the fluid that collapsed my lung is getting close to doing that again. If so, they will probably punch a hole in my chest and insert a tube again. In which case I will be in hospital with no wi-fi for most likely several days. I will never stop responding to your emails if I can so if not, you'll know that I can't.

Re the phone calls, please understand that I have a large family and they take priority over my friends dear as they may be to me. So no, I'm not giving out phone numbers to anyone except close family, I appreciate your concern. I really liked that name "Cleo DeLeon", we had such fun together sweetie, thanks for the memories and the continuing contact.

Luchia: Hi I will write more later have lots I've been thinking about but just wanted to let you know that my friend did not hurt me in the way it might've sounded. I had been drinking some wine that night and slipped on the rocks. I hit my head and got a concussion and the effect was so sudden and so severe that I thought I had been drugged. I was unable to stand or sit and could not stop throwing up violently. I begged for him not to leave and he agreed.

The result however was that as soon as I had stopped throwing up for five minutes and was lying quietly he slipped out the front door. I woke up the next morning with my face in a pile of vomit. I was to have been cared for all night long woken up every 20 minutes etc. instead I was left completely alone. I have never felt so alone so humiliated so abandoned.

You were the absolute night in shining armor it makes me wonder it's so amazing people do these things all the time out of see their basic goodness and decency however I realize now they often don't realize what an impact they have made on someone else's life. Please understand that you were there for me a stranger in my absolute hour of need. I cannot ever thank you enough nor can my family who was frantic when they heard about all of this.

It would be lovely to see you when you come over please give me notice when you find out when the appointment is so I can book the day off regardless of whether you come I will be available on that day. The attachment was a word document you may not of noticed it but I'll resend it tomorrow.

Marcy: My Very Dear Michael, I am speechless. Thank you very much for thinking of me and for letting me know of this truly life-changing event. I consider you one of my dearest friends as well, and I know our paths will continue to connect. Whether you are in this world or the next, or the next, or the next. I've been crying and processing all morning since reading your note. I'm moving through some very deep feelings, which I am sure you more than understand.

I am so grateful for my job, and the opportunities I have to deeply connect with such amazing people as you. I feel very blessed and honored to be part of your close circle of friends. We have shared some very sacred journeys.

I fully accept your journey into the light, and I also hold the space for a miraculous change in course for you to have a miraculous mind blowing healing. Both are beautiful options. If you choose to explore any possibilities to stay here longer, I can direct you to some options. Obviously my prayers of the highest good are with you always.

I would like to share a bit about my life as well while I have the chance. A few months ago I went through a pretty severe depression and felt myself leaving the earth plane. I wasn't suicidal exactly, but I had no will to live and didn't feel anchored to the earth. This was due in part to some intense relationship challenges and a feeling of helplessness for some things that were happening around me. Then in September I had a dream that my husband died suddenly. Of course that thought jolted me back to reality and I knew I had to do my part to fix some things here. Step one, I had to forgive my husband and all the people who had initiated me in suffering. I knew it was important to be on good terms with him. Then I got practical. I started thinking I needed a better life insurance policy just in case. But that didn't happen (long story), and even the idea didn't feel good. I knew I had to shift the energy.

I knew that the solution was to create my own sacred space on the planet, and/or have a project that would really inspire me, and/or to create some abundance so I would have more freedoms and be able to follow my inspirations for ongoing spiritual training etc... To do what I came here to do. My internal guidance was that I would need to take some big leaps of faith in order to create the changes I need to make in my life in order to stay here and do what I came here to do. Along this line I have been guided to do an elite training class with an amazing healer from Australia who may be able to turn things around for you if you choose. His training is next August and it costs $10,000. Also, I am guided to go to India and attend spiritual training (another $5,000 - $10,000). As this guidance came to me of course my head was spinning and I began to pray for signs from spirit to see if I would be supported. It wasn't about the money as much as it was the question of whether I could come alive again.

I went to Turkey with Catherine of the Magdalenes and my sister who you almost met. We had an amazing time there. And on the trip, a lovely woman (who had just received an inheritance) gifted another woman $25,000! That was a beautiful sign of the flow of abundance happening somewhere. I started to feel the magic again just to witness it. Then I came home and was introduced within two days to a lovely group of women who are working on projects to help empower women and create prosperity using the paws of attraction. I got involved and I now feel myself feeling alive again and hopeful. Thank God!

So I am connecting with some beautiful, interesting people and my creative juices are flowing again and I am more clear than even about what is important to me. I feel that somehow, I will co-create what Ester-Hicks talks about. Well being. I am hopeful again. You see, most people spend their lives trying to get rich, but feel hollow spiritually until the last part of their life. I did the opposite. I worked endlessly (but not necessarily always wisely) on my spirituality, and now realize finally that the manifestation of abundance is really important to be fully anchored in the material plane.

So then about a month ago I started having shortness of breath and difficulty breathing again. I know I'm allergic to cats etc.. (We have 3) and I have had asthma symptoms most of my life, and I have had many lung issues, but this... this... I just couldn't put my finger on it. Until today when I got your note. Now I understand that I have been feeling the effects of your experience. I know it all sounds and feels surreal. I've been feeling uneasy the past few weeks and knowing something was going on somewhere, with someone I cared about. It all makes sense now. I feel emotional and also a wave of grace moving through me. Thank you again for sharing your journey with me.

I have a few questions for you. First of all: where are you right now? Second: I would love if you would continue to write to me as you are able and let me know what you are experiencing and feeling. As you know, I teach dying consciously classes and this path you are on is very dear to my heart. Third: I would like to ask you to continue connecting with me and teaching me from the upper realms as well. Maybe you can in time help to open more prosperity doors for me and send me messages to inspire me on my path. Fourth: please give my contact information to someone close to you to keep me updated with you if you are not able to do so.

You are dear to my heart and I love you! Godspeed! Love, Marcy

M: This is a beautiful message Marcy, thank-you for sharing so much. Many of 'us' (those I think of as my spiritual family or group soul, including you) have been experiencing much of the same at about the same time. Yes, it's almost uncanny that you were having the shortness of breath exactly as I was, but hopefully not the cancer, that's *my* job sweetie, it's in my script.

I love what you expressed when you wrote: *"I fully accept your journey into the light, and I also hold the space for a miraculous change in course for you to have a miraculous mind blowing healing. Both are beautiful options."* My family of course quite naturally want me to "fight" and rage against the dying of the day. But not so, I will go gently to the rim of the shadow, the line where light begins, and do my new dance there. And you dear one respect that desire where many others would not. Yet because you are healer you also offer an option should I choose to follow that path. Yes, there is an option, the final pages of my book are not yet written, we'll see how it winds up knowing all along that for me it will be a happy ending regardless of the disposition of my physical body, that you understand fully.

I'm glad that you got to travel with Catherine of the Magdalenes, that must have been an awesome trip, say hello for me, I met her once.

You are curious for the expansion of new knowledge into your awareness and continue to try on new wings to see if they will balance the one you were given. If any other is more or less powerful than yours you can only fly in circles and thus get a limited understanding because the view doesn't change much that way. You could of course choose instead of another's reality to create your own, grow your own balanced wing, and fly straight to your chosen destination, or journey, time after time without fail. You are not here to learn from others, there is little lasting profit in that, you are here to teach and to do. As you relax into your own strength perhaps your guides need not shift and change so much and you will become stronger and more useful, and more content? But those are just the meanderings of one man, nothing compared to your own inner knowing. I offer just one more thought dear one. If you are discontent with a present moment, with your imagination create a new life in the next moment, and choose happiness in it. We need never fight anything, in choosing joy and thus love we transcend everything else and abundance flows freely unresisted. Does that make any sense at all?

I would be pleased to share my dying experience with you and your students. Ask me any specific question of yours or theirs and I will respond until I am no longer capable of writing. But know that I will not be held back but will fly as high and as far as I am capable. I have already peeked into heaven and it and we are beautiful there. I feel so blessed Angela, be happy for me, we will surely meet again...

1. I am in a rented one bedroom apartment in Victoria, British Columbia, Canada, very close to the sea, an excellent location, I love it here. Jen is with me. I have told her about you, she could always update you in person when she is home in your city. We divorced about one year ago and will not likely remarry but remain good friends.
2. Ask me any questions and I will respond openly. That will give you a firsthand authoritative resource for your students.
3. As mentioned, I will fly high once my spirit is permanently detached from this body. Meanwhile I am pleased to connect with you on any level I am capable of.
4. Your contact will be Jen, she lives in your city. You can reach her via email to me and later transition to direct contact with her if you both so choose. She is Mormon but reasonably open-minded most times, I think she would welcome your visit/s to her home when she is there.

I love you too dearest Marcy, we are no doubt soul entangled, be well my love.

M: (to myself) Early this a.m. I have spent the night alone in my bed, Jen having turned to contention last night and the night before. Last night she was raging after I went to bed that I cared about "all the other women" in my life who I considered great but don't care even a tiny bit about the challenges she herself has faced in her life. (Which indeed were challenging when she was married to other men.) Yes, I suppose it's a very difficult time for her to be with me in my dying, especially so soon after the death of a different former husband. I almost sent her home two nights ago when she was so riled and raging unceasingly at me for hours, and I discovered that she'd secretly been into my computer and snooping at my emails then accusing me of things falsely. When I got up today I went to her where she had spent the night on her computer and said, *"You could have cuddled your man all night, is this how you want to remember these final days with me?"* She has now gone to bed a few minutes after my arising, I will not disturb her.

I offered on her first day here to marry her but she shied away with just a few now forgotten words. I will not make that offer again or bring up the subject, she is obviously not wanting to be my wife though claiming to love me, the only man she wants she says. Sometimes I see her as unrefined and immature rather than the choice ancient soul my Eve is likely to be. Yes, I'm sure she'll be offended when she reads this, she wants to be presented in a really good light, but I write it as I see it at the moment of scribing and that's the way she often presents to me when we're alone together. But I will continue to reserve judgment and try my best to retain my own integrity and direction, for I am becoming Adam. I picture sometimes my beautiful Eves and I weep with joy for us to soon be together. Perhaps we shall and I and they will be content...

What a lovely outpouring of good will from my dear friends of the past 14 months. I feel as though I have done some good 'out there', at least I have been an angel. Where's Suzanne/Suzette again?? Is my tilting at windmills now done and I soon to face reality? I must start the search for another literary agent to work on getting my books published, there's not a peep from the one I sent my query to on December 3rd. Will my books be accepted by the buying public? I don't know. Can I trust Jen to get that underway without altering the manuscripts should I die before it happens? I don't know. Who else could I trust my manuscripts with? I don't know yet, maybe I will attract such an one. I think possibly Elaine, but she's not a high energy fighter so I don't think so. And my children would judge the books by Mormon standards and most likely not follow through. The precious-to-me files, like my life, might grow dusty then forgotten. I need some help with this. Kris maybe??

I see that Jen sent me two messages before going to bed at 6 a.m.

Jen: If you are not going to live or except the church teachings then you should not come back to the church in a lie for the sake of me or your children. Be true to your self.

Jen: These are my stories you do not want to hear me talk about because you feel you heard them before. These are some of the things that have molded me in what I hope is not to negative of a way. I know you do not want to hear them and I hope your really meant for me to send them in a email and if not delete them but tell me you did. I am sorry but when you tell me of your lady stories with great compassion it causes sometime my memories to surface and I make you very mad when I mention them. Maybe just maybe I have not had anyone listen with compassion to my hidden abuse stories. Maybe just maybe I though I had a husband that would listen and understand the depth of abuse I went through as he showed great empathy toward those women that were barley strangers. I spent my life hiding it. Maybe if you tapped Jen as you tapped other women maybe you would understand why you can't find Jen. Very few people have ever expressed sympathy for anything I ever went through. I hid it so well and I felt so unworthy of sympathy.

Story 1. My first husband. Coming home one day from the store I walked in the door and he said why did you tell my mother to not register me for school. He was right, I told her he was to sick to go to university and he was. The next thing I knew he was beating me. All I could do was curled my body around our small two week old baby I was holding the whole time. He only stopped when he saw the blood on me and that I need stiches. At least when he stopped he took me to the hospital and they called the police and the police at that time did nothing when it came to domestic violence and advised me to leave him. I did for several days until he was picked up and treated. Yes this was not the first time.

Then another time I was under such stress I through a wooden chair down with no one else in the room. He walked around the corner into the dinning room about the same time and he grabbed me and a knife and held it under my neck. The spirit told me not to move or say anything and he would not cut my throat let me go. I was so traumatized by that experience I told no one for 15 years. I could not speak the words to tell anyone. I lived day after day knowing that this poor sick man could kill me if I did or said the wrong thing. I could see it in his eyes and I knew he was possessed. I knew if something was the wrong color it would disappear. Even my clothing. He would go on about conspiracy's happening and I would get calls at work from the police for crazy things that he was doing and they would hull him off and put him in a straight jacket. I was in such survival mod with no family support around me. I remember one day at work I over heard a woman say is that the only pair of paints she owns. It was! Their was so much stress in my life that one pair of pants was the least of my concerns until I heard those degrading words. (Is that the only pair of paints she owns) The truth is it was. I soon realized my children and I could not live in this situation any longer. I planned and left the safest way I could. I went to visit family back east and from there we disappeared for several years. Maybe you have heard the phrase "I feel like a ton of bricks were lifted of my shoulders." Well it is real. That day I left I literally felt a ton of bricks being lifted of my 26 year old bodies shoulders. I never blamed him but I did blame the illness.

You tell a heart felt story of a woman left by her boyfriend after a horrible accident in BC. Thank God you were in contact with her by email and encouraged her to move forward. You truly were her angle. BUT, Was my story that much less that you could not listen. I will tell it as you instructed me to do by email.

2 story. My second husband. We were driving home from Calif. to Utah. He started getting up set about something miner and pulling over to the side of the road reached over the seat and started pounding me in the face over and over with his fist. When he stopped and left my laying on the set against the door. He then stared the car and was once again driving, I asked in a low voice please leave me at a motel. He said nothing and would not stop. I did not wanting my children to see my bloody swollen face. When we got home. It was late and they were asleep. When I managed to get myself to my closet I laid down on the floor. I remember it felt good to hid so no one could see my face.. He left my laying in a closet for a day and a half. A couple times he peaked in and said are you going to get out of their. Your kids are asking where are you. When I managed to crawl out of the closet to get to the bed. My children saw me and asked where and what happened I lied to them

because I was so ashamed of what he did and wanted no one to know. I laid in bed for a week because I could not stand up. It left me with virago. When I tried to get up ad go to the bathroom I would struggle to the bathroom and often fall and when I ask for help he would say what do you want me to do about it. I would say through me a pillow so he did not have to get out of bed and help me. He would just let me lay on the bathroom floor to sleep or I would eventually crawl to the bed again. I finally I had to go to the doctor to get medications for the virago. I never heard compassion and over heard him tell our marriage counselor on the phone. That I was hurt and he was worried he might be excommunicated from the church again. Hearing him express his only concern was for himself sunk very deep that he was only capable of caring for himself. I never told and I never shared for years and it sunk very deep.

Maybe I am doing a bit of emotional cleansing that often happens as we get older. You tell a heart felt story of a woman claiming to be raped by her husband in Florida and of course you made it possible to have her cured out of the kindness of your heart.

This started very early in my second marriage. I also was subjected to what I would say was much worse. I was a sex slave to my husband and nothing more. I allowed him to have sex with me every day in a manner where he never touch the private parts of my body or touched me in a loving way. I despised what was happening and bared those feelings and did my best to give sex for just him pleasure. Truth I was afraid to say no. I was trying to do the right things the best I could. He told me after being married one month that a prostitute, a cook and a baby setter would be cheaper than me. To survive I pushed my emotions and feeling down deep within. He was very cruel and selfish in sex and one of the best put down artist I have ever known. Never in my life had I ever heard such deep cutting remarks. I knew I could never compete. I tried so hard to be a good Mormon wife. Even a Relief Society and Young Woman president at that time. He had one rule. I was not allowed to tell him he ever did anything wrong because he said he was perfect. If I tried to share discontent he would take a pillow when I was in bed and put it over my face and hold me down knowing I could not breath. He told me he used a pillow because it would not leave marks on me. He had been excommunicated before for hitting three different women and could not take a chance on leaving marks. This was early on in the marriage. Toward the end of the marriage is when he started losing control and would hit me.

When I was 7 months pregnant with our daughter he came into the house and said go out to the garage and load the van with cases of soda pop. I did as he instructed but started to have cramping pains. I told him I was cramping and his comment was. I do not care if you lose the baby load the van. When I did go into labor he took me to the hospital dropped me off and went home and went to bed and would not come back until the next day evening when all was over. My doctor told me to not have any more children. I often wondered if it was his nasty comments and actions that prompted the doctor to say those words to me. I feel the doctor may of done something to insure I would not have any more children with such a man.

Yes there is more but is this enough unappreciated dumping. I am a person also that had a ruff road as some of these other women but you make excuses for them and me well what I do and feel is just unacceptable to you on so many levels.

M: Yours is a story of cruel abuse sweetheart, it should not have happened that way, I wish I had a magic wand to make it all disappear but I don't. Knowing me my guess is that when you first told me such stories I was sympathetic and expressed it. But obviously how I reacted was not sufficient to meet your needs, I'm sorry that I failed you in that respect.

Please understand that I do not get "mad" when you tell me your stories. Please understand that in my human frailty I do get not mad but *annoyed* that they are told over and over. Yes I failed to be the listening shoulder you needed so you could better heal yourself from that terrible abuse. Please understand too that it is my belief that negatives dwelt on are energized and made stronger, that it is best to forget them and focus on love and joy instead so the negatives starve and melt away of their own accord.

I love you darling, I wish I could have been better for you. I so much appreciate the time and attention you are giving me when you could be elsewhere, thank-you for that. I'll try to have more patience and understanding when you speak of yourself. Your message is in Book 4, thank-you for sharing with me and with our readers a better understanding of where you are coming from. Please never hesitate to do that, we eagerly want to know you sweetheart, everything you write to me goes into my books as does that of those "other women". I love you.

DeLeon: Michael - what is your full name - my computer crashed a while back and with it went everything... I know I had all of that at one time... I appreciate and would always respect your privacy with family. I wasn't wanting to intervene in any way - just wanted to be able to have some sort of communication re you, dear one. I'm still in a tough mode at this point, for so many unknown to you, reasons.. Will take me a bit to go into that spirit mode, as I am in human right now. What are the name of your books, and the last one - are you going to have help getting that printed and available, as would so love having all of them - as you gave it your all getting it done.. Where can I get the books? Allways....

M: I understand a bit about the challenges you have DeLeon, it is my hope that you will find relief and great joy and satisfaction. Jen has agreed to keep you and those other ones who are particularly dear to me updated when I am unable to do that myself should it come to that, she will have your email address. When my books are published you will know how to get them but until then I hold them close to myself, even Jen has read only a few paragraphs, that's just the way I am.

I am trying to find a literary agent to represent me and my manuscripts to the world of traditional publishers. Failing that my plan is to self-publish e-books and possibly move into soft copy books from there. So far I have sent out only one query to an agent but I haven't heard back from her yet. I feel a sense of 'mission' about these books and believe that the right people and circumstances will arise to get them published and marketed properly. There are messages of importance between the lines of entertainment. I think that is the best way to potentially attract a larger audience and not just write for the already converted.

I understand your pressing financial needs honey but I am always short of cash for my own needs so I can't help with that. But if the books sell well it is my hope that those who take over when I cannot do it will remember and tangibly reward those such as you who helped me write them. That's the best I can do to that regard even as I strongly encourage you to keep in mind that your own basic financial needs have always been addressed all of your life and will continue to be - you have not starved to death and you cannot die until you yourself have set the date and time. So I encourage you to go forward with that good mission of yours and write away with fervor and eagerness. You will be deeply inspired line upon line as you make yourself available and useful to the higher powers (that's multi-dimensional us) that want to help this world and its people make the transition to a glorious Golden Age. You are an excellent writer DeLeon, there may be many waiting for your messages. All I use is a laptop and a free limited version of Microsoft Word (Starter.) You most likely have that already and the time as you settle into the task to become content that you have done what you are prepared to do. *Hunt with us again Lioness, we care deeply for you...* Enjoy the day DeLeon, please keep in touch, I'll update you as events unfold for me. Jen will continue to do that should I become unable.

1: Likely most of us have multiple email accounts. I am offering to help us all sort out our preferred email addresses for the issue of Dad's/ Michael's health, etc. When you receive this message please reply to me with your preferred email address or addresses. Would each person also let me know if there is someone else, a spouse, etc, who should be included. I think that we're all feeling our hearts be softened by and opening up more to Heaven.

M: (to list) By way of update, I was informed by telephone this a.m. that I do not need to go to Vancouver for a PET scan. Dr. 1 may correct me but my interpretation is that they don't need to know where else the cancer is in my body because I already have a fatal dose that cannot be treated except perhaps to gain a few days of remission? I am now waiting for a call to go to the cancer clinic where I will get a better idea of the anticipated timeline. The caller from the doctor's office said that call would come "shortly" but I interpret that to mean in less than ten days rather than later today.

My spirits continue up and I am not in pain except a bit at the spot where they put the tube in. However, with that new perspective I am now much more aware of things happening in my chest that are not normal. It would be easy enough I think to latch on to that as internal proof that what the docs are telling me is correct, and move closer to slipping away painlessly with no effort, I think I am capable of that. Eventually that may come but I'm also open to do family visits and a few more cruises etc. should that much time appear. I accept whatever, except pain.

Thank-you all for being here/there for me. I feel your love and concern and return it as best I can. God bless us all to come out of this better, more loving, and more united as a family. Dad/Michael

1: Thanks for the update Dad. I'm hoping to see you at the end of the month.

M: (to Kris) We only met once but it was a good meeting and we've swapped a lot of messages so I thought I should let you know about a change that has recently come into my life. About ten days ago I was admitted to hospital for a collapsed lung and spent seven days there while they drained the chest cavity. Along the way they did CT scans etc. and before I was released from hospital I was informed that I have inoperable lung cancer. I am home now, still walking around looking and feeling healthy (with *two* lungs why not) and am waiting for a call from the cancer clinic to find out where this is headed and when. I'm quite cheerful and accepting, my only fear is pain and apparently that is taken care of in hospice programs. I just thought I should let you know.

Meanwhile my ex Jen is here for several weeks and is providing tremendous support. And one of my daughters is on standby to come when Jen needs to be home in Utah for business. So I'm well taken care of. I wish you the very best Kris, I've enjoyed our interaction.

Kris: OM Goodness. That must have been an incredible shock. I am glad that you have support. PLEASE let me know if there is anything I can do for you. I am back home now and would be happy to support you in any way I can. You will be in my thoughts and prayers. If you need help and family is not there... just call I am close by. Caring thoughts.

M: I am hoping at an appropriate time that you will visit so we can renew acquaintance as friends. I always felt 'good' about spending more time with you but unfortunately made decisions that kept us apart, at least one of those times being that I was ill. Please keep in touch if you will Kris, I feel that we are connected in some ways. I would like to talk, perhaps you wouldn't mind visiting while Jen is still here but sometime after I have been to the cancer clinic and am aware of the time they are allotting to me. I greatly appreciate your kind words and "thoughts and prayers".

Luchia: here's the 'guided document' Michael, how are you today?

M: My customary response to that question is "I am well". And so I am, except that a couple of doctors told me I have cancer, otherwise I'd never know. With two lungs now available I feel much improved. The next step is an x-ray on Monday to check the fluid, and a call to visit the cancer clinic. It is the latter that will give me a much better idea of an arbitrary admittedly but possibly useful time line. I got a call yesterday that I do not have to go to Vancouver for the PET scan so it's now unlikely that I will visit you in your home unless they prognosticate long-term functionality. Maybe you can come visit sometime, I'd love to see you, but I need that timeline first. I sure appreciate your interest and concern Luchia, it warms my heart to have such a friend as you.

I did receive the same file earlier but the photo does the same as in the earlier version, it appears for a tempting second then disappears when the text displays, perhaps you could send it separate. But in that second I see a lovely woman, and oh so sexy. Enjoy the day sweetie.

M: (to list) I had three CT scans including the long one while the biopsy was being performed. They took three samples with a pathologist present but within range of the same needle insertion (additional wobbling) so almost certainly from the same growth. That was the biggest mass close to my right nipple. I was initially told that there were two growths, one quite a bit bigger than the other. But when I was told that I had cancer and that it had spread to other parts of my lung and behind the lining my guess is that the second CT done after the lung was inflated told them the story already, they just wanted the biopsy to cover telling me that I had cancer rather than a fungus or whatever. I was told clearly that removing the lung would not be helpful, thus the "inoperable" label.

The fluid was not in the lungs but in the right chest cavity. There was about three liters, the pressure of which had collapsed the lung possibly weeks before I went to a doc, maybe even months, I typically tough things out thinking my body will heal itself but noticed some shortness of breath as long ago as Yuma about a year ago. I adapted to it by taking deeper more frequent breaths or just putting up with it. I am not aware of unusual fluid in the left lung or left chest cavity. It was much more difficult to breathe while lying on my left side, I suppose the weight then being on the good lung. I was told that there was a bit of abnormality in the drained fluid but it was within range of normal. Otherwise I am not aware of any other test results than the biopsy, in fact the doctor who was a holiday replacement said the results from the fluid test were good. I do not want pain so I'll for sure closely consider all the options (including hospice) that will address that concern. I am not depressed in any way though I can allow myself to slip into emotion, being the kind that comes from joy. Strange eh?

I am not planning to aggressively "fight" this. In some weird to others way I suppose, to me this news is a gift. It is already easy for me to allow my mind to drift to places that are beautiful, a going home after a great war. I belong there more than here though I love you all, know you love me, and know that my death will cause tears, that's normal. Please do not prolong the sadness, a day or a week at best, man is that he might have joy, rejoice that we had so many years together.

Jen and I visited my sister today, it was a nice visit and the Tom Ka soup at a nearby Thai restaurant was good though more bitter than usual. Yesterday I bought a 40 inch flat screen TV and a headset for Jen to watch movies and not disturb me. So, daughter of mine, should you become my baby sitter when Jen is not here, you won't have to read the entire time you're here. No, you can't bring a cat along but there are always dozens of dogs in the leash free area of the Dallas Rd. walkway along the sea. Everybody pets them and gets their dog fix, owner or not. I saw a Siberian Husky there a while ago, it glanced up at me with deep blue eyes that looked human, incredible animals those. Well, duty calls, a movie at home with Jen, ice-cream, and chips and homemade onion dip. Not so shabby... Good night all. Dad/Michael

DeLeon: Dearest Michael, I'm going thru an incredible experience - that has been reenforced by you, Precious One. I attached a 57 minute oral presentation. Hoping you get a chance to listen before going into hospital/center.. as it's my message to you - on my going forth in life..... If not, all is aokay,,,,,

I met her at a huge church in Colorado - 30years ago - and again at a seminar and, and, and... put on. I so deeply connected with what she says - and for once in my life didn't feel alone on this planet. 30 years later - on Dec. 22nd - she gave this talk. And shook me back in to MY REALITY.. As I know my life has been about what she describes. And the one thing she said that shook me to my core - was "don't die" -(we have much to do, regardless of this thing called age - this is my translation) ..... I'M NOT SAYING THIS TO YOU, SWEETIE, this is about me. I know why I'm here and what I'm to do.. and now is the time.

I finally got the Contempt of Court action in the mail the day before your 1st email came through. I'm pulling that together on a lot of levels - putting my efforts into it - on all I can do,,,, and then it's in the Hands of Grace. And I am done and on my way. IN Love........ DeLeon

I don't know, why, Michael, but I am experience the greatest grief I remember, in a very long time. It's not about you making me sad.... so no worries ....it's something soo much deeper and beyond words. Something so deep in my soul - feels like a volcano coming forth..

M: Re the grief, several others I am in contact with including myself have recently felt that grief, perhaps the passing of the world we grew up in? Several of us have been exceedingly close to dying but we live yet each of us as do you. Jen and I listened to the attached audio. Congratulations DeLeon Lioness, welcome to the hunt!!!!

Carrie: hi there... all is well with my trip and my experience here... happily received and in the best place ever in our dance together.. not looking to the future, just enjoying the now and Being together... please keep in touch with what's happening... i will hold you and your path in the light and do hope your dance here will continue IF that's what you want... gentle hugs,

M: I'm happy for you Carrie. Be sure to visit if you two come up this way. It's interesting how you use the words "hold" and "dance" because yesterday I wrote the following to a dear shaman healer friend of mine.

"I love what you expressed when you wrote: *"I fully accept your journey into the light, and I also hold the space for a miraculous change in course for you to have a miraculous mind blowing healing. Both are beautiful options."*

My family of course quite naturally want me to "fight" the cancer but not so, I will go gently to the rim of the shadow, the line where light begins and do my new dance there. And you dear one respect that desire where many others would not."

I'm glad that you got to travel with Catherine, that must have been an awesome journey to Turkey. Say hello to her for me. I met her once, took her to dinner in Las Vegas, we had a pleasant chat.

I love the gentleness of your hug dear one. I'm almost healed in the wound that looks uncannily like where one would thrust a spear and see fluid flow out. I've had plenty of that happening, symbolic of stigmata though I am not He. Hello to your man...

Kris: Hi Michael. Yes let's get together. Just let me know when it works for you and i could come there or we can go for tea. Whatever works best for you. Much kindness.

M: (to myself) I think I have heard from everyone now except the one I once called "Kira" who I never contacted, I think it best that way. After my appointment at the cancer clinic and a finding out of a realistic timeline, I will have my friends come visit, except Elaine who is coming tomorrow. I don't know what to expect from Elaine after her long silence and with Jen here. I'm quite curious to find out if we still have a connection. There is still a gift waiting here for her, horsey socks from me and an angel pin from Jen. I will decide during her visit whether or not to give it to her. I'm hoping she and Jen will become friends, or maybe Jen and Kris, or possibly Oresha. I suggested that after I die Jen keep my apartment for a few months and show my significant others where I loved to walk and the ancient trees I loved. In addition to the breakwater they may scatter some of my ashes in a grove in the park, Jen's suggestion, she hugged each of the ancient trees there.

Jen is in agreement that my friends should come visit me and she meet them, I'm grateful for that. We're now enjoying our time together. Today we walked the long walk through the park and to the sea and back, the walk that once almost did me in with breathlessness followed by angry heart beats for a half hour when I laid my body down on the sofa, it was not pleased that I had overextended with just one lung working. I did not know that at the time but of course my body did. I am most grateful for Jen and for our coming together now, I think this time it will last. But she will not marry because it would mingle our financial assets and possibly cause difficulty when I die. And she being Mormon, that means we do not have the fullness of sex available for our pleasure and my comfort, though we cuddle at night when she comes to bed with me and is not up on her computer as it was the night before last. It was pleasant last night, and a nap together this afternoon. God bless you dear Jen, I do love you. You asked today why are together and I reminded you that your spirit man told you he was your Adam because you could have children. That is why we are together Jen, because you want lots of children, and I am becoming Adam.

Carrie sends a rather confusing message regarding my last email to her and I respond.

M: (to Carrie) Oops, a misunderstanding. I copied you in to an extract from a message I sent to a friend of mine yesterday. I copied you in because of the way you and she used the word "hold" and the way I responded with the use of the word "dance".

M: (to Catherine, formerly known in these books as "Corine") Catherine, You may remember me as the man with the motor home who took you for dinner in Las Vegas. I am a friend of Marcy, have known her for several years. My ex Jen lives in Utah but is with me for a few weeks at my home in Victoria. Tonight she expressed to me an interest in the Magdalenes. Please let me know if you have any workshops coming up, particularly any in Utah, Las Vegas, or southern California that she could attend, or how she could otherwise meet you for a chat when and where you are both available, thanks.

M: (to list but not sent) It is my hope that nobody will be offended by how openly I write about living out my dying and other subjects for that is the way I am. Get used to it or unsubscribe from this list because I will tell you plainly about me holding back nothing, and if you judge me by your own (religious) standards I will almost certainly fail you. What I write will become part of the fourth book that I am living and writing at the present moment.

Over the past year I wrote 850,000 words into three novels and self-published another in 1984. That first one was written in one setting during a spiritual initiation in Victoria. I call Victoria "Womb of Michael" (Michael is my pen name) because every time I come here for any length of time I emerge a changed and better man. Perhaps now I can also refer to Victoria City of Victory as "Tomb of Michael" for they tell me I am dying.

Those who do not know me well (does anyone including myself?) may not be aware that I have quietly been a mystic all my life, shy and clinging to organized religion but curious and always seeking new knowledge in my private moments. I am now ready to share some of that knowledge, it's in my books. With this list I'm trying some of it out on you. Feel free to respond openly on the list, and ask your own questions of myself and each other by always replying to *everyone* on the list so nobody is left out. I will follow the back and forths too and participate when I have something to add.

Humor and back and forth banter of course is welcome on this list. I'm really hoping that nobody indulges in sadness and mourning when I die for more than a week max. I believe that man exists to know joy, not extended sorrow. Be grateful that we knew each other for as long as we did. Are you ready for such an open discussion? Or would you sooner this list be just me writing a few words now and then about my last experiences in this world? Let us know... (above not sent)

M: (to list) Jen and I enjoyed a long walk yesterday, a stroll through Beacon Hill Park then to Dallas Road and the seaside walk back to James Bay Square. I had previously written that I do not want a traditional funeral or a service of any kind other than the quiet gathering of my children and perhaps a select few others to interact happily with each other and scatter my ashes into the sea at the end of the Ogden Point Breakwater. (Which I used to walk to daily, seeing many forms of sealife.) From there symbolically my ashes would move through the levels of plant and animal life and eventually occupy all the seas. So (symbolically in the imagination) my loved ones could find me anywhere near an ocean. Or, I suppose one could stretch the analogy to the evaporation of sea water and rains over the land masses. Thus parts of me would be everywhere on earth and in the twinkles among the stars for surely my soul would reside and play there. I would like that but am also ok being forgotten soon so nobody grieves for my passing, we exist for joy.

But before the breakwater idea I had thought of a certain place in Beacon Hill Park where there is a grove of ancient trees. Jen wanted to go there yesterday and we did. She hugged each of the giant trees and asked for my permission to scatter some of my ashes there. I agreed as long as it is not done in a ceremonial ostentatious way because that could perhaps be considered littering a public place? Just a quiet enjoying, each dropping a few ashes from their hand as they wander individually about the grove along the way to the breakwater to settle the major part of what remains of the tabernacle that served me well for an entire lifetime.

Ok, I've imagined it and here's how it could play out: A day or so before the event somebody picks up my ashes and stores them at my apartment. At the appointed time on the chosen day, my children and spouses gather in that little apartment. Just before going on the walk, everybody who wants to receives a pinch of the ashes to clutch in their hand and secretly drop wherever they want knowing that there is a special grove of trees along the walk where they will most likely want to drop their individual memorial maybe at the foot of a favored tree that calls to them or anywhere in the grove. Dress will be casual, perhaps blue jeans for that is how I always dressed, rather than an attention drawing parade of people in suits and Sunday best along the streets and casual paths of Victoria. Anyone else wanting to join in that day's events will meet at the end of the breakwater say two hours later. The grove is just for my children and their spouses? (Siblings? And Jen of course if she wants to join it.) It could be revisited and shown to my grandchildren and others later on a casual basis.

So, the group takes the ten minute walk from my earth home to the grove in Beacon Hill Park each who wants it with a bit of ash clutched in a hand, and each individual does with that ash what they choose to do for their own personal memory and memorial, they can keep it secret if they choose. Somebody carries the rest of the ash with them or it is taken to the end of breakwater by someone else (Les representing my siblings?) in an unobtrusive container, even a paper bag. We don't want a public funeral or service, just a quiet gathering of those I knew and loved and a simple dropping of the ashes into the sea when most others there who are not in our group of 'tourists' don't even know what's happening. Maybe the one doing the dropping will go down to the rocks close to the water while others look over the rail above, only they knowing what's really happening below.

There is a café at the entrance to the breakwater, perhaps refreshments there on the way back would be in order? If you like carrot cake with a quarter inch of gooey cream cheese icing, I recommend that you share a slice, they're huge, I used to sometimes carry a slice home for a meal until I discovered whole cakes for purchase right across the street from my home.

So, from the grove of ancient trees my children and those with them make their way through the park and across Dallas Road to the seaside walk. They'll take their time, go down to the water for a while perhaps, and meet others at the end of the breakwater at the appointed time. People who are interested but unable to get to Victoria might be able to pick out our group on the Ogden Point internet webcam.

It is my hope that this entire day will be filled with laughter and banter. My most loved activity was the rare times when I could lie on a sofa with my adult children gathered nearby interacting cheerfully with each other, I lived through them. I do not see this as a formal or sad event. Sure some will grieve a bit it's natural, but the opposite of sadness is my hope. Enjoy each other's company, make it a fun happy memory, we *exist* for joy.

Maybe when my sons are here visiting soon we will walk together that way and in our minds each rehearse the role we will play for that event, perhaps I'll walk it with my daughters later. I love my individual part, for me it's to die for... :-) Those are just ideas, enjoy the day everyone.

M: (to myself) It is now almost 2 p.m. Sunday and I have not heard from Elaine, she said she'd let me know yesterday what time she was coming today. Perhaps she is not emotionally equipped to come see me? Anyway, if she does not come or communicate an excuse I will never again attempt to contact her in this lifetime being content with what we had and her extraordinary gift of a few words that showed me how to rewrite my books.

She called an hour later, it was a misunderstanding on my part, she'll be visiting Tuesday afternoon.

1: We don't know about the legalities of disposing of human remains in the Province of British Columbia. The ceremony or funeral or funeral-like events celebrate the life Dad and are also for the living. Regardless of your desires not to be missed and not to be mourned I will mourn and I will miss, but you are not dead yet. That missing and mourning will finally end for me in the resurrection of the dead. For me there is only One Source of Healing, only One True Physician. His Light is for me, for all of us.

"And God will wipe away all tears from off their faces". (See The Holy Bible, King James version, Isaiah 25:8 and Revelation 7:17 & 21:4) *"But there is a resurrection, therefore the grave hath no victory, and the sting of death is swallowed up in Christ. He is The Light and The Life of the world;*

yea, a light that is endless, that can never be darkened; yea, and also a life which is endless, that there can be no more death." (The Book of Mormon Another Testament of Jesus Christ, Mosiah 16:8-9 Church of Jesus Christ of Latter-day Saints.)

As my wife says "The sentiment is lovely" about your desires. We are so grateful for your thinking about and being willing to express your thoughts about what to do after you die. Let's hear what your siblings and children and grandchildren and great grandchild think, but also what they need or may need. That, I think, will best help you achieve your goals Dad. We are so happy that you are going for walks, talking to Jen, allowing your feelings to be expressed, communicating. Please don't forget the plea to record memories, stories the generations before you told you like my name-sake great grandfather etc. Why did he change the spelling of our surname?

M: (to list) In the days of your great grandfather and earlier it was often only the lawyers and priests who were literate. And census takers wrote down what they *heard*. So it's common for family names to be different.

Re the recording of memories, as you know I kept a book of remembrance for many years and was always a prolific writer. I think it best that someone visit me with a video camera and a list of questions and hold an interview, I'll gladly participate in that if I am able. Perhaps someone could gather those questions.

God will have no need to wipe away tears that are not there. The way I see it, we are each responsible for our own happiness. That comes by habitually choosing only thoughts that come with positive emotions, quite easy actually. Would you as a parent sooner see your children be responsible for and taking care of their own happiness, or would you sooner provide boxes of tissue each time they visit? You'd think that would apply to God as well.

The bible says that God is love. When we cultivate love by choosing always the happiest thought then playing in the theater of our mind we are becoming more like God, and along that way is much happiness. I think it would please God that his children become as independent and responsible for themselves as they can be. Do you really think that

God mopes around because His/Her children "sin" during their earthly experience? How dare man suggest that he man can hurt and make sad our Heavenly Parents? I think we should focus only on love, that brings joy the purpose for our being. Then the tears will depart of their own accord with no need to "fight" to overcome our perceived 'weakness'. Just love, that's the whole solution. But this is just me rambling for all it may be worth...

My Cousin: What a shock to receive this email and read of your condition. Certainly we will keep you in our thoughts and prayers. Please keep us updated on your condition and we will, in turn, keep my side of the family informed. Thank you for forwarding your address and our telephone numbers. We will update our records. Again, know that we are thinking of you and keeping you in our prayers.

1: "Jesus wept."

M: (to list) I didn't receive the following messages re my photo but Jen did and forwarded them to me. Please always check to ensure that my email address is in every message sent to this list, thx.

1. *Trying to compensate for the lack of hair on top of your head by growing it on your face? Ah..., I know that trick all too well*
2. *Shave*

When I was in hospital and raised my arm to wash an army pit my wound started to pour (yellowish fluid not blood) soaking what I was wearing and gathering on the floor. So I never attempted to shave. And now that I'm home I'm quite liking what I see in the mirror.

Jen and I walked to the end of the breakwater this afternoon and saw a pod of sea lions passing by. It was extra nice for me because I hadn't been able to go there for about a month. We walked slow but I was not breathless so perhaps the fluid is not filling, an x-ray tomorrow will determine that. If it is filling fast and threatening to collapse the lung again I will probably end up in hospital without internet again, maybe tomorrow. But Jen will keep you posted should that happen.

Like everyone else I have known tiredness in my lifetime. But the last two or three days I feel a tired coming on that is different than anything else I have ever known. It is a deep one that feels different, more clingy, more lasting, inexorable, making me force myself to keep going to get home while I am able, though that may be just psychological at this point. I just thought I'd share that and other experiences with you as I go along this path. As one who is living out his dying (which eventually each of you must do as well) I am an expert on the present happenings of this particular body. Maybe it will be helpful, but if not my first hand information will at least add to your knowledge of the process leading to the death of the physical body. Don't hesitate to ask any questions you may have, or to make comments, but please always respond to *everyone* on the list (reply to all), thanks.

One would think that the rapid approach of death would bring close encounters with heavenly beings sent to help prepare the way. But I recall visiting my step-father in hospital a few days before he died. I asked him if he had seen angels or deceased relatives. His eyes faded a bit then he responded "no" looking a bit puzzled. Perhaps he did see them after I planted the suggestion that he might? We can empower people with the knowledge to be themselves, which is vastly greater than consensus reality would have us be.

As for me, I have always been a mystic because I was born with the ability to fly (astral projection) at night as my physical body lay in a cold bed or a wind was blowing. So for me the world was always different than the adults said it was. I developed to the point where I can now find almost instant joy in peeking into a place where I see myself and others dressed in glorious white robes enjoying sociality. We the men there are as beautiful as the women, all of us truly glorious. I think a part of each human being lives in that state, our "higher self" perhaps. So because of that ability I may be deprived of those personal visits from angelic beings though I have seen them in vision and dreams quite often. I once saw my "guardian angels" or spirit friends or "guides" reclining comfortably on loose hay, male and female, in a wagon pulled by oxen. The message to me was to slow down, that it takes a while for the universe to catch up with my desires. Strange? Most likely, but there are almost certainly many who have the same experiences and just don't tell or share like I do.

M: (to myself) Can't sleep, up at 2:30 a.m. and sent a message to Jen with the email addresses of all the women in my books plus the nurse in Texas who flat-lined and got me there in the beginning with a trail of chocolate emails. She is not in my books because she went silent a long time ago after thinking I was sexually interested in her 24 year old daughter. I met them only once to interview for a non-fiction book I was planning to write on near-death experiences. Soon after that interview I switched to the thought of writing fiction and soon after that met Suzanne.

This morning I am thinking the cancer is advancing and I'm thinking the chest cavity is most likely filling. I may not be so brave about not taking chemo or radiation or dying when the serious pain sets in. But then again, I may welcome death even sooner. It's still unbelievable that I'm dying. I keep asking Jen if I am dying and she keeps saying "no". It's hard to wrap my mind around it. *Am I dying???*

I'm still troubled with the fact that Jen does not want to marry me. I'm feeling rejected by that, prone to wondering if I should be looking for another. (But not really, my time is short it seems and it wouldn't be fair to any other to burden them with my dying.) I thought Jen would be eager to marry while we can so I offered the first day I was home from hospital with her. But not so, money has always been more important to her than I am, at least that's what I felt over the years of our marriage. I'd sometimes tell her that she'd sell me for money and she'd always deny. I do have some manageable debt (to finance the book research and motor home) and she doesn't want to be legally saddled with that. I understand, it's just that some things should be more important than money. She proudly wears the rings she wore while we were married but denies us formal marriage even as I die. And although we cuddle in the night she denies us the fullness of sexual relations because it's important to her to be a temple worthy Mormon. (No sex outside of marriage.) *Yes, it frustrates me!*

What am I to think of her wearing those rings and saying she feels as though we are married when legally we are not? So I will go to my death a single man, but one loving women and children, one *wanting* to become Adam. How am I going to get a happy ending for this book, the final one in the Becoming Adam series? I wish I knew, perhaps it will unfold soon. And maybe the happy ending will be just for *me*, and will come when this body is dead.

I surely hope my books get published and sell well, I don't know how that is going to happen yet. Should I consider marrying another because Jen won't have me? Would that break her heart, again? Do I need to be formally married? I think not actually. (As an aside, I almost blacked out as I wrote that sentence sitting at my computer. This dying may not take long.)

I am grateful for Jen though, it's good that she is here. She genuinely loves me and I love her even though it seems that by her choice we will never again be husband and wife. I will not push it, I asked and was denied, I must leave it at that. I thrill with the thought of what is to come when I finally push through the veil of forgetting and become who I really am. Maybe Jen and I will meet there in better circumstances. But at this point she does not meet my definition of "Eve" being the woman who exactly shares my dream. She is Jen, the woman I left tending the roses in my back yard some 14 months ago, the woman who secretly filed for divorce a day or so after I left, or maybe even while I was still there? She could have been the 'acres of diamonds' in my own back yard but that remains questionable. Will I find Eve or Eves? Is there a better love for me somewhere? Will I become Adam? *How will this book end?*

Chapter 4

Catherine: Of course I remember you. I entertained you at dinner. Since we went to dinner I have become involved in a relationship and we have moved to Texas in the last 3 weeks consequently there are no workshops planned in those areas at this time. In a few months I expect there will be workshops scheduled in southern California. The best thing for Jen to do would be to join my mailing list. That way she will receive all the announcements of upcoming workshops and events. If she wants to have a chat she could send me an email with her contact information and I would be happy to talk with her. Hope you are staying warm in Canada. It has been below freezing here, way colder than we expected but then again the weather is weird everywhere. Blessings.

DeLeon: I shared with Rev. Nancy - about you... as she was impressed by you, when you were here and of course, she remembered.. So - you are in the prayers and Love of Unity in my city. I have to say this - no man, in my life time, has treated me as beautiful and sacred as you. I thank you forever..... Loving... Always....

M: How's a man supposed to die with all those prayers floating around? Thanks, you're so sweet DeLeon. Please express my thanks to Rev Nancy and the others. At the time I met her I sure didn't think I'd be the one needing prayers, life's full of surprises. We had some happy days, I particularly enjoyed our beach time. The water was surprisingly warm, the woman on my arm delightful. We'll meet again in better circumstances than mortal life offers, it's better that way. It should be a nice hug that first one there, I hope your hair is still long...

M: (to list) I just got back from hospital for an x-ray to determine if my chest is filling with fluid again. My guess is if it is I'll be looking at a hospital stay while they drain it, but don't know yet. The next step is a few minutes from now, a two minute walk to the clinic to have sutures from the chest tube removed. Then the biggie, first appointment at the cancer clinic where they'll tell me what stage my cancer is and how long the stats say I'll live. I can plan life from there, I'm waiting for a call for that appointment. As for how I feel, I am still trusting that the docs got it right otherwise I don't feel that my body is dying. Except, well, there's always an except or a but, but no pain. It's very nice to have Jen here, remember her kindly for that. I do need the help getting around as I almost blacked out while up early this a.m. so I'm probably better off not driving for a while. Enjoy the day.

List: Please delete me from this.

M: (to list) I understand the emotional turmoil that some of you may be experiencing from the unexpected events of the last couple of weeks and the desire perhaps to make it all go away. But I don't understand if what I am writing to this list is something I should not be doing? I say that because within minutes of sending the message above I received a request from someone on the list to be deleted from it. Should I be more discrete with what I write or do you want to know what I am experiencing as this moves along, painful as it may be? A bit of feedback would be helpful, thx.

Also, I missed the call but apparently I have an appointment at the cancer clinic on Friday. That means that perhaps 1 can accompany me, ask all the right questions, and then interpret to all of us after. I would like that and Jen says she doesn't mind stepping out if 1 is here to go with me. It seems completely appropriate for our family medical doctor to head this list and provide expert commentary to my lay descriptions as the process rolls along. I will try to make Jen and 1 my authorized contacts with the establishment. Any objections?

Lynne: I'm sorry to take so long to get back to you... I am just planning my week and I can be available for a reading with you at your convenience from tues - fri. I look forward to hearing back from you.

M: How about Wednesday at 11 a.m.? Jen is visiting me, would it be ok with you if she came along to listen and take notes? Please confirm and resend your address, thx.

Kris: Was thinking about you this morning and wondering how you are doing? If you have had any more news from the Dr.? Caring thoughts

M: It's nice to have caring friends like you Kris. I just got back from hospital for an x-ray to determine if my chest is filling with fluid again.

My guess is if it is I'll be looking at a hospital stay while they drain it, but don't know yet. The next step is a few minutes from now, a two minute walk to the clinic to have sutures removed. Then the biggie, first appointment at the cancer clinic where they'll tell me what stage my cancer is and how long the stats say I'll live. I can plan life from there, I'm waiting for a call for that appointment.

As for how I feel, I am still trusting that the docs got it right otherwise I don't feel that my body is dying. Except, well, there's always an except or a but, but no pain. It is my hope that you can visit soon but I'd like to have that cancer clinic appointment over and a timeline in place first unless you are leaving town soon, let me know. Enjoy the day.

Kris: Good.... things are moving forward and soon you will have some answers. I am around for awhile... no trips planed as yet. Let me know what works. Glad you are not in any pain! Much Kindness

Carrie: will check out the links and thanks... always open to new inspiration... and, yes, I am full up at the moment... but... there is always time to explore and expand my spiritual connection... I hope you are in a place of loving support as your travel the road of health alternatives... love and bless you... and, of course, send sweet hugs...

M: (to list) I just got off the phone with the cancer clinic. My appointment for a two hour consultation is on the 16th. So 1, if you can get to it with me and right after the consultation tell me and Jen and your brothers who will be here as already planned what happened in plain English, that would be wonderful for all of us concerned. We will then prepare and send a report to this list soon after so everyone's in on it. I gave Jen and 1 as my emergency contacts.

M: (to 1) We will be seeing Dr. K for a two hour initial consultation. My hope is that you will go with me, ask all the right questions, and report to me and those on the list. I'm so pleased that you are already planning to be here then. I love you lots my son, I'm very proud of you. Dad

1: It continues to astonish me at how Majestic is our God. I am happy to go with you. As to discretion and the list, I would think that sentiments to your children are always okay. So attention to which list is of the essence. The list I was volunteering to coordinate should probably be limited to close intimates only. Could you please advise me as to who wants off the list? Love

M: It was one of your siblings. I understand that your sibling is most likely wanting to escape thoughts of dad dying but it did hurt as if I was being rejected. Now I don't know if that sibling of yours will even visit though I think so. Please be easy on your siblings if you follow up, I love my children so....

M: (to myself) I went to bed at 10:30 last night and for the first time in perhaps decades I slept an entire eight hours, Jen beside me. At first I described to her the beautiful sunsets I was seeing over a lake and rays of light shining through the trees. I accepted my death, told her there was "such peace" for us. Then in the night I thought that I am a powerful man capable of organizing my body and my life as I will. This morning I am thinking I might do just that!

Last night before I went to bed I found a contact for a different literary agent to send a query to and I think I will do that today. It breathes new life into me to think of my books selling well and to have the financial means to live the best things of this world. Maybe I will.

Elaine comes to visit today. Jen has been cleaning and getting ready to present her best self to this lady who was important to me. I don't know what to expect of her visit or what feelings to anticipate. I feel closer to Kris in some ways right now than to Elaine, don't know why, just imagination I suppose, let's see what the day brings.

Lynne: Okay Michael... Wednesday it is.

M: We'll be there Lynne, a few minutes before 11.

1: Ok everyone. I believe that this is the correct family group email list. Please reply to me if anything is not correct but again when doing so do not "reply all" If I do not hear from you then I will assume that this is correct. FYI I will also send out an email group for Dad's children as a separate group called "Dad's Family Group" With Love 1

M: (to 1) Do you think I should just ignore your sibling's delete request, or should I remove the name when sending to this list?

M: (to myself) Elaine visited and stayed for almost four hours. For me it was enjoyable and I thought from their conversation that it was good for Jen too though she got into a bit of Mormon preaching. But within minutes of Elaine leaving, Jen displayed her jealousy. She said that if Elaine visits me when she Jen is not here then I should never invite her Jen to come back! I'm dying but Jen will not marry me and she will walk away if I invite my friends over when she is not here. I feel distanced from her whereas it was well for the last couple of days. Truly I am a single man and need to live my own life what remains of it separate from Jen, or be controlled by her as usual. My heart moves again, my imagination wanders, not to Elaine though I like her, but possibly to Kris, for there is no other...

But my body now validates what the two doctors told me after shaking my hand. The wound punched into my chest is as painful today as it was a week ago, I will need pain killers for the night so I can forget about it and rest. The way I am feeling now, if they hadn't told me that I am dying I would think there was something wrong with me!

I sent a query to another literary agent, it has been too long without a response from the first one.

Dear Agent. *"Becoming Adam"* is a series of four fictional books based on current real life people and events in USA and Canada, as embellished by the author. Four women who live thousands of miles apart and have never met are followed by an exchange of private emails that are peeked into. The common link is "Michael" who used to be a strict Mormon but has strayed. Michael is searching for "Eve" the woman who shares his dream, but he sometimes thinks there is more than one Eve and he is glad of that. Will Eve be the wife he left behind or someone he picks up along the way as he travels the USA in his motor home? The women are in love with Michael, and he with them. There are others as well.

The real life woman who is "Suzanne" in the books is a traveling hospice nurse who tells true stories of courage and love as her patients live out their dying with an angel at their side. The stories are poignant and beautiful. In real life Responsible Nurse goes home to an empty house in Texas each night, her ex turned out to be gay. For balance she sometimes turns into wild anything goes "Suzanne", the woman she really wants to be. She reaches into her toy box and writes to Michael, he back, they know the drill, they've been there before. Nothing much is redacted from the messages they swap and readers peek into on such sultry nights.

The author (me) LIVES his books and writes them into his journal of a million words which he has now compiled into the first three manuscripts. Book 4 will end with the death of the author in real life. So the story I am currently living and writing should be eagerly anticipated by readers of the first three books who don't know that yet, but a publicist or blogger could spread the word before book 4 is published. Yes it's true, two weeks ago I was diagnosed with inoperable lung cancer. Would you like to read the story of my dying and how the four women react to that? Trust me, they *are* reacting! Would you like to LIVE the story with me? Would you like to work with me, get to know me in my final weeks, advise me as a literary agent, and make these books come alive and HUM perhaps for millions of readers? *This story could go viral...* The first three books are ready to submit. Book 4 is being lived and written concurrently.

Copied below are a few of the opening pages. I am looking for *aggressive* literary agent representation for all four books. Thank-you for considering my series of books, enjoy the day. (Insert first 4 chapters of Book 1.)

M: (to list) The hospital called re yesterday's x-ray. There is some fluid building in my chest but nothing to be concerned about. So, no hospital with another chest tube, great news for me. The next step is a visit from my four stalwart sons some arriving in two days and then a Friday a.m. meeting at the cancer clinic with Michael. I'll let you know how that goes.

5: Thanks for all the updates Dad. We are at Epcot right now enjoying the fireworks and the gorgeous weather! Luv you. Here are a few pics from our day. My niece and I got some princess tiaras that we are wearing and will continue to wear throughout the life of the tiaras. I may bring mine with me to Victoria and wear it while I am the team!

M: (to myself) Jen came to bed with me contentious last night but nowhere near the level it once was. I am appreciating her being with me to no end. She's very jealous of Elaine even though we both assured her that we had not been intimate. She considers Elaine "a threat". I guess she just can't handle me having female friends. I find love for her and she for me but we won't marry again, it's not her choice to do so. As she ranted last night I several times told her when she said all I want is women in my bed: *"I'm aged and I'm dying, I am not wanting another woman in my bed, I have nothing to offer a woman."* I don't think I convinced her though. She's now expressing interest in not Al and not her former ex who she inquired about but in her next door Mormon neighbor whose wife is dying. I'm encouraging that, such a man could give her what she wants for the rest of her or his life.

Given her reaction to Elaine's visit it may be best that I do not invite anymore of my friends while Jen is here. Except perhaps Oresha and Kathy, Jen doesn't consider them a threat. Maybe next week after my sons' visit I will invite others. Regarding Elaine though, I've had closure with her visit yesterday. Much as I like being in her presence, at this moment I am ok if we don't meet again.

1: Okay here is another fix. We had my sibling's email address wrong (another person of the same name in Canada oh the shock of it). From now on please ONLY post to this group and archive or eliminate all other emails/threads if you want to communicate to Dad and his children. (Until I have to fix this again) There is also a general email group that includes Dad's siblings, etc.

M: (to list) I am not finding my own email address in the list when I reply to all. Is that normal and I always have to add it manually? But oh what a relief that none of my own children are wanting to be removed from the list, I failed to understand that, it was a shocker. I'm so pleased that you now have all the email addresses correct, and agree with your comment about the person who was receiving our emails in error. Enjoy the day everyone, I love you all. Dad

7: That is actually quite comical of a mixup when you look back at it. I imagine someone reading all of those soliloquies dad lays on us and wondering what on earth is this about. I thought 3 was pretty gusty pulling her name from the list when she was in the dark the entire time. Happy to see that cleared up but I had a good laugh to myself thinking about it.

M: I'd like to hear from windy 3 that she is now caught up with the rest of us. Dad - laying it on thick - building my legacy one pile at a time.

M: (to list) I tried to think of an appropriate number for me and since I am one of two who came before the 7 perhaps I could be known as 007 and the other one as 07. What do you think 1,2,3,4,5,6,7? 007 layering it faster than a speeding bullet, leaps tall buildings in a single bound. (insert link to old Superman series intro)

M: (to myself) Jen and I went to see Lynne the clairvoyant today. Jen likes her, they hugged, it felt good to be in Lynne's home and presence again. About my statement that I may make a decision to die soon or heal Lynne said, *"You'll look back on it and say I honestly did feel that way at the time, but I don't anymore."* I'm not so sure, there are huge attractions waiting me if I follow the road the doctors say I am now on though my preference would be for this physical body to be made immortal, I like it. But whatever, I want to have my dying documented just in case I heal, that could be a great story. Lynne gave me a blood stone to carry in my pocket.

This afternoon I told Jen I wanted to walk the breakwater and she chose instead of going with me to go shopping on her own. I go much slower but it's good to be able to do my customary walk again. I still feel as though I am needing someone who loves me unconditionally as I am. Much as Jen and I find love and loyalty for each other, I'm just not getting that something special that satisfies body and soul. And obviously, since she doesn't want to marry me and still threatens to walk away, it's a mutual condition.

M: (to list) For those of you traveling today, my guess is you'll have GPS in your rental car so can navigate Victoria just fine. The drive from the airport is about 40 minutes to Inner Harbor where I think you are staying. I'm really looking forward to seeing my sons, hopefully you'll come to my place tonight. 1 and I will attend the cancer clinic meeting tomorrow. We can take my car for the ten minute drive to the cancer clinic. Hopefully my last son to arrive will be with us when we get back to my place and I will brief us all re the meeting. If you are planning to give me a blessing my suggestion is that you tend to that on Sunday just before you leave? See you soon, enjoy the snow-capped mountain views on your flights, they are magnificent.

2: We do intend on seeing you tonight. I understand that 7 gets in early this afternoon, will pick up the rental car get us checked in to our hotel and then pop in to see you. He will then return to the airport to collect 1 and I at 6 p.m. following which we will all go to your place. I am not sure when 4 arrives tomorrow. See you later today.

Elaine: Hi Michael and Jen... Hope that all is stable and that you two are making it through this difficult time. I wanted to say thanks again for the sweet and thoughtful presents you both gave me. I didn't even notice that the Edgar Cayce book was new and a present, but when I got home, I realised that it was. So a big thank you for that. I would love to come and visit again... Next Tuesday? Let me know. Love to both of you..., Elaine Prayers to you Michael for strength and comfort with all changes...

M: (to Elaine) Three of my sons flew in today, the 4th will arrive tomorrow. They will stay until Sunday. My oldest son will accompany me to the cancer clinic consultation tomorrow a.m. That will give me a much better idea of what to plan for my life and I'll be better able to get back to you re getting together again, thanks so much for your care and concern and your prayers. Also, my sister from Nanaimo will be visiting my Victoria sister on Monday and Tuesday so I'll keep those days open for them. Take care.

3: It sounds like I missed a few e-mails over the past few days. I'm planning to come visit on the holiday weekend. Looking forward to seeing you then. Have fun with the boys this weekend.

M: (to my sister) My sons would like to meet you, most likely on Saturday if you are available. Someone could come and pick you up. What do you think? Tomorrow I'll send an email to the list after the cancer clinic appointment. That meeting should give me a much better idea about how to plan my life going forward from now.

Sister: Yes I certainly would like to see your boys. Let me know what time. I did not receive your email until this am even though it says it was sent yesterday.

6: Hi Dad, Things are going ok for me. I'm planning to try for a job when I get back from visiting you. One can only stay still so long. I'm enjoying my time with my boyfriend. I'm still not positive it will work out because we are so different...... but he is kind to me and I love the attention. Sigh. What I do know is that change is inevitable, so I'm enjoying my life as it comes to me. Sorry I don't always answer in the thread. I'm used to checking emails only once a week. I'll step it up. But please do have someone text me or call me if things take a turn because I may not see an email. I was glad to see your picture. I love it.

6: You are funny Daddy. My man loves to pun it up..... he keeps saying "These aren't your Father's Puns.. these are turbo puns".... I know I roll my eyes every time and usually have to tell him that I've heard my Dad Punning on the exact same thing. LOL.... and we know it takes #6 a few extra beats to catch puns.... Miss you Popps, Your Daughter 6 PS sibs... .any fav. Dad puns.

6: 007 Dad. Really? Did 3 ever tell you her "Dave Bond" dream? I think it was a recurring dream wasn't it 3? LOL. Your going to have to dye your hair back to black Daddy Dear if you want us to start calling you double 'O' Seven. Or we could all petition for a new James Bond Film with Sean Connery or Rodger Moore so it's more believable! 7 and 7+ were so clever to think up that team numbering system for the family reunion. I love it. Love you Dad, and Sibs... you're all ok..... giggle. Ps on a more personal note; update on my health. My Doctor and I are working to reduce my medications and eventually have me just using the injection. (6 is bi-polar) I'm still experiencing some "downs" and heavy sleep cycles, but I'm hoping that will improve with the medication change. All in all I'm much much better than before. Loves to all.

M: (to 6) Shhh, don't blow my cover 6. I'm glad life has improved hugely for you. As for me and mine, it's to die for... Three of my stalwarts are in town, we enjoyed chat and Vietnamese last night. 4 arrives this evening. What a treat for me, four sons together to see me, this has never happened before, I'm thrilled. Gotta go, someone's picking me up in a minute or two for brekkie at their hotel, Jen's staying home. Enjoy the day.

4+: (4's wife) 4 will arrive in Victoria at 6:30 PM.

M: (to the big list) 1 and I met with the oncologist at the Cancer Clinic this morning. It was a short meeting because my questions were answered in the first few minutes. Cutting to the chase in plain English: The final/worst stage of lung cancer is stage four. I am at stage three only which means that I will most likely live at least one year. The next step for me is a chest x-ray in one month to see how much fluid (caused by the cancer) has accumulated. If it has, I can have a device implanted so I can drain it myself when I get short of breath. Then a CT (cat) scan in two months. Meantime I can travel except no flying for at least one month while the hole in my chest heals at all levels. As for the cancer, there are large tumors in one lung only, it would not be helpful to remove the lung.

So, breathe again, there's almost certainly at least a year before I get to the point where I'm going to need closer attention. 5 you're off the hook, I can live independently on my own, thanks so much for standing by.

How am I taking this? Not sure yet, it means that I must be responsible for ordinary life again for at least a year. I'll handle it, already have all my adult years. Ok, I'll admit, it's better this way, there's time to prepare. There's no rush to visit me. I'm dying yes, but I'm doing it slowly. I hope this is good news for all my loved ones who of course want me to linger. Hopefully this summer I'll be able to spend time with each of my children who have children so they can get to know their grandpa better. I love you all, this is good news, enjoy the day.

M: (to sister) Sorry to be so late getting back to you, they've been keeping me busy. There are some things planned for this morning. If you are ok with it one or more of my sons will come and get you about 12:30. I think the plan is for us to have lunch together somewhere.

Sister: Sounds great.

M: (to Suzanne and everyone I informed that I am dying) The final (worst) stage of lung cancer is stage four. I was told yesterday that the lung cancer I have is progressing but is still only at stage three. That means that I will most likely be able to travel etc. for at least one year. I'm good with that, it makes it easier for family and friends after my sudden announcement and will give me the time I need to get my three books published and the final one completed. I appreciate you and wish you well, please stay in touch. Enjoy the day.

Suzanne: Are you choosing to have any treatment? Can you tell me the specific cancer type?

M: There is no treatment offered at present, a CT scan in two months and an x-ray in one month for the fluid concern. Surgery and radiation are useless and although chemo could prolong duration possibly maybe, I expressed the choice for quality rather than quantity and that is respected. It is squamish cell with two large tumors and several others in both upper and lower nodes of one lung, one tumor is penetrating the lining, it is the cancer that is causing the fluid. A later solution for the fluid concern is to have a tube inserted that allows me to drain it myself, that is not needed at present. It's always good to hear from you Suzanne, I sometimes still feel our connection, I hope you are well.

Carrie: wonderful... how about exploring alternatives now that there is time for them to work for you??? or do you want to move on after you finish the book? all is progressing here... not sure in what direction but trusting the process... we are in open honest communication and spirit is guiding me so all is well in the big picture... sending love and a bit tighter hug.

M: Yep, tighter hug works, almost healed now. You can run alternatives by me but hey, I'm getting good mileage from this dying thing, might even help sell books. I'm pleased that things are working well for you, there's a lot to be said for living in the moment with no concern for the future, trusting that only good can come however life unfolds. I'm still hoping to meet you some day but can't fly yet and am not going anywhere by road until spring has sprung. Maybe Jen and I will track you down sometime. Enjoy today Carrie.

7: Ok, no prob for us to go get your sister. Update, we will prob be there closer to 10.

M: Suggestion. We convoy to my sister's, Jen can drive my car. We pick up my sis along the way and do lunch at the seaside bistro in Sidney that I showed you before we picked up 4. (Good fish and chips there.) Then drop sis off on the way back to my place for the biz meeting I think you still want to hold?

3: This is good news Dad. Love you lots.

Kris: Thank You for letting me know. That is good that it isn't stage 4. Have you thought how you could reverse this? Any help I can be... let me know. Much Kindness

M: I do want to meet with you Kris, I know you are a healer. I think that would be better left until about the 24th when my company will be gone. Because I am now independent for possibly a year I don't need my daughter to come stay with me as originally planned so I'll be on my own from that day until the 13th of next month when my daughters will visit for a week. Hopefully you'll still be around and we can get together and chat, maybe even walk the breakwater again or stroll the park if you'd prefer not to visit in my home.

Luchia: Thank you for letting me know that. It is a big relief of course I hold out for other things. I wish you smiles belly laughs and hugs all day take good care the Luchia.

Elaine: I'm really happy that your news is such. Your family has come together for you, which is very loving... and you can get away feeling assured now too. I am in rest mode after last night's shift, 2 more to go. Must go rest. Prayers and loving thoughts to you.

Suzanne: Thank you for sharing your test results. Did anyone suggest hospice care. You are very appropriate and they would monitor your symptoms and manage your energy. You could use some of that million dollars for your own hospice nurse as well as a critic for your writing. I could tell my hospice stories in person. Please feel free to ask me any questions along this journey.

M: If I was on my own without loving support from family and local friends I would take you up on your kind offer Suzanne, thank-you for that. My four sons are still in town, they all fly to their various homes tomorrow. It has been a great visit, my three daughters will visit next month. I will keep in touch with you Suzanne.

Suzanne: You should make your goal of finishing your writing in 6 months.

M: I agree with you that the stats are weighted at both ends and can go either way for any individual. I have the oncologist telling me verbally that I should be able to keep going for a year and yet wanting CT scans each two months, my body speaking loudly that something's gone terribly wrong, and stats revealing that 14% of people with my type and stage of lung cancer live five years. So it's difficult to plan though it's certain that without intervention of some type what I have is fatal at some point in the fairly near future. I hope I am able to continue writing for six months, thanks for the counsel. And again thank-you so much for your offer to be my hospice nurse, what a wonderful way that would be to spend my final months. I know you are an angel to many, perhaps it will come to that, we'll see how this unfolds as time goes on. God bless you Suzanne.

Suzanne: What sweet blessings you have around you. The love of the constant people in your life here will be in the next life as well. Relish all the sweetness. I pray for you.

Carrie: (she sends links) ok... here you go for a good start check out this web site... etc. let me know how you feel about these resources and we can go from there... love, hugs, health and some fun for today...

M: I'll check this out, thanks Carrie.

Carrie: i hope it gives you some valuable resources... hugs

Kris: I am happy to come to ur home or walk... whatever works best. Yes would love to talk and offer any support i can. I am around now for awhile... no trips planned until the end of next month. So just let me know what works for you and we can connect. Much Kindness

Lynne: Thank you for your message. I'm glad to hear your good news. Life has many good things and triumphs ahead for you! If I can help in any way, please let me know. Have a wonderful day!

DeLeon: Thank You, Thank You, Thank You... Creator for this wonderful news for Michael and his family/ friends/ soul mates/ beloveds. How great to know you will be getting those books published and the current one completed. I know that brings great joy and great satisfaction and great peace... to you.

Last week a Dr that is working with patients to wean them off drugs referred 10 patients to me for counseling - for a while he had sent 1 or 2 a month, if that.. then the client feedback and his staff's reaction to me was so strong, he is now sending all of them in my direction - am a bit overwhelmed, but thrilled in doing what I have been so gifted with.... It's taking alot of adjustment and focus to stay on top of it all.... and the ability to rest in betweenst it all.

Friday - got this incredible text - from a guy that is dealing with huge pain issues - and referred to me, was with him about 1.5 hours (my usual time for first session) - and didn't know till the end that he's a chiropractor - now can't practice, because of the pain induced by a screw up in surgery, etc. etc.. He said "U r a True Blessing, ur therapy is over the "TOP" with genius and Love ! My life has changed forever with ONE visit with Dr. Cleo! ps. I have a new patient for U., my wonderful friend needs U like everyone else does."

Michael - Cleo (and then some) is back! Now - need to go do this pile of paper work. Thank you for bringing Life to me - when it was so.... dark - thank you for being there, literally at my feet. Loving You Always, my Blessed friend.... And Holding you in Light and Love.

M: What wonderful news for both of us Cleo DeLeon. You are for sure on the hunt again Lioness, *you've got your groove back*, I joy for you. Please stay in touch.

M: (to list) It was a wonderful visit with my four sons, my heart was warmed immeasurably even though they acted like siblings sometimes. Thank-you so much for coming.

M: (to Oresha) Jen and I are free all day and evening on Tuesday this week. You and Kathy are welcome to drop in for a chat if that would work for you.

M: (to myself) My sons left yesterday after the remaining two and I and Jen visited my two sisters on the way to the airport. It was a wonderful visit with my sons, we walked to the grove and to the end of breakwater, the path I suggested they walk with the ashes of my physical body. But today I'm rallying and thinking again of taking charge of my body and my life and becoming immortal Adam. So I don't know if I'll die, maybe, maybe not.

Where's Eve? I set out to find her... Or is she even to be found in this mortal world? Maybe we'll get together in the next. Maybe there will be more than one Eve for me. Jen won't even allow me female friends in this lifetime. But when confronted with the Mormon view of one man several wives in the eternities she says she'll conform to that when she is there. She does not speak of my dream, my fantasy, except negatively. How can she be Eve when she will not share my dream?

Jen watched movies and slept on the sofa all last night. It had been a wonderful day but the spirit of contention arose in her last night and she got angry, using a four letter word, calling my friends "whores" and saying she doesn't want to be my Eve or even in my books because of the "circle of immoral friends" I have chosen. I reminded her that she has had the penis of several men inside her body thousands of times. Who is she to judge and put down another? She thinks I will write about her negatively and of course she doesn't want that. She is quick to judge and put down but admitted that DeLeon and Suzanne's recent messages were very nice. All she did with the blaming pity party tirade last night was as usual to drive us further apart and for a while at least to destroy our peace.

She seems far from being Eve Mother of Nations, woman with the exact same dream as mine. Our love and interaction nowhere approaches a perfect love gone right, the subtitle of these books, I'm still searching and hoping for that. But she has been helpful, affectionate at times, and allows me to be affectionate with her. That's a need of mine but there has been no sex of any kind for several days, she makes no effort to prompt that and the feelings don't rise often in me anymore. But all in all our visit has been pleasant enough. She will fly home on Saturday this week and says she won't return until I invite her to come back. It will be strange being alone again but I've been there before and will handle it. She asks what I will do when I get lonely (obviously probing to see if I will ask my friends to visit – she once said if Elaine comes again that she will walk away from me permanently.) So I guess

I have little choice but to keep secrets if I am to have a continuing relationship with her. I try to calm her fears about me having sex with someone else by saying, *"I am aged and I am dying, I have nothing to offer another woman."*

At present I think it would be wrong of me to go back to singles sites and look for another friend, though I suppose with full disclosure of my condition there could be mutual enjoyment for a while. I'm looking forward to seeing Kris again, I'd love to have the confidante that Jen can't be because my shared secrets often return as an accusation or put-down of me or my friends. I love Jen, she loves me, but she won't marry me again for financial fears she says and won't allow the fullness of sexual relations outside of marriage, so we sure are dragging out this divorce! *How about that offer from Suzanne eh?*

I attended a Sunday meeting at a local Mormon meeting house yesterday with Jen and my sons. It was pleasant enough but there was no emotional pull for me there. I see life (and death) so differently now that I've stepped back from organized religion and allow myself to see a bigger clearer picture. My sons laid their hands on my head and gave me (then each other) a priesthood blessing in the Mormon manner. It would please them and Jen greatly if I returned to activity in that church. Who knows, maybe I will? Now what do I do about Jen?

Oh, another thought. How about I get rich then take a luxury world cruise with Suzanne as my hospice nurse and and and *someone*? Or maybe just me and my nurse? Yeah, raunchy Michael's not quite gone yet...

Oresha: Thank you for the invitation. I just spoke with Kathy.... how does tomorrow sound to you for a visit? I'm pretty open... Kathy has other commitments through the day... so 3:30 works best for her.... I'm looking forward to seeing you and to meeting Jen. I'll bring back your DVD's in case you'd like to watch them... perhaps I can borrow them again at a later time (they've been at Kathy's the whole time since I borrowed them this time ...lol) Please let me know if this time works for you .... Hugs..

M: 3:30 tomorrow works for us, looking forward to seeing the two of you.

Oresha: Great! See You then... Cheers!...

I did it! And that surely proves it. *A man who is capable of cutting his own toenails is capable of living independently!* (Write that down, that's pure country wisdom from a city boy.) It's not that I think that statement is particularly inspired, it's that when I said it to Jen she suggested it go into my book. And not being one inclined to ignore Jen... (Smile a bit for me?)

7: Pops, I was wondering if you could send the words to the song you used to sing us. Also, any pics that you have from this weekend would be great. Thanks.

M: The song I'd sing each early weekday a.m. when you guys were little went something like this:

> *Safe within the family circle - Safe within each other's arms - Safe within the family circle - There will be no outside harms - Let each member of the family circle - To each other be a light - Pray together, love together - And always choose the right.*

We would then say prayers and read the Book of Mormon aloud each in turn. I tried lots of different ways of doing that so nobody would be asleep by the time it got to be their turn. One verse, two verses, one sentence etc. trying to find a balance but inevitably someone would need to be awakened. Those who got there first would lie near a furnace outlet and pull a blanket over them. This was in the big house mostly. Your mother and I owned that house but I don't think she ever liked it, we sold it soon after we separated that final time.

Your comment when your mother announced that we were separating was *"that sucks"*. By then I had rented a place in the city and all of you got a key for it, even your mother visited when I was not there. 4 and 5 came with me because I thought the younger ones would be better off with your mother and because they went to high school in the city. When I dropped 5 off there first time she walked in like a princess and soon ran for student pres. 4 walked in with his head down. I still feel bad that I obviously never spent enough time with 4. (Or any of my other kids, too busy trying to provide for a large family.) But it worked out, everyone goes through stuff in life, I feel content with mine though would like to crown it with my books being published. I love you lots. Dad

M: (to list) Attached is a photo of me and my sons in Victoria. I want to thank my cousin for the nice card and healing wishes she sent. We were kids together what seems like a few years ago, not sure what happened. But I'm content with the process, life's good, real good even as we live out our dying, no worries. I have seen the destination - *wow, just wow...* I love you all.

Oresha: I have to tell you that I had a rough night last night.... I woke up in the middle of the night coughing and stuffed up! Looks like I got my self a Bug! Ugh! So Kathy and I won't be coming over this afternoon .... I want to make sure I'm all better before we get together.... How long is Jen staying? I think it's best to get together sometime next week, if possible.... I was so looking forward to seeing you & to meeting Jen..... Kathy's going to bring over an arsenal of "De-Bugging" stuff for me a bit later today.... Take care.... please let me know that you got my message.... Ciao....

M: Thanks for letting me know. Be well Oresha, we'll get together some other time.

Elaine: How have you been last little while. Family surrounding you.... are you getting peaceful rest time? Kind thoughts to you and your family...

M: My sons left on Sunday after a brief but wonderful visit, my daughters will arrive for a week soon. I am needing to mentally adjust to the probability that life will go on reasonably normal for at least several months. With Jen here it is difficult to find quiet time and inclination to do the meditation I need to find a comfy me center again. Also, Jen's (still) quite jealous of my female friends and I hear about it. I was hoping she wouldn't be and would make friends in Victoria but she struggles, wanting me exclusively as if I was her husband, but not wanting to remarry. So it's best I think that I don't have visitors when she's here.

She'll be flying back to Utah this coming Saturday and may not return for quite a while. I'm hoping that you and I can get together now and then after she leaves if you would like to do that. Enjoy the day, thanks so much for being you.

Elaine: No problem, I understand completely... Go with the flow, Try to carve out some of that quiet time wherever you can. I am the same as you! Best thoughts to you PS. I will do either a painting or poem for you soon... I promise, as it's been on my mind... Love, in this world as a stage... Here we are, jumping into scene after scene, doing our best in our steady, even ways You are doing so well.

M: (to myself) Such happy thoughts as come when my friends send me messages like that. I feel cared for, I feel loved, I feel good about me. Today the thought came with emotion that even if the teachings of organized religion are true and there is a God who punishes his children when they die (horrid thought) and I am judged unworthy, wherever I go after the death of this physical body there will surely be beautiful women there and I will be beautiful too. Some of those women will want to be with me and I with them. *What more could I ever want?* All is well, all is very very well...

I thought tonight too as I opened a curtain and gazed out at my beautiful city, the legislative building lit up how honored I am to die here. Victoria is the only city I consider to be my home. I have come home. Have I come home to die this time? I wonder...

Jen and I just watched a movie about the secret lover in the life of author Charles Dickens. I saw some parallels in my own life. I could yet picture myself doing readings and discussions should my books become well known. I could yet picture myself wealthy and doing the rich things that money can buy. I could yet picture myself becoming immortal Adam. And yet, and yet, should I die it's possible that much as I say I will cling to the thought that I am becoming or am Adam, I might find there in that realm something (or someone) that is even *more* desirable. Will that finding be my happiest ending and you dear reader will never know? I promised a happy ending and so it will be, at least for me. Will I be able to tell the end from the beginning? Perhaps someone else will need to write the sequel. And perhaps these books like my first one were written only for *me*? I love it when I choose not to remember how something ends...

3: Thanks for the pics Dad. Beacon Hill park looks lovely even in the winter.

M: (to myself) It's early morning and Jen is asleep on the sofa behind me. I would much prefer to write only positive things about her but feel that I should present the truth and let you dear reader decide for yourself how she and I are progressing towards that perfect love gone right that I am seeking. Among other things, yesterday Jen said that readers of my books by now know that she is Eve. In her discerning way she asked me if I had heard from Elaine. (Or is she cheating and secretly reading my emails?) I responded that Elaine is going to write a poem or paint something for me. That seemed ok and we watched a long movie together. After the movie she came to bed with me. But after only a couple of minutes she said that if Elaine is painting something for me she is planning to come and see me. She then got up, went to her computer to play games and spent the night doing that and probably watching movies. Sometime in the night she covered herself with a blanket and slept on the sofa.

Is this Eve Mother of Nations, the woman with my exact same dream? If she loves me as much as she proclaims she does why does she deprive us of these last few nights before she leaves, knowing that I may die before she returns? What strangeness this is. Is she punishing me, herself, us? She is obviously very insecure with me and I can't blame her, I can't hide my feelings and disappointments. There is nothing much new in our relationship: she is up most of or all of the nights while I sleep, sleeping somewhere other than where I sleep, eating as much or more than she did before while nowhere near her stated weight goal, provoking contention but blaming me for it, denying us fulfilling sexual relations, etc. Yes, I am ready for her to leave much as I enjoyed her company and help most of the time and do love her. I guess she knows that in some ways we are close but in others far apart. Will we ever fully reconcile and enjoy each other effortlessly? Or are we just continuing to drag out a divorce that should have been complete a long time ago? I don't know...

When Jen got up this a.m., without even a "good morning" she instantly launched into a poor me contentious thing which concluded in her saying she is leaving and not coming back. She gives as her reason that my friends are more important to me than she is. She may be right too, I'm not handling well the way she has become though I am loyal and do love her. If she'd put her energy into being the beautiful woman I know she is inside and stop being contentious, there'd be no reason for the growing distance between us. She seems almost deliberately to be sabotaging our relationship and driving me away, though she invariably tries to make up soon after an episode of contention. That's where we're at this morning with three nights to go before she flies home, possibly never to return. Eve? You decide.

M: (to Kris) My company is leaving on Saturday so I'm available Saturday afternoon and evening and all day Sunday and Monday if you can find time for us to get together. My preference would be for you to come to my place where we can chat, maybe walk a bit, and perhaps go out for a meal on me if you have the time and desire to do so. Please let me know, I look forward to seeing you again.

Suzanne: I pray for you daily. If you have to go back for pleural fluid draining, you should have a tube placed, it will provide more comfort with breathing. Such a blessing to enjoy all your children.

M: I really appreciate your kind thoughts and prayers Suzanne, thank-you so much, you're precious. Yes, rather than endure the placing of another tube and subsequent days in hospital I will opt for the pleurex (sp?) so I can do the draining myself and maybe be able to do some traveling when I'm allowed to fly again. I have an appointment with the oncologist so will most likely stay in Victoria at least until then. Not so shabby actually, this is a seaside garden city and glorious in spring and summer. Winter days hover a few degrees above freezing with not much sunshine, I'm ready for warmth and light.

I still have intermittent but frequent pain from the tube wound healing deep down I think, I don't need pain relievers to handle it, it's mild. That makes me think I'm not well but I don't think the pain is from the cancer. I am however fatigued easily and rest a lot. Is that mainly psychological at this point do you think? Should I ignore it and stay active to prolong quality of life or is it just something that comes with the territory that I need to learn to live with and give in to?

The photo is me and my sons about to go to church last Sunday. My boys have grown large with western living but they are precious to me as your children are to you. Our children are our greatest accomplishment in life aren't they...

Jen flies home on Saturday and will probably not return for a couple of months at least. She's still jealous of my female friends I discovered after one visited, so it will be refreshing to have friends visit again. Jen wants to have me exclusively as if I am her husband but doesn't want to remarry. So there's conflict, I need some breathing space. Her departure is welcome though I'll probably miss her, especially the cuddles at night. There's nothing much better than the touch of a caring woman. I welcomed each night we had in Las Vegas sex or not, I could never forget you. Thanks for keeping in touch sweetie.

M: (to myself) To Jen's credit she did come to bed but not until 4:30 a.m. just before I got up. I had earlier seen her covered and asleep on the sofa. Hugs though pleasant don't connect a lot anymore, I feel that we have slipped far from each other. She can become contentious in a moment with no warning, apparently from stewing over stuff in her mind when I thought all was well.

This dear lady is insecure and troubled, my dying of course adding greatly to that. But because I'm not feeling much connection with her I am welcoming visits from my friends, maybe even hoping for a travel companion. My guess is that Jen and I will get together again though, she now says she's going to return and plans to leave clothes in my closet, up and down typical of her. I do need to hold her and encourage her to talk about what she is feeling without judgment or comment, just listen. I haven't been good at that, going on the defensive, and she's leaving soon. I am feeling remiss, she's surely got a lot of unexpressed feelings pent up. Maybe I'll try to get that happening today, maybe it will restore some substance to our love.

She asked about and I encouraged her to attend singles events in her city and befriend her neighbor. She thinks and I agree that her having one or more male friends might help her overcome her jealousy of my female friends. I continue to think that her neighbor might be an ideal husband for her after his wife dies. She doesn't want to marry me so even though she wears her rings I feel that the engagement is off, we're both single, we each have every right to do as we will. Perhaps I'll suggest that she not wear her rings? Or would that hurt her? Only a woman would know how to advise me and there's no woman here. I'll say nothing.

As for me individually, dying man that I am (so they tell me) other than getting my book manuscripts in the right hands there is nothing more important than the right woman or women in my presence. I am still wanting to become Adam.

Kris: I have company all weekend... so Monday would be best. Would later in the afternoon work... I do have an evening event to go to.. but that would still give us lots of time. Kind thoughts.

M: Sure, Monday will work. Enjoy the weekend.

Kris: Ok perfect... see you then.

Literary Agent 2: Thank you very much for giving us the opportunity to read your submission. We appreciate you considering us for representation of your work. Unfortunately, after careful review, we have decided that we might not be the right agency for this project. This industry is incredibly subjective, and there are many agencies out there with many different tastes. It is for this reason that we strongly encourage you to keep submitting elsewhere, in the hopes of finding an agent who will be an enthusiastic champion for you and your work. We wish you all the very best of luck and success with your writing.

M: (to myself) It's going to be more difficult to get published than I had hoped. I'll keep trying to recruit an agent. If that doesn't work in a reasonable time, I'll self-publish and hope for success with social media.

Or maybe the books are just for me? I don't know, I just want to become Adam.

M: (to myself) Jen and I cuddled last night and good feelings are restored, we'll stay in each other's lives I'm sure. And I'll visit her now and again after I die if it works that way, at least until she settles with another man. I did that day of no judgment no defensiveness with her yesterday and she did talk a lot, saying I was giving her a day of "closure". She asked for additional details about my sexual relationship with Suzanne and DeLeon and seemed content to let that be from now on. This morning she thanked me for the day of closure.

Yes she loves me deeply I'm positive of that. Interestingly she told me this morning for the first time ever about a man she slept with for one night only. I asked her why she was so judgmental with me, trying to make me feel guilty that I'd had that one night stand with Suzanne, when she'd done the same thing herself between husbands in her younger years before she met me. She got into differences such as her man hung around the next day so it wasn't a real "one night stand" for her as it was for me. She says she regrets that experience with him and I said I will never regret my experience with Suzanne. To me that first hug was a spiritual experience that unloosed the chains of orthodox religion that I'd allowed to tie me so tight all my life. Whatever happened between Suzanne and I it was revealed to me during the hug was ok with God. I needed to know that, I've never looked back on the matter. To me now sex between consenting adults is beautiful, not a matter of fear and guilt, heaven and hell like most priests and their craft make it out to be.

Just one more night then Jen goes home most likely for quite a while unless I relapse. My guess is that I will eventually need to have a self-administered drain tube installed in my chest and will probably be in pain for three to four weeks while that heals. I still have pain from the first one hopefully healing deep inside. I'll work on getting some more query messages sent to literary agents, wish I could just forget about it but I'm the best one to take care of it. I guess once I'm dead the publication and success of my books won't mean as much as it means to me right now, it may be completely meaningless. I still think the books will sell but I don't know that.

I'm going to miss Jen, even up and down as it has been with her. I hope I can stay disciplined enough to not feel sorry for my dying when I'm on my own. And I hope some of my friends will visit fairly often. I'm very curious especially to see how it will go with Kris, much more so than picking up with Elaine again. Monday's visit with Kris will tell me a whole lot about how it's likely to be with me and her. I hardly remember our first meeting except that it felt good and she was quick to put her arm around me when I put mine around hers. Could there be love there for us and fun travel when I'm not with Jen? Kris is in Africa fairly often with her children's charity project, I'd love to go with her. And I'd love to have a confidante who I am positive will keep close everything told between me and her so I can even talk about my up and down relationship with Jen, and about my books. Could that be Kris? If not, probably nobody though possibly Elaine because I'm not about to find someone new at this stage of my earth life. Well, who knows, if I had the money maybe I'd hire Suzanne as my hospice nurse and we'd travel a bit together, I could tell Suzanne *anything*. There's really nothing to tell though that I haven't already shared with Jen. I'm always way too open and am just now discovering some of the things she has kept secret from me.

Jen says she'll be expressive with emails when we're apart so maybe this book will grow, it's still only 54,000 words and should be at least 200,000 to match the first three. Will anyone be interested in this stuff? Dunno, dunno, dunno…

One thing is clear though, harsh as it may be to her when she reads this, if Jen is my Eve, *there are others too!* Those others however may not be in this mortal lifetime and surely Jen understands that if she's going for the Mormon dream - as per the early Mormon prophets, in the next life she's going to have to share her man. Guess I'll be finding out a whole lot more about that soon.

Jen and I walked to the Empress Hotel yesterday, she took me to buffet lunch at the Bengal Lounge. While there I covered my about-to-shudder lips with both hands, ignored the threatening waterfall, and told her again how I felt so blessed to be dying. That process is the greatest adventure we will ever experience in this life. I feel honored and thrilled to know that I will be wide awake and aware over the next few weeks or months of my dying and will experience it to the full, hopefully with minimal or no pain.

I mentioned to Jen while we enjoyed our curries and mangoes and pan bread that an expiry date had been placed on my forehead when I was in hospital and it would soon reflect from my eyes. But they opted for a digital indicator, red lights, rows of numbers that move sometimes rapidly backwards or forwards counting the seconds to my death according perhaps to how much I am enjoying the experience of dying. I don't believe that I will die a moment sooner than I have planned for that grand event, nor later. But I keep the time and date hidden from my physical self. If I didn't, the parts I will leave behind to disintegrate could panic or rebel and no longer serve me so well, I might choose to go sooner than later. My attitude about this dying of cancer? Life's good, oh so very good. I cherish and treasure each moment while looking forward with great anticipation to the fullness of freedom that comes with its inevitable termination. *(Or is termination really inevitable? My books indicate that it is not so. How will this book end?)*

M: (to myself) Jen is flown, I took her to the airport this morning and am alone in my James Bay apartment. There was no sex of any kind in the night, my choice most likely, and we awoke each feeling good and together. She had packed only a carry-on bag, left almost all of her clothing in my closet and her suitcase in my storage room, she planned to return soon. But life with Jen is not like that. I was warned when she casually commented that what she wants of me is to be *faithful* to her. (Meaning don't have sex with any other.)

While she stood at the mirror in the bathroom she asked me a couple of questions and took my honest responses as bitter. You know how it goes from there. In a moment the spirit of contention was alive and well and it never leaves easily for Jen. She hastily threw everything she was planning to leave into the suitcase she was planning to leave and demanded that I drive her to the airport right away instead of waiting the planned hour or so to leave. She said she would not be coming back, that my friends would console me. (She later retracted the not returning comment, saying she would return to "care" for me because she loves me, but not as a lover.) I commented to her that we were feeling good about each other a few minutes ago and that I had not changed. But that didn't give her pause. I don't even remember what the questions were, they were insignificant to me but they did what I guess needed to be done.

At the airport parking lot she wanted to talk in the car, asked among other things if she should continue to wear the rings she wore during our 18 years of marriage. I told her that she is wearing a wedding band (soldered to her engagement ring) and we are not married but if it comforts her to wear them I didn't have a problem with it. The conversation steered to a point where in response to a question she asked I mentioned that there are "some things" about her that I don't like. She instantly said, *"And with that I take my departure, you needn't walk me to the terminal."*

Of course I did walk with her, pulling her suitcase, and we sat together in a lounge for a while holding hands but not saying much. I gave her a somewhat lingering kiss at parting and she went into security without looking back. She looked cute with her raincoat-matching black roaring twenties hat perched on her head, the one she had left behind last time she was here, and had planned to leave behind this time too but didn't.

On the way home from the airport I analyzed what had happened and came to the conclusion that as usual the women in my life read me completely and give me exactly what I *really* want. Now that Jen has distanced herself from me and I don't feel that we are even engaged (being engaged means planning to marry and she refuses that) I am single and free again. Should it work well with me and Kris or Elaine or some other, as a single man I can take what comes, perhaps even travel with one or both of them whereas had Jen departed in good order the way we awoke this morning I might feel guilty about doing that and refrain. I think there is much excitement to come in my life and my higher self remains in control. *I believe the universe continues to unfold as it should.*

Here's what happened a few hours later when I awoke from a nap and opened my email.

Jen: I think one of the things we should acknowledge is the blessings in our lives or the good. It was good that I had the opportunity to care for you in what ever small way it was. It was small in comparison to the blessing it was for me. I enjoyed our intimate moments of conversation we had and regret your feelings of discontent with me. Maybe meant to be to make the parting easier.

I will pray for your will to be as you wish it to be, may you have little pain as you grow closer to the end of this mortal experience. School is almost out and you will be graduating with honors soon. May you continue to find joy and contentment with your life, as you choose it to be. I apologize for seeking more than your heart has to offer. Maybe I seek to much. Find joy with those that bring you the pleasure you need. I apologize for exposing me meaning the part you do not like. That cuts very deep with in me. I don't understand love that is conditional but it must be if that is what you express toward me because that is what I hear in your words. Even in the heat of discontentment I feel deep love for you. This is being you and me being me. No walls and nothing hidden. I wonder how often two people experience this or is it an earthy condition.

You have expressed deep spiritual experience with several other women that you have never said you experienced with me. Maybe I was the wrong woman you settled for and you soon realized that was what you miss and soon were in search for. All unfolded and you don't regret your life but could there of been chooses that would of brought you more joy. If we would of know some of the trials we would of faced. Would we of chosen to marry. Please tell me the truth with out saying you don't regret your life. What went wrong that you would say you are leaving with the weakness of a email. What was the realization of that decision. Yes Michael, even though you do not believe in taking responsibility of another persons feelings. We sometimes hurt those we claim to love the most and we the perpetrator need to repair. I understand some like my former husband can't see it and other don't take responsibility for their actions because they choose denial.

Silly me. You left because you felt we were not right for each other and only wanted me back because it is not that easy to find the perfect love that went right. My sin is I loved to much and made the scene difficult when I should of walked away for many reasons. Maybe soon the choose will no longer be mine. I can not be a woman with a man that only loves the woman he is with. I know that is not the case now that you think you are dying. Live as you well know you will. Enjoy your time alone until Elaine, Oresha or your daughters come for a visit and give a moment of comfort.

I don't choose to be a creature or person you talk about that just loves those. Those are the ones that come for a moment then left in the memory of sweet thoughts or not. Why choose loves that disappear with occasional emails. Do these emails leave you feeling the contentment you seek. II f I think again. They must offer something to feel that spot in the heart. Is that your choose. Did you seek others that found safety in virtual love. A love that you found disappears with the push of a button. What do you have left. Are the memories more satisfying than a woman that looks deep into your eyes, and washes your back. Again how foolish I am to want the fullness of love from one man that does not have the same dream.. Kind regards, from the woman that is learning, Jen

Jen: Hope I do not miss my connection. Many are being rescheduled for late flights. Almost wish my flight was canceled because I am that foolish woman that wants your arms to hold me. Yet sorry you see me with such deem eyes. I wish I could walk away with dignity and bury my disappointments and loss of a dream as many have before me. I am sorry I do not measure up to them in that way, but yet again, I justify saying they never felt as deep a love as I. Yea I know you heard that before.

Jen: See I not even out of the airport and you are getting emails. I must be a sicky!

Jen: I want you to know how deep I feel your pain and cry alone on your behalf when it comes to the love and/or disappointment's of your books being published. I know you will not give up. I would like to be selfish for a moment and think they were for you and me. So now, I ask is their something in those books for me to discover. If so why hid it from me. Is it possible you fear my reaction. Why fear when with a click of a button my messages are deleted. Even with our situation I can be deleted as your first wife was. Do I have to wait until you are dead? You see, you are magnificent writer. I have dreams for this writer's legacy.

Jen: My emails from Victoria would not go out but did when I got to Seattle. The plane in Victoria left so late I missed my flight in Seattle. It is going to be a long day. I won't leave here until 4:00.

Jen: I think I will go to bed for a week when I get home.

Jen: Do you think you will die as quickly as you want to? OR Have you decided to live. I mean really live and do the things that mean the most to you. Your books are done. What is important to you beyond your books.

Jen: You say you had no closure with Jackie. Do you really think after two dates you need to have closure with her. Do we need closure? I feel my being over weight makes me much less of a person in your eyes or in other words less desirable. True is it not.. You ask me to loose weight to travel or cruse with you. My knowing this makes it hard for me to want to loose weight for your ego. I want to loose weight for me. I am unhappy about the way I eat when visiting you. Lets say I sabotaged myself and not sure why.. Knowing it is me does not make it easier knowing how you feel. Wonder why when you look in a mirror and see an old man that you would put that burden on me to be beautiful and slim but thanks for saying wrinkles are ok.

M: That's what I did, went to bed, but had to get up before the week expired and discovered your messages. Sorry it's going to be such a long day for you, hope you get a shuttle connection sweetie. I really really appreciate your coming to be with me, I enjoyed almost all of our time together. I love you, please stay in touch, we aren't done yet...

Re your unexpected "decision" I needed that, we needed that, it was the right choice. I wasn't feeling close to you at the time but did after. In fact it's that giving of yourself to me that caused me to decide that I would visit you after my death if it works that way, to comfort you and let you know that you are indeed a woman who is deeply loved. You are extremely important to me, always will be. But I do not know how conditions will be after we die, hopefully the Mormon dream is true and we both qualify, if so I'll be waiting for you if you still want me by then.

Oh, by the way, I watched you closely as you walked away to security and never turned to look back. You looked so cute in that hat, your lips were soft and good to kiss and linger upon just before you walked away. I am not angry with you, you're only being insecure you. I love you, please stay in touch. Your Man in Victoria

Jen: Hope I sent enough emails for your comfort of getting emails. I hope I can go silent for a long time. We know a click of a button one is gone. Hope you go to Alberta to die where your loving children will properly care for you. Then I won't be so tempted to come back and care for you. It will be hard not coming back. Feel we had a good visit at times. But we left each other with bad feelings and I am tired of those bad feelings and want them to stop. It seems we are drawing them out in each other even though you feel its all Jen's. Not much left and no closure for us. Now Jen goes to her pity party as you call it. For a man that grew up with women and wants only women for friends knows little very little about a woman and a woman's way. Yea you get it as I feel it. It only takes a push on the delete button. What a simple way to end a love relationship.

M: I never even thought to check the board before you went to security to see if your flight was delayed. I would have liked to have gone back to the car and held and kissed you. You are dear to me, I'm missing you.

M: I hope you got my messages, I don't want us to end like this...

M: (to myself) And that's all she sent. I surely hope she got my messages before catching the flight from Seattle to Las Vegas or it will be a high flying "pity party" the whole way for sure. If she came back today and was willing I'd marry her and hope above hope that we were never physically separated again. That's just how I am, much as we quarrel I know she loves me and I love her dearly. I don't need friends beyond that. But there's that matter of us not being physically together, that is all important to me. Much as Jen hates it, I will consider myself single and free to do as I will when we are not physically together or married. I continue to be astonished that she doesn't want us to marry. You'd think with such a great love as she expresses to me that she'd want us to marry more than anything else in life, especially considering that my time on earth is so short. I'd throw myself entirely into her for the balance of my life, I just know that I would, she'd have everything she wants from me but she continues to deny us and to blame me for it. I am baffled and must question the strength and depth of her love for me. As I've noted before, she says one thing and does another, *what am I to think?*

M: (to Jen) I expect by now that you are 7 miles high on the way from Seattle to Las Vegas, Nevada then home. And if you didn't get my earlier emails today I expect that unless you are asleep you are enjoying a delicious pity party on me. I'll have you know that I just got back from the pharmacy where I bought pencils, a pencil sharpener, and a sketch pad. They're in my bedside drawer waiting for your return. Be well sweetheart, I'm thinking of you. Michael

Chapter 5

———— ✦❖✦ ————

M: (to myself) I watched a movie, one Jen had watched when she was here, about a writer trying to persuade a famous one to write again. I felt to question again if I am really a writer or just a book keeper, passing along messages from other people. I want to be wealthy and free and to have the right woman in my life, one who will love and accept me unconditionally and lead me in the pathways of fun and becoming myself before I die or am made immortal. I don't think that Jen is such a one as that and she knows it, I think there may be another. On Monday I'll find out if it could be Kris.

Now I must read in Book One again and try to convince myself that I am a writer and it's worth trying to get my books published. I do that sometimes in my doubting, to reassure myself that the books are worthwhile.

Jen: (re the sketch pad) What a sweet thing to do. I do love you.

Jen: I would of loved to go back out to the car and be held in your arms and be showered with kisses..

M: Were you able to catch a shuttle and get home?

Jen: I was able to get a late shuttle. Then my daughter picked me up.

M: I'm glad you are home safe. I truly don't know what that tiff was all about just before you threw everything you had planned to leave behind into the bag you had planned to leave behind as if you were never coming back, and asked me to rush you to the airport so you could get away from me. We woke up feeling good about each other only a few minutes before.

It's true that I will never understand women, at least not in this lifetime. Delightful and essential as you are you sure act strange sometimes. There is no logic or reason to such behavior unless in this case it was you wanting to release me to enjoy life as I will while you are away without feeling obligated to you? I'll chalk it up to you being your 'normal' insecure woman self faced with the horrendous reality that another of the men in your life, this one the man you loved the most is facing death. That can't be easy, I feel for you.

I wish you well in setting and meeting new goals and finding the friends you need to fulfill them and enjoy your life going forward. I love you lots, I very much doubt that we are done with each other, please stay in touch, I'm missing you already.

Jen: I was thinking the same thing. I don't know what upset me. What ever it was it sent me for a loop. I was in a deep depression for 10 hours on the way home to the point I didn't talk or eat and drink on the way home. I think I was having a hard time leaving you not knowing how much time you have left and I want to spend as much time as I can with you. Yet I knew you and I knew I need to go. As you said I am not your wife but feel like your wife and I don't want that connection to break but realize I need to let you be free to say your good-bye's to all you choose to associate. Please keep me well informed of all happenings. I have much crying going on deep with in me. I try hard to not show it in my face or body movements.

M: I've been resting and going to bed to sleep even during the day and not feeling guilty about it like I used to do. Maybe because of that I walked to the end of breakwater this afternoon and felt filled with energy like it used to be, no breathlessness and walking fairly briskly. I spotted Lynne but she was busy texting and didn't see me so I kept going, my hand in a jacket pocket wrapped around the heart-shaped bloodstone she gave me. There's little connection between us anymore, it was a sweet goodbye with you there beside me feeling the same thing, there's no need for anything more.

I just got back with carrot cake, chips and cheezies. The store was filled with people, ten to fifteen waiting in line at each register. Life's good, I hope there are many more days like these filled with energy and well-being. And yet I feel so blessed with this news that so much I wanted in life and only got the shadows of will soon be alive to all my senses. I thrill with the thought that I have a paid reservation on the longest and bestest of journeys we can ever take, far better than a luxury world cruise, I am so happy. Be well sweetie, life's too good (and too short) to dwell in anything but..

Jen: I am glade you are resting so you have the energy to do the things you like getting out and doing. I miss you much.

Jen: I have you on my mind constantly. I worry I am missing out on quality and valuable time with you. Went to my daughter's for dinner. Didn't really want to. I just want to be alone.

M: Today I'm thinking I'll live a long time yet. As I walked the breakwater I was thinking too that I'm going to so enjoy the spring and summer here that I may not want to leave this glorious city. But if another winter approaches I'll be wanting to do that one somewhere much warmer. Time will tell it true, I'm accepting of whatever comes except pain. Speaking of which I took two pain pills today first ones in many days. Maybe that contributed to such an easy walk this afternoon, I wasn't feeling that something was wrong. But I've been sleeping much too often today (just woke up again) so I'd better not go to bed until late if I can, probably can't. Maybe I'll try a movie. I watched one of yours about a writer trying to encourage another writer to write again, it was good. Who knows, by the time we get together again maybe I'll be into movies and you'll enjoy me even better. I discovered a top and pants of yours in the laundry basket so you're going to have to come back to get them sometime. See, there's your excuse! Enjoy your beautiful home sweetie, gardening should start soon.

M: (to myself) I must admit that as I walked today I felt free, a single man again. It might even be romantic like in the movies to talk with a purty woman then reveal at an appropriate time that I am dying. The thought passed through my mind that maybe I should go to some of the events at the cancer clinic, meet a purty lady who is dying too and spend our last days together loving and encouraging, sharing all. It would be sweet if I had the money to travel with such an one as that. Am I doing the right thing to encourage Jen? We love each other but our times together are not the best, there's a wealth of life remaining for me elsewhere, is there for her too?

I was getting so excited about the thought of her new slim body from a distance but that disappeared into the reality of her eating as much as ever before and looking the part. It didn't seem that she had lost weight at all though she said her pant size is smaller than when we were married. It's rude of me to write that I suppose, my lady readers will not think well of me, but when have I ever not been open with my readers? Jen must not read my books until I'm dead I think, they are not flattering of her even though I love her and know she loves me. The truth is often inconvenient, I will continue to tell it the way I see it. And Jen knows that I'll publish everything she writes to me so she is able to present it the way *she* sees it too, I won't hold anything back from her or you who are reading this.

Yesterday I bought a bottle of bourbon, tried a few sips and decided to pour it down the drain but didn't. Tonight it's calling and it's open near the keyboard, tasting good, a blend of nuts and fruits it says, seems healthy, as if I should care. A new experience for me, a solo event with hard liquor, hiccup, shhheee you tomorrow. Oh, my sister said that medical marijuana comes in pills, wonder if they'll offer me some later on? If so I'll not likely turn it down. *Who am I becoming?*

Jen: I slept in. Church was at 9:00. What do you plan to do with all the down time you have. I have lots to do. The problem is making myself do it.

M: I'm reinventing me not being a starving writer working 18 hours a day. Not sure how that's going to work out just yet but I'll think of something I'm sure. Remember my impression in the night that I should stay away from the lofty peaks for a while and experience earth like normal people do while I can? Probably take up reading again, walk more when the sun comes out and the temps creep a little higher, maybe throw in an African safari or something normal like that. Dunno, but wish me well experiencing it whatever comes moment by earthy moment. Meanwhile I wish you luck making yourself do what you know needs to be done.

Jen: It is good you are dissatisfied with being a starving write. You sure looked like one. Please keep eating and remember to eat healthy with all that junk food. Enjoy reading your books. I suggest a few Mormon writers. Keep reminding me I have to do the things that give me a securer future. I seem to have a difficult time with that responsibility. Do you want to do some traveling with me. If so lets start dreaming it. Do you love me.

M: Although it may not please you or easily blend into the way you see it or hope it is/was, I will always write frankly the way I see/feel it, that's just the way I am. I never deliberately try to hurt you but of course you (like everyone else) can choose to take offense at anything I say or write or am. I think personal communication should be a process of getting to know another human being as they really are rather than a process of trying to make that person fit into our notion of who/what he/she *should* be to fit better into our own bubble world. We can choose to *enjoy* diversity and take delight in the way others are different. Yes I know I need to work on that one too, I all too quickly go on the defensive when the truth about me as I know it is not being presented properly and someone thinks they know me better than I know myself. I suppose the solution is to be non-judgmental and to always accept others as they present themselves. They too are playing a game that often requires the wearing of masks so the *real* we remains concealed in no danger of being discovered. We can choose to play along with them, or move along to something/someone more entertaining, or go into ourselves.

In your chosen insecure judging doubting blaming way you ask if I love you rather than accepting that I do, getting on with life where you are, and looking forward to even more enjoyable times together in the future, which is likely. You could choose to enjoy today where you are and do a little secret smile those times when you feel particularly close. Or indulge a fond memory, a secret something only you and I know and loved. You could choose to discover happiness and contentment within your own self, your own safe matrix in a world that must always change and expand, going with the flow of life renewed daily, drifting with the stream rather than fighting it and paddling furiously upstream, trying to remain in one spot or return to the past, it cannot be so. To cling is alien to our being, life is not a static state, it's a *process* leading to enjoyment and fun, a fullness of love and joy moment by delicious moment. There is no demand for sorrow or sadness or pity when one has 'let go and let God' and is flowing with life *abundant,* accepting life fully, we *are* life.

The truth is that I haven't changed, I continue to love you as I loved you when we were married. I think each time we get together it will be as if the divorce never happened, we both feel married but in fact aren't. You were content with me for the most part during most of our married years and we enjoyed our lives together. Although you felt justified at the time you sought out a lawyer to fight me I will continue to think that the divorce and separation of our properties was not essential, we could have just separated for a while, we were already living physically apart. We would have been drawn together again like we continue to be. But I did need to get away to live and write the books that mean so much to me (and maybe nothing much to others.)

I am not ready to think of travel but that may come. I can't even fly yet and spring is not far from Victoria. I may want to stay here in the beautiful seaside garden city I call home.

Jen: If you were here I would be laying in your arms. But realize you need to be free to create what you want and time is of the up most. I know you have several friends that may want to come and spend time with you and for that reason I need to be out of the way so you will feel comfortable with them. You are a single man and I am a single woman. I thought we were a couple but not sure you want that any longer. Took my rings off. I felt from a comment you made it bothered you.

This I want to share you were most likely unaware that your leaving me and your emails created a mental and emotional disturbance within me. You became such a different man that choose to take a disturbing road as I saw it. I did not judge it. I just excepted it as a temporary state of mind. Soon I was playing a roll in your world of mostly emails. I know this was your process for inspiration to write books. What I learned from you is if most men think and express two faces of love as you did I will never trust a men's ways again. I felt like a sickie on a mare-a-go-round caught and could not get off. I am still on it. To the point I don't see relationships in a healthy way and I am very emotional most of the time. I never know when it will expose its nasty head. I don't like it. This has effected us both greatly. You call it a pity party but I see no way to get off when I see no way to get off. Then you through in cancer and dying and I can hardly handle it.

I believe you love me but I question what you mean by love, as you said it means something different to a man. For that reason there can never be a love that has gone right. I wish I could squash my feelings of insecurity. As I told you when I am threaten and I want to run. I know I should keep my mouth shut. My leaving for a time out might be best and have my own fight with myself. When my emotions flear it is a cry for help but what I get from you is, i don't like you right now. I often wonder why you didn't take me in your arms and sooth my emotions. It would have calmed my feelings to feel your love. I feel you are dissatisfied with me. The rejection I felt from you for being over weight hurt continues. One time you rubbed my feet and legs. I was grateful for that attempt but knew it was an attempt of something you really did not want to do. Often we do do things we don't want to just to please another person. I will not return until you want me to. I admit I am threatened, confused, and not sure why you want me there. You have your freedom to chase what ever winds that bring you joy. That I want for you.

I am grateful for many wonderful moments we spent these last three weeks. I really enjoyed our wonderful open conversations and getting to know each other a bit better. Hope to have many more. That part of our relationship was like two people in a healthy loving marriage. I felt very close to you. I know having a spiritual connection, falling in love, and being attracted to another person is something that can not be forced on another. I am not sure I express my self clearly or in a manner that gives true feelings.

M: Well expressed, thank-you for sharing that. You write *"When my emotions flear it is a cry for help but what I get from you is, i don't like you right now. I often wonder why you didn't take me in your arms and sooth my emotions. It would have calmed my feelings to feel your love."*

Taking you in my arms of course is what I *should* have done rather than going on the defensive because buttons from the past had been pushed and I (like you) was feeling insecure in myself. I'm learning, I'll try better next time…

It's a foggy day, almost magical. The gulls have been calling for hours, reminding me how close is the sea and its creatures, and how parts I once called "me" may soon merge into that life ever renewing while I go on.

Jen: Just a thought. I have no doubt you are a wonderful writer (magnificent) and your books are great books. But also had thought that maybe your books were draining the life out of you. They took your health in two ways. You would not go to the doctors until they were finished and you would not take the time to eat properly that resulted a very weak thin body. If you had died I would of blamed the books. Even with the knowledge of you having cancer I would still blamed the books for draining the life out of you. Of course I would always follow your request regarding your great books. But know this no book is worth losing you over. You look wonderful now. I was glade you went and picked up more food. Don't forget to eat the salmon and cucumber in your fridge.

M: Had salmon last night, forgot about cucumber. I love my books and what they have done for me.

Jen: (re an Abraham quote about attracting money that I forwarded to her) I agree we must not talk the talk of being poor or think we are poor in any way. Except remembering, At the same time when it comes to financial matters we should kept to a budget that except our thinking to say "buying a ice cream cone makes me rich because it is in the budget." This program move one along to being able to afford a hamburger with that ice cream, followed by new opportunity that change our financial ability and we buy a car. Meaning positive thinking with prudence. If we decide to buy that car before it was prudent we may not be able to buy the ice cream that made us feel rich. Where with prudence and timing you get the ice cream, the hamburger, the car, then a house and then all the vacations you could ever want. I think your youngest son is a good example. With his prudent business methods he will have all he desires and a retirement too. His brothers are further down the path than this youngest boy. But rest assure her will be there or possibly have more than his brothers because of his prudence. I believe he feels rich with prudence and is enjoying the journey that gives him site for a better future. What journey can we enjoy with prudence and get what we want. It may not be a world cruse but it might be a trip to Alberta, or Hawaii or possibly a Mediterranean cruse. And we will say we are rich. And we aren

Jen: Sorry I sent the email in the middle of editing it by the wrong push of button. I think you will get the jest of what I meant.

M: Surely you jest madam. Or perchance you are not up to speed with four letter words, not being given to using them oft enough. I feel certain however that you now get the gist of what I am wont to communicate. Or something like that...

Tried to do laundry but all the machines are in use. Then fell asleep, again, getting to be a habit, an hour here an hour there, adds up but at least time moves swiftly along and I did sleep the night last through. Fog's gone outside though not internal, was thinking of going out and disturbing its settle, maybe even push it aside the length of breakwater but didn't get to it. Maybe it will reappear tomorrow and I will.

M: I would love a Med cruise, maybe linger a bit, do Venice, Rome etc. while there. Someday when I'm rich and not so prudent maybe... I hear you about my son, but they are spending huge amounts of money on websites, offices etc. that could have gone to their own personal pockets and memories better than be shoved into the business perhaps fruitlessly. That's how I see it, especially when memory is much of all I have left at the seeming end of my mortal journey, and it's rich. I'm glad I wasn't always prudent, the cruises I paid for are among our fondest times together. Life's overflowing with abundance if we will only grasp it and enjoy while the fruit's available for the plucking.

M: (to myself) Today I sent author queries to four literary agents picked somewhat at random. If none of them expresses interest in representing me to publishers I will most likely self-publish my manuscripts as e-books and go my way having done what I can to get them out to the public. It's possible that I wrote them just for me as part of the process of preparing for the death of this physical body and what is to come beyond that. I thought to hide my pen name and thus the books from my children because being Mormons they will judge me and what I did harshly. But of course they will have access to my computer and papers when I'm dead so it will likely get out. I continue to hope that they will love me, I love them and am proud of them all, they will remain my greatest accomplishment.

As I think that soon I will be in the company of billions I wonder why women like Jen in this lifetime are so adamant that the man in their life be exclusively theirs even after the years of child bearing and raising when family is so important. But it is so, I must respect that and maintain my own freedom as best I can. Sure, I'd marry Jen and live out my days with her if that is what she wanted. But it would complicate her financial affairs as she sees it, and that is more important to her than marrying me again even though she knows I'm dying. So be it, I accept her as she is but continue to look for that perfect love gone right that she denied today could ever exist. Will it be only in the next life that I will find Eve?

Kris comes in two hours. I wonder what that visit will bring, I'm open to anything that feels good and right. And I long for the touch of a caring woman now that Jen has distanced herself again and left me a single man. I expect that Kris and I will hug when we meet and part, I'll enjoy that. I think I'll find her warm and loving but busy, it should be a good afternoon today.

Kris: On my way.

She stayed a couple of hours and yes we hugged at greeting and at parting. I'm not feeling a close connection but the hugs were good. She travels a lot, is going to Dominica next month and back to Africa in May. She travels with a friend who looks real good in the photo I saw of her. Now I need to catch up on a bunch of messages from Jen.

Jen: As you read you will maybe understand where I am. It is true one should except one as one excepts them self. I am non-judgmental but you can not expect me to see you as you think you present yourself. None of us see you that way. We just try our best to put ourselves in your place and hope we are close to understanding. We call it seeing through another persons eyes. But can we truly. I am very simplistic and may even want to fix it. As you read the two sides of me that tear at my heart below don't judge me to harshly. You may not perceive my heart felt feelings as I failed to express them in poorly written language but I gave it my best shot. I am not the gifted magnificent writer you are. (She writes between the lines of my message.)

Is that really true. You hiding your writing from most and keep it a secret. I am so grateful you shared a small amount with me. I do except and love you wholly as you revile glimpse of your progressive thinking process that creates changes and even more questions.

I do not choose to be static. Are you in this state of abundance? Should i not be free to judged betrayal. Yet you put judgment on me. Yes I do judge you as I feel your betrayal to me and listened to your expression of that betrayal. How can I forgive betrayal when you are so fond of it. You expressed with great delight in the good that resulted from mostly bad sexual experiences. You choose and cherish them over me. You express no sorrow in your chooses. Will you ever feel sorrow for those decisions or is it a fact you went to far and the distance to come back seems so far away and clouded and you can not see the path. But is not. You have not forgot how to pray. God forgives us when the heart is filled with regret and desire to change. The slat will be wiped clean and all forgotten. As I will forget all also.

You believe as my ex does. Us feeling married when together and single when out of site. I do not waver in my feelings as you do. It was very important to divorce and have a separation of assets. If I had not. I would now be in jeopardy of losing the little income I have. Do you not see that. To pay your debt on the motor home and credit cards, if still married, I would have had to sell our house or a rental property or two to get out to pay off your debt in this market. Do you feel I should pay off your debts. I worked hard all my life but did not prepare properly for retirement. You believed in spending, enjoyed and live as a wealthy man. Thinking wealth was to be come from thought. I do wish you continued wealth. Just might not be money. But would sure like it to be.

You might find someone like me and your children that are your real wealth in the last days of life. Don't get caught up in something else and forget to pick those precise diamonds waiting in your own back yard. How I would love to cover you with a blanket as you quietly swing on the swing in our back yard. I would excuse myself and I walk a few yards away and pick a flower and bring it to you with a smile on my face and a deep expression of love in my eyes. Leaving no devotion I will be with you always. My dream continues as I go to bed and gently take you in my arms for many a nights and quietly say share our thoughts and as time passes I hold your hand and encourage your passing from love on thru the door (veil) to much greater love. With my hopes you will come back and take my hand when it is time for me to put my hand out and wait for your touch that will usurer me to meet others love ones, than to our home where we find rest in Christ, comfort in each other and learning for progression. For women that are sealed to their husbands as I am to you have their husbands take their wife through the veil. For I know we will be in the same place because I want to be with you. I can not see it not being if that is what we both want. Is that what you want? Will you promise to come and take my hand and take me through the veil and be together for eternity. I want to have many children with you that I was denied in this life because of our age. God has a plan that allows our dreams to be. He wants us to be happy and find joy.

On to another subject of this life. I thought you believed a piece of paper meant nothing except a government control. We could of easily stayed married and see each other on rare occasions for business and that would have been fine with you because you choose to be single when in fact you were married on the words of a paper. You said a marriage paper was a government control. You considered your self single when in fact you were married not only by a government paper but also sealed in marriage by God for eternity. Now we are not married by government paper makes no difference to me. It did made you legally a free man. Emotionally I will always be married and be faithful to until you die. I am sealed to you in marriage for eternity. I choose to not have that changed. It is a matter of the heart. I know you have other priorities and travel is not one of them at this time. What are your priorities?

Again on to other thoughts. Why do you change your mind about being like Don Quixote when your experiences might have been different your search was not. You related yourself to him in your books. Do you not think the point and success of the book was that men found them selves foolish as he was, and see themselves and his man servant in them on some level. To see we our selves are as foolish at times chasing what does not exist. But find great adventure. You your self often chased phantoms with just as much foolish hope as he had. Other saw it but dare not wake you because you enjoyed the foolishness that took you far. Often it was a great journey and well worth going on. A few caused great wealth and others a loss of wealth over time, that included your marriages and now onto the final frontier. You and your magnificent writing ability took you to a place that you lingered to long and (almost) took your life.

If only you stayed with me and was willing to worked on us. I would of loved being a part of the journey with my magnificent writers imagination took him on. I would of never stopped your desire to travel alone if you only talked to me and showed prudent plan. I am not stupid as you try to invent your reasons for leaving. I was not invited because your search was for the inspirations of other women developed into virtual lovers followed by immensely wanting the reality of their bodies followed by disappointment. You are a strange man that has no regrets. I do not judge the past. That you can discuss with your maker. It is a bang of a way to live and go out. Did it give you want you were looking for. I want you to have joy! Good memories give us something to cling to on lonely nights. I did and do love you well and that made life worth living for me. Lets make many memories for my lonely nights.

M: Wow, you put a lot in writing with this one, very well done, thanks for sending this message. I respect your feelings and how you see events that we have in common, we each have as much right to our own opinion and perspective.

The bottom line for me is that the person you tell me you are is pretty much exactly the person I want as my eternal companion. But then you do things or don't do things that tell me you are in fact someone else. And when we get together it's good and I want much more of that but as you know we don't go more than a couple of days before you become contentious about something and threaten to walk away from me, Saturday being a particularly nasty split with you indicating that you'd never come back. So what am I to think? Should I accept what you say and write, or pay more attention to what you do and don't do that so often contradicts what you say?

Anyway, I wish you were here, I'd surely hold you if you wanted to be held. Or would you prefer to be up all or almost all night doing other things, as you were when you were here? We both need to learn to not only talk the talk, but also to consistently walk the walk. We just had three weeks together, it ended with a blowout rather than a lovely parting until we meet again. I'm just telling it the way I see it. Do you really think you can be the person you say you are? I have not found any other. Can you be beautiful soft-spoken loving caring tender feminine Eve Mother of Nations, half of a perfect love gone right? Can you want to be with me more than with anybody else? I wonder...

M: Although I understand the importance of investing some of the profits back into a growing business there is of course another way to look at it, one that I have been familiar with for decades having read motivational books on the subject of making money since my youth. (Napoleon Hill "Think and Grow Rich", Og Mandino etc.) Generating a profit is the great motivator of the free enterprise system, it creates and motivates entrepreneurs and business leaders and the companies that manufacture and distribute products and services that we rely on daily. But everyone at all levels needs to be paid along the way.

In your case, from my point of view you were hugely blessed to have had our real estate investment company pay your way through life entirely so you could reinvest in and grow your own private business that you held by yourself. It would not have gone so well over the years if you had had to take your personal expenses out of it. I do not begrudge you that, I'm just pointing out a fact. I really appreciate your messages sweetie, I'll respond to the others later.

M: (to Jen) Was I too harsh with my comments? I know you are hurting and I should be much gentler with you. I wish you were here with me even though we have some rough times with the good ones. I love you sweetheart. Your Man

Jen: I see your point. But feel our threats that are similar to each others feelings. I understand your concerns about me. I am also concerned about my self.. I Would love to be something more to keep your interest spiked in me.. Don't know why I lack the motivation. When younger I never sat still and was always involved with little down time. Most people would be amazed at what I could accomplished. I worked out several times a week, went to collage, cared for children, worked hard in a business of locating and fixing up houses, kept a clean home and cooked meals almost everyday and took care of a yard that had two acres and on top of that I sold real-estate and was the Relief Society president.. Well may I did not do all that at the same time but most of it.

I request only one thing of you at this time. To not feel threaten when I get up set and just take me in your arms and reassure me you want me and I love me the most. I would soon calm down and all fears and hurts would melt away and you would have your Eve. I ran the other day because I felt you tired of me and don't want me around any more. I knew you were ready for me to go home and I needed to go home to take care of my personal life but even with that knowledge my emotions at the last moment flared at the thought I would soon be gone and I could hear you saying she is not with me and when she is gone I make no promises and Adam is looking for another Eve. Even though I know with your illness that is most likely not true but at the same time I know you will have Elaine over and if she said the right words you would take her in your arms and tell her you love her also. And I become a lonely woman or a old friend with even more of a broken heart. The chances of this is slim on her part. But you would just melt with joy if she gave her self fully and promised her heat to an old man like you. That is why as long as she wants to come over you have a secret hoping in side. That's part of my fears.

From what you write you are not sure you want to cement us as one. I ask my self why do you linger with this man whom is not satisfied with you. Even in these finally hours you linger. Is it in hopes of another Eve or are you. When I don't go to bed at the same time as you it is because I feel frozen inside and sometimes can't move for hours to go to bed. I used to say I did not want to give up the day. More truth is I set frozen inside. Please take my hand and I will always walk to the bed with you and climb in for as long as you want to hold me. I might get up later but you would have me to hold until you fall asleep.

Even now I set frozen since I came home in hopes by tomorrow I can move. I will take something to sleep tonight and maybe by tomorrow I will awake thawed and become mobile and accomplish what I came home to do. it is a form of depression. Michael I became frozen long ago in the marriage and not moving forward and accomplishing my purpose in life. What will it take to awake me. Thank you for buying me a pencil, eraser and paper to draw on. I think it would be a start. I should ask Elaine about different directions I could go to learn different skills. When I return and it is a bit warmer I just might go out and set by the sea side or park and draw for hours in the warmth of the day. Maybe you would go with me and lay on a blanket in the park with the warmth of the sun and your body soaking up the rays of the sun and finding joy in the book you read.

True I did those things you say I did. Next time take me by the hand and lead me to bed. I would love that gesture and lay in your arms. When my voice gets loud and ugly fear shows its face take me in your arms and I will be become calm. Tell me what gift you ask for regarding this subject.

M: (to myself) I responded to the message above then Jen responded between the lines and I responded to her so I'll put her and my messages in sequence as follows.

Jen: Thank you for writing such heart felt message. It touched my heart deeply. You have every right to feel the way you do. I am glade you shared every word. With such a letter I will not justify. I did respond to your remarks below. Enjoy your days.

M: Wow, your message is beautiful, you've almost got me crying. Sure, I'll take your hand and you to bed but I want you to be free and I sleep long before you do.

Jen: I understand a very long time.

M: And it would mean the world to me if you would come to me instead of the other way around.

Jen: When and where?

M: What I mean is when we are physically near each other that you walk over to me, touch me, touch me, touch me, speak tender words, caress me, sit with me our bodies touching, talk to me, linger long unhurried your mind not on some silly computer game running on your laptop. *You coming to me* instead of me walking over to you and rubbing your shoulders, caressing you (as I often do) is what I need most of all.

M: I don't think anyone has ever come to me like that except my children when they were little. When I came home from work in the summer I'd go outside and sit in the sun, hoping beyond hope that the mother of my children would come to me and talk and touch, but she never did. And often in Utah I'd sit on the swing day and night and dream of you coming to me. You may have come a time or two over the years but then in a minute you'd be watering or tending to the plants, not touching me, talking with me, wanting to be with me more than anything else in the world. You were busy with other things that were more important to you. We didn't satisfy each other's needs very well did we?

Jen: Very true. Were you just as empty as I was. Were you just as starved for love as I was. Did you want to make love as much as I did. So sorry I let you down.

M: Not always making love as in sex (though that too) but just tenderly sharing thoughts and time and touching each other in the meanwhile (you sitting on my lap?) never in a rush to walk away to something else that seemed more important, like watering plants (or computer games and movies.) Yes I know, there's too much female in me, but at least you know. Why do you think I liked Elaine sitting on the sofa reading to me while our bodies touched in a non-sexual way? There, got you jealous didn't I? But learn from that sweetie, learn what your man craves from you, he's quite simple and easy to satisfy if you would only forget the power struggle you engage in but deny doing so and be instead tender loving feminine WOMAN, Eve Mother of Nations. Can you not grasp the vision of HER and be that? The woman's role is not to fight and argue and contend with husband and children but to quietly lovingly tenderly *nurture* and set that example of womanhood. You seem quite rusty on that from my point of view.

It's not busy I want from you, it's you in my arms, wanting me, touching me tenderly like women do to men they love, *coming to me, coming to me, coming to me...*

Jen: I was trying to do those things. I took your arms often when walking. I washed your back, I cut your hair, I gave you a back rub, I often rubbed your feet and legs and I tended your wounds. Were these the busy things that don't count. I will remember the difference. I thought I did at times touch you tenderly but must of done it wrong. I like you putting your arms around me in the kitchen. Does that not count. I sat at the table often so you would have the couch to rest and sleep with out me disturbing you by walking around the room. I know one big mistake was I played games way to much.

M: As usual you are completely wrong about me. I don't have "a secret hoping inside" for Elaine's "heat". I don't really care if she visits at all. But sure, I'm lonely when I'm on my own, I won't say no if she wants to visit.

Jen: Sorry if I am wrong.

M: You are right though about your leaving, I tired of fighting with you, of losing my peace, never knowing when the fight would come, only knowing that it would.

Jen: I finally understand and won't come when not wanted.

M: You don't understand at all. I did not say I don't want you to come back just that I try to live in constant happiness and peace and that was disturbed sometimes when you were here. After three weeks I needed a break, and so did you.

M: And I was hugely disappointed when you had told me you'd lost a lot of weight then when you came it didn't seem you had lost any. I'm not likely to change that attitude Jen, I want you slim, it means the world to me, you knew that all those years, you know it now. I wanted you to sit on my knee. I wanted to be able to carry you to bed. But you were too heavy! Why is it a fault in me for wanting that?

Jen: Yes it is a very big relationship fault. Now after saying that I understand your desires and wants. Just not sure why I can't find the state of mind to make it happen. It has brought me great unhappiness knowing I embarrass your ego. I feel the lack of passion you have for me. Of course I dream of being slender and beautiful for both you and me.

M: It's not like you couldn't do it, you were on the way, then when you get with me you crash and seem to turn into an enemy instead of the one who loves me the most.

Jen: I do not sleep with the enemy.

M: Cute.

M: Why? Why? Why?

Jen: We both have many why? Maybe cause and effect.

M: It seems that you try to punish me, or yourself, or us, or make our togetherness unpleasant. Hey, you're pretty good at that sometimes. It COULD be nice for us *all the time*. Why isn't it?

Jen: Sorry I don't know the answer right now. I never have thought of punishing you but my emotions punish me and then you by effect.

M: I don't know what it will take to "awake" you. My death maybe?

Jen: I hope not.

M: Will you become slim and pleasant for the next man then? I think you will, and I hope he is vastly better for you than I have been.

Jen: Not sure but I don't think there will be another.

M: Sure, I continue to dream of a perfect Eve. But now I think she can only be found in the life I will soon move on to.

Jen: Does that mean you will not take my hand and invite me through the veil. This new light hurts.

M: You are referring to the Mormon belief that a man who has been sealed to a woman for all eternity in their temples will stand at the "veil" of forgetting and welcome her to the 'other side' when she dies. Sure, I'd love to be there for you if it actually works that way, and I do remember what name to call. I'll do my best sweetie but I can't promise something I'm not certain I can deliver. I've told you many times that my door will always be open to you even though (in the original Mormon way until politicians forbade it) there may be other 'sister wives' gathered with me too. There is no "new light" to cause you to hurt, just your own seemingly desperate attempt to conclude that you and I are not for each other. It's (as always) you yourself who comes up with such things from what I write, things untrue that I never intended to convey. Maybe that "perfect Eve" will be you but only when you cross to the other side (at your appointed time) to be with me?

M: You could still enrich the days I have left (they may turn out to be many.) Why don't you try a little harder to be the woman you keep telling me you are but always fail to be?

Jen: If you only knew how I want to be that woman for you. But feel you prefer another on the other side of the veil.

M: I'd hold you and love you so much if you were here right now!

Jen: Thank you for those words but they flee so quickly from your desires.

M: You do read my desires and indeed they often flee. But it remains constant that I want to become Adam and to know a perfect love gone right, or perfect loves if it works the original Mormon way. I invite you to be with me forever, my door is always open. But it is you who must come to me, that's the way it was with Adam when God brought to him his bride. And that is the foundation of why it is so important that you come to me when we are within physical distance of being together. And why the coming of Kira was important to me, *it was the way she did it!* Jealous again? That one is over and buried in past books, we do not communicate or have a connection of any kind whatsoever, she has a husband already and loves him and he her. I am content with that, I did not know she was married and in love with another when she came.

M: But then, when you come again what will the tomorrows bring for us? Based on our recent history I never know because you are so often insecure, doubting, fearing, blaming, jealous, angry, contentious. Just be beautiful for me all the time like you are sometimes, that's all I need to bring out the depth of love that resides untapped inside me, as yours does inside you. As death approaches do you not think I will become even more tender and loving? And more needy? Why not try to complete your physical fitness program as quickly as you can? Even if it doesn't work fast enough for me at least you'd be ready for another man and you'll be pleased with yourself for having done it.

Jen: I respect your wants and will stay away as long as possible to not wound your ego. I got it when you said I embarrassment you because of my weigh. Six of your seven children are over weight and you don't get the connection. Do they also embarrass you as I do.

M: Ok, harsh words again, but that's what I'm feeling right now so please allow me that and look to *yourself* for happiness.

Jen: Yea you have the right to say it as you feel it. I sure shot the emails the way I see it. But it is not fair to say look at your self for happiness when you just blasted. The purpose of your words were to destroy those feeling.

M: I never deliberately write or say or do anything to hurt you. But I do tell the truth as I see it, painful as that may come across to be. Your fight is always with yourself. Emotions are your guide. There would be great peace in only choosing and following thoughts that FEEL happy. Should you do that consistently you will no longer struggle with doubts and negatives, they will disappear of their own accord. Try it?

M: Yeah, I'd love to lie on a blanket in the warm park and watch you draw as the ancient trees beckoned above and around me, me not resisting their pull much anymore. You could draw the trees, the flowers, the ducks, the great blue herons, the squirrels, the peacocks, the people, the ponds and flowing waters, the man on the blanket... We COULD have it all yet you and I. But I keep thinking that the change must come from you. And perhaps you keep thinking it must come from me?

Jen: Well with the conditions you put on me to loss weight will most likely put off any plans for some time. I would not feel comfortable coming back knowing I might of not lost enough weight and in your minds eyes I lost none. Leaving you feelings of disappointment and betrayal of your vision. You snatched my park dream and other dreams away tonight. I feel very lost and not very motivated.

M: Oh well, that's life I guess. But does it *have* to be that way?

Jen: You set the rules for me to change. I can only do my best. My fear is I might not be able to live up to your rules of making you happy in our relationship. I was never allowed to request changes in you that would make me happier. They were always used against me to find my own happiness.

M: My belief is that we are responsible for creating our own happiness. We do that by choosing happy thoughts and lifting our vibrations. Works for me...

Jen: Thought I would share me exchange of emails with a friend.

Jen: (to a friend) For the last two weeks I have been thinking about you. I just returned home from being in Victoria Canada for the last few weeks. These last two years have been full of constant life changing events in my life. I hope you do not mind if I unload a bit. I have always seen you as a trusted friend in the past. For now we both are on different busy paths that don't bring us together often. I would like to share how much I respect and honor you and your husband in your partnership in marriage. I as a woman I know the power you hold as a help meet to your husband. I to was once that woman for my husband. Once married he soon found his talent and we created a wonderful life and business. He had the desire and ability and I saw the direction for us to go. When he left me I divorced him for two reasons one being financial. He created his great escape and adventure to write books. But in spite of that He has always been the love of my life thru thick and thin. He has always been very kind to me.

Then most recent back in early December at his request I went and visited him and I knew he was very sick. But would not go to the doctor until he finished writing his books. Finally he went to the doctor and was sent to the hospital with a collapse lung that required draining. Test showed his lungs and lining are full of Cancer. He lost a lot of weight and was weak but looking much better now. His 3 daughters will be visiting him and making sure he is all right. When I am caught up with business here I will go and spend as much time as he needs. He told me he is looking forward to dying and will reject prolong treatment that takes away from quality of life but will except treatment for pain. His son that is a doctor came from Edmonton to go with him to the cancer clinic to make sure his dad understood the best options for him.

I have missed him so much this last year and half. This has been a tinder sweet and bitter reunion of reality. We have sat and shared our deepest thoughts and feelings. Michael is a very intelligent and complex thinker. He just gets lost in life sometimes. He always said he did not fit in this world well but was so pleased and happy to have had 7 children. They love him as much as he loves them. His 4 temple going sons flew into Victoria from all over US and Canada to gave him a powerful priesthood blessing. They are brilliant strong loving men like their dad. I am keeping my self on call to go back for what ever time he needs. Sometime we are given sweet and bitter moments to grow in, I feel only blessed to be able to tell this man how much I love him. Again thank you sweet lady for just being the wonderful understanding woman I know you are. Love Jen

Friend of Jen's: Dear Sweet Jen, Oh sweetie, you are my precious friend and sister and I feel honored that you have shared so much with me! I have missed your love and friendship -- but you are I will always have the kind of relationship where we can just pick up where we left off. I am so thankful for that!! Life does change and can change in a heartbeat, it seems. I am so sorry to hear of Michael's terminal condition. So many are leaving us -- I guess it's part of getting older. Michael is so lucky and blessed to have you, Jen. I know that life has not always been easy for you both. I can relate to him in a way, because I've never felt like I really fit in anywhere either. I feel different from most people and oftentimes misunderstood. I'm sure he has felt that way, from what you have explained in your email. What a wonderful blessing it has been for you both to be able to talk and just lay it all out on the table. That is a very healing and trusting process for both of you.

I am grateful that he has always been kind to you -- you are such a Christlike and selfless person, Jen! It's got to be so difficult to have to divorce the love of your life, and now, to have to watch him as he nears the end of his life. You are so strong and courageous and I'm sure an anchor and "rock" for him as he passes from this life when the time comes. How wonderful that you have been able to tell him how much you love him.

Oh, Jen, life is never what we expect it to be. I have often told my children that my life has been harder and more difficult than I ever thought it would be and sweeter than I ever imagined it could be at the same time. I told my daughter a few weeks ago that I sometimes didn't know whether to be sad or happy, because sometimes the good and the bad are going on at the same time. She said, "Mom, we live side by side with joy and sorrow our entire lives!". That made so much sense to me!

What would we do without the knowledge of the Gospel Plan? How hard it would be to believe that our loved ones died and were gone forever! At some level, it sounds like Michael knows that. He's not afraid to die -- in fact, he is probably relieved to soon be free of the cares and woes of this earthly existence. Knowing that he's surrounded by his children and his loving wife, has got to be such a comfort and blessing for him! His passing will be a sweet experience. And you will see him again!

Jen, how grateful I am that you reached out. I love and appreciate you so much! I am here for you, whatever you need -- whenever you need it! We can stay in touch via email, if that's the best way. But let's stay in touch for sure! How long are you going to be in town? You probably aren't sure, but maybe we can get together and just talk sometime? Let me know and please take care of yourself! Hugs.

Jen: (to friend) What comfort you bring to me by your words. It brought tears to my eyes. You should really write a book. I am serious. There is such a need for your words regarding this subject to be heard and held close. They would change lives. You would find where you fit. I think many don't feel that they fit. I know God has a box we all fit into. That is if we choose to call it a box for this example. We just get stuck hanging on to one corner some times. Afraid to let go. Once we let go we realize we created the box and it has no walls or bottom. And we are released to flow and create. I feel like I am hanging on to a corner even though I know its not a real box. I just don't know where I want to flow. I feel lost so I stay. But you. Awe you know where you would flow or are you flowing to similar places we all go as women inside. With your way of words would help so many women find comfort of not being alone. To many like me need to hear your words of wisdom. They would be healing and give promise.

How ever you are different. That is what endears you to me. Who ever misunderstood you were not listening with a open mind. Would be good to talk some time. Thanks for writing me back good friend, love Jen

M: (to Jen) I'm glad that you have such good support. And that you are becoming such a prolific writer as well. Now it's *you* who is encouraging others to write books. Maybe you'll get into that yourself someday, you're coming along real well. You mention to your friend that you divorced me for two reasons, one being financial. What was the other reason?

Jen: Yes your words hurt me as much as mine hurt you. You are just as much up and down as I am. Are you not aware your emotions are off the chart just like mine are. The only difference is I express mine in a ugly way but you use words to de-announce all affection.

You would think you are dying or something by the way you act. Can we not talk about what was good when i visited. I don't ever get built up much by you. I don't think you see much worth in me. I even question that myself. I was hoping I did some good when I visited. I came to you as quickly as I could. Just like Kira in Utah did but mine was for a much more worthy cause. That was to be at your side when you went home from the hospital so I could be tenderly at your side and care for you.

You made it clear that you want me when you feel loneliness but in reality you don't want me hanging around because I am fat. Then you requested I stay in Utah until I was expectably thin. Is that even possible in your eyes. I will honor your request and not come. I really don't want to embarrass you or damage your male ego any more than I already have by walking beside you in public. I guess my feeling of taking my belongs was right on. May you always find happiness in yourself.

The request to lose weight as a condition to coming to see you will burn deep within me for the rest of my life. You know what it does to a woman and I feel you stuck a knife into my stomach with this possible last request.

M: There you go, I tell it the way I see it and feel it and you take offense and walk away again, this time (yet again) threatening that it will be permanent *("this possible last request.")* I guess you get what you really want inside, to walk away from me permanently and to blame me for it, it has seemed that way for a long time. I have tried to reconcile for many months but you won't. Sure, you'll 'sacrifice' and come to Victoria to "care" for the man you divorced while he dies because you never stopped "loving" him even as you filed for divorce and to take control of everything he owned however justified you kept telling yourself it was to do that. That story of your sacrifice, caring for a dying ex, looks real good to others, it's a wonderful tale of womanhood to tell of you, there are similar stories floating around in the Mormon world. Harsh yes, true, it seems so. I'm not wanting your 'selfless' sacrifice, I'm wanting you to be my Eve Mother of Nations in every beautiful sense of the concept.

I was hoping you'd come to care for me yes, but much more importantly I was hoping you'd come to me because you genuinely want to be with me more than with anyone else. But instead of the reconciliation I have sought and been denied since May of last year you indulge yourself in critical judgments, misunderstandings, attempts at manipulation (weak), contention, self pity, jealousy, blame, and anger. That's how I see it, I'm just expressing it honestly. You are beautiful, I want you, but as I said while still in the car at the airport, there are *some* things about you that I don't like. Your response to that was to say, *"And with that I take my departure, you don't have to follow me into the terminal."* Pretty weak for an excuse don't you think? But it does reveal your intention to get away from me and to blame me for it. Well, GO if you must Jen, but why do you need to blame me for that going? *Can't you face up to the person you have become when it relates to me?* I'm sure you will do well with another man, I was just hoping you'd give US a chance while there still is one.

Yes I know, by writing so openly and honestly I am quite possibly getting you angry enough to never come back to me, but I'm willing to take that risk. I want only *beautiful* you, not the garbage. I'M TRYING TO WAKE YOU UP!!!!!!!!!!

Enjoy the day and your life Jen, it seems we may not see each other again. That was not my desire, you are welcome to come back anytime. And just so you know, I am not embarrassed being in public with you, not at all, I'm proud to be with you, you're pretty, you're cute, sometimes beautiful. It's just that when we're in private passion is not easily aroused when it should be as I look upon the body you have abused with too much food for decades. (Harsh but true, I don't hold back.) I do have strong sexual feelings for you when we hug long and I think you feel them too. I repeat, we COULD have everything we want but you choose instead to pity yourself and blame me and come up with wild excuses not to be with me. I would throw myself into you for the rest of my life if you would only be the person you yourself *want* to be (and say you are but aren't) and come to me truthfully and fully, wanting to be with me more than with anyone else, nothing else mattering more. But that would be *un*conditional love wouldn't it? That's very difficult for you much as you'll deny it.

Really, what's so hard about losing weight? Especially when you yourself want to do that. Better to blame me for how I feel and put it off until there's another man beckoning you? That's how it looks to me and that's the truth. So, knowing that you could have easily slimmed down over the years and even more easily now that you live by yourself, I must logically conclude that it's not losing weight that is your problem but that you have a deep down fight with yourself or an anger on for me that is keeping you from US. Do you hate men because of what your other husbands did to you? *What is it Jen?* Or better yet, stop fighting yourself and me, forget the negatives, and choose and follow only thoughts that *feel* good. I do love you babe, wish you were here... Michael

Jen: Ok you got it out. I can't take much more. Please lets stop fighting.

M: (to myself) Today I am resolved to allow Jen into my mortal life as much as it works for us but to *focus* on my goal of becoming immortal Adam with sister wives. That's my fantasy whether Jen fits herself in or not, it's the deep burning desire I shall take with me to my dying, or better yet to this physical body being made immortal. That's what these books are all about, that's who and what I really am. Will the universe fulfil this deep desire? I don't know yet, but I'll surely tell you if it happens while I can still press these keys...

M: (to Elaine) I spoke with Kris yesterday and mentioned you and your departed friend. She told me to ask if you know Matt. I hope you are doing well Elaine.

M: (to list) Happy birthday 7! I want to once again thank my four sons for the wonderful visit, I'm still thrilled with it. And looking forward to my three daughters appearing soon, two of them planning to stay a week I think. Also, thanks to two more of my cousins for the nice card and well wishes.

Jen flew home on Saturday and I'm getting used to being a bachelor again. Thankfully I internally stored up some of the delicious food that was laid on while she was here trying to fatten me up. She was an enormous help to me during a time of difficulty. It is my hope that she will visit again, she remains a very important person in my life.

I am getting around well, walking to the end of breakwater with no breathlessness though I can feel that I'm not back to the way I once was. I rest and sleep a lot, maybe too much, giving in to a psychological rather than a physical need? I don't know which it might be. I'm feeling good about life and accepting whatever comes except I'll do my best to tame the pain should it ever make an appearance.

As for upcoming appointments I have a chest x-ray (re the buildup of fluid), a CT scan coming up, and an appointment with the oncologist at the cancer clinic. And I can't fly for six weeks anyway so it's not likely that I will leave Victoria anytime soon. At which time this glorious seaside city will be in full bloom so I may not stray at all, we'll see. You are all welcome to visit anytime. Dad/Michael

Cousins: we will continue to keep you in our thoughts and prayers...

I'm beginning to think I'm a fraud with all those people praying for me, *I don't feel like I'm dying!*

1: Dad thank you for the update on what is going on. What you just sent was exactly what I was wondering about just before you sent it. Not a coincidence to me. Please keep sending regular updates. It helps me to be able to focus on my work.

I don't think that I can adequately express how thankful and grateful i am to God for how well the trip your sons just went on to see you. I'm so thankful for Jen's help to you. I remain so remarkably touched by getting to visit with your island sisters and to hear about family experiences. Your sisters are so delightful. I feel I've lost out over the years by not being as connected.

I remain delightfully struck by the mannerisms and appearances that must be our mutual heritage that I could see in you and your sisters and that I see or did see in other living and deceased family. We are blessed with a good family. Cancer may kill but it can also heal. Dad your daytime sleeping is probably part of the disease process. Any part that is psychological is okay in that it would be part of the expected normal reaction and response. A little 'anaesthesia' from sleep would be welcome particularly since you are not the person to likely stay there. Just don't delay setting into place what's needed as your disease and it's consequences of fatigue, etc, are likely to progress (that's doctor talk for 'worsen') making it harder to accomplish tasks.

I was so impressed by your candour and willingness to tell your sons how you feel and what you think; as also to stick to what you want and to express it well even when hearing some few differing desires from your sons. I can't and won't ever be your Medical Specialist in Psychiatry but I am one and consult to the highest level of cancer/palliative care so I do have some experience in the area and with that experience I can say as a highly educated son that you did well Dad. Please keep considering the expressed hopes of your sons to minimize the things we will need to do after you die. You know your Victoria Bishop and Church congregation seemed pretty nice. Maybe you should consider some limited connection with them. As promised that will not and did not come from your sons.

M: Thanks 1, nice message. I appreciate your counsel and will snore some more. I used to feel guilty about not working hard at something all the day long but need to adjust that attitude. Could be fun, there's a book or two I haven't read yet. Just got back from a walk to the end of breakwater, nice sunny day, temps are picking up with buds on the trees. Life's good...

5: Dad, I also was wondering today how you were doing. So thanks for the update. Did you get the pictures that I emailed you? I haven't heard from you about them. My trip went well. I am grateful for the record breaking warm weather! Anyway, that's it for now. Luv ya.

M: I did get photos, thanks, was negligent in responding. See you soon, love you lots.

Jen: I spent a lot of time adding extensive comments to what you wrote and did not send them. Face it you are a dying man that has much to offer by creating wonderful memories with me. If you choose stay in Victoria until called home that's ok. I want you to be happy and as comfortable as possible. I don't want head games from you. I want you to be respectfully honest in sharing with me your needs. You don't have to make me into something you think is better or I make you into something I think is better. If we relapse we say "fluffy kitten is it not." or something else. At times we did laugh together and it felt good. I loved taking your arm when walking. In a moment I will send you my conditions.

Jen: Thanks for the very sweet words about me in your message to the list. I want to cry.

Jen: This is a request not a demand: Remember God and his son Jesus Christ, read the Book of Mormon or other Mormon books and pray as your father did.

This is my offer: Take me as I am. That's the only real thing I have to offer that means anything in the end. I do need to know your answer. Now share with me what that means. I started to list the beautiful benefits but what does it mean to you to take me as I am.

M: As for your "request" it is noted. But please keep in mind that I have already read or listened to the Book of Mormon at least a hundred times. I am very familiar with it. Are you? But I understand that you are thinking of my spiritual well-being from the Mormon point of view, that's ok, no offense. I'd be willing to listen if you read church books to me.

And as for your "offer" I was thinking of that earlier on today. Sure, I'll gladly spend the rest of my life with you the way you are if you care to hang around most of the time, you are welcome to return anytime. My conditions are that you give me a smile and a hug (when I'm not hurting) at least once each day. And that you don't get after me if I eat chips and cheesies and ice-cream and carrot cake whenever I want, get as fat as I want, laze around as long as I want, and don't shave if I don't choose to. And that you wear the headset to watch movies when I'm on the computer. Oh, yeah, and that I get at least half of the closet space until I can't cut my toenails anymore.

1 indicates that I may soon run into even more fatigue etc. so the "year" I am expected to live may turn out to be far from a year of reasonably good health. If we're going to travel, we should do it soon. (And yet I could fit into the 14% of people who have what I have and live five years. And I could be permanently healed too, it happens...) What would you *really* want for me? A quick death so you can get on with life after grief, or several years with me maybe not even being able to travel? Ask yourself truly, and let me know.

I think you could find friends here sweetie, and I'd go to the first Sunday church meeting with you while I can if that's important to you. If time goes on we could find a better place to live in Greater Victoria (though probably not a better location while I'm mobile.) I'm tied to British Columbia for my health care and I consider Victoria home, though it's possible that I could/would spend a few weeks at a time at your Utah home too. *Promise to come sit with me on the swing?* Your Man in Victoria if you want him.

Jen: (received just as I sent the message above) My heart softens today and I want you to know I miss you and I love you.

M: I miss you too darling. I love you.

Chapter 6

———— ❦ ————

Jen: I just got home from the grocery store. Bought two loaves of sprouted bread. At least I got dressed and went out. I will start looking at trips also.

M: I forgot about sprouted bread, might check for it across the street, it makes wonderful toast. Re the trips, now would be a great time however I can't fly yet and don't want to drive in snow. I can't miss the CT scan and doc appointment. We'll take it from there with that new information.

Jen: I ran into our old Home Teacher' wife that came to visit us with her husband. I told her about your cancer. She said she was sorry and to say hello to you and that her and her husband really liked you and enjoyed visiting with you. Laura called and we visited for a time. She does not think she wants to get married again and doesn't even want to think about it. I told her later in the future we should go to a temple night session with the older singles group. Just to make friends. Most will be women. I guess I do have friends.

M: (to myself) Ok, she's looking into the future for herself, but not replying to my message about accepting her as she is, and not saying she's coming back to Victoria. I feel that she will though and we'll plan the rest of my life together. I'll dedicate myself to her if she comes and doesn't leave me alone too much from then on. After all, fantasy is just fantasy right?

Dinner time. Cucumber (left over from Jen) sandwich on fresh Seed Lover's bread generously spread with real butter and a few drips of salad dressing sound good? Actually that's quite elaborate for me, I've never done such a thing before. (Can of nuked spaghetti and one toast for lunch.) Proud of me a bit? I am, but missing Jen's meal preparations.

But now that I've opened myself wide to Jen, gone wholly to her, and left myself completely vulnerable will she move away from or towards me? What is your guess? What is the woman way, to move towards the one she loves and has not yet conquered, or to move towards the one she loves and has hopelessly vanquished? It is my hope the latter prevails. Today I want Jen and if I get her firmly and she treats me/us well and stays with me long and often, I will keep her for the rest of my life however long or short that may turn out to be. Why does she delay her response to my submission and invitation to come back? Does she still need to think about it? In writing with urgent implication *"I need to know your answer"* she indicated that she has an early exit plan if I don't come through. Is her preference the exit with blame as I've been saying all along it most likely is? Or does she truly love me and want to be with me the remainder of my days? It is my hope that before this night ends we will both know how this is going to go down. With her I will most likely turn hugely back to family and back to being Mormon because they and she are. Without her I will probably continue my search for Eve and a better love. Which will it be Jen? Do you really know how much power you have over me?

Elaine: How are things going... how are you feeling? Good to hear from you. Yes, I know who Matt was... I have been in his hot tub, while Lila was house sitting and Matt and his wife away on holiday. He moved from there. I remember him, but never got to know him well, or his wife. Let me know how you are.... Kindly

M: (to myself) Sure I waver, my desires are fleeting, but I'm still single right? I know that 18 years of acquaintance with Jen will without a doubt prevail should she choose me wholeheartedly and put in a long harmonious appearance. But in the meantime why shouldn't I have friends and friends over? Maybe Elaine will read to me and we'll enjoy each other's company like we used to do.

M: There is no question then but you and Kris were acquainted with the same Lila, I'll let her know. As for me, other than sleeping and lazing more I am quite well and back to walking the breakwater each day never breathless and feeling no pain. (No, nothing to do with the bottle of bourbon I bought a couple of days ago, first time in my life, just curious, and still thinking after a couple of sips I might pour down the drain. :-) And getting fatter from acquiring the rather pleasant habit of consuming chips and carrot cake in prodigious quantity while Jen was here, thinking all the while why not indulge, *what's it going to do, kill me?* More easily fatigued but doing well would sum it up I think since there is no scale in the house to weigh myself upon.

I'm on my own again, can of nuked spaghetti for lunch and cucumber (left over from Jen) on buttered Seed Lovers bread for dinner, and of course carrot cake as I write this, sip possible, gotta give the bourbon a reasonable attempt, after all it's a blend of nuts and fruits it says, should be healthy enough. But yesterday I indulged in the protein drink you recommended, so should stay healthy for a while yet, do need to get some more of that delicious kale drink you brought though. I think I can walk to a kale smoothie dispenser on Government Street, maybe do that tomorrow instead of breakwater. And spring has almost sprung, reason for gaiety and goodly spirits in this gorgeous seaside city. How can you tell that I've been reading Man of La Mancha today and am immersed in an archaic (you might say primal, at the least antediluvian) form of word telling?

Kris stayed a couple of hours yesterday, only the second time we've been in each other's presence. We may or may not become friends, she's busy, was headed to a Native American naming ceremony when she left. Like somebody else I'm better acquainted with she morphed me into a rather poorly species of host by taking only a glass of water from my hand and talking nutrition part of the time, everybody wants to help poor ailing me. (I appreciate and love my family and friends, need them.) Come visit if you will when you can sweetie, you are welcome here.

M: (to Kris) Elaine writes: "Yes, I know who Matt was... I have been in his hot tub, while Lila was house sitting and Matt and his wife away on holiday. He moved from where he was living. I remember him, but never got to know him well, or his wife." So there is no question but it's the same (now deceased) Lila you two are acquainted with. I enjoyed your company yesterday, perhaps we can do that again sometime.

M: (to myself) Perhaps I'll get to meet Lila soon? Should I ask Elaine if she'd like me to pass along a message to her once best friend? Wonder if Lila's beautiful. (Grin, yep, still here, Jen hasn't completely spoiled me, yet...)

Kris: Yes enjoyed our chat. Quite inspiring actually!! Yes it must be the same Lila. Yes lets connect again. Much kindness

M: (to myself) It's after midnight where Jen is and still nothing from her. But I don't want to get into holding my breath for a message from *any* woman again. I wonder if with her "conditions" message she was trying to get me to send her a list of all the things that I see as good in her? I mean it's reasonable to conclude that from the following sentences that she wrote is it not? *"Take me as I am... Now share with me what that means. I started to list the beautiful benefits but what does it mean to you to take me as I am."* Maybe she's not really serious at all about being with me other than to care for a dying man so she looks (and feels) good? Is she racked with internal guilt about filing for divorce two days after I left home (or sooner?) and misleading a judge to give her control of my finances and cash flow and my company and properties? Or does she really care? I never know for sure. She talks well, she acts contrary to what she says, but I think we both love each other. *Do we?*

Maybe she'll come roaring back with excitement and enthusiasm, tell me she's coming soon and we'll plan the rest of my life together as an item. (Sure, I'd marry her if that was important to her, but it doesn't seem to be.) Or is she too pained that I'm dying to feel excitement and enthusiasm? Maybe it's just my misunderstanding. Maybe she doesn't need to respond to my message telling her that I'll gladly spend the rest of my life with her just the way she is and that she's welcome back anytime? Maybe it's time for me to indulge in some sleep and see what tomorrow brings...

Elaine: I am going for a kale smoothie today at Mayfair mall. Do you want to meet up? I am busy until mid day, but we could meet up then. We could leave that mall and go for quiet walk on the gorge...? Are you up to it?

M: Yes, nice, send details.

Elaine: Hey you. Can meet up at 2... I had to add laundry and swim to chore list after casting an eye around here after driving daughter to school. So, can we make it a 2 instead of noon... We'll get our smoothies, then head over to Gorge walkway as it's supposed to be clear and dry. If you are weary, we don't have to go far, can always sit at Gorge ours Coffee outside where we first met. Dress warmly! You did look a little thin... even if you say you gained weight... Let me know, I'll check back to my email before 1100. Will be good to see you again! Smiles and kind thoughts,

M: My webmail service was under virtual attack the last couple of hours or so but is up now. We'll meet at the Mayfair Mall west entrance. So what you're saying is finish off the carrot cake so I don't blow away if a gust of wind comes up? See you soon.

Jen: I need my daily dose email that you miss me and you love me. Cause I sure miss you and love you and want to gently hold you in my arms. Keep me informed of what you are doing and how you feel. With that I can pace where you are and if I should to you sooner. I am feeling peace at the moment but my heart never stops yearning for you. I haven't felt that in days. I felt so depressed leaving you. I realize it took a toll on me. But today I am moving and doing things. Love Jen

M: I was expecting a response from you to my message yesterday in which I told you I'd accept you as you are and invited you back anytime. If you did reply to that message please resend it. This will confirm that if you are silly enough to keep on loving me and to spend a whole lot of time with me while I live out my dying (or healing whichever) then I am committed to you and we'll plan the rest of my life together as an item. It is my hope though that your motivation is not simply that of a caring Mormon Relief Society sister giving service, but a genuine interest in being physically with me the next few months or however long it takes to resolve this cancer issue. I do believe that you love me, I do know that I love you.

We quarrel sure, but the weight of that 18 years of history trumps everything and everyone else regardless of how emotions and desires may come and go. I WILL commit fully to you if we can be together much of the time from your next visit and you keep telling me you love me. Be sure to bring your hat, that's the image that floats into mind when I think of you, the way you were at the airport, peanut butter on your purse and all. Gosh how I love you, why do we quarrel?

There are so many people praying for me that sometimes I think I am a fraud because I don't FEEL that I am dying. However, it's undeniable that I do tire easily, sleep and rest a lot, and breathing is getting more difficult at the top and bottom ends of a deep breath as most likely fluid continues to seep in and compress the lung. Getting the self-draining tube installed and the weeks of pain while that heals will most likely be my next ordeal. The pain from the other wound is largely gone now though it flashes briefly on occasion. It's no longer the dull aching constant reminder that there's something gone wrong with this bod.

Who knows, maybe this thing I've got will bring families closer to each other and do some good, I think it's doing that for us. I'll do my best to set the example of how happy an ending can be. That won't be hard as I contemplate the wonders that I am about to experience. The thought of that fills me with joy and causes tears to hasten, we're such glorious beings.

Come when you will sweetheart but there's no great rush for you to abandon unfinished business to be here. Maybe you should visit your grandkids for a few days first just in case you get tied up with me should my body decide of its own accord to accelerate its disintegration and so release me?? I love you sweetie, enjoy the day. Your Michael

M: (to myself) It was a nice walk along the Gorge with Elaine, I really do enjoy her company and the touch of her. I bought kale shakes for each of us (delicious) and followed her car to where we walked. She was very responsive, putting her arm around me each time I put mine around her and never shying away from physical contact. I was tempted to kiss her lips but didn't, just her cheek at parting. I reminded her when she said she wanted to go to Hawaii that she is the woman who turned down a cruise to there. She replied, *"I didn't know what your intentions were."* I didn't say it but my intentions were to have fun! I suppose she was concerned about me wanting to sleep with her, I continue to think she has problems with that. But she says she wants to find a man to settle with, she thinks she will. I was ready to come home after being away for a couple of hours, the energy drained away suddenly, and with it the connection.

M: (to Jen) I was out for a walk and a kale shake and noticed that you called. Do you want me to call you back?

Jen: Yea I did, I think I was listening to an old message from you and it got me worried. I can still call back if you want me to call.

Jen: I do, I do do do !!! You ask about responding to something but not sure what email.

M: (in response to Jen sending links for cruises) I'd love to go all out on a 45 day or so Mediterranean cruise with you but I can't miss the CT scan and doc appointments. I wish I could fly so we could go right away because today I'm thinking this thing is progressing faster than they thought. I sure get tired easy, never experienced that before. But maybe that's normal and I can still do things for a long time yet, push myself like I used to instead of giving in and sleeping like I'm doing this week. But in a way it's exhilarating, I'm beginning to think that I really am dying and for me (much as I know family and loved ones will grieve my passing) moving on is a pleasant thought. I'm so curious, so willing to explore the unknown... Keep sending me suggestions? We could book a long cruise and get cancellation insurance just in case I can't make it.

M: (to myself) Jen called and we chatted a bit, she seems solid with me. She resent the comments I had been waiting for and never received. Not much, between the lines, here it is.

Jen: Sure I will read a bit to you each day. This sounds good. I can't see any of your conditions being a problem. Thanks for the reminder that I am welcome. I do love you. You are my one and only man. I think you will have good days and some not so good. But most likely not shorten your time. Your son said you can get pills to pump up energy for travel or special events. And better pills for the pain. Don't live with the pain. Take your pills. Use the meds for a better life style. Sounds good to just go to the first meeting at church. Where you are at with the church is fine with me. It would be fun to look around for a place. You know I like looking at property.

M: (to myself) There's no doubt that I enjoy being with others too but I *will* commit to Jen if she comes and stays a long time. So what if we quarrel now and then, the important thing is to be together physically, that's what I've been wanting for many months.

Jen: Tell me. What have your books done for you that is obviously vital to you? I am curious to know? The story, the message, meeting women, or is it the legacy you want to leave at the end of your life. I would like to think, it was the journey back to Jen that you once made a eternal promise to.

M: (to Jen) From my journal:

I continue to not know exactly how my books are going to move along. I do not know the end from the beginning, just the expressed desires of the characters and their history, which makes for somewhat accurate predictions but no certainty. So the stories themselves could have been quite different. It might not matter if there was a Suzanne or a DeLeon or a Carrie with the stories they provided, much as I love and appreciate the real women behind the characters for those. It could have been "Anastasia" or "Tania" or "Helen" who provided the entertainment that allowed the 'mission' to be fulfilled, the message I thought vital to be taught between the lines. In fact in some ways I wish the stories *were* different because the books are pretty much the same story repeated over and over, that's what I was attracting as I wrote the manuscripts.

I told you several times that only you and I getting together permanently would change the stories and (hopefully) move them towards the better story of a perfect love gone right - if Michael and Jen are capable of creating that in this lifetime. (Not sure, we'll see, maybe my dying will bring out the tender energies needed to flow such a great love as that?) A change did happen when I closed my singles site profiles, the story became *only* the story of Michael and Jen repeated seemingly endlessly. Michael and Jen are still not together, that's still pending, it's still uncertain. Quarrels could still erupt and change the ending - you know how Jen departed in a swirl of shadow just a few days ago and how Michael or she could with a mere thought and the press of a few keys or silence make that parting permanent.

You and I as writers Jen experience the *feelings* of our book characters in full (we *live* the books) so it's not necessarily boring for us, but it could be for our readers. There's endlessly too much up and down in the major characters and no final satisfying resolution of the conflict. Will Book 4 the final one have a happy ending? Will Michael find what he set out to discover? One thing we know for sure, the author had better get on with it, time is now of great essence. He's not just packing his bags but is moving them across the river some call "Styx". But he sees no underworld, no boatman there but wings that work and love and light and climbing, and a fullness of joy.

It's true, I am moving on from the story as it unfolded in the books to the reality of this body dying and me moving on to the awareness of a much bigger much better reality; the universe must expand and each of us. Former priorities grow weak and uncaring, the ancient trees whisper now with new power to my soul, the approach of Spring and rebirth, the dropping of former pretensions, the promise of newness. Another season approaches, it comes swiftly, inexorably. I feel it all around me, I cherish its coming, I greet it with fullness of accepting, I relax into its lovingness. Gentle giants in the park call to me that the time is soon to release claim to that which came from the soils that nourish their roots. They claim their own, it's *theirs* they say, as does the sea by the breakwater. This body I once fancied "me" still moves of its own accord so I must interact with this world, but internally my awareness is shifting to that which is largely kept secret from those whose physical bodies are not yet dead or dying. It's a grand and glorious venture, the greatest any human will ever undertake, our escape from that which binds us to this planet. As the ships of our time rise on tails of fire bound for moon or planet we are but symbolically unfolding wings and living out our dying, our thrusting for that which is more, our reawakening to that which is us.

Consider my sense of 'mission', my wanting all my adult life to be a writer, to teach knowledge that could have a positive impact on many people. The message in my books includes how to harness Law of Attraction, how to find chronic happiness, the possibility of immortality in our time (fountain of youth discovered), and for those who have the desire, the possibility of becoming Adam and Eve on into the eternities, populating new planets the gods made then rested. That last one, becoming Adam is the biggie for me, it is Michael's greatest fantasy, and mine the author of these books. I lay claim yet to what is written at the top of each of my books and hope to soon carry into the eternities.

"It matters not where my consciousness centers in this life or the next, or what anyone teaches differently, or however I may be challenged and criticized by others who see it differently and want to sway me to their way of seeing it, or who say my dream is impossible. As my soul roams the universe it will always be with the utmost thought and fixed determination that I am becoming or that I AM Adam!

Only in that manner can I create the reality I want for myself. Only with that strength can I attract the Woman to me who shares my dream exactly. That's what I want, that's what I am becoming regardless of any other soul who would tempt and beckon me into worlds of their own choosing. I am not theirs, they are not mine. The gods keep the timing, when the time is right for me, my well-beloved Eve will appear, and we will be ONE..." Michael Demers

I still don't know if these books will be published and discovered. If so, the 'mission' will be fulfilled. If not, then I will think the books were just part of the process of preparing me for my dying and moving on to the next stage of my life, and it doesn't matter if others read them. Yes I know you personalize them, as well you should because you are "Jen" and Michael's stated purpose for the past 15 months is to find "Eve", the woman with the exact same dream as his. Is Eve Jen the woman Michael left behind tending the roses in his own back yard? Or is Eve someone else he finds along the way? Or is there more than one Eve? Or is Eve even to be found in mortality?

Of such is the stuff of fantasy, the worlds we enter when we watch a movie or read fiction or sleep or day dream to escape the boredom of consensus physical reality. (Some love it.) Even the hoped for Mormon dream is uncertain, nobody knows until sometime after they have left mortality how that really is going to play out in the eternities. No mortal can tell you with certainty what that ultimate dream (expressed in the Mormon concept of "exaltation") consists of, or if it's different for every individual according to their desires and hopes and longings for. I think it is the latter. For me "exaltation" is becoming Adam, and maybe eventually moving on from there should we ever tire of our children. But how could that ever be? Our children are our glory, our life, we live through them and they are ever changing. But ok, in the Mormon way we could create bodies of spirit as well as bodies of clay. (Would Mormons really claim that, to be like God?) Perhaps exaltation is to create the first or both?

The author writes at the beginning of each of his books: *"As we follow Michael we'll peek often into his private emails and we'll know in the end if he found Eve and became Adam, and what became of Jen left behind alone in her garden. Was Adam's Eve all along the woman growing roses, the acres of diamonds in Michael's back yard? Or is this story of a perfect love gone right the story of Michael and another woman he picked up along the way? We'll find out because this story is true, it really happened...."*

Shall we live a bit more then Jen, and together write a happy ending for this series? Will you play Eve Mother of Nations while I play Adam? Will you come to me and BE who we could be? Will you want to be with *me* more than with anyone else? Will you love me and call me magnificent? Will you touch me? Will you, will you??

Jen: (I received this later, her only response to the above) I feel your dream goes on.

M: (to myself) Elaine called, she will bring me a painting tomorrow instead of today as yesterday she said she would. She does not invite me to go with her to walk her horse along the beach today, I would have enjoyed that. I am looking with eagerness for Jen's return, she will not be too busy for me. She is the one by far with the greatest and most enduring love for me. Can we find that perfect love I seek in each other?

Or is such a phenomenon not of this world? I can easily imagine it in the next.

Jen's message below arrives just as I send the above to her, strangely similar to "the other" Suzanne who is once again silent. Jen's message gives me direction as to which way to go from here, what to write about. Jen is without doubt my most prolific and best 'counterpoint'. Is she Eve?

Jen: I was thinking today how at times I let my jealousy take hold of me and bring out a side of me I do not like. I am working at releasing those feelings. I want you to know I do not judge anything you have done in the past. I see two, three, and more sides to your experiences and mine. I am far from being perfect. How could I possibly think I could judge another. God did not send me down to this life to be a judge but to learn, observe, experience, change and yes repent.

Is there such a thing as being in the Rest Of Christ in this life or is it the next. I know there are writers that have written about it. What does being in rest of Christ mean to you?

I hope Jen (me) can step up and encompass becoming a more loving person but at times I feel I am back sliding. Not sure why except new difficult challenges take a bit of time to adjust. I find the most difficult ones are the ones that are matters of the heart. In the past I never felt I had no time for me or others that indulged in self-pity. As I have slowed down with age I find myself going into that room. I have learned what it feels like in that room. There is a season for everything and a little pity party can be indulged for the healing process. I now have patience and compassion for those that do. To help another we must be capable of compassion and understanding that comes from experience. For one must remember to not let it linger long for it will feel like home.

In my mind and thoughts. I want to be perfect in everyway for you and for me. I really do. Then the state of human conditioning and old habits slip in and sway me away. I can't always live up to what I want to present for a special as special as you. I hope I have the wherewithal to see and meet as many of the things you desire. I always have good intent. In my eyes you are a wonderful and great man. It is my honor to be with you when I can. It makes me happy to be around you. They way out way the flair ups. At this stage of the game the only thing we have left to give each other is accepting who the other is. Love Jen

M: Loyal Christians tend to view everything through the lens of the particular Christ Concept that has distilled upon their minds. So for each Christian the phrase you use "Rest of Christ" could have different meaning, and for those not Christian it could be meaningless, quickly tossed aside as mere jargon of the unthinking 'brainwashed' robot masses. An internet search comes up with a vast quantity of responses, one being that "soul rest" is needed more than physical rest, soul rest being release from worry and tension, from stress, from fear, from bitterness, guilt, anxiety, a state of simply BEING, the "I AM" Concept. That type of rest can be found in meditation (calming one's mind, suspending the world) and in the exercise of imagination to increase the rate of one's vibrations. In such an easy state of mind the world of fear and stress dissolves into happiness. The answer you seek is found inside my books, I just revealed it yet again: meditation and raising vibrations, *accepting* yourself for who and what you really are and are becoming, judging nobody including yourself, ever flowing with fresh abundant life and loving it, always following the happiest thought in your awareness.

I am thrilled that you find yourself changing, moving towards a nonjudgmental love, towards being *yourself* (uniquely you there is no other) instead of the tightly contained person you have been taught you *should* be.

You write, *"For one must remember to not let it linger long for it will feel like home."* To me that means you have come to better understand that a belief is simply that which we keep repeating. Cease to repeat the things that keep you chained, limited, restricted, feeling guilty that you are "back sliding" when you are in fact growing and spreading your wings. Tell a different story, the story of freedoms found, and you will soon release yourself from the old binding attractions and can move on.

You write, *"at times I feel I am back sliding"*. I say *rejoice* in such a feeling! It's marvelous, the coming of Spring, you knowing that you are more than what you were told you are - you emerging from a cocoon so tight you could never spread or even find your wings or know about them unless you pushed outside the box that held you for so long. I say *flow*, flow with the newness of life as it comes moment by delicious moment. *Accept* that your nature is not to be static but to be ever changing. Pay attention to the emotion each thought brings, that is your unfailing personal guidance system. Is "back sliding" a happy thought? Is moving forward to new heights of expression and being a happier notion? It feels real good to me that you are making what I see as wondrous progress, and that you will come and be with me when you are ready. Come, we can learn and grow better *together*... I love you Jen.

M: (to Jen) Does the stuff I write make sense to you? Do you think it would be of value to those who might yet read my books? I've already done most of the writing I think I should. I am grown weary of it, careless and sloppy, not expressing every thought that comes to mind, another needs to be appointed to my muse, I no longer *want* to fulfill. I look forward to your coming and our living life in the real world. Let's do some travel, I am months behind the vacation I wanted to take when I moved to Victoria. I was already worn out by then but the travel companion never came, or she never stayed long enough for us to begin a vacation, or I failed to recognize her, or the universe unfolded as it should and I was already marked for a greater rest so the vacation didn't matter. It matters now, it matters to *me*...

M: (to daughter S cc Jen, subject "The bucket prior to kicking it.") Depending on the state of my health at the time of course, Jen and I are toying with the idea of doing some traveling together for maybe as long as 60 or even more days if I can get the meds I need, leaving soon after my oncologist appointment in Victoria. Our focus is cruises and cruise tours and possibly timeshares around the Mediterranean. Family company in separate cabins is welcome anytime (canasta?) as long as I'm not kept too busy to rest often. I'd like to include Rome, Venice, Casablanca, Morocco, Monaco, Barcelona, and other movie/romantic spots, with Israel and Arab countries optional except maybe a taste of Istanbul? Oh yeah, and of course an African safari while we're in the neighborhood. (Jen might balk at that one but I'd seriously like to do that someday health permitting.) I thought if we came up with a goodly itinerary on an ocean view type budget we could book ahead and get cancellation insurance just in case.

Anyway, don't put too much time into it but I know you were interested in being a travel agent so any ideas you can come up with are welcome. Ask questions and run prelim ideas by me anytime, my guess is that Jen will go along with whatever we come up with as long as the budget is reasonable, she'll be paying her own way I expect. Dad

5: Let me see what I can do....

Jen: Most everything you write makes since and is good. Much of what you and I write back and forth is of the same stuff with a twist. I think readers would tire quickly of it if to much is repeated. The best should be selected with a flow of purpose and learning as we go and excepting what we can not change in the end.... Does this make since to you my magnificent writer.

M: The first three books are fine as they are I think but book 4 if it grows long could be pruned. I like what you write though, and I like the words it elicits from me. I'm just tired of playing writer, I'm wanting a long rest with no responsibility. And I want real world travel in warmer places than this is right now. Let's see what my daughter comes up with, could be good if my health holds. I slept long last night and much of the day but did get to the park for a short walk. I'm tiring much too easily much too quickly. May walk for a kale shake tomorrow, they're delicious.

M: (to myself) Jen is not writing much the last couple of days. Is she feeling pressure from me to come back to Victoria? She's not commenting on the travel either and I don't want her to be burdened with a big bill to be my travel companion to the Mediterranean. So that trip may not happen and I'm ok with it. Better let her know I guess. Sure wish my books would place and sell well, I could use the cash for travel and pay Jen's way.

When my sons were here they didn't express any interest in inheriting my USA business and assets so if my daughters are also lukewarm on it and Jen is determined to spend the rest of my days with me, I may will all my USA assets to her? In which case, I'd better get to work improving my business website and sales. Maybe that's my task for the next few weeks, or maybe wait for her to join me and we'll build a new website together? I wish I knew when she is returning and how long she'll stay. If she was willing to marry and live with me it sure would make it simple, I'd turn everything over to her except the books, she would manage my cash flow much more wisely than I do. (I'd most likely become an active Mormon again too.) If the books sell, the royalties would be my parting gift to my children, divided equally among them, that is my desire. I wish Jen would come so we can do my life together. As I distance myself from writing the book series I'm losing all desire for the female friends I made and looking to Jen exclusively. I believe I can now give her everything she desires except perhaps a long mortal life with me.

M: (to Jen) Cruising the Med looks like quite an expensive affair and I don't want to burden you with a big bill to pay after I'm gone. So unless you particularly want to do that I'll let 5 know we're not going. Maybe we'll just explore Vancouver Island and the nearby islands when it warms up like I was wanting to do last year, and possibly drive to Phoenix and on to Alberta and family visits in the summer. When you're here we could do a couple of nights in a Vancouver hotel, possibly Seattle too, maybe musicals, opera or whatever. What do you think?

Jen: You are wise. What ever you want to do.

Jen: My daughter and her husband are doing a River cruse through Europe next year. It will take them thru many countries.

M: That would be fun. Do you think you might join them? Not sure if I could but would...

Jen: I don't think so. They did not invite me.

M: (to Jen) Lynne wrote that my daughters may not be coming until later. So you are welcome to come as soon as you want to. I'm missing you and wanting to get my life in better order, we can plan it together. Perhaps we'll work together on redesigning the business website and get all of your properties listed too? That way you can carry on after I'm no longer able to work it. I have some ideas if you are sincerely planning to spend the rest of my life with me (however short or long it turns out to be) and are motivated by genuine love and desire to be with me rather than just a service project. (Can you assure me of that?)

As I distance myself from writing the books, the friends I made are becoming less and less important and I'm moving exclusively to you the way you say you want it to be in all respects as if we were married. (Why aren't we? I'm willing.) That may include a return to the Mormon way, it would mean so much to my family and you I know.

I think the major reason why we quarrel is because of your insecurity, not knowing if I am exclusively yours or not, and for me the living alone without you. If we can make the living together arrangements more permanent perhaps the quarrels will disappear? I love you sweetsie, come soon and make me yours entirely? I'm willing. What do you say to all that?

M: (to Elaine) Further to your offer to bring a painting to me today I felt that I should let you know that for my part there is no obligation to you to do so or to see me again if that would best fit into your life and plans. I do enjoy being with you but I am drawing ever closer to the woman I already have 18 years of history with and she is drawing closer to me. I expect her to return to Victoria in the not distant future. Given her insecurity over me having female friends I want to offer you an opportunity for a clean exit from meeting with me again should you so desire. We could swap messages now and then. Just being open, how do you feel about this?

Elaine: I have no problem with that, especially as you wish to be open and honest with Jen at this point. Just say hello now and then via email and stay well... find happiness now! Enjoy a holiday when you are cleared to go on one, and best wishes in all ways. I'll keep the painting if this is the way you want it, because Jen would see it and it might upset her and make for some bad feelings. The thought was there anyway. Very kind and loving regards, Elaine.

M: (to myself) And thus Elaine disappears from these books. I'm a bit surprised actually, I thought she might come over as a friend anyway but it seems she was inclined to go her way, can't blame her. Must get my own kale shakes now, maybe this afternoon. Kris doesn't seem to factor in at all and no others are writing me. I hope Jen comes soon, I do need the frequent loving touch of a woman. From now on it seems it will be exclusively Jen's, the way she always wanted it, I'm ok with that.

Sister in Law: We've been receiving a lot of e-mails and it sounds like everything is fine. We had a very relaxing time in Cuba. I wrote to Jen since I did not get to call her when she came to see you. It was nice of her to come and cook a few meals for you and to be with you. It was also very good that you saw all your boys. The picture is great. We hope you'll have as wonderful a visit with your girls. Since we've been back, we've been quite busy too. I have now volunteered to do some reading at a school. I go today at 12:00 and am looking forward to it.

My husband has been busy at work. He is anxious for the day he turns 65 so he can retire too. He hopes to work until the end of this year so far. We both have nice tans now but I'm sure that will fade fast. We are so pleased you'll be around for a bit longer. We still hope to go to see you but we will discuss that further when it is closer to summer and when we know that you will be home. It seems that you plan to do quite a bit of visiting. That's great. You should enjoy your children and grandchildren as much as possible. Keep the e-mails coming, we enjoy them, and we hope all goes well. Oh by the way, my cancer was a stage 3 also. That sounded encouraging. Take care of yourself, eat well and keep positive. We're praying for you. All our love,

M: I envy you the tans, I've lost mine after twenty years of wearing one. I'm glad you enjoyed your vacation, thanks for writing. Sometimes I feel like such a fraud with so many people praying for me and wishing me well, and you yourself having been at stage three with cancer and not complaining. Maybe I'll live another twenty years, who knows? If I am able to I will almost certainly drive to Alberta this summer and can see you two then. But it sure would be nice to have another sibling reunion here on the Island. You could stay at my place if you'd like to. Jen and I are drawing ever closer, there's a possibility that we will yet live together again. I know my family still loves her and accepts her as my companion, wish us well. Enjoy the day.

M: (to Jen) I'm counting on you being my forever love and am getting my affairs in order. Elaine offered to bring a painting today. I knew it would make you insecure to see it and suggested that she and I just swap emails now and then. She agreed and wished me well. No other of my former friends are writing me, including Suzanne and DeLeon, I haven't even heard from Oresha. So if I'm ever to get the loving touch of a woman again, it's going to have to come from you. I'm very ok with that but am still a bit insecure about cutting all my ties when you and I are still not together and you last left the way you did. Can you assure me that you'll come fairly soon, love me, and stay a long while?

Jen: You are so sweet to think of me that way. If you would like a picture Elaine painted I would be ok with that.

M: Please respond to my question in the last sentence, thanks.

M: (to myself) Gosh, I guess I'm still quite insecure with Jen, our communication hasn't changed much, still lots of talk but little by way of action and concrete plans. In truth we're still where we were months ago in many ways, still apart, still nothing concrete planned on her part to get us together long term.

By cutting off my friends I am not abandoning my dream of becoming Adam. I am making a clear distinction between my fantasy and my *real* life with Jen and my family. Should she ever choose to play along with my fantasy and be ok with me having more than one wife in the next life, I will play with her of course. But so far when we've been together she has not played that game with me, and may never. If so, it will remain inside my secret thoughts as I visualize myself Adam with several wives on a beautiful planet given us to populate. I so look forward to that even as I get my temporal affairs in order for a short or a long mortal life.

I feel free with Elaine gone, I don't even have to shave today. Kris is not completely gone I don't think, but I can take care of that with a message about my commitment to Jen should Kris write. As for Suzanne, DeLeon, and Carrie, well, all my friends knew I had some assets and may have (including Elaine) been attracted to my money as much as anything else?? I haven't written about that much before but it was in my mind and most likely in yours dear reader. As for my part, much as I deeply felt every feeling I expressed in these books, all the ups, all the downs, perhaps I was mainly interacting with those women for the story? And now the story's told except for Jen where it began, she in the back yard tending to her roses when I left. Should my books generate a great deal of income and I'm still able, I might get all the major characters together for that "Island Event" I wrote about. In which case, it would be Jen at my side. *Perhaps I've found my Eve...*

Jen: You are not a service project. When I am with you of course it is work but most likely less work then my home here. I just want to spend wonderful times being together with my sweetie.

M: Good answer, I am reassured a bit. Any plans to come back to Victoria?

M: Or am I pushing you again and making you uncomfortable?

Jen: I want to check my options about renting the house. Then get my taxes done. I think it is a very good idea to work on the business and get some money coming in.

M: Ok, good. I'm thinking of buying some software and using it to create a better website. Would it be better if I waited for you to come so you can learn how to do it along with me, and have your say in how it will look? It would be a together project for us.

Jen: I don't think you need to wait. You will just be a bit more familiar with it.

Jen: I will come as soon as business is taken care of here. Unless you really need me. Other wise I want to do something about the house so my finacail burden can be a bit litter.

M: Well, I really need you because I miss you when you're not here. But I am still independent and will probably remain so for quite some time yet so you're probably smart to get your business taken care of that can't be done from a distance. Thanks for being available though, it's hugely comforting to know that if I must have help that you will come. I love you.

Do you think you'll ever marry me again sometime, or are the financial and other concerns just too pressing for that? I'm just thinking that with the exchange rate most likely going to go to 25% between USA and Canada dollar that if we married here you'd probably not only be able to get B.C. health insurance but with our income from USA worth 25% more we could possibly live quite well in Canada for at least six months a year and maybe do a warmer place for the winter??? Just sayin, I can't guarantee the length of my life so it's difficult to plan but if we're living together long term I'd be willing to share my SunSpring cash flow with you and maybe we could build that. And if you sold your house in Utah you still have other units to fall back on when I die, or stay in Canada should you choose. If you can't afford to keep the former marital home, could you move your furniture to the main floor of the house where we married and make that your USA residence? Talk to me about it?

M: (to Jen) Social Security cancelled my Medicare as of September, 2014 so it's a good thing I stayed in Canada. That means that it is a risk for me to be in the USA though I think my B.C. insurance would cover *some* of my medical costs there if I incurred them. I doubt that I will ever again qualify for travel insurance. But I think my B.C. insurance would reimburse some of a cruise ship doc's charges for example?

I'm looking forward to hearing from you regarding my questions and suggestions in the last email. I figure we should talk about the options so you have all the facts before you make major decisions about your house etc. I think we can get together in an orderly and financially beneficial way if you are certain that you want to spend the rest of my life with me, living together most of the time. Are you? (Yep, I'm still insecure...)

Keep in mind that using USA currency we get an automatic 25% discount if we buy a condo or whatever in Canada in the near future. E.g. we'd pay $150,000 for a condo purchased for $200,000. Time to shop around?

M: (to myself) Jen is not responding to my specific questions, marriage etc. so I still don't know for absolute sure where she is with us living together long term. Will I ever? Will I ever know what it is that keeps her from throwing herself at me the way I am wanting to throw myself at her? I'm almost regretting turning down Elaine, I could have touched and been touched by a woman today, it would have been nice. Are you coming soon Jen? Would it have been better if I was not so open, leaving an element of Jen needing to chase me? *A dying man, right!*

Ok, in all fairness to her, I looked back at a message she sent today and she did say she'd come when she has her business in order. What more should I expect from her? God bless her, I love her, I think we can carve out a good remainder of my days for us.

M: (to 5 after an exchange about cruises that she might go on with me and Jen) The cruise to London is inexpensive but most of the trip is sea days on the Atlantic in early Spring. The thought of sailing into warmer and warmer weather instead sure is attractive to me. My choice would be 34 days cruising from San Diego to Hawaii and Polynesia but Jen might balk because she and I have already done that run. We need your input Jen, please pipe up.

So I gather you'd go with us then 5? That would be a delightful treat for me, and you and Jen could do stuff when I'm needing to rest or not wanting to take (yet another) class on embroidery or petit point. Now macrame maybe (not). Yeah, I'd like that a lot (you going) but please don't feel an obligation on your part, only go if you really want to. You could bring along a video cam and do the interviews 2 was writing about. Get questions to ask from your sibs? People around might think I'm some famous writer being interviewed, good for my ego, should I grow the beard again?

I'm liking this idea a whole lot but will only go if Jen is along, she's my girl. Coming Jen? Have you already been to Bora Bora and Tahiti? Dad

Literary Agent: Dear Michael: Thank you for your email. While your project sounds interesting, I don't think it is right for my list at this time. I appreciate your querying us and wish you good luck in finding the right agent who can successfully champion your work.

M: Thanks for the fast reply, best to you. P.S. I've just been diagnosed with inoperable lung cancer, do you happen to know an agent or publisher who might be interested in a book of the final days of a writer living out his dying? Michael

Literary Agent: Hi Michael, I'm very sorry to hear that. You might look at agentquery.com to see if you can find someone who would be a good fit. However, most publishers are looking for books closer to 80-100k and I think you will have a hard time finding an agent who can take on such a long project. Best,

Jen: I see you are amongst the living again. Love it.

M: I'm not sure what prompted that but I am thinking of possibly traveling a bit after I see the doc. Will you be responding to some of my other emails or are you wanting to avoid any serious planning just yet?

Jen: Just nice that you are planning a bit of life to enjoy.

M: You didn't answer my question but ok be you. Gone to bed good-night, love you.

Jen: I like most of your thoughts. There is so much we can do together. I need to get Utah problems going in some directions so I can see things better for us. It is the house I am living in that is holding me down. I know it is so important to do for any financial stability I am going to have. It is so hard for me to give it up but realize I would be much better off. I just need to get myself moving.

M: Here are some thoughts for you to consider, everything is open for discussion. This is assuming that you are sincerely solid in wanting to live with me (most of the time) for the rest of my life however long or short it might be, formally married or not.

I am willing to give myself to you exclusively even to consider becoming (reasonably) active in the church again so I have a claim on the Mormon temple blessings if they turn out to be valid and vital in the next life. Yes when you die I will be there to take you through the veil in the Mormon way if it works that way. In short I am offering everything you've told me you want because I am ready for that now. It is my hope in turn that you will continue with your body shaping program. That's all, it's important to me but it's not a deal breaker, I can accept you as you are. Just love me, live with me, have fun with me, travel a bit when I can, and touch me lots when I'm not hurting there.

Once we are living together with the expectation of it being long term, I am willing to turn over management of my company's cash flow again the way you used to do it and to work (a bit) at making more sales. My personal allowance could be my pensions. You witnessed that my sons have no interest in inheriting my USA assets so I am willing to leave them to you including the company, the accounts receivable, and all land owned. I would ask that you send daughter 6 a bit of money now and then and keep an eye on 4 while his kids are little just in case. All my other children are well provided for. We'll figure out what to do with the motor home as we go along and we'll budget to pay out my (currently zero interest) credit card loans, it shouldn't be difficult. But it is my hope that our emphasis will be on quality of life and having fun rather than denying that to get debts paid swiftly or to accumulate savings, I may simply not have the time for that, we'll see.

Assuming acceptably good health and several years of life, my desire is to live in Victoria for at least six months each year. We could then have fun renting a different warm weather place or places each winter, maybe southern Italy, France, Australia, South Pacific Island, Bahamas, Cabo, etc. To live in Utah would be too cold for me in the winter, I want to feel the tropical sun on my face and body. But if you really wanted that, like everything else it would be up for discussion. So consider that when you decide to sell or not to sell your house. Maybe it would be best to just rent it furnished for two years while we see how it goes with me and your desires when I'm gone? You'd then have the option of refurnishing and moving back in to that beautiful home with (hopefully) delicious lifelong memories of you and the man who once lived there with you.

I hope that helps you make decisions. I love you lots Jen and look forward with eagerness to your return to this glorious seaside city and the man you say you want the most. He's here, he's available for you, he wants you. Coming?

M: (to Oresha) I hope you are recovered Oresha. I'm not meaning to ignore you it's just that I tire so easily now that much of my time is spent resting and sleeping. There's no need to rush back with the DVD's, enjoy them. I do have excellent support from my family and Jen is on standby to return anytime I need her, so I'm doing well all things considered. I continue to think that life is great with a whole lot to look forward to. Now somebody come up with a magic pill for this tiredness! Enjoy the day.

M: (to Jen) You have been very uncommunicative lately not responding to my serious emails, saying nothing personal or heartfelt, no terms of endearment etc., all warning signs from my recent experience that something's not quite right. However, I'm going to trust you completely as if all is well between us and update you with what's happening today.

Much as I want to plan for a long future you may recall that right from the beginning I said that I didn't think this cancer was going to take a long time to do its work. Here's an exchange of emails with my doctor son today as written in my journal.

M: (to 1) I tire so quickly now, can't go more than a couple of hours without needing to lie down even though I'm eating pretty well and rest and sleep a lot. Is that to be expected and lived with from now on or is there something I can do about it? Dad

1: That seems too fast. Something's going on. Go see your doc now to get checked out.

M: Oh shoot, I don't want to be hospitalized again. There's probably nothing much they can do about it anyway and I've already lived a really good life so I have no fear of dying other than pain. I think I'll just live with it, I can still do long walks and get home ok.

What do medical marijuana pills do? My sister mentioned it. Would they help with energy or just pain and make it so your mind's fogged up? But I agree, the way I'm going I'm not going to be doing a year of reasonably good health. No pain though, thankfully.

Based on that sense of urgency, today I contracted to publish all four of my manuscripts in both e-book and soft cover. I'll send the first three manuscripts within the next few days and then I'm about done with it except for some author input along the way, that will be a relief. They can get the books on shelves (print on demand for the soft cover) within 90 days so there's a chance that I'll get to hold my books in my hands. I won't have time to soften the sex scenes like I was thinking of doing so it will just have to be as it is. Please forgive me as needed and don't judge too harshly, they were meant to make the books easier to market and sell. The manuscript for Book 4 will be sent later, I'll leave instructions for you to do that if need be. Book 4 will end most likely with an announcement of my death? Please do not share these health concerns with my children, tomorrow I might feel a lot better, just having a rough day today perhaps, need to sleep it off (again), thanks.

M: (to Jen) Will you share your thoughts and feelings with me? You've been so distant the last couple of days that I wonder if I'm losing you. What's happening?

M: We shouldn't treat each other that way, please share with me what's happening.

Jen: I have just sent some answers and I know some others I have not answered. I am not distant I am depressed. You will not loss me. Just can't see my future so how can I see our future. Please give me time. I will eventually see it clear.

Jen: Why did you not call if you are concerned. I have been on the computer for a long time with tec support and my new program to make my accounting easier requires time and knowledge I don't have. I had to wait at least a half hour after talking to a live person for an hour then a tec chat that lasted 2 hours as he worked on getting it set up on my computer. That's how I spent my afternoon and I feel frustrated.

M: Sure doesn't seem to be a user friendly program you bought, it should be saving you time not stealing it. Can you return it? I've been thinking about calling because I was getting concerned but wasn't quite there yet. Yes, I'm still insecure when we're not physically together. But all is well with these messages, I am reassured again that you still want to live with me and not reluctantly. I love you sweetheart, sorry you're frustrated. Spa tub with candles?

Jen: Fore most important thing is are you OK as far as your health goes. Written below, you may like some of my comments and some may be questioned by you, but none change my direction toward wanting to be with you. I guess I get up set when you do this to me and should of deleted some of my comments. They are controversial.

(She writes between the lines.) All is well. I am feeling at bit lost and just need some time. My love, my concerns for you and my wanting to be with you has not changed. Just not sure what to do or how to Secure my future. Probliblly I am not motivated. But each day I move one more step forward. I hope I am.

Then you must go to the doctor tomorrow morning and take your phone and call me right away. If all is not well, I need to come right away. I want you around a long as you want to be and I hope that is a long time. I don't think you would be hospitalized unless it is a procedure. Most likely given meds.

Of course I will handle Book 4 as you desire and send it later as you direct. I can not wait to get the books and read them. I will keep in mind what you said about the sex scenes. Free sex can be very alluring and hot. I will believe what you wrote and that is what you felt in fantasy and in the matters of the heart. If I said otherwise I would be lying. I guess I must set aside the fact you traveled to find a greater loves. For me it will continue to hurt me even after your death and especially those who read your books will know I was less important. I fear you are exposing me in a very negative way as Michael uses me as an example. Those we know will know I am Jen. I shared many emails of disappointment at times caused by feeling of rejection and then told to be happy. Especially about your freedom to love other women. You do have the freedom to love who you want.

I fear I will be shamed in many ways by the books. Is this so? Let me read the books before any one else so I will know if I need to go into hiding. What is it about the books that I am unaware that people are going to love. I know you are a magnificent writer but that does not tell me the story. Are you proud of Michael in the book. Are you revealing yourself through Michael. Will you hold your head high and be proud to say this was my great path. I want you to be proud of your work. I think you are. I know the book is not about me. Jen may be spoken about all times in the book but it is really about Michael's journey. Would you not say.

Men? Many will betray you by eventually finding others they search to love more. As you said men can love many. This has been going on since the beginning of man. Women with this type of man learn to settle and learn to contain love, they learn quickly what not to expect, so they go a place of respect for the marriage. Just sorry you joined their club at the ending of your life. I was effected deeply. All is forgiven and I just love you so very much. Its just that the heart takes time to heal. But with love coming back from a man like you healing should be much faster.

My plan is. I will be with you to the end if that is what you want. My hope is you will want to be around for a while longer. My giving is to lovingly care for you, touch you tenderly, and hold you in my arms. At least once a day but could be convinced to do it any time you want. My out look is to not think about how short time is but to find the things that bring us joy each day. What do I want to remember to thank God for, is when I wake up each morning seeing you are beside me and say I am hungry where is breakfast. (A female friend) ask me if I would like to co write a book with her. I told her I could hardly write a decent email.

M: You write, *"Just not sure what to do or how to Secure my future."* Did it not comfort you when I said I would share my company's cash flow with you and will give you the accounts receivable, the company, and all the land when I die? Add that to the income you already have and you should feel quite secure. You can continue to build the business and make sales over the coming years, you will even know how to edit the website. I should think you will be quite comfortable. Why worry about money, it's almost always an unrealistic worry, you've always had your needs met, you are in fact quite wealthy, *accept* it!

Jen: Its more than money. Its doing the work. I hope I can come to a place that I am motivated. What you are offering to do is wonderful and would be wonderful for us now and my future after you are gone. I am great full for this. I don't feel poor. I just don't feel motivated to do what I need to be doing. I just want to do nothing. I hate being that way. I am a doer. I will get there. Thanks for helping and understanding. I love you.

M: I can't go to you because of health insurance. So why don't you come back for a while and we'll each do nothing. That's how I'm feeling too, may as well do nothing together. Grab the papers you need and catch the next plane, return when you need to and feel up to doing something?

1: Like I said "That seems too fast Something's going on Go see your doc now to get checked out" There are lots of reversible things that they could find that do not require a hospital admission. FYI 6 told my wife about the cruise you have planned. Way to go Dad. That's definitely something to look forward to and something to get the investigations/examinations for so that you have improvement in energy and stamina (less fatigue ability). Dad I don't want to pry but I am your loving son. Have you and Jen considered re-marrying with a pre-nuptial agreement?

Now as to cannabinoids, you don't want them at present as you have no pain, adequate appetite, and want to keep you cognitive abilities from being dulled. If you had pain that was not responding to pain killing medicines, bad side effects, or some other reasons then maybe but that's a maybe. Of course if you smoked some form you wouldn't have to worry about developing cancer of the lung. (By the way that's a joke, there wouldn't be a reasonable reason to smoke cannabis). Why don't we start talking regularly by phone, Skype, or FaceTime? Your grandchildren would like that, and I probably need it. Love 1

M: As you know, it's difficult to get an appointment with a specialist. I don't have a family doctor and they'd most likely be clueless about this anyway. Also, the cancer clinic doc would need to have an updated ct scan before I saw him to see what was going on. That's scheduled in the future. I didn't go out today, just laid around mostly and slept a bit too. Perhaps just a 'bad' day, maybe tomorrow I will have more energy. I think it's partly psychological, I'm *expecting* tiredness now, maybe gotta get a grip on it and keep on trucking...

5 is exploring the possibility of a cruise or all-inclusive resort for me and her and possibly but not sure yet Jen and 6 if they are willing and come up with the money. I have been trying to reconcile with Jen for months and continue to suggest that we marry. She seems reluctant to discuss it but wants to be with me as much as she can. I remain open to the possibility of marriage but can't push her into it, it's something she needs to be comfortable with. She wears her rings and I think considers

us married. She will most likely return to Victoria in the not distant future.

I tire very quickly on the phone. Email works best for me, I'm used to it and can respond at leisure. I appreciate your concern and your love for me, I'm so proud of you my good son, you have done well.

1: Go to the medicentre next door. Simple blood tests can be done. I keep you and Jen in my prayers.

Jen: I can't leave unless you really need me. My cousin is coming next week. That should to get me motivated a bit to do a few things. Then I can come if you want me. I am happy with you.

M: I'm certain your cousin would understand so that is not a valid excuse for not coming. However if there are urgent things that can only be done with you physically in Utah that I can understand. I just thought it might be fun to aimlessly spin our wheels for a while spaced out with our arms around each other. Isn't that what you need more than anything else right now? It's not all that expensive to fly here and back. Just some thoughts, I'm not wanting to pressure you to come, I'm still independent.

M: If you need to often be back and forth between here and Utah how be you always buy a one way ticket here and I always buy your one way return?

5: (re our ongoing discussion about taking a cruise or an all-inclusive resort vacation) I like them both. If it is Mexico, I would stay a week longer than the 7 days though. You can go home, but I will soak up that Sunshine and beach! I think 6 would prefer the cruise. At the end of the day, wasn't this about crossing things off your bucket list?

M: Jen? Are you in for the Med cruise? Or for the Mayan Riviera? (If so, seven days or 14?) Or none of them?

M: (to 5 and Jen) Much of my inspiration comes while I'm in the shower and I've been there, just came out. Regardless of who else goes or doesn't go, if 5's in for 14 days at the resort we've been considering then so am I. (Assuming there is internet in the room that is.) I can absorb beach and sun and warm water and unlimited food and drink all the day long and continue to write my final book while I'm there. THAT'S FOR ME! Anyone other than me and 5 in?

5: I was just talking with my husband, and if we are going to do the Mayan Riviera, we should think about a different resort that is about $400 cheaper CDN for the same dates (28Mar15) and if you look at it, it is a beautiful resort. I am a follower here, I just want to make some memories and spend time with my dad (Jen and 6 are a bonus!) Just let me know where and when and I will book and be there!!

M: Pshaw! Just because your husband can't go doesn't mean we have to downgrade from 5 stars to 4 stars so we can keep four more photos of a dead politician in our wallet. (Canada $100 bills.) I'm for 14 days at the Five Star!

5: I was just checking, the prices have gone up some though. I am ok with that! Does that change anything? The price now includes absolutely everything except any optional excursions (which I do not necessarily need, except to go to the new permanent Cirque show there!!)

M: (to 5) Now that I'm decided, I'll pay the price. But I need to know for sure that there is wifi available to the public daily even if it's not in our room, so please confirm that. Also, maybe I should fly to Calgary a few days before and stay with my bro or 3. Then anyone wanting to visit from Edmontown can come see me before and/or after we fly to Mexico. Everything of course is assuming my health is acceptable and I'm cleared to fly at the time. Cancellation insurance is most likely advised given my uncertainty.

Chapter 7

————◈◦◈————

Still no word from Jen so I don't know where she is on this. I hope she responds soon and hopefully comes with us. But I don't want her to feel any obligation, money is of concern to her right now. *But then, life's short eh?* It would be loads of fun if we can consign dead politicians to their proper status and go all out for *fun* with careless abandon... Two decks for canasta, or three or four?

5: Flying to Calgary is a good idea.... if it is just you. Hopefully Jen can come... if not then you and me for sure, I would have to check on 6, she will probably do it to spend time with you, she will whine about the destination as she has been there a few times with me already and done all of the stuff.... It's not really about the destination (besides the sunshine) it is about the dad! 2 decks for Canasta with 2 teams of 2 or 2 individuals.

M: Yeah sure, bring Hoyle! I don't know where 6 can come up with the money other than to borrow it somewhere and I can't help her with that. As for me, if she came to visit while I am in Calgary I would be content. Are you three still thinking of visiting me in Victoria? I guess with this trip in mind it's no longer so crucial to me, but would sure be nice anyway. Any word on internet at the resort? The Dad

5: 6 is looking into $$ cuz she would like to spend the time with you. The girls are changing their flights cuz 6 wants to spend Valentine's Day with her beau and 3 & I want to ski! The hotel's website says that they have wifi in each room. The reviews that I have read say because of the construction, the wifi is only available in the main place and is spotty. Once the renos are done, things should go to the way that they are described on the official website.

M: When are the reno's done?

Jen: What would the cost be for me. This is not a cruise but a trip to Mexico. Alaska airline goes to Cancun 3 or 4 days a week. We could possibly use my companion ticket. Is this a 5 star resort.

Jen: Oh, I see you may want to go from Calgary. That would be fine then you could spend time with your brother and your kids. It would be good for you to rest up. Maybe after that we could fly someplace and use my companion ticket. I want you to do what makes you happy.

M: The total cost including flights and all-inclusive food etc. is about $2500 US each for 14 days in a 5 star resort on the Mayan Riviera. It works out to about $119 per day including flights etc. so about the same as a cruise but in a warm place on a white sand beach. 5 has stayed there and says it's fabulous. If you are here we could fly together and stay at my brother's in Calgary before and after we join 5 for the flights to and from Mexico. (I'd like that a lot.) Coming?

7: (he includes a link to a video about being like Jesus Christ) Dad have you seen this yet? Love 7

M: (to 7 cc Jen) I don't mean to insult you 7 but you are so *me* when I was your age! (I consider that a *good* thing.)

I may yet come into full fellowship in the Mormon church if there is time. But is it possible do you think that individuals each have certain experiences they need to have in preparation for their dying, and that we should never judge or criticize or try to change them for having those experiences regardless of what they may be? I wrote in my journal today:

> *I love my journey and my dream. It's hugely cathartic after a lifetime of piety and religious faithfulness to stark repression and denial of that which is human me. I have discovered roots, am now of earth, stooped from a lonely mountain where the air's rare to the sultry valley where soils are deep and fecund, and my footprints are. I tolerate more. I accept more. I judge and condemn much less if anything at all. I love better. I know that I AM all things. I am ready to die and meet God. Perhaps I will discover that I am much like He, and like He I will go on. Perhaps I will discover that I am becoming Adam on another planet...*

I love you my son, I know you mean well. Dad

Jen: Maybe this should be a father daughter trip with me out of the way. Your family would most likely feel a bit more at ease. We are not married. We can do a trip when you get back. Driving down the west cost. It sound fabulous. You have wanted to stay in a 5 star resort and I want to live in a 5 star home. I love you sweet heart. Maybe in the fall we can go to the meditation or a Europen cruise down a river.

Jen: Please don't miss understand I love being with you and it does sound like a great deal. Just feel this should be about you and your kids this time.

M: This would be a trip with most likely only one of seven of my kids so for me it's all about being in the tropical place I've denied myself and craved the entire winter. I understand that it's really all about the money for you and that's acceptable. I was expecting that actually, as well as your expression of ongoing determination not to marry me for reasons you no doubt feel comfortable with. It's entirely your business who you formally tie yourself to or not regardless of any depth of affection you may have for someone. (You might get quite bored with beach and canasta anyway, whereas I thrive on my own internal rhythm and my writing.)

But sure, let's take that drive if I still can later in the spring or summer, I'd like that too. I do love you but you continue to baffle me with the difference between what you say and what you do. If our roles were reversed and I'd made up my mind to do it, I'd most likely never leave your side. We'd be an item regardless of *anything* else the world threw at us except one of us dying or becoming unaware or uncaring of the other. But I understand that you've been deeply injured by me (as you perceive it) and are still in the process of healing from that. I hugely appreciate the love you express for me, it gives me hope. I want that to continue and to grow, hopefully not with mere sympathy and desire to be of service to another. Come when you can, you know where I am, I'm waiting for you.

Jen: I just walked out side and felt the warm sun. The concrete was warm to my bare feet. It is like a warm spring day. One could almost sun bath.

M: Yes, spring is about upon you where you are but I cannot go to you Jen. I'm not even allowed to fly let alone the medical insurance consideration and ongoing testing etc. Enjoy the warmth, breathe some in for me.

7: Wow Dad now that's writing and that's your writing. Maybe we should make a book and/or documentary about the journey of discovery. I'm not sure what you mean by insult as I don't see that.

M: I *am* making books my son and in them is much of such writing in the whole million words of them. In fact some who have seen it call my writing "magnificent". But if nobody reads it why would it matter?

I wrote "insult" because even though you are my son I do not really know you, we've had so little contact over the decades and my guess is that you are disappointed that your father didn't turn out the way you'd hoped. (Faithful Mormon High Priest, obedient, sacrificing, *enduring* to the end as goes the ideal image.) In writing that I don't mean to offend you, just to be open and honest in how I see the matter. There is much of Mormon influence in my writings, I will never regret having been Mormon almost my entire life. If anyone is going to affiliate with organized religion, that's a great group to walk with. But like most others it's really all about obedience to the prescribed rules and donating money all your life with the promise of *maybe* getting to some ill-defined higher heaven or avoiding misery after you die depending on how obedient you were to the church and its leaders in this lifetime. Sure there's the sociality and fun, but all institutions offer that. Anyway, meandering here, enjoy the day.

7: Thank you for telling me this Dad. I don't get the comments about being disappointed in you. It was your courage to follow, to change continents, to hear, believe, and obey. As for me I am who I am. Not much but working on more. If you see yourself in me then see it as a compliment.

Jen: I noted in one of your emails you would be spending time writing on your trip. Is it book 4. Is it a sequel of the other books. It would be great to have a book not about sex. But if the other three have sex than your readers would expect it. Well this will give you time to rest. I do appreciate you asking me to go but felt this was not my trip.

Regarding marriage. Why marry now? I plan on loving only you. If a viable plan is put in operation that does not put me in jeopardy of taking responsibility of your debt. Yes we live in two different countries. That is an obstacle. How am I suppose to figure out how to make it work for us. As you are living exactly where you want to live. Now you have serious medical issues. We could get together and work your business. I would not want to be a partner. I would be a employee or a independent contractor. I will ask my accountant about the tax consequences.

I can visit often. I would like to rent or sell my house so my financial burdens are not so heavy. Maybe when I don't feel so burdened down I can think about marriage. I was sharing my feeling of love long before I knew you were ill. *"I'd most likely never leave your side."* Is that why you left and moved to Canada? After three weeks, Michael you were wanting me to leave when I left. Who's actions have really kept us from being an item. Our ducks are not in a row to marry. Of course I am will to put them in a row but are you. You have made some wonderful suggestion that could work. I must get my life and obligations under control before I can be expected to help you with the business. Please do your best with it and I will help when I can. You must do your best if you want to enjoy travel. Sweetie, enjoy your trip with your daughter. Enjoy the sandy beach and warm Sun. Find a shell or a stone on the beach for me.

M: (to myself) Jen called and and, hang, nothing has changed has it? She has no plans to return to Victoria, just makes excuses. But I'm tired of it, I want to finish this book here and say something like: *"Michael died today"* and be done with it, we'll assume he's happy wherever he is. But it didn't happen and I *live* my books so can't. I do know though that I will go to my death with the fixed determination to become Adam so I will attract to me women with the exact same dream and we will be happy together forever.

Should I be looking for another woman? At my age and dying? I think not. I do love Jen, but she is not wanting to play married couple with me and living full-time together is what I want whether formally married or not. It's a simple choice for me, apparently a complex one for her. Indeed, as she writes, *"Why marry now?"* What other woman would say that of the man she professes to love and wants to be with more than any other?

Enough, I'm done, I'm going to pretend that everything is well between us, and see what comes with the rest of my mortal days. I'll try to keep my mind open to *any* possibility that feels good and right whenever Jen is not physically with me. Meet someone at the cancer clinic who has a similar expiry date to mine maybe? Anyway, women are extremely important to me. Jen remains Number One but she's not available to be a couple. Maybe she never will be and I'll always wonder *why*? So where's Eve?

5: Dad, I saw that there is a 2 bedroom unit available immediately in the tower next to yours. It is $1500/month. If this is something that you would be OK with, I would pay the $$ above what you pay now a month. This would work better for those of us that would be coming to take care of you..... Think about it. They may let you upgrade if you sign a year lease??? Let me know.

M: I pay only half that where I am and it would cost $900 to break my lease. I already tried to get to the top floor in this tower and it's the same manager, they won't let me make the upgrade even though a new one year lease would be signed. But who knows, maybe the manager would cut a deal for me if she knows I'm dying and family will honor the lease on a two bedroom that's needed for my caregiver/s?

Sure, I'd jump at the chance to move into a two bedroom for in effect the same rent as this one. My air mattress would look great on the floor of the second bedroom! Hey, I'd even give up the Mexico trip for that deal. You might have something going there though, maybe others in the fam would like to have a furnished James Bay place available for vacation and would be willing to chip in on the monthly rent? You can't "sublease" dirty word, but you can always have "friends" house sit when there's no fam around.

Jen says she's not going to Mexico. I'm never really for sure positive where I am with her. I don't know when she'll be coming back here, she just makes excuses that I see through. She says and writes one thing then does another. I don't understand it, must be a woman thing. Maybe

I will be needing that help from family rather than counting on her when my condition worsens? I just don't know. But I want to stay in Victoria not just for the existing medical coverage but because it's the only city where I feel like I'm 'home'. A good place to fly from...

I like what you're suggesting, much better than a trip to Mexico or a cruise. I'd even pay the $900 myself if need be instead of doing Mexico. Are you serious? I'd need some help moving and furnishing the other place.

5: Dad, 6 was talking with 1's wife about our trip to Mexico, and she is interested in joining us. She could only come if we went the 2nd week of the next month because she and 1 will be in Tahiti before then. Tough life, I know. I priced it out from Calgary because you said you might come here first and visit people.

If Jen comes, us 3 girls would share a room. If Jen doesn't come, we will book as 2 people in each room and then figure out sleeping arrangements when we are there (it is cheaper that way). Most likely you will get your own room. Only if 6 snores too badly will I have a cot brought into your room and hide from the snoring!!

5: Oh we are going to Mexico!! I will email your apartment manager and see what we can do. It is only $700/month difference which is not bad at all. I can do that, or see if 1 would split that with me. It would save all of us $$ in hotels and make things more comfortable for whoever is there helping. Let me see what I can do!!

I love my scheming kids! I'd enjoy being in a larger suite higher in either of the towers. I'm thrilled at the thought and it makes a lot of sense too. Maybe me not having much cash flow right now in addition to an expiry date is going to unite my kids even more? Yeah, right on!!!

5: (my daughter writing to the lady who manages the two towers where my suite is located) My name' is (5) and I am the daughter of the man who lives in (suite number) a 1 bedroom apartment on the 2nd floor. My Dad has recently been diagnosed with terminal cancer. He has been given a year to live. The reason I am telling you this is because my siblings and I will be taking turns staying with my dad to help him get to doctor's appointments and treatment, as well as cooking, cleaning, shopping and all of the things that he will need help with. To this end, I am hoping to move my Dad into the available 2 bedroom unit so that there will be space and privacy for each of us as we are in Victoria. I will happily sign a 1 year lease to accommodate this.

My siblings and I are all professional people that include doctors and lawyers, so you know that the apartment will be well taken care of and the lease will be honoured if my Dad dies before it is up. Also, if there is an available unit in the tower my dad is in that would be more preferable as it would be easier to move his things that way. Anyway, please let me know if this is a possibility and when it could happen and I can fly in from Alberta to take care of it. Thank-you.

S: I just sent your apartment manager an email. Hopefully it isn't too sappy. I blind copied both of us. I will let you know when I get a response.

M: I'm thrilled S, truly thrilled, thanks so very much. The suite I'm in is so noisy, right above the heating and water equipment, I just put up with it. I love my scheming kids...

S: Let me know what you think about moving Mexico two weeks later.

M: I don't have a problem with that at all if we're still going. (I back off paying the $900 lease breaker though in that case, much as I'd love to live in a less noisy suite higher up.) It would be nice to have 1's wife along. I'm sure we'll talk a lot and it will be passed along to 1 who I feel I hardly know at all, or him me. We've hardly seen each other over the last two or more decades. 1's visit here in Victoria is the first one he made to his dad in twenty plus years even though he travels frequently worldwide. I love him, he's my son, but I don't know him other than when it comes to religion, I see him as myself at that age. Just unloading, telling it the way I sees it...

S: Fellow Travelers, Here is the scoop on Mexico. We will be staying at a 5 star resort for 14 days. It's an awesome place. The prices include everything except any side trips. There is a new permanent Cirque show in that area that I am interested in seeing. Other than that I have done everything and don't need to do it again. If we get bored after a while we can book something while we are there. My plan is to read, soak up the sun, enjoy their gorgeous white sand beach, snorkel a bit (I will bring my own stuff), and play a lot of Canasta!!!!! !! Let me know if you are committed and we can proceed to book this!!

M: I'm in, subject to: 1. Hoyle's rules for canasta in our room. 2. Somebody else shuffles the cards when it's my turn. 3. I get a private bedroom where I can crash as needed. (Do we need a bigger place?) 4. Wifi somewhere nearby on a daily basis. 5. Health permitting, meds available to take with me if needed, and health not likely to seriously change during the 14 days. (Cancellation insurance should address that concern, I'll assess a few days before and decide to go or not go. If not, the rest of you can arm wrestle for the bedroom. I'll plan to be ok though, sounds like great fun.)

I'll make my own return flights Victoria/Calgary and will likely stay with my brother two or three days maybe coming and going, but at least *before* we fly to Mexico. So what happens now? Do you need to do all the bookings so we get the same room/s and we reimburse you by check/chequeh? (Do you have an installment plan? :-) Wish I could practice my sun-tan, I'm rusty on that, maybe it will come back.

5: Dad, you've already got cancer, so there's probably no harm in fake 'n bakin'!! That's how you practice your tan!! We would book from each city. Room wise, the girls can share a room and dad can have a room, except if/when I can't take the snoring and will have a cot or have 2 double beds in dad's room to crash in. Canasta wise, we play family rules that we predetermine before (yes I know) we start the 14 day tournament if kings (in which I play the winner!?)

M: Somehow I thought we were all in the same suite. Is there no bedroom at all then and maybe we'll be located in different buildings? Do we need a bigger place? Do we need *two* sets of Hoyle because I don't know family rules that you make up on the fly? Ok, if you're playing winner I will too - *team!*

5: No, we would be getting 2 junior suites, with either 2 double beds or 1 king bed in each. 1's wife has emailed about possibly only coming for 1 week. I priced it out for her and it comes out to almost the same price as 2 weeks... So it may be 3 people sharing 1 room for a week.

When we get to booking, I will talk with one of the travel agents instead of just booking online and seeing what we can do, and making sure that the rooms will be beside each other.

Jen: What's wrong sweetie. Either you were very tired when I called, or needed to go to the bathroom or something else. I felt like you were being nice but something not right.

M: I just prepared a long email responding fully and openly but you might not like it, it may open old wounds. Should I send it to you? I continue to love you but yes, something's not right, nothing new, just festering.

M: (to Jen but not sent) Yes of course you sensed that something wasn't right. It's my reaction to your several days of not responding to my serious emails and the constant excuses you give for not being with me. As usual I'll be (perhaps brutally) open and honest so you know where you are and can make better choices for your own best interests. It's always the *lack* of communication that causes the most problems.

From my point of view we are exactly where we have been since last year when I attempted to reconcile with you and take up where we'd left off and you rejected that. You talk purty but I never feel that you are *committed* to me. Simply put, you continue to tell me you love me more than anything and you're everything I've ever wanted. *And you continue to keep us apart!* You say you'll visit often but even on the phone today you were sliding away from coming anytime soon and indicated that you wouldn't even likely be here when I have my ct scan and doctor appointment almost two months away. You wrote in your email that you weren't going to the resort with me and then on the phone you led me on as if there was hope that you would. You'd fly from Las Vegas and meet us there you let on. I don't believe that you were telling it true, you just dangle me and I see through it all the time. (Much as I believe your love to be sincere.) I suggested since you were indecisive and unmotivated that you go careless abandon for a while and come veg with me, that's what I wanted to do too. I even offered to pay your return flight. But you won't come. I have no idea now when you might come next, you know

I'm lonely even though I'm still independent and don't need nurse or caretaker. Maybe you're waiting for that time to do your 'duty'?

You know that I want to live with you at least *as if* we are married but you are not willing to do that – after all, married couples live together! You sometimes say you are willing to get us together long term, but as always you are not available for that. You confirmed that today when you said that you will visit "often" meaning not make it long-term. Your last departure a short time ago after a three week visit during which we quarreled almost every second day and you threatened to walk away several times was in a cloud of anger and jealousy over what? I don't even remember the excuses you made for that sorry scene, you seem so mixed up, so conflicted. You never looked back after I kissed you long at the airport. What else could I think but that I'd lost you maybe forever? I know, you'll come up with excuses and blames but what I write is how I see and saw it.

My kids must have sensed the change in me today too because just minutes after I hung up the phone with you I started getting emails. They are thinking of renting a two bedroom suite for me in this same or the next tower and paying the difference in the rent because: *"It would save all of us $$ in hotels and make things more comfortable for whoever is there helping."*

So, much as I love you and dearly hope you will be with me over the coming months of change and uncertainty, I know that your 'responsible' mind almost invariably prevails and prevents you from being who I think inside you'd like to be. It's that denial of your real self and your trust instead in the arm of flesh rather than what your heart is telling you that causes you so much conflict, and keeps us apart. What do your feelings tell you *right now*? Is it a happy thought to remain a thousand miles away from the man you say you love? Or a happier thought to abandon all and rush to me? My guess is that you can do everything you need to do from here by phone and email, so you'd not be totally irresponsible to come and veg for a while and see if we can reconnect better than at your last visit.

My children are rallying behind me, they are willing and preparing to take care of their dad when that time comes. So here's your chance to think deeply and to *feel* as well for the right course for YOU. Take no thought for me, I am well cared for and loved. This is your chance for a graceful exit, a bit of pain for a while, and getting on with your life as the unattached single lady you are. I'm offering you an out if you want it. Please think carefully about this, it will impact your future. I know you love me and I love you, but there are temporal things of great concern to you that you need to consider thoughtfully without concern for me.

Let me know your choice. But there's no rush, you know where I'll be and that you are welcome. There's no other woman in my life, no pressure on you except that you are confused and discontent about something, and that's never a happy situation. It would be better to resolve it *permanently* don't you think?

Now as I finish writing the above I begin to think that I should just delete it. I love that you love me, why mess with that? I think with time you will work through your stuff and we'll be better prepared for each other. It's just that, how much time do I have left?

M: (to Jen) I've decided not to send that long message to you, it would just open old wounds. I am well, I love you, there's no other woman in my life, it's you I love, no pressure. Off to bed now, hope you are well.

Jen: Yes, I had a good nights sleep and I am ready for the day sweetie.

M: (to Jen) You keep expressing concerns about how you will look in my books even to the point of thinking when they are published (anonymously) that you will have to run away and hide. But I think they are beautiful books Jen. And since Elaine showed me how to rearrange them, *you* are the major counterpoint in them all, you are the heroine. I'm copying an extract from Book 4 below. Try standing back and consider yourself a woman reading those words with no personal connection to the characters or the author. Don't you think it interesting? Don't you think women will relate to how *you* the woman he left behind see Michael's experiences? You write beautifully just the way you are, just the way you do. We're telling a lovely story that may yet end with Michael finding the perfect love gone right that he is seeking. Can't you see that? (I copy from where she mentions Don Quixote to where she sends her exchange of messages with a friend.) Etc. etc. I think it's a beautiful book. Don't you?

Jen: I am going to make a list of the things I think need to be done before I come back to you. I will let you know my progress and I think once I get into doing the things I need to I can give you a date of return and book my ticket. I love you. Please send me your long email.

I received the above email from Jen just as I sent my message with extracts from book 4. I do not want to send the other "long" message to her, it's just a repeat of the same old same old and she addresses most of the concerns expressed in it with the few words she just sent.

M: (to Jen) In those few words you have addressed almost all of my concerns, thank-you for that. Yes, please keep me up to date on your progress.

Jen: (re the message I sent with extracts from Book 4) My writing might have some heart felt meaning. But my sentences are not always easy read or as clear as the message I was hoping for. Yes your writing is beautiful.

In this story we communicate as two screwed up people. With a lot of nonsense going on. I think the problem in the story is hashed out to long and no conclusion. A clearer direction of progression would help. Neither seem to have a real light bulb come on to the real problems. Women readers don't want this amount of emotional ups and downs unless they can see it moving in a clear direction. One way or other. It is great information for a self development book. It could be one of the stories of what is wrong or what could be right, or both. Some of the writing is very heart felt. But I see this as a relationship problems. Both have hope and desire to make it work. The reading is a bit depressing and I feel sorry for both. As a reader. I don't want to read a book that makes me feel depressed no matter how good the writer is. Are your books about character development more than plot?

From reading their email conversation. Michael express little patients and much patience (I know wrong spelling) in other areas with Jen. Michael is a bit paisa. Never gives up his vision of his Eve. He hopes she is the right Eve. He desperately wants Jen to fit the mold Michael makes. Jen wants to fit the mold but finds it doesn't really fit her as comfortable as she or he would like. She then backs away feeling lost. Neither want to give up. Drama goes on. When will something else happen. Like the trip you are going on in Mexico. What lessons will you learn and take back to cement Michael and Jen. I don't know if this is a fair opinion or not. YOU are my magnificent writer.

M: I appreciate your comments, thanks.

Jen: I hope I did not offend you. Did you see anything that made since or am I off.

M: You have not offended me in any way whatsoever. I always appreciate your candid feedback and frank and open comments on my writing and everything else including my health and our relationship. To hold back anything is to stem the flow of honest communication and cause misunderstandings and poor decision making. *Lay it on me baby!* Are you planning to let me see your check off list of things to do before you return to me?

Jen: Yea I will as soon as I get it finished. Doing accounting because that seems to be the hardest for me to do.

Suzanne: How are you???

M: Nothing much has changed since my last message except that I tire quickly and am settling while on my own into a routine of resting and sleeping a whole lot with a walk of a few blocks most days, not too hasty and no breathlessness. There is still some deep down pain in the vicinity of the chest puncture but it's fleeting and the oncologist said to watch for *consistent* changes and let him know. So I'll sometimes pop a couple of Tylenol, it helps remove the reminder that my body's got a problem that I'm told it's not likely to recover from. Otherwise I'm doing what comes naturally, keyboarding.

I mentioned the tiredness to my doctor son and he thinks it's coming on too soon, that I should get blood tests to see what's happening. But each day is different and I've never been one to rely on the medical profession for my ailments (have to now) so I'm more likely to just adapt to it and rest as need be. A few days ago I was doing a pleasant walk and chat with a friend and enjoying it immensely. Then about two hours from when I left my home energy seemed to drain from me and along with that any interest except to get home and get to bed or sofa, so I did.

I'm planning a 14 day trip to a resort on the Mayan Riviera with three family members so I'm not neglecting setting up forward looking psychological reasons to remain as healthy as I can as long as I can. (Trip cancellation insurance in place of course.)

Last week, thinking the undeniable tiredness meant that I might not get that year of acceptable ambulation and clear thinking, I arranged irrevocably to have all four of my books published and made available worldwide in both e-book and soft cover formats even should I not be capable of submitting the manuscripts myself, which I have not yet done. My plan is to very soon submit the first three manuscripts so they can create appropriate covers for the series, then hold back on Book 4 which is still a work in progress. But they'll all get out there. Whether or not anything sells commercially remains in question.

Jen calls my writing "magnificent" but even if she is correct why should it matter if nobody reads it? Anyway, I've done all that I personally can do to ensure that the manuscripts are eventually published as is. I have no interest in further modifying or polishing the first three even though I know I am capable of doing better. It's possible of course that the entire process was just for me, I continue to show nobody anything other than a sample chapter or two to a very few. My guess is that I will live to hold the first three books in my hand, for all they may be worth to anyone else if anything at all. Thanks so much for your vital part in getting me going, I always wanted to be a writer, you were there when I needed what you gave.

I'm intrigued by your comment that hospice nurses can "manage the energy" of their patients in addition to their pain. Please explain, thanks.

5: So your 7 children have decided that we will have our family reunion this year as originally planned. We will be doing it in British Columbia and preferably on the Island. Just so you know!!! And we will be doing it this summer. So, I have spent the last couple days looking for something cheap and that will fit us all, as we have not had the time to save up like in previous years.

M: You guys are astonishing, I am totally thrilled and in favor of having this cancer! But check out the west coast, Ucluelet to Tofino and around Sooke (close to Victoria), it might be a lot more fun there, open ocean and rain forest. First though, run it by 3, she and her hubby know this island well.

M: (to list) I received notice today that my scheming kids are not only planning a family reunion but planning to have it on Vancouver Island. I just want you to know that you guys are thrilling me to no end! It makes having this cancer seem worthwhile! And not only that but the biggest schemer of all is working on a couple of other delights, including a 14 day stay at an all-inclusive Mexican resort and a possibility that I won't even mention yet because it would be such an unexpected bonus for me. My kids are rallying around me, life's so good, thank-you, thank-you, thank-you.

By way of health update, I continue to spend much of my time resting and sleeping, and of course keyboarding and reading a bit, but do get out for a walk most days. There's often a dull general aching in my chest that's easily alleviated the few times I break down and pop a couple of pain pills. It's the only reminder I have that my body's apparently got itself into a scrape it may not easily recover from. I'm ready and accepting of whatever comes except pain and it's my understanding that such a thing can be managed nowadays. The forward looking events that are on the horizon are psychologically good for me I'm sure, giving ready reason to hang in there as best I can and not just quietly slip away in the night as it seems it would be so easy to do, just a relaxing into it. (But when I do don't blame me, blame the cancer. And don't mourn too long, I've had a wonderful life already, 24 years more than my own dad had, I am content.) Enjoy the day all. Dad/ Michael

1: We'll mourn, like it or not. Don't forget that your "kids" include my wife who is struggling with the news of your cancer Dad. You're a father to her. She pointed out that you've been a father in her life for 25 years that's longer than you were not in her life.

M: (to Jen) Today I submitted the manuscripts for the first three books to a publisher. So that's done and what a relief! The three books will most likely be available worldwide in e-book and soft cover formats in less than 90 days. Book 4 is ready to submit anytime but is still a work in progress. So if I am unable, please make sure that my Word file titled "Book 4" is uploaded to them with a note announcing the death of the author. Contact my representative at the publishing company.

In addition to having that done and finding out about a family reunion coming up, 5 is not only arranging the Mexican resort vacation but is trying to move me into a two bedroom suite in one of the two towers and pay the difference in the rent to make it easier for family visitors and caregivers. I'm not sure if she'll be able to swing that one but life's good, I love my scheming kids!

Jen: I will keep this in my records for you. What a sweet daughter you have. She sure loves her dad. I hope you get the 2 bedroom apartment.

Suzanne: Thank you for the update. You sound positive and realistic which is healthy. You have reachable goals and embedded in family and friend... wonderful. It's important for you to listen to your body as you are doing. Much of your energy is being used by the disease process and that will be. Use the energy you have to write, enjoy family and friends. Stop and rest as you need. If you push too hard you will get more tired. Control pain. Pain uses tremendous amounts of energy. Don't hesitate to take medication when needed. How's your heart dear one?

M: You ask about my heart. Today it is warmed muchly with your caring message and endearment. Thank-you for that, you know how pleased I always am to get a message from "Suzanne". I still sometimes feel waves of fond feelings for that (frustrating) woman I once met in Texas.

On the physical plane my heart has not been abnormal for several weeks. As I look back on the experience it was the heart pounding explosively, literally shaking my body, that finally got me to the medical clinic where I was told: *"If you have a ticker problem you've come to the wrong shop, you need to go to emergency."* The clinic doc then did his listen/tap routine and told me one side of my chest was completely shut down. I was in hospital an hour later. My imagination says the explosive heart was a warning to get the breathlessness addressed. (And thus find the cancer.) And who knows, maybe it was also an intelligent-beyond-comprehension body clearing out cholesterol or whatever so there'd be fewer complications in what was to follow? It's not quite that simple of course, in addition to the explosive heart there were quite a few bouts of much quieter and more prolonged heart irregularity, but nothing lately. I couldn't ignore the pounding heart and had to lie down for the duration, sometimes at least a half hour. But I was getting used to the irregularity and it didn't trouble me, no fright, just a quiet accepting that I could drop dead any moment from heart failure, type on. Nonetheless it is a comfort not to throw possible "ticker" problems into the other situation as well, I'm grateful for that.

Thanks for your counsel to not push through the energy stops and keep on as was my lifelong habit. I'll continue to rest often then and take pain pills routinely, your explanation is satisfying and motivating. Where I'll ignore my specialist doctor son, I'll listen to Suzanne. :-) Should long walks be optional then? Of course I enjoy the sea and the ancient trees and flowing streams in the park but are the walks beneficial or needlessly energy draining? Enjoy the day sweetie, thanks for writing.

M: (to publishing rep) This is a just in case because I am diagnosed with inoperable lung cancer. Should I cease to respond to your contacts this will authorize my son (2) and (Jen) to interact with you and represent my interests. They have been given your email address. 2 is instructed to take care of transferring royalties to my estate and Jen will submit the Book 4 manuscript if need be, thanks.

Rep: I'm not sure what say. I'm sorry to hear what you are going through. I'll take note of the contact person mentioned on your email. Thank you for letting me know. Also the Book 1-3 already passed content evaluation and we can immediately start with the design and layout process. I really appreciate your time and effort yesterday on sending the materials and providing the complete information online. I will keep you posted. Have a great day!

Jen: Why did you not tell me the others were going to Mexico. I thought it was just you and 5 going.

Jen: See it is turning into a family event. It will be wonderful in Mexico. 5 must of decided to pay 6's way. So what will be the room arrangement. Be careful but mostly enjoy. To bad 3 is working. Do you know when they will be having your family reunion? How will it effect our travel? So much is happening with you and your family.

M: Yes my family is rallying around me, mostly 5's doing. I think 6 is paying her own way to Mexico somehow. It's not booked yet and I only recently found out that 1's wife wants to go too. My understanding is that we are getting two separate "junior suites' without even a bedroom in them. I will have one to myself it seems and the three women will have the other. I'm not sure yet but we're all apparently sharing the cost of the two evenly. I was under the impression that you do not want to go. Is that not correct? The first I heard about a family reunion this coming summer was a brief message from 5 yesterday. I don't know when it will be, we can work our driving trip around it, I do want to travel with you.

Jen: I would consider going if I can leave from here. It would help me with the cost.

M: I guess that means that you're already decided that you will not be in Victoria anytime soon?? I sure don't understand you or where you *really* fit into my life much as I do believe that you love me.

Jen: I plan on coming to see you later if you want me to come. The trip is not until two months yet, I thought.

M: Ok, I understand better. Your plan then is not to stay with me long-term just to make short visits and get back to your normal life. Is that correct? We sure are different Jen...

M: I do love you and want to spend time with you, maybe travel a bit, but I need to better understand how to plan out my life from now on. I had been thinking you and I would be together almost all the time but my understanding now is that it won't be like that so I need to consider other options. Rest assured though, my children will make sure I am well cared for so if you need to get on with your life and future planning without me in it except maybe for a quick visit now and then you can certainly do so without concern for me. Let me know where you are with this openly and honestly please, we can remain good lifelong friends, thanks.

Jen: As you know I am working on getting my life here taken care of so I can be with you. I don't have all day to just do as I please. I have work to do and many things to do, I don't want to do.

Jen: Once I get situated with my life here. I will know better. I planned on a one way ticket but may need to come back to Utah at some point. If I don't go with you on the trip then I need to go home. Anyway, Just can't make decision on who will be where. You have a lot happening with your family. If I get my house rented then I can stay full time with you.

Jen: The used vehicle I am buying is roomy. We could take a ice chest and have picnics on the beach as we travel and rest in the van away from to much hot sun.

M: That would be fun, I'd like that.

M: I need to understand you clearly and correctly.

1. Is it your desire and your plan to live with me almost all of the time?
2. If so, will you attend family events with me as if you were my wife?

(My children would get used to that and accept it whether we are formally married or not, you would fit in.) Please answer each of those two questions honestly and make it a commitment either way so I know for sure where I am with you and can plan my life accordingly, thanks.

M: (to myself) Is she just a friend, travel companion, part-time lover? Or is she my wife (formal or informal)? I want to know if I am morally and ethically committed and bound to her exclusively or if I can as a single man leave my mind open for Law of Attraction to bring in other opportunities regardless of what the doctors are telling me. My guess is that she will avoid directly answering those two questions with invalid excuses, or not even respond at all. If either, much as I love her I will consider myself not bound to her, enjoy her when she visits or we travel together, and will watch for what else comes through the door and keep my own counsel. Life continues to flow exciting. I am not a slave to the parasite inside me, my higher self will determine the moment of my dying and the tool. I have been trying to black and white separate my 'real' life and my fantasy life, with Jen being real. Perhaps I should go back to simply allowing life to flow. In that way the two worlds become one and I am healed of present limitations. Does Jen remain "my greatest temptation" or is she my wife?

Early this a.m. as I sat at my keyboard and meditated a moment I was prompted to finish the following message and send it to Jen. But emails started arriving and I didn't get back to it until now. Is there significance to it or is it just my uncertain needy mind wondering which way to focus?

M: (to Jen but not sent) In my fantasy world today for the first time I caught a glimpse of you *inside* my bubble, an equal with me and with my family of spouses on another planet rather than being as usual outside, me always having to leave the rest of my family to go somewhere else to play with you. You never came in to join us until this morning if that glimpse of you among us lying on the grass was real. I was always willing to go to you and play for a while before getting back to my real world. My door was and will always be open to you, I'd love to have children by you. It's just that you've always written of yourself as different, as greater than my sister wives, and with your spirit man greater than me, creating both spirit and physical bodies while I did only physical. You elevated yourself, called yourself "Eve" and your sisters merely "budding Eves". Did that change?

Publisher Rep: I understand that you are still working on Book 4. I would like to know when is your estimated submission for the 4ᵗʰ book. Let me know if you need assistance. Have a great day!

M: I was premature in buying a package for book 4 but you will understand the situation and my desire to get everything taken care of that I can while I can. I will continue writing the book 4 manuscript possibly for quite a few more months if I can, it will end the series. Can you hold it open for me without manuscript submission that long? Otherwise I may need to cancel the book 4 package. Or perhaps end Book 4 somewhere along the way and open "Book 5" as the final book of the series? Please advise.

Rep: Please take your time with Book 4. I completely understand the situation. The publishing package you've purchased does not have a deadline. I just asked for documentation purposes. Feel free to contact me if you need assistance. Thank you for letting me know.

M: (to Kathy) It's unusual for Oresha to not respond to emails. Is she well?

Kathy: Hi! Michael ... Oresha was sick with a cold but doing much better now! How are you doing I am holding you in my thoughts and prayers sending healing energy your way. I am sure she will get back to you and you are always in her thoughts and heart. The email must have got lost among all the ones she is receiving from her admirers. In Peace and Love

M: Your well wishes are much appreciated Kathy, thanks. Other than tiring easily I am doing well, walked to the end of breakwater today with no problem.

Kathy: YEAH!... If you ever want company for a walk let me know!

Carrie: how are things going? any new directions in your health care? book development? love and hugs,

M: I tire easily but otherwise doing well Carrie, thanks. Are you still in California? What's happening with your house?

M: (to 1) Energy was fine yesterday though I rested a whole lot and today I just did a long walk and am fine. So, false alarm, must have had a bad day or two there.

1: In general it sounds okay. You do need to pace yourself, like it or not. Pain and the cancer will sap your energy. I doubt it's a false alarm. Rather it's real consequences of having cancer.

By the way I did not hear indifference from your sons about your business. I heard expressions of lack of expertise, lack of experience, lack of time. I heard compliments to you about your achievements and about your abilities. I also heard about the complexities of inheriting the business between tax and legal implications. I heard a willingness to help you put your affairs in the best possible order before you die using the gift of time, God's further Assistance, and your expertise and experience. Given that you feel you don't need the money then I think you should explore the possibility and implications of a trust or holding company. Once you die the $2000:month income covers the annual tax bill on the property.

Have you thought of hiring someone to adjust the website and web pages. We know people who do that for work. I did learn a powerful business lesson from my two years in the summer jewelry business. The 'paradoxical' result of raising prices on what's not selling, The business should play up the extensive track record AND the dwindling supply. Fewer properties - greater price. Gotta go help friends who are trying to manage the fallout of death without financial affairs in order.

Luchia: hi Michael, how are you feeling? I have something I wanted to send you, could you pls send me your address asap? Thanks so much.

M: It's good to hear from you Luchia. I am doing well just tire easily and need lots of rest. You needn't send anything, just the thought of you as a friend who cares is sufficient. But here's my address.

Wow, I open my mind a bit and today I hear not just from Jen but also from Kathy, Carrie, Luchia, and Suzanne. Life *is* good when it's allowed to flow... (And later I hear from Oresha too. All that after many days of only getting a few messages from Jen.)

Jen: I feel pressured. I will be with you as much as I can. Pretending like we are married to your kids is hard for me to do. Feeling like your wife is easy to feel. In some ways I am in the fact that we are sealed but you are also sealed to your first wife. I am sure she does not feel that way. Don't know what we can do yet. I think your family would be nice but not except it because we are Mormon. I am extremely busy doing accounting. Sooner I get these things done sooner I will be with you. When I am done I will make an earlier appointment with the accountant and ask about tax consequence toward debt of us remarrying.

M: (to myself) I'm not sure how to accept this. She does mention the possibility of us marrying but she also avoids the question about us living together. I think I'll keep my mind open and see how it flows. I'm willing right now to be with others rather than think exclusively about Jen. I think she expects that actually though she doesn't approve. It's just me who closed myself off with the thought of the inevitability of spending the rest of my days with Jen. (I'm ok with that though.) I might even walk with Kathy.

M: I might take you up on that offer of a walk Kathy, I do walk most days. Why don't you come over some afternoon for a chat and I'll decide on the walk or not. Some days seem better than others, today was comparatively high energy.

Jen: I was wondering about your RV. The other day I had a great idea but forgot the details. What I do remember is. Maybe 5's lawyer husband can write the bank on you behalf and tell them the situation, living in Canada, and you are ill and dying. In that letter he could explain you would of liked to pay off the loan but no longer have the means. Would they discount the loan about $30,000 or $40,000 depending on the offers that come in. It would be sold through a dealer or privately or would they prefer it go on their books as a repossession. They don't like that. Years ago you could work that out on 2nd and 3rd deeds of trust. They discounted them all the time. its worth the letter.

M: (to myself) I forwarded Jen's message to 5. It seems like it would be worth a try. The RV has been preying on my mind a lot, my outstanding loan on it is still higher than it could be sold for. That debt is certainly part of Jen's concern about marrying me. She has a good business mind and is highly motivated by money.

Jen: I was just thinking maybe just maybe the IRS would… (she outlines some possibilities to make my business transition more orderly.) What do you think. I will ask some accountants that deal with this. Are we wanting to make this a success so we have money to go to Europe and other wonderful places. Give me time to get my life here taken care of and my financial burden's lifted. I would help you the best I can with the company. If we can get your financial situation under control then we could get married. That means mine and yours. Does this help?

M: You dodged the question about us living together but I'll assume that you are sincere in saying that if finances get straightened out you'd agree to marry me. And if we marry then my guess is that from then on we'd live together. So sure, it's encouraging even if conditional and iffy. I shouldn't be putting time pressures on you, it's just that I wanted to know for sure where you *really* are with us. I had closed my mind to everything but you and no longer allowed Law of Attraction to work in me. This morning I opened my mind a bit once again, decided to let life flow and see what happens, and after weeks of getting only messages from you (and lately family) today I got messages from *five* of my friends!

Oresha said she was getting over a cold. Kathy (Oresha's friend) wrote to say she'd like to walk with me. (I might do that, it's interesting talking with her.) Luchia is sending something in the mail and wanted my address. Carrie wrote a long update and expressed care and concern. And Suzanne after another long silence sent some good advice on managing my energy.

Suzanne wrote: *"Much of your energy is being used by the disease process and that will be. Use the energy you have to write, enjoy family and friends. Stop and rest as you need. If you push too hard you will more tired. Control pain. Pain uses tremendous amounts of energy. Don't hesitate to take medication when needed."* I agree with her and will rest without feeling guilty and take pain relievers more often.

I'm munching on a fresh spinach and goat cheese salad for dinner with strawberries, nuts, pumpkin seeds and and... You should be proud of me, I didn't even automatically nuke it.

Suzanne: Your walks are too special to cease. You may need to keep them at reasonable time. Enjoy the beauty you described to me.

M: Thanks hon, I'll do that. Hope you are doing well.

Oresha: Hello Michael :) I'm SO sorry for not getting back to you sooner! :(You are on my mind and in My Heart :) I understand that your energy may be rather low these days.... and that you need to take Good Care of Yourself and amp up that Healing Energy!...

Thanx for the heads up on the DVD's... they are still @ Kathy's... I hope to get them from her soon and start watching them again! They are So Wonderful! Please let me know if at any time you'd like them back in the near future... I take it that Jen has flown home now? Which daughter is spending time with Dear Dad?... :) Marijuana may not be such a bad idea! Have you talked to your Dr. about the possibilities? ... lol

I'm still doing some coughing/blowing! Ugh!... lol However... I am feeling SO much better thanx! Almost human again!... lol That's what I got for burning the candle at both ends while on my mini vacation in Vancouver!...ha! ha!... ;) As soon as I am sure that the bug is ALL gone.... I would love to come over and spend some time with you, when you're feelin up for a visit? Kathy would like to come and see you too :)

Please keep me posted on how you're doing? Any time you'd like to chat, please drop me a line. If there's anything that I can do for you... PLEASE just let me know! If you need a ride to a Dr.'s appointment, or to have me pick up some groceries... or anything! How do you feel about some "Natural" assistance at this time? Have you heard of Adam? He is a young man from Vancouver who has been said to have some rather remarkable "healing" skills! He is now a naturapathic dr..... I'll send you a couple of links to take a look at.. to see if you may be interested in exploring the possibilities.....??? Sending You Much Love and Healing Comfy Thoughts ...

M: My dear 80 year old sister in Saanich who doesn't even have a car offered to catch a bus and walk across the street here to bring me groceries. So I've got that one covered, thanks. :-)

I'm glad you are getting better, I hadn't heard from you so contacted Kathy for an update. She kindly offered to walk with me so I might take her up on that now and then though I continue to get along well on my own, just tire easily. Do you think she could carry me if need be? :-) You are welcome to visit too of course.

Jen is in Utah tending to a load of business matters. Since the cancer clinic doc gave me an expiry date a year away I've become quite independent and my kids are just on standby, I'm on my own and doing well with it.

I'll look up Adam. Maybe when my daughter (the one you met) comes we'll go see him together if only for the fun of it, I'm always curious and welcome new experiences. Thanks for the tip. Stay in touch.

M: (to S) One of my friends (Oresha, you met her) suggested I see a noted naturopath in Vancouver. If you come this way to see about getting me into a two bedroom why don't you allow enough time for us both to make an appointment with him in Vancouver? Might be a fun experience if nada else... Dad

Jen: All sounds well. Good to hear friends are sending caring messages. You need that. Just don't make your walks to long. Set if you must in the middle of your walk for a half hour or so and visit. All is coming along just fine for us. I am finally putting very long days into getting my accounting done. Then I will work on getting the house rented. My sweet love I am working to be with you.

Carrie: my house won't close for another month or so at the earliest, so right now, i'm planning on staying in the states until i have to go back... david has offered to go with me and help me move, though to where is still quite up in the air...

Carrie: are you getting any kind of treatments? is that what you are tired from? are you alone now, or still have family members with you? i hope and trust your health journey is taking you where you wish to go...

i've been in California for almost a month now... just before i left south america, i was contacted by a man from the spiritual singles site... put him off for a while as i was getting ready to leave, but did take a bit of time to connect before i left and since i've been here, our connection has expanded and we are both very much looking forward to meeting each other soon... i am holding off being excited until that happens, sometime within the next week if all goes well... his name is david and he is a coach to heart centered entrepreneurs... lives in arroyo grande cal, so just up the coast from where i am now... we seem to speak the same language - he's a strong abraham proponent - and he's sweet, playful and extremely present... we hit a new depth in our connection last night and it seems as if we can't help but be friends and most probably more if there is even a small spark of chemistry to get us going...

i've been with robert for about a month now, helping him get some directions established and settled in a new place... we have had a really wonderful new experience with each other, yet not one that will yet lead us into the quality of relationship i can see as possible... it's ok for me though as i am allowing spirit to guide all things in my life now and trust things will unfold as they ought to with both robert and david and whomever else is right to be in my life... i will leave here on friday to spend time up the coast with friends from topanga to the bay area and probably come back here for more time with robert... we are working on a project together that could be amazing in both it's service and money making capacities...more as that develops... meantime... consider yourself warmly hugged by me.

M: Does there come into everyone's life a time when they need to 'settle' because anything better is elusive, and *stability* is more important than ideals? I resonated instantly with the name "David" for all that may be worth if anything. I wish upon you the very best in finding what you want and what you need. But maybe it's the *flow* of life that makes it so exciting and stability is foreign to that? (Unless you attract someone who will flow contentedly in your stream or you in his.) Please keep me updated sweetie.

5: My thought is, let them know that you have no assets and that you are dying in Canada, and to repossess it. It doesn't affect you so that's what I suggest regarding your rv. ..

M: No letter from your husband then?

M: Maybe I'll run it by 2.

M: (to 2 my lawyer son) Jen sent the following suggestion re disposing of my RV. It makes a lot of sense to me. If 5's husband won't send a letter would you do it?

5: I haven't shown my husband yet, he's got the flu. I will show him tomorrow.

Oresha: God Bless your Sis!.... If she can't make it... please keep me on your "back-up" list... :) I'll also walk with you if you're up for it :) A Boy needs his exercise... after all!... lol I'll see if I can find a Little Red Wagon for you to ride in... if you get tired....;)

I wouldn't take much stock in the Dr.'s "expiry-date" guesstimate!.. A friend told me that a friend of hers has a sister in the US who's been living with the diagnosis of stage 3 lung cancer for 4 yrs now... and doing OK!... :) As we know, a LOT of it is in our "belief system".... Have you looked into what Abraham has to say about such things???

I will now send you a few links/articles to read about Adam & his clinic in Vancouver... It may help to do the visualization of the "heat/ flames" burning up the cancer..... if it speaks to you..... Much Love ....

M: I could make a crack about us playing in a sandbox and me allowing you to pull me around by the handle of my little red wagon. But hey, it's Oresha so I won't. :-)

A few months ago I met a lady near Victoria who had a book written about her. She was given the classical "six weeks" to live. That was ten years ago. She attributes it to nutrition. One of my sons is an MD. He tells me that 14% of people who have exactly what I have at stage three live five years or more. So of course there is no need to settle into anyone's prognosis regarding longevity. It's not quantity that I am after, it's quality.

But being of Abraham I am convinced that I will not die a moment before my higher self has decided to schedule that event. The parasite inside me will not necessarily be the tool that governs that event either, it has no power over me that I do not allow. However, at this moment I am accepting and allowing. I may (slowly) move over to the other side but I'm not there yet. This dying thing is kind of fun actually, the greatest experience, the longest journey we will ever get to have, hard to turn down when you're content with it...

Jen: You just don't know how to make a girl feel secure do you? Or are you looking for more drama for your book. The fool I play to allow a man to control my emotions. Is it not enough to know we love each other and will be together. So this morning the law of attraction is called upon you to find you a woman. You pressure me so if I do not dance your dance. I can't stop you. I don't mind the communication you have with these people. I don't mind if you walk with Kathy. What I am up set about is you are basically telling me you opened your mind to other women. That's the only thing you are really interested in. Other than travel. You were pressuring me hoping I would give you an excuse to set me aside while you open your mind and check the playing field once again..... I don't get you. Things were settling. I was working almost around the clock hopping to get back to you sooner and you through in a wrench.

M: Ouch, here we go again! You caught me by surprise, I thought from your other emails today that everything was fine and moving along well with us. You were even giving me hope that we might marry and live happily ever after, today's the first time you've done that since the divorce if I recall correctly. But I guess my mentioning that I heard from friends got you jealous and insecure again, I need to learn not to be so open with you, you can't handle it.

Yes, before I heard from you today I too was insecure, you gave me cause for that the last few days with your lack of open communication, everything seemed as it was months ago, you not available, not committed to a together life for us. I wasn't sure where you really were and wanted to find out, thus the absolute clarity of my two question message. Before hearing from you I did what I do best, allow life to flow through me, accepting whatever comes, knowing that it will always be good. I'm going to continue doing that and let you handle your own emotional battle as best you can.

I do love you, I want to live my life with you. But I want to live it in peace, knowing that we accept each other for who and what we are and flow with it. Yes for goodness sake, if we marry or live together I will be sexually faithful to you! At my age with me dying anyway how could it be any different? What more do you want? Why the insecurity and the blame/feel guilty game? Does it make you feel more, or less secure to indulge in such things? When you do it makes me feel that you don't really want me, that what you want is to blame *me* for us not coming together, and to justify yet another weepy poor me pity party. *How nasty of me to control your emotions!* Get real will you?

What do you *really* want Jen? We're back to that again. You don't know how to make a man feel secure do you? Kiss and make up?

Jen: Instead of using that life flow for attracting women. Use those life flowing juices to contain the cancer from stealing your energy. I am glade you have friends. When you feel insecure you pressure me. Then you don't get what you want you write insinuating email that include ex lovers and old girlfriends. You well know it will get my hirer up. You knew exactly what type of response you get back. I want you to promise to be faithful not because we are married but because you love me most. I want you to be patient until my life is in order. I want you to trust I am coming back. I want understanding of how difficult my situation is. I want someone to help me. These are the things I want most in that order.

M: I will try to trust that you are coming back and that you will eventually get your life "in order". I can't help that I attract women. I'm just that kinda guy I guess. :-) But once again you accuse me of deliberately trying to do something negative to you. I do not do that. You could have chosen to be happy for me because five of my friends wrote today letting me know that they care about me instead of blaming me for provoking you into some kind of a negative emotional response. You could have chosen to be pleased that I shared that with you.

That's quite a list of "I want you's". How be that you accept me as I am and deal with your emotional problems on your own instead of expecting me to 'control' them in some acceptable-to-you fashion? Will you ever accept that it is you yourself who is responsible for your own emotions and that you have a choice in the matter, a choice of attitudes? What do you mean by your wanting someone to "help you"? I can't go where you are, you know that.

I'm cheered that you are now actively engaged in doing your taxes, I know that's a tough one for you to get to. It's just as hard for me to get motivated to work on the business website. 1's pushing me real hard to do that, it seems that I got the wrong impression that they don't want to inherit my USA assets, I now think they do. But I don't know how they think to run it after I'm gone, 4 doesn't want to have anything to do with it. I don't think they clearly understand that the land will default to the state if taxes aren't paid and that it's worthless unless it's marketed and sold. Maybe it's the accounts receivable that is attractive but at least half of that will need to go to the politicians for property and other taxes. Divide that portion among seven people and it's nada. It makes more sense for you to take it over if you want it.

Anyway dearest, I do love you, I hope you will come as soon as you can and that we'll cease to quarrel like we so often do. What a relief that would be... Thanks again for giving me some hope that you may want to marry and live with me some day.

M: (to myself) In the nights and dream states I am becoming Adam with many wives and children. Jen seems to be contrary to that, always wanting me to be exclusive to herself, jealous, demanding that I love only her. There is a stark contrast. Do I mentally put her in the "real" column and Adam in fantasy and accept the divide? Or just flow with the power that creates planets and enjoy what comes and goes, being who and what I really am moment by delicious moment? I love my wives and children, I have many. Is that fantasy, or reality in some other time space or dimension and I am just becoming aware? It is my hope to maintain an unbroken stream of consciousness and memory. I continue to want this physical body to be made immortal and to flow in joy with the newness and power of that. Am I destined for such a perfect love? *Am I becoming Adam?*

Jen: It was nice that you heard from old friends and it is nice that Suzanne helps reminding you to take medication for pain. As she said pain steals your energy. Go for a walk with Kathy if you desire to. It would be nice for you to have someone to talk to. I am sure she is very lonely for good conversation.

I wonder who 1 inherited the idea of pushing people in the direction he thinks they should go. He is right. This is your business and you have a responsibility toward it and should be working it to keep it going. I heard 7 ask 4 if he wanted the business and 4 said no. I seem to be the only one that is willing to help you bring it back. I am the only hope to keep it going. The business will die unless you train me to run it totally and keep the website up. By no means work at it long hours. Just a few a day when you are welling well. Then if you want leave it to your children in good shape. Maybe one of them will step up and run it or they can divide it 7 ways.

In no way do I mean to hurt you or disrespect your wonderful writing ability. I realize your purpose of writing the books is to get your message out there with hopes by adding sex will attract more readers. The truth as I see it is. There is a bigger chance you will make more money with your real estate business than your books. The reason. The percentage of authors having great financial success selling their books is much less than you selling one of your properties. You are a magnificent writer but that does not guarantee success. There are hundred thousand great writers out there that make little money at writing. There are thousands of people that would like to say they own a piece of land in the USA.

If you have an emergency I will get on a plane and be their as soon as I can. Mean time take good care of your self and go to the doctor. You must not be afraid of them putting you in the hospital. They can not do that against your will.

Meanwhile I have business and obligations here to take care of so I can freely go to you and stay as long as we want. I have been extremely neglectful of my responsibilities and I am paying the price now. It is going to take time to catch up. Please be understanding. If you could only be here it would be wonderful. I know you can not at this time. You also have a responsibility to see the doctors. Oh, by the way, stop attracting those women. It makes me nervous my love. :-) Let just love each other OK.

M: That's a very nice letter sweetheart, thank-you for that. It's the "kiss and make up" that I suggested.

M: (to Jen) You write: *"I have a feeling today we are moving forward and that cancer is not going to stop you. There is much for us to do together. Lets enjoy the journey."* That's real world. Leap with me now to my rich fantasy world where I wrote two days ago into my journal:

> *"In my fantasy world today for the first time I caught a glimpse of Jen inside my bubble, an equal with me and with my family of spouses on another planet rather than being as usual outside, me always having to leave the rest of my family to go somewhere else to play with her. She never came in to join us until this morning if that glimpse of her among us lying on the grass was real. I was always willing to go to her and play for a while before getting back to my real world. My door was and will always be open to Jen, I'd love to have children by her, I think she wants that. It's just that she has always written of herself as different, as greater than my sister wives, and with her spirit man greater than me, creating both spirit and physical bodies while I did only physical. Jen elevated herself, called herself "Eve" and her sisters merely "budding Eves". Has that changed?"*

Keeping in mind that my fantasy fits with the original Mormon Dream of Joseph Smith and Brigham Young before the politicians banned it, do you as Jen care to comment?

Jen: (responding to my forwarding flight schedules for a visit from my daughters) This is wonderful news. Have fund with your girls. Looks like 5 and 6 will get to spend a couple different days alone with you. I am sure they want that. I will shot toward coming the last week of next month. Any problems let me know.

M: I'm sure I'll enjoy the visit with my daughters. I'm thrilled that you are planning to come soon. I love you lots, want to hold and cuddle you.

M: (to list) I was informed today that my three daughters are coming to visit. How lovely, I feel so special!

I must admit that much as I love Victoria and it's no doubt the best place to winter in Canada, after twenty years of living in much warmer places the winter here with hardly any sun seems long. Should I fall among the 14% of people who get the same type of cancer I have and live for five years, I will want to summer here and winter somewhere warm. Sure, I'll own up to the title "wimp", never did like the cold. Life's good though, shouldn't complain, especially not when I have kids that care for their dad as much as mine do, I love them lots. Dad/Michael

Jen: I just walked out on the back patio and it is warmer outside than inside. My feet love going out side to warm up. I love the warm weather we are having. This morning it was over cast and I was not sure if it would be a nice day.

Jen: I forgot to ask if the girls are staying with you.

M: I hope so, I expect them to.

Jen: Listen to this fantasy I just dreamed up. It is great and funny.

I was thinking a bit earlier about your dream to become Adam. It appears there are no requirements or price to pay except wanting to become Adam. Then would not most men want this as soon as they become aware. I see the different Adams standing in your doorways (of their earth) waiting for and expecting Eve's to come that chose a program. There are many intelligent, creative men out there that would put those talents to work creating unbelievable worlds. The spectrum of worlds would be so vast and so interesting to see and experience. The Eve's only have to choose. How's world would they choose. Such a vast variety to choose from. My imagination could go on and on. Be careful you may get all the fat ones that want to set and rest with you. And you would not be able to send them away because you are all equal.

I love the freedom you give women in your world. There wouldn't be a day go by that it would not be revamped by a different woman. Since they have their own thoughts and thoughts will progress them. I do not believe what you think will happen exactly the way you want it to or I do not believe Joseph Smith or Brigham Young saw it the way you do. Yes they did have wives in this life and the next. There are laws to be abide.

I would love to hear what type of worlds your old lovers and friends would dream up. I bet it would be greatly different than yours. I think they would put different rules on men. As you told me most of them have been damaged and hurt by men in everyway. Could write short stories of called. WHO CREATED THAT WORLD! I bet the stories would be funny and fascinating. Or you could call it WHO CAN CREATE A WORLD IN LESS THAN 500 WORDS. OR THERE IS MY WORLD - THEN THERE IS YOUR WORLD. Can we combine them. This was fun.

M: You seem so bitter Jen, striking out and making fun of that which you do not understand. Your fantasy bears no resemblance to mine. You create a state of anger and chaos rather than like attracting like, love, fullness of joy and beautiful children. Is there no heaven for you? I was sharing something special with you, I cast a pearl your way, you trampled on it.

Jen: WE ARE TALKING ABOUT FANTASY NOT HEAVEN! You told me it was a fantasy. We all have fantasy's. Your is a very nice fantasy based on your desires. Mine is thought's, things to think about or just a fantasy not a desire or want. I am not bitter I was just having fun.

M: Not to worry, I love you and look forward eagerly to your return.

Chapter 8

---◆◆◆---

Kris: Hi Michael, I was just thinking about you and thought I would email and see how you are feeling. How is the writing project going. Maybe one night you could come for dinner?? Kind thoughts.

M: How nice of you Kris, I really appreciate your invitation to dinner. Alas I'm going to have to make it a rain check because I found out yesterday that my three scheming daughters, not to be outdone by a recent visit from my sons, are all coming to visit and stay awhile. They will be followed by Jen who I'm guessing will be here several weeks whether I need the help or not. They're rallying around me and I think the siblings have several events planned possibly including shopping for a larger place for me to live so they can visit more comfortably. And I'm hearing rumors of a couple of weeks at a five star resort in some tropical place. What can I say other than life's splendid? Take care my friend, please stay in touch.

Jen: My daughter came over tonight, her husband is out of town for business. It is their anniversary. I told her I want to get the house rented so I could be free to leave for some time. She suggested I have her daughter come and help me move some of the big stuff into storage down stairs. There are several options. I am to tired to go into the details. I had so much happening today that I could not get much accounting done. My cousin will be here on Friday for a few days. I will need to clear stuff from the basement so I can get what I want to keep and put it down their. I am trying to free my self up to be with you. When I can get my to do list done I will share it with you.

I talked to my daughter about how great our life was together most of our years. She agreed she thought so also. I told her all the great things in Victoria and how we want to travel the West coast. I told her I want to be with you until the end. She said she understood. Love you sweetie.

M: Our life together was good sweetheart, I'm hoping there will be more. I'm committed to you if you are willing to take time for me.

I can't promise how long or how short my stay will be, the tiredness and other indications are undeniable much as I tell myself that I am in control. I'm now taking pain relievers fairly often otherwise there's a general ache that I was ignoring but I now understand draws from the energy available for me. I'm also finding that a few sips of red wine now and then really do help the stomach as goes the common lore. My thinking is that even though I may turn more to being Mormon, given my condition I will consider *anything* I eat or drink to be medicinal and not to be denied because of some clerical principle.

I'm glad that your daughter is supportive and there for you. It seems that you are now on a roll and doing what you can to get us together again, I appreciate that. Give my regards to your cousin, she too is a good friend for you, I'm glad of that. If you stay here a while you may make friends, perhaps from church or possibly from among mine though the local ones are dwindling because of my neglect. I turned down a visit from Elaine who was going to bring over a painting so may not hear from her again and today turned down an invitation to dinner with the author of that book on healing that I have. I'm just not feeling up to it but because I walk most days anyway may invite Oresha or her friend to accompany me sometimes. If there's time that is, my daughters arrive in a few days and possibly you a few days after they leave. Then it's off to Mexico I think, nothing's booked yet, and soon after should be warm enough for us to take that driving trip. If you want to travel with me further while I can maybe we should use up that companion ticket of yours before it expires? Where would you like to go?

M: I've been watching some of the movies you watched when you were here and am struck at how indoctrinated western women are and how ignorant about that men are who don't commonly watch such films. Although of course I've watched such films before I didn't analyze them like I do now. So I understand better today where it is that you are coming from when you speak about romance and "love" and how it should be for a woman. In an age when chivalry and the way women of higher class used to be treated (maybe still are) is largely unknown to males, there is certainly a glaring gap in what women expect and what men provide. In my books I write a bit about Tantra and how males should change their attitude towards women. But that will remain a long way from being fulfilled for a long time I think. The feminist movement a few decades ago unfortunately brought women down to the level of men and to be treated equally. They're still stuck there and left with deep feminine longings perhaps particularly when they see the kind of "love" that comes from Hollywood's silver screen fantasies and are not getting that from the males. Am I making any sense?

Kris: Glad they are all rallying around you. Enjoy your time together. Kind thoughts.

S: (to list) So, I booked a place for the family reunion. Like my husband said, it is better to have somewhere to go than to have nowhere to go. As long as we give them about a month notice, we can cancel.

M: This is wonderful. Let us know when and how to make payment. For those interested in history, when I graduated first in my class in the military I was given first choice of where to go. Among the choices was the same location we are having the reunion. I seriously considered that but picked Manitoba instead, to the great relief of everyone else in the class none of them wanting to go to Manitoba. Had I chosen Vancouver Island I would not have dated your mother and we would not be having this conversation. Just thought you might be interested in knowing that. It's little individual choices such as that one that determine how generations of human beings are organized possibly for centuries and possibly amounting to hundreds of thousands of people and zillions of interactions that otherwise would not have taken place based on that single almost spur of the moment choice.

S: I guess this brings it all full circle then!

Jen: What a great message to your family.

M: (to Jen) There's nothing to worry about but sometimes, like an hour ago, I get unfamiliar aches that even pain pills don't take care of. So, no need to come but please keep in mind that if I don't respond to your emails within 24 hours (unless I provide a reason ahead of time) that I may be in trouble inside my apartment. So, if you don't hear back from me within 24 hours try phoning me in case internet or my laptop isn't working. If no answer after a few tries, call the apartment manager and ask her to go in my apartment and see if I'm ok. No worries, this is just in case so I can rest easier when these things happen, I'm doing fine right now. Please don't pass this along to my kids, they'll just worry without need and 1 will insist that I go to a doctor. I am not asking you to come sooner or even suggesting it, there's no need. I might last for years yet, I just don't know my body well anymore, there's a lot happening that is unfamiliar. I appreciate you.

Jen: I got the message and I will call you.

Marcy: Hello Dear Michael, I'm checking in to see how you are feeling. I'm sending you lots of love and light and grace from the divine. All is well here. I leave today for the ashram in Tennessee to learn from a guru. I'm very happy about that. You are a treasure! Love,

M: It's always nice to hear from you Marcy, I really do appreciate your kind words and blessings. I tire easily and need to rest a lot but still get out and walk most days so can't complain. Support and well wishes from family and friends is almost overwhelming, I've never felt so loved and cared for before. Maybe you should try dying sometime, it's great. :-) Take care, enjoy your seminar. Please keep in touch, you are precious to me.

Marcy: Thank you Michael, Yes I will try that some day. But not for a while:-) You are precious to me too. And I love hearing from you!

Jen: Good Morning, I wanted to let you know you are loved and I am sending you a big kiss and gentle hug.

M: Hi sweetie, thanks much, loving you.

1: (to list) The following is from an article that I just read: *"Grief does not change us, not really. It is infinitely more powerful than that. It has the amazing ability to connect us not only to others but also to the lost and forgotten parts of ourselves. It has the power to bring us to awareness, to show us what we have forgotten and, ultimately, to make us whole again".* Like I said cancer has not only the power to kill but to heal.

5: (to list) That's an awesome article. Thanks for sharing it!

M: (to myself) I was amazed today when the sign off forms for all three of my books arrived in my email inbox. I thought it would take several weeks and I'd have to supply images etc. With only a few changes to the covers, I *signed!* In addition to e-books, the books are soft cover 5.5 x 8.5 inches perfect bound with 806, 604, and 544 pages.

Jen: I was talking to my sister today and she said you are often required to put life insurance on large vehicle loans. Just don't know about California laws.

M: When you come you could look over those papers again and check, I don't know. I've been overdoing it today reworking the business website and am paying the price, super tired, need to lie down a whole lot and not doing enough of it, doesn't work. So when we travel, I'm going to need to lie flat a lot, your vehicle should work well for that. Hope you're having a better day sweetie, I think I'm going to turn out to be even less fun than I used to be. :-)

Jen: I understand. Rest. I was just going to email you and say I think we are both back on tract getting things done and creating a future for us as long as you are here. Just take it slow. Set a timer or something and stop when it goes off and rest. Pace yourself. As far as having fun. Being with you is what makes any travel worth it. The cruise deal has some great trips.

M: (to list) I want to wish 4 a very happy birthday today even though my guess is that his kids are more excited about it than he is. Happy birthday my son.

I tuned in to 6's radio show last night at midnight. It was nice to hear you 6. You certainly have a talent for the radio arts, you kept things moving along well, expressed solid opinions and have an enjoyable personality. In my opinion your voice is much more pleasant than that of the co-host. I didn't stay tuned for the entire show because it was way past my bedtime and although it was nice listening to you, I am not among the target audience for your subject matter. :-)

Strangely, late yesterday afternoon after putting up with persistent tiredness much of the day I got a burst of energy and finished making improvements to my business website some of it thanks to suggestions from 1. The extra energy was nice. I don't know what to attribute it to, maybe thanks to those praying for me and friends who are healers doing what they do from a distance. I was carried along on the strength of others and felt pretty much normal. I hope it continues today.

I'm getting excited about my daughters coming to see me next week, my guess is that 5 has every moment scheduled for something. :-) I really appreciate how she takes the initiative to move things along in such a good way, I love my kids. Jen too is saying she may come towards the end of the month. I'm looking forward to her visit, she is precious to me and brightens up my days when she is here. Please get used to and accept us being together, we had our troubles but I doubt that we ever stopped loving each other. I hope to travel with her in the future, maybe including family visits.

Enjoy the day everyone, you especially 4, I'm thinking of you. I'm proud of you my son, you do so much for your children, there aren't many dads who would work such long hours as you do to provide for their family. I love you and wish you great happiness and contentment. And time to make the music you do so well. Several years ago you made an MP3 of your songs for me and I didn't take it. I don't think I ever explained that I wanted to listen but didn't have an MP3 player at the time. I'd welcome any of your songs you care to send by email attachment or whatever in a format I am likely able to play. Are you preparing something for the family reunion? Dad/Michael

Jen: Michael, Could you do me a favor. Would you send me a Hi message each morning so I know you are alright and made it through the night. Love you.

M: I'll try to remember to do that. I sent a message to the list this a.m. Did you get it?

Jen: Yes, that will do also.

2: (to list) Dad, Glad to hear you are working on updating your website. This will assist us all after your passing. Thanks for that. I am sure I speak for everyone when I say that we have and always will accept Jen as part of our family. All relationships have challenges but those are best kept between the individuals involved and should never affect the relationship of either individual with surrounding family and loved ones. Our family hopes to maintain our relationship with Jen for the remainder of our lives and beyond.

M: Thanks so much for that 2, well put. I will accept that you are speaking for all of my children. Jen was not certain that you would still welcome her though I always felt that you would, our troubles were mainly my fault not hers. She is copied into this, she should be comforted. Wish us well. Dad See, I told you Jen... :-)

Jen: Yea, you did. It was kind of you and 2 to say what you did. It means a lot to me.

M: (to myself) I am not easily duped, but I do sometimes go along with those who think I am to see what new learning or adventure that may lead to. I agree to play in their sandbox until it's not fun anymore. Although I will continue to communicate with my friends I am now totally committed to Jen and will be faithful to her as if we were married. I sent her passwords etc. how to edit my business website and carry on when I am unable. I look forward to us spending the rest of my days physically together as much as she will give us the time for that. My strategy to avoid contention in each other's company will be to say *"love me a bit?"* and to hug and hold her when the contentious spirit threatens. I think that will work for us and will give us enough peace time together that calm will become our customary interaction.

I forgive and forget the past other than to finish this present book which may yet lead to some drama that I will record to get us in an entertaining way to the point where I die or heal. But I wrote it true when I express that I do not deliberately do anything with the intent to provoke Jen. I do however record what takes place, and publish her written messages faithfully. So all is fair between us and it is she herself who determines how she presents to my readers. It's most likely that female readers will take her 'side' against the way I see and present mine. But if so, all is well. I am merely telling it the way I a male see it, there may be some value in that to my curious female readers. I admit though that I am not your typical male, so judge accordingly.

M: (to 5) Sensory deprivation was big in the 80's, I'm surprised to find it thriving in downtown Victoria, saw it in a magazine today. You float for an hour in a tank of salt water that you can't sink into. No sound etc. With no sensory input the mystics say the spirit leaves the body. I've never tried it but heard a lot of raves back in the day. I might try it sometime, just wondered if it might interest you? Could be better than a massage??

5: I don't think I could do that if you truly are in pitch black. Hubby said he would do it cuz he would get to be naked. Weirdos, the lot of you are weirdos!

M: Yes, that would be us. I might try it when Jen's here now that I know it's around. Back in the 80's two people tried to persuade me to get one and rent it out, they'd do "anything to float again." I had an appointment to try it out in Vancouver. Not sure why but cancelled. Weird huh? Cancelling I mean, Vancouver's ok, nude beaches there, stumbled upon one when out for a walk with your oldy sibs while at UBC. Fellow student wanted me to go there with her, told her I was married, she didn't care, didn't go, weird huh?

1: (to list) The God of Heaven Is Kind, Gracious, Merciful, and Willing to Act on the righteous petitions of His children. Your experience with energy Dad is consistent with the Love He Has. It is evidence of these things that I have outlined. 2 correctly expresses our thoughts and feelings about you and Jen. My wife, our children, and I hope for the touring visits to all your children and, of course Jen is welcome in our house, although we wouldn't want you both in the same bedroom, but that sentiment is not particular to you two, rather it would apply to all parties not married to each other. Now go sell your lots well.

FYI I am in total agreement if a sibling were to ask for a single lot to be transferred prior to your death as long as you concur Dad.

To myself and to our family let me be very clear that I have a singular resolve to act to protect and preserve your wishes Dad insofar as there are no 'moral' factors associated with them, even if I personally would wish otherwise. That includes end of life issues and so I am pleased to be the required consultant to any decisions by your health care agent Laura. I have told Laura this. I will attempt to hear and understand you correctly Dad and I will also try to encourage, assist, and yes also influence you. With Love 1

M: (to Jen) Further to 1's recent comments to the list, you and I know where we will *not* be staying overnight. :-) But we already knew that didn't we? I think 1 has a hard time facing the death of loved ones. I hope he doesn't have such a difficult time with his own dying, I'm quite comfortable with mine. I've now had two days with good energy. I don't know if it's relevant but yesterday morning I received the following from Marcy the healer in Utah who knows your ex. She was involved with the distance healing of Luchia, the artist who moved to the mainland.

"I'm checking in to see how you are feeling. I'm sending you lots of love and light and grace from the divine. All is well here. I leave today for the ashram in Tennessee to learn from (the resident guru.) I'm very happy about that. You are a treasure!"

Anyway, I'm grateful for that renewed energy and hope it lasts. I walked to the Bay Mall today to get a kale shake and when I sat down picked up a magazine lying there and it fell open to an article about floatation tanks and they being available in downtown Victoria. During my initiation here in 1984 I was approached by two people who wanted me to get one. I didn't and never tried it but I was intrigued with the idea that during sensory deprivation mystics say the spirit leaves the body to play outside. Maybe when you're here we'll try that experience if it interests you. (insert links)

M: (to Marcy) Here's a message I sent to Jen today. (insert above) I trust that you are enjoying your new experience, take care.

M: (to 1) I think you are having a hard time coping with the thought of your dad dying, personally I am very comfortable with it. It's the greatest experience we will ever know, I'm loving it. There's nothing shabby about dying at all, especially after seventy years of good living, I go wide awake and rejoicing. Re the land, several of your siblings and my brother have purchased land from me over the years. Let me know at the appropriate time and I can try to find you a property that is close to theirs. What would be those "moral" factors you mention associated with my "end of life issues"?

6: (to list) I want to thank you Dad for tuning into my show. I know you aren't my target audience for that show... thanks for your kind words. I want to echo what 2 has said about your relationship with Jen. I love her dearly and hope to have her part of my life forever too. I don't always keep in touch with her.... but that is our common practice. Please pass on my love to her. And I can't wait to see you... I'm having fun choosing outfits to match 5's fun plans! See you soon.

M: (to list) "5's fun plans" eh? Somebody had better clue me in so I too can go shopping and be ready for whatever's coming along with those scheming daughters of mine. Anyway, don't bother bringing an umbrella. I got caught downtown today without one and bought the fifth or so to hang in my closet. Fortunately they're to be had in this city almost anywhere for about four dollars, invariably just inside the store entrance. Had a kale shake today, they're to die for really... My energy continued well today, very nice. Sometimes I feel like a fraud with all those people wishing me well and praying for me. It's great to have the attention and get the visits of course, but I don't *feel* like I'm dying. (Except sometimes...) Dad/Michael

M: (to myself) It's after midnight where Jen is and I'm missing not hearing from her since early today. In the olden days I might have thought she'd gone somewhere with Al or whoever. But now I'm thinking she's just secure, knowing she doesn't have to chase me and doing her own thing. She's most likely alone in her home watching a movie or bathtub and candles (maybe toys) whatever, she's a woman. It's amazing what a change of attitude will do isn't it? But it's true, I'm lonely and missing her tonight, I wish she'd write and tell me what's she has been doing today, she doesn't share a lot. My three books moved to the printer today, they could be on the shelf in less than a week. And I finished tidying up my business website, my projects are complete. What will the morrow bring I wonder?

1: Dad I don't think that I am having anymore difficult a time than anyone else. The moral issues part is a generic covering statement since we do not know all future possibilities. That's how I and other physicians think. I was not asking for a property for myself. Again everything is up to you Dad. I think that 6 may want a property transferred to her before you die as something of her Dad's to hold on to. That's what I was saying but it was a more public forum than you and I. But we're getting ahead of ourselves since the hope is for you to live for some time and get to sell lots yourself and 'see' more of your dreams realized. Canada's economy may go down but the US economy may be recovering enough to see revamping your website begin to literally pay off.

M: (to Jen) I'm up and letting you know, as you asked me to do. But where are *you*? I'd like to hear more often from you, it always seems that the more secure you get with me the fewer and slimmer your messages get. If you are insecure and think I may be off with another woman you start chasing me and sending lots of messages. What am I to do? :-)

So what did you do yesterday? In the olden days my insecurity would have led me to think you were with Al or some other man and that's why you didn't write. I'm no longer concerned about that (you assure me that I needn't be) but please at least respond to my emails. I went to bed lonely last night wondering where you are, wishing you would write, and up early this morning hoping that you did. (You didn't.) Please take some daily time for me, I'm important too...

M: (to myself) While she was visiting, several times Jen asked me if I now repented of my sins in the religious way, meaning felt sorrow for them as well as forsake them. Each time I told her that I did not regret my life, that I cherished it. I could not find sorrow for having sex with Suzanne and DeLeon. That remained my attitude. But this morning I am beginning to realize that yeah, I could feel an element of 'sorrow' for those sexual indiscretions. Not because I felt they were sinful and offended God but because with the passing of time they were no longer important. So ok, sure, I'll admit, it made for a good story but I could have done without the sex. *(Did it really happen or was it my imagination? Was I a Casanova or a Don Quixote? Or just a fiction writer?)*

But if it really happened, is my change of attitude a proper element of "repentance"? I'm not sure, it's approaching it I guess, a Mormon bishop might think differently if interviewing me for a temple recommend. But yes, as for the forsaking, my guess is that I will never again have the fullness of sexual relations with a woman other than Jen. Unless of course she forsakes me and runs off with another man while I remain alive and active. I suppose I could be willing to have sex with someone else if that happens. At my age? Dying??? Hmmm, meet a lady at the cancer clinic with a similar expiry date as mine? Consider the possibilities. Isn't life grand...

So, could I become an active Mormon again if mainly to please Jen and my children? Yes I could, but in a limited way. Mormons who attend the temples are required to abstain from tea, coffee, alcoholic drinks, and smoking. I've never smoked so no problem there. But I think with my illness that I would want to consider everything I eat and drink as medicinal. If my body craves a food or drink I'll most likely provide it. I'd attend the first Sunday meeting at church with Jen if I am able. I'd abstain from sex with anyone but Jen. What else? Oh, this morning I was reading an article about Mormon leaders doing a survey to see about making changes to the undergarments Mormons wear after they've been initiated in the temples. The intention I think is not to do away with them but to make them more comfortable and practical to wear day and night as is required. I'd probably not do that because with age and illness the body wants as little restriction as possible. I sleep naked and most of my day alone at home I wear only a light summer bathrobe to cover my nakedness, nothing else. That would be hard to give up, I probably wouldn't. So, active Mormon? You decide.

Jen: Good morning. I slept in late. My cousin came in for a visit about 3 in the after noon yesterday. So I won't be on the computer. She is leaving Tuse. or We. Not sure. Love you sweetie.

Jen: My cousin and I are going for a walk out into the desert. She has lost 40 lbs. and looks good. She is inspiring me to stay on track to losing more weight.

M: Invite her to stay?

Jen: Maybe you now know where you are getting your energy with that healthy drink. Keep drinking your shakes also. I am going to buy a Kale salad mix today. Should be really healthy. Love you Lots

M: Chicken comes before the egg. Energy came before the kale.

5: Oh, and the whole "huh" thing is American. We Canadians say "eh"!!!

M: Split personality. Weird huheh?

M: (to my sister in Victoria) 5 writes: Thanks about the umbrella info. I was going to pack one. Now I won't. As for Aunty, I have her booked to do secret stuff with us Saturday morning through lunch and then we go home to rest. She will need to wear shoes that are comfy to walk in, but dress cute (which she always does so no worries there). Could you please let her know? Thanks. She does not need to bring her purse!

Sister: Ok sounds like fun but pass on to 5 that I refuse to wear my tutu with running shoes.

M: What's this about tutu's? I've already tried ballet, wasn't good at it, schedule something different 5

5: Dang it. I guess I should tell my sisters not to pack their tutus. I may still bring my tiara though...

M: (to Jen) Could you ride back with your cousin to get the vehicle you're buying? When is your daughter expecting it, or can you borrow it back for our trip?

Jen: My sister is not ready to let it go until she gets her new suv. Most likely in another week or two. I have not given my daughter a date when she will get it.

M: I'm looking forward to our road trip, I think we'll have a lot of fun, your SUV will be almost ideal for me. I do want to see that big tree you drive through and walk in the forest of giants. Maybe we can get a place and stay there three or four days? Whatever we do I want the trip to be slow and lingering where we enjoy it and each other the most, trip of a lifetime kind of thing. Mount Shasta would be one place I'd like to visit.

Should we use that companion fare of yours and go somewhere warm *before* the road trip? I haven't heard anything further from 5 about going to Mexico, I'm assuming that's still on. After many days of cloud and rain I'm very ready to see the sunshine again much as I love this city in the warmer months. I'm having a sluff day today, didn't shower, didn't go out, didn't get dressed, it happens, guy thing, you wouldn't understand. Don't want to winter in the north again if I'm granted as many months as that and can get around. I got the business website finished, worked on every page. Enjoy your company, it helps to get frequent messages from you, nobody else is writing other than 5 and sometimes 1.

    M: (to Jen) I was up at 4:30 a.m. and polishing Book 4 from the top to where I am now (105,000 words), still working on it, cuppa white tea nearby. I lie often on my sofa reading "Casanova" for the first time. I'm finding it interesting but can't read for long before I put my e-book reader down on my chest to meditate on some thought or fall asleep. I watch or try to watch movies in the evenings and sometimes get through one but often get bored and end up turning it off. I eat a lot, am up a pant size, but there remains a great emptiness inside me that food, much as I eat of it, cannot fill. Maybe it's a longing for you with me physically, I don't know, that seems a good explanation. I count the days to when my daughters and you arrive. Enjoy the day, please take the time to send frequent notes and tell me how your day is going.

    Did you enjoy the long walk in the desert with your cousin and your many conversations? Have you told her about the abuse you suffered from the other men you married? Had you not had so many buttons to push maybe you wouldn't have been so hasty to divorce number four? Or maybe you would have anyway, you saw things quite grim at the time. Topic for a cathartic discussion with your visitor? Maybe you've already gone over that with her. Anyway, I expect that she's your angel right now to help you heal. Don't resist, she's not likely to break confidence unless she too has her own 'mother confessor' and confidante and you never know where it might go from there if it's of concern to you. I'm sure you'll do what's right. Talk to me?

    M: (to myself) I don't write it to Jen but because I have sometimes expressed my notion of what romantic love is to a male, my female readers might be interested in the following. In his apparently true autobiography Casanova falls "in love" with a 14 year old girl (marriageable age in those times) who he sees dressed in finery. Later he discovers that the clothing was redeemed from pawn for the day and the girl lives in poverty. When he sees her looking less than made up he quickly falls out of love and concludes that love to a male is merely a feeling of *curiosity* combined with the sexual feelings that nature provides to preserve the species.

That observation does give pause for thought but it leaves out the fine feelings that can come with love and romance. (Except that I can find them for more than one woman at a time. Maybe women can for men too.) I do continue to think that "in love" means something different to a female than it does to a male. Perhaps generally speaking, the woman is focused on 'nesting' and settling down with one mate while the male though he may go along with that has eyes that see more than the woman who claims him as her own. I sense a great and wondrous love for each of the 'sister wives' in my dream world, not just (but including) lust. I'm getting curioser and curioser to know how it will really be when we're together.

Jen: We had a walk in the desert. She is still not able to go as far as I would. She is aware of some of the abuse from other marriages. It is nice having her here.

Maybe Elaine *is* a friend, just a very busy one.

Elaine: (she attaches two photos of a painting she made) How are you making out now? I have been thinking about you and hoping that things are stable and you are still getting support from family. Are you well enough. As for me, I just finished 3 day night shift, but things got quieter this weekend, so it was more civilised and not so crazy. I sure hope that things are stable with you. PS. I did a nice big painting, just to get warmed up. A copy of some of another artist whom I adore! More color injected into mine... but love practicing her style. Here is a photo of my messy tabletop studio.... Kind regards,

M: That's so interesting. I see the woman not sitting on the horse but a tall centaur standing behind resting her elbow on the horse's back and mulling why Elaine would paint her like that. :-) (attach links to woman with mechanical horse feet and centaur art)

As you know, Jen is/was jealous of my female friends but I would like to have a painting or drawing done by you. How could she not like it if she herself was in the art and she would inherit it? (Yeah, I know, scheming me... :-) This is just an idea but I would commission you (say up to $300 including frame?) if you would create a work that would include recognizable faces of me and Jen. (See attached photos, artist license agreeable.) Ideally it would be the two of us sitting on horses (optional) or on the grass in a sunshiny green glen with trees surrounding (blurry trees ok if it takes too much time to do realistic.) Old riding habit as attached? Or maybe by a lake or stream? What do you think? No obligation though, this is just a notion...

I didn't mean for the last message I sent to drive you away Elaine. I am doing quite well, even walk to the Bay Mall for a kale shake now and then. I'm on my own until next Wednesday when my three daughters will begin a visit each arriving on separate days. Jen is saying she will likely come the last week of next month and may stay a while. I'm still hoping that she will want to take art lessons from you when she's visiting, maybe pay you with visits to galleries in Vancouver or Seattle etc.?? She has a talent for drawing but almost no experience, just a great interest. Last time she was here she did a two minute drawing of me with my beard sitting in the recliner. I was surprised, she'd never done such a thing before. I'll show you next time you come over. I'm glad your shift was more humane, take care.

Elaine: Wow, you see things I didn't! I will wrap my head around the picture idea and tap into my intuition. I can do faces sometimes, it's not my forte.... realism. Thanks for offer of paying. I can still do you a non commissioned painting as I promised. If Jen would not be upset. I understand that is why you want both of you in the painting. Would she want lessons? I would love that! I can teach children to paint beautiful watercolours, so with Jen's talent, she would happily produce most beautiful paintings... it would be so happy and a beautiful memory. I'd be so happy to go in that direction... and will think about the commission, if I could do it.... I'm off work now, rested in a day... let's touch bases again. Cheerio,

M: (to myself) Elaine didn't offer to get together though. It would have been nice to feel the touch of a woman today even though it would be non-sexual. She could have come here and had a restful day chatting and cheering me, that seems like something a friend would do. I know, the world doesn't revolve around me but I would have visited her often if our roles were reversed and my visits were welcomed.

Jen sure doesn't make it a priority to write me even though I frequently ask her to. I wish she would, it would be a small thing for her to do and I'd be much less lonely. At least I know she is not off with another man. I haven't heard back from Kathy since I sent her that last message. And it has been several days since hearing from Oresha. I'm beginning to wonder if Kathy didn't want me to mention to Oresha that she had offered to walk with me. Have I caused trouble between those two? Anyway, I'll be largely unavailable from Wednesday on with my daughters coming and (hopefully) soon after Jen will arrive. I may yearn for private time again. But with 18 years of living together behind us, I can pretty much be myself with Jen around. I surely hope we keep the peace this time.

Jen: Just woke up from a nap after church. I Love and miss you.

M: I feel such a fraud today. Just got back from a walk along the sea and haven't been low on energy all day, I feel normal. I think what's happening is that I switched from one pain pill to the one that worked miracles for me when I had pleurisy. They're doing it again, two pills last for hours. I don't need more than two doses a day to make me feel as though this body doesn't have a problem. Maybe the docs got it all wrong... But come visit me anyway please. :-)

Jen: See you needed that anti-inflammatory. I will bring you a big bottle of it. So glade you are feeling good. It will make the road trip a lot of fun. Just enjoy and it may last a long time. I will come see you but will need to pick up the SUV before I come up. I am waiting for my sister to tell me when I can pick it up. Miss you sweetie, Love Jen

M: I would love to go to Costa Rica with you, especially to have a few days at the Baldi Hot Springs Resort, Arenal. We could fly to San Jose then get a private driver to take us there and later to a beach resort. I think you'd really like it, it's so peaceful they don't even have a military. I have a contact in Costa Rica (the woman from Canada who was promoting my now unpublished e-books.) She lives in Costa Rica and runs a tour company. I could get a price from her if you'd like to set a date, maybe 10 to 14 days in the country? What do you think?

M: (to myself) I just paid for three years of hosting for the website BecomingAdam.com. I was a bit anxious to be sure nobody else took that name. It's premature but I have time now and the inclination to get it started if even only to put in a link to my bookstore page at Trafford Publishing where I get the largest royalty on book sales. I may add a blog later if my energy keeps up like it has been the last few days. I'll most likely start the blog with quotes from my books and maybe later open it for comments and feedback from readers. Book 4 may contain a link to http://www.becomingadam.com if there are sales happening and the books are not just ignored or only Book 1 is sampled with no orders for the next books in the series. Will my readers want a blog I wonder? Could I persuade the real people behind Jen, Suzanne, DeLeon, Carrie (maybe Marcy and Luchia who are public figures?) to respond to questions and make comments on such a blog? There are so many possibilities but the books must first become a commercial success and pay royalties. The first (now unpublished) e-books did not sell, my fingers are crossed for Becoming Adam. If you're reading this please consider favorable mention in social media, thanks.

M: (to Jen) Checking in. Out and about.
Jen: I don't think I could enjoy Costa Rica. Not when you took Cleo there for a week and met this woman before for the same reason.
M: Ok we won't go, but go with someone sometime when you get the chance, the hot springs near Baldi are marvelous.

The magic continues. I hadn't heard from Cleo (DeLeon) in a long time but in the few seconds that it took to write my message above, an email came in from Cleo.

DeLeon: While I haven't been communicating - my thoughts are with you so much - in gratitude for our every moment together. I've been gratefully overwhelmed by adhd, add and addiction clients referred to me by a DR.. So grateful to have some money coming in - and back to doing what I love... saving lives and helping them remember who they truly are. Most of the time there they have no insurance - and of course I'm not set up for insurance, often not employed, so I charge such a small amount - but it gifts us both. The Dr. who was referring - had broken up with his lady friend, to whom he was referring, now they are back together and my referrals have plummeted. Am behind on the paper work, so grateful for the time to get paper work back on track.

I started doing treatment for my brain, as the memory has plumeted... most likely due to the 8 times under anesthesia in 2013 and 2014. Low Energy Neurofeedback - which is Brain Mapping and Neurofeedback has opened the door to my bringing in clients to help with anxiety, depression, add and adhd and of course addiction - as it is one of the "slowly" but very effective arising heailng modalities outside the system. They want to help train me - to do the process - and in the long run, I want that to be a major part of The Encouragement Centers of American.. I am starting to answer my phone Encouragement Center!! It has begun.

Got to jump in the shower and get ready for another Dr appointment, as I want to change my meds for thyroid into bio identicals - a natural support, which I hear is amazing.. How are you, on all levels.. Always, Forever.... Love Cleo

M: (to Kris) A friend in Florida tells me she is taking some courses to add to her alternative healing armamentarium. I glanced at the website and noticed the mention of nutritionists so I thought you might be interested in the following. Apparently it's leading edge, you may already be aware of it. Let me know if you get involved, a friend in Victoria (she's clairvoyant) has a 24 year old autistic daughter living with her, perhaps this would be helpful?? I'm just networking in case there's some synchronicity here, the message from my friend just arrived. (insert links from Cleo's message)

Kris: Thanks Michael. Will check it out. Happy thoughts.

M: (to DeLeon) It seems that you have found something leading edge to add to your healing armamentarium Cleo. I passed the link along to an author friend in Victoria who is a professional nutritionist. Indirectly, another Victoria friend (she's clairvoyant) has an autistic daughter who lives with her. If the first friend gets involved with neurofeedback, who knows what synchronicity your message to me this a.m. may have brought...

It's good to hear from you and to know that you are moving forward towards your goals with no thought or fear of the aging myth. Take care my dear friend, please keep in touch. Oh, as for me, the last few days I have renewed energy and zest for living. Could the docs with their CT scans and biopsy have got it wrong? I doubt it, but I sure don't feel like my body's dying. Thanks for caring.

M: (to myself) My softcover books are available on Amazon tonight but not the e-books yet. My first three books are published! I'm a bit disappointed in the quality of the covers but I suppose later on if they are selling I can commission a better cover.

Jen did not respond to any of my emails but she did call tonight it seemed to persuade me to become active Mormon again. I dragged it out of her that she will not be coming this month but most likely will come next month, she had already made her plans but had not shared them with me. This is not a woman who wants to be with me more than with anyone else, I seem to be a low priority. She now has three weeks to herself, will she be with another man or men? She has the right to be of course, and with me dying (apparently) it would be prudent of her to be looking for another man. Something's not right with her silence the last couple of days and her hiding her plans from me. I am insecure and unsure of her again, she is keeping secrets. And yes I'm jealous, I had given myself totally over to her as if we were married. After all she keeps (or kept) telling me she has no other man in her life or desire for one, might never. Am I such a dupe or is she sincere? Is it all a power thing for her, her desire to control and manipulate me at will? And when she feels she has me in her grasp she backs away and ignores me?

My heart yearns yet for Eve, yearns deeply for the loving beautiful woman (or women) with the exact same dream as mine. Perhaps I will have to die to be with her. But will I die? I don't feel as though it will be so, but it could be. I am lonely tonight but can't go looking for another woman when I have the sentence of death overshadowing me, and still a hope for Jen. How will this book end? Ok, this moment I feel that I must die, and I easily find the pains within to validate that. It would be a final solution, a complete release for me and for Jen. I think I'll sleep on it...

Jen: (Re 2's grandchild who is in hospital from an accident yesterday) Thanks Michael for forwarding this. I also shed tears today for the child but mostly for her parents and grandparents.

M: It's the mother I am most concerned about because she will blame herself for what happened while the child was in her care. Don't bring pain pills when you come. I did a test between what I buy locally and the pills you left last time you were here. Only the ones I buy locally work for me. And they work very well, that's what is keeping me thinking and acting normal, I've tried with and without several times, there is no doubt. It's possible that the difference is that mine are 400 mg and I take two at a time. (Once sometimes twice a day.) The pills you had and put in a different bottle may only be 200 mg so I'm only getting half the dose with them - doesn't work at all.

M: (to Jen) You've sure been silent lately, are you trying to punish me for something? Am I not important enough to take the time to write to or to respond to my emails? What's happening? 5 arrives tonight, I'll pick her up at the airport.

M: (to longer list) My immediate family is occupied right now with sad news about a serious accident that 2's grandchild was involved in yesterday, but I wanted to pass along some good news too. My siblings will be joining us for the last two or three days of our family reunion. I thought my children would be excited about hanging with all of us oldies for a while. It looks like it's really going to happen and I'm hugely pleased about that. You guys are all so great, I couldn't have a better or more supportive family, my inconvenience is surely bringing us together. Here's a message I received from my brother's wife a few minutes ago.

"Ok. (Our Manitoba sibling) and I finally reached each other. She will stay in Calgary until we go to Victoria. We may only go on the 7th to the following weekend. That way we can get to see your entire family. I personally look forward to that. She may even bring some of those albums she's been working on. They are very impressive. So we will look at that Motel you told us 5. Thanks for that. Ok that's all for now, rest well Michael and we'll talk again soon."

(my message to the list continues) My suggestion is that everyone get a room at the same place we'll be at because it's quite a long travel distance between there and Victoria and Nanaimo. That way we can all talk into the night. It should probably be done soon because apparently that location is popular.

The good news continues with my having found some over the counter pain relievers that work splendidly. I am back to normal energy, taking stairs two at a time etc. And my lungs feel clear, my guess is that the x-ray next week will confirm that there is no fluid buildup. Thanks for all the prayers and well wishes.

I'll be picking up 5 at the airport tonight and 3 and 6 on Friday. I think my Victoria sister is joining us on Saturday for some secret event in which said sister refuses to wear her tutu I understand. I've already warned 5 that I'm not good at ballet so we'll see what actually happens, I do have the requisite walking shoes.

Take care all, we're praying for you and your family 2 as you wait for news on the little child's condition. Dad/Michael

Jen: We will need to plan where to start for this trip. Since the SUV is in the South maybe we should start either in Phoenix or San Diego. What do you think. love you

M: If you're serious about spending a lot of time with me, I (or both of us if you are here at the time) could fly to Las Vegas. From there we'd drive the SUV to Phoenix so I can meet my new grandson. From Phoenix to Yuma, to San Diego, see the girls, and up the coast and inland to see the giant trees, Mount Shasta etc. going only short distances each day, staying in hotels sometimes several days at a time if we really like where we are. We could use the same hotel chain and get and use points. You could get a device so we'd always have internet even while driving. (Or use your phone??)

Then ferry the SUV to Victoria. I check in with doctors. Then explore Vancouver Island for ten days or so. Then ferry to Vancouver and (stopping at places in the mountains) on to Alberta to visit my family. Then to Utah and decide what to do from there but fly back to Victoria for the family reunion. (5 assures me that we are welcome to stay at everyone's home - other than with 1 we know.)

It's an ambitious trip and would have to wait until about May when it's warmer, we'd be starting in the south. But it would be the trip of a lifetime for both of us and hopefully we'd have a lot of fun together if we take our time along the way so I can stay rested. It might be better than a cruise or resort. What do you think?

Jen: That sounds like a plan. I would need to go to Utah to pack the Suburban before leaving on a trip.

M: I just talked to 5 about the Mexico trip and that is totally optional for her. So it's on the back burner and we can think of setting off for the road trip if and when the docs clear me. I hope you will still come and visit me as soon as you can though, and stay as long as you will. I do love you and want to be with you as much as you will allow us to be, everything is up to you.

1: (to list) We all want to be together. The place, and the distance from Dad's home and medical care may be an substantial issue since we do not yet have enough information to predict Dad's care needs by then. We don't know where your level of comfort will be. I know we can't predict all things but we may need to be getting together much earlier. Your chest x-ray, then your CT of the chest, then your next Oncologist appointment should give us the information that we actually need in order to make short term plans. That's only a handful, or less, of weeks away. My concern is that it is premature to put significant plans in place. All of us do need to, and know that we need to, keep the next few months and at least the next year as available as possible. This cancer beast is unpredictable. In the interim we pray, hope, and prepare as best as we can.

Dad I'm so impressed that you've had a bout of improvement and that you have been able to get some work done to help to reduce the burden on us when you die, and I hope that it will also help you because of a longer life. I re-iterate that the healthy and frank conversations already by this point are class A good. Love 1

1: (to list) Thank you 5 for bringing Dad love.

M: 5 says she didn't bring me love she brought me exhaustion. :-)

5: (to list) Hello all! I thought I would share some pictures of my day with Dad. We went to Walmart and bought a camera thingy so we can video Dad answering questions about his life. I brought a couple of books with questions so we can all take turns interviewing him and videoing him. I will leave the books (book marked) and the camera here so when people are here they can do some interviews.

We did Thai food for lunch. The only dish with coconut milk had a lowest spice level of medium. Dad really likes the coconut milk dishes and can't do anything hotter than mild. He asked if they could do it mild and they said they couldn't. So Dad said that he would "man up" and try the medium. It was hot. Hotter than I like and I do medium. We did it and aye almost the whole thing. Funny times! We came back and rested, then went for a walk to the ocean. We spent the time looking for sea glass. I loved it because it reminded me of Grandma.

We came back and rested and then walk to the Imax theatre and saw the movie, Journey to the South Pacific. Dad has been wanting to see it for a while and it hasn't been playing, so I checked, and it is playing this weekend! Awesome. We came home and dad fell asleep right away on the couch while I warmed up our meats pies for supper. I guess he was more worn out than he thought. He keeps telling me that he feels like a fraud (so 1's email was well timed!), and I just kept trying to slow down our pace a little. I think Dad will eventually realize that his body has some different limits now.

Anyway, enjoy the pictures. I will keep you all posted as the long weekend of daughters continue. Tomorrow 6 and 3 fly in and we are going to a Death by Chocolate Buffet (very fitting for the occasion!), which is the only activity Dad knows about! Your always scheming sister/niece/daughter,

Jen: I went out side and it was warmer out side then in. Did some yard work. Now back at accounting. I opened the doors to let that fresh air in. Miss you lots. Have fun with your beautiful girls.

M: The girls say "Hi we miss you". So better get yourself here girl, we're all missing you.

M: (to list) We're about to leave to pick up 3 at the airport after doing same for 6 this a.m. This afternoon 5 and 6 and I walked to the end of the breakwater. Along the way we watched a drama as a man pulled in a fish about one foot long and a huge ling cod (at least three feet long) kept trying to swallow the smaller one. The man had two chances to land the cod with his net but never let the rod go and with only one hand failed to catch the cod. Eventually he did land the smaller fish but the cod got away. That's our story and we're sticking to it. My guess is that the energy level is going to peak for a while when the third of my daughters joins us tonight. I'm told that on the way home we're going to stop at the Bengal Room in the Empress Hotel for the death by chocolate buffet. My mouth is watering already....

Jeannie: (A lady I swapped a lot of emails with when I was living in Yuma. I never included her story in these books because she's a public figure and didn't give me permission.) Hi Michael, I hope you are happy and sharing with a sweet Valentine this weekend. Just thought of you and wishing you happiness. Life is full and lots of beauty. My city is always glorious. Many blessings,

M: What a treat Jeannie, thank-you so much for writing. I'm still in love with you because of your beautiful music you know. :-) It's early a.m. and my three daughters are visiting me in Victoria, British Columbia. They're moving about now for the day's activities as I play your Wind Poet album. My four stalwart sons visited two weeks ago and the girls didn't want to be left out.

I surely wish we had met. Now it is unlikely because I have inoperable lung cancer and they tell me I am dying though I don't *feel* that it is so. The news struck me as a wonderful gift, school unexpectedly let out early and vacation time begun. I finished book three of my four book "Becoming Adam" series only hours before I took a cab to hospital emergency knowing that I wouldn't be coming home soon. It turned out to be only seven days while they drained a collapsed lung and incidentally discovered stage three cancer along the way.

My valentine would be my ex who at present is in southern Utah, I expect her to visit soon after my daughters leave next week. We've been getting together now and then but it's not likely that we will formally marry again though we may spend much time together. My health permitting it's possible that she and I will take a USA road trip together and may eventually pass through your city. If you are there at the time I'd love to drop in and meet you, you continue to be important to me. But please tell me what you are up to, when we were in regular communication you were indicating that you were wanting to move somewhere else.

Due to my circumstances I rushed my three books to self-publishing. They did come out but are now being revised due to a publisher formatting error. If you are interested I'll send a link when the revised editions are ready in soft cover and e-book. Book 4 will be the final one as I write the story of living out my dying. I wanted to anonymously add you to the books but we had a virtual tiff or two and I never did get permission to publish your emails, so you aren't in the books other than perhaps casual mention.

I hope you are well Jeannie. I feel to bless you as best I can. At some levels we are close, you still powerfully call me to "come home" with your beautiful song that is playing as I write this sentence. You assure your listeners that all is well and that is how I feel about how the universe is unfolding. I'm happy sweetie, it is my hope that you are too.

Jeannie: Michael, My dear what a challenge in your life to bring about all the gifts that need to explode from your heart. In the last six years including myself, I have watched many people reverse cancer with (ionized water.) I did that. By the time I had a hysterectomy I got a clean bill of health of cancer and I would not have needed the hysterectomy. Anything is possible. People have even had stage 4 reverse. I will share with you only this in this email today and give you a free website to watch detail about this. I can mail some things to you as you wish. If you find after any interest in seeing this we can talk further about it. For five years I've never had any other water to drink... period! There is not a cell in my body that says you are going to die from this! Many blessings, M: I appreciate this information Jeannie and will have a look at it.

DeLeon: Hi Sweetie, hope your Valentine's Day was gentle, in peace and with smiles from life, family, beloveds flowing like a river thru you. I'm slowly catching up with the overwhelm that hit with clients/patients being sent... past week many less were referred (as his girl friend came back - and he is now sending most of them to her). It was a gift for me, as a few minutes ago, I finally finished the last patient report that I had been behind on.... My mind just doesn't function like when done before. And actually have 5 clients set up, already, for this coming week - so all is good.

I finally started going to a place called... I had heard of them well over a year ago - and finally had the money to start the process that they do to help with memory, add, adhd, addicts, sleeplessness, depression, etc.. called... I've had 3 sessions with them and this week, they will do the bioneurofeedback. That's a 2 hour session - where it starts cleaning out ancient memories within the brain, body, etc.. Anticipate great healing occuring. Talked with them about bringing that into the clients that I am working with... As most of the addicts are ADD or ADHD diagnosed as well. C for B want to work with me as well, including teaching me how to do work the machines to do the process - lot of Visions are flooding thru me - and they are getting it as well. They are part of the future for healing.

Also have a meeting tomorrow with 2 of the dance instructors that left the studio - they are very spiritual and we are going to do some vision work - as think they are interested in being part of the start of my dream. Exciting, my dear friend. Tired and going to bed.. In Love and Gratitude for you in my lilfe. Let me know - always, how you are.

Jen: I was so surprised when I opened the door and saw red roses in the delivery mans hands. I knew it had to be you., had to be you, do toot da do, had to be you. Remember that song. I didn't send you anything. I feel so bad. I would call you but you are most likely out with your girls. I was not trying to remind you of Valentine's day when I sent that message. Any way the chocolate strawberries I was going to send will not be as good as what you will have today.. I will be thinking of you every time I look at those roses and in between. Love you sweetie have a great day with family. Love

Jen: I Can't wait to find out what you and the girl's did on Sunday. Love you

M: Church today then symphony. Just back and headed to Spaghetti Factory for dinner when I'm rested a bit. Pain pills are working well but wow I can't be off them or I know about it. What have you been up to?

Chapter 9

M: (to list) Carousels, high tea, and opera. That's how the closely guarded secrets evolved yesterday. We picked up my sister along the way then did a walk through of Butchart Gardens complete with a carousel ride, I got the lion. That's the first time I've ever done the complete garden, I didn't even know there was a carousel. Now I know how to go about walking the walk. When we finished the walk there was a time when I realized the others were killing time. Everyone except me was in on the secret that we were going for high tea at noon and we did, it was great, good food, lively company.

We dropped off my sister then rested at my place after leaving 3 at Fisherman's Wharf for a solo walkabout. My three daughters warned me that I had to put on a suit and tie as they were dressing in beautiful gowns. The day was complete with my and 6's first opera, Lucia Lammermoor. For me it was better than ballet but not near as addictive as musical productions such as Les MIserables, Mama Mia etc. It was in Italian with English subtitles. I got more into it after intermission, they saved the best for last.

It was a great day with my daughters, huge thanks to always generous 5 and her husband for covering most of the expense, much appreciated. And to 3's daughter for comic relief from other events happening concurrently with texts to 5 as she was skiing, hopefully not doing both at the same time. We're all of course tuned in to the updates from 1 and 3. We sorrow for 2 and his family and pray for them while going on with life.

Today has dawned sunny and the girls are bustling about getting ready for church, three girls one bathroom. Who knows what the rest of the day will be like, they don't tell me, my family keeps secrets, sometimes delightful ones. Enjoy the day. Dad/Michael

Jen: Other than working on taxes I haven't done much. I was just looking at the flowers you sent me and in the middle they have a tall cinnamon branch that I noticed look like it was budding and now small green leaves are appearing. It is so beautiful to look at. It makes me feel loved. I don't think another man could please me as much. Love

M: Thanks sweetie, have a good day. I'm off to hospital with 3 for the x-ray. I'll forward a message from 2 that I just read.

M: (to DeLeon) My three daughters were visiting on Valentine's day so it was a memorable time for me. One of those daughters planned secret activities and I'm well cultured now with opera, symphony, high tea, etc. I'm doing well, take care.

Jen: Please let me know what the x-rays say. I am so sorry about 2's grandchild. My heart goes out to the parents. How are the girls holding up with the news. Are they having a funeral and are you going. You should. You will see a lot of family you don't normally get to see. Love you sweetie

Oresha: Hello My Friend :) How are you doing these days? Is your lovely daughter there with you? Have you had a chance to take a look at the info from the naturopath that I sent ? If so, does any of it "speak" to you? I have a couple of books if you're interested in reading them? I thought I'd pass along this healing herb recipe for a home made tea... it is said to help heal the lungs...

Are needing to replenish your supply of hotdogs or anything else in your kitchen?.... lol ;) Pleas let me know if there's anything that I can do to help out?.. or if you're up for a short visit sometimes? ...or a short walk around the "hood"?.... lol Are you getting any more of your writing done? I can't wait to read your book(s)! :) Take care.... much LOVE..

M: My three daughters have been keeping me super busy and my cupboards, fridge and freezer packed! Two left yesterday, the youngest is with me until Friday. I'm interested in the naturopath in Vancouver but am not likely to take the energy to travel there, maybe sometime in the future. I appreciate your friendship Oresha. There will likely be a few weeks between my daughter leaving and Jen returning, we could get together for a visit or hood walk then. Take care.

M: (to Jen) The funeral will most likely be on Saturday somewhere near Edmonton. I still can't fly so no, I'm not going. It's good for the girls to be together, the topic is discussed but life goes on and as I write this 5 is planning part of the funeral service. I talked with 2 on the phone today, they are holding up. The mother's family is abundant and all there with her. We walked for kale shakes today then drove to Willows Beach and two other places to make up a longer day than I needed but with two doses of pain pills it's ok. Take care sweetie, hope to see you soon.

5: Dad, I put something in your freezer for you. Don't share. Also, I made sure to stock your house with as much food as I could get away with so that when you're alone there will be food for you. Please do your best to make sure that it all doesn't get eaten by someone that is not you and that has some eating compulsions...

M: I hugely appreciate your thoughtfulness and your generosity 5. I'm sure I'll continue to be well fed for a long time now, maybe until Jen comes. Thank-you so much for everything. I love you lots.

M: (to list) This morning after dropping 5 off at the airport we went to a beach and watched a glorious sunrise over the water and the islands. This afternoon 3 and I went to the hospital where I was living for a week not so long ago. She took sheet music with her and played the grand piano in the lobby for me. It was wonderful to hear her play, she is so talented, from Beethoven to contemporary and jazz. As I listened I looked out at the patio near a chapel that the hospital complex is built around. A woman was sitting there in a wheelchair basking in the sunshine. She was dressed in white and had what looked like white wings coming out of her shoulders at the back. It was a glorious scene and I easily imagined angels all around as I listened to the compelling sounds of the music 3 was making seemingly effortlessly. A young boy came up to 3 and she paused a moment while he gave her a flower, a dandelion, a magical moment in time. After her performance 3 asked me if all the money I had spent on her piano lessons had been worth it. I assured her that it had been, well worth it.

We then walked into the chapel built in 1909 and from there drove to the beach where I picked up sea glass to add to Jen's collection and 3 searched for sea anemones in the tidal pools. It was a good day, ending with her flight being delayed and she and I and 6 eating dinner at the airport terminal. She should be home now and at work tomorrow, it's a small world after all.

Michael Demers

This morning I indulged in the last of a delicious cherry cheesecake the girls made, just right, not too sweet like it often is, double cherries, double cream cheese, half the sugar I think is how it went. Earlier we dined on 6's chicken curry, we ate well these last few days my daughters and I. And my fridge and freezer are full, these girls take care of their dad. I like that, I like it a lot.

It's 10 p.m. as I write this. 6 just finished watching a movie while I read in my bedroom. We'll play a round of canasta before I go to bed. Life's good even if it does come with tragedies now and then. Dad/ Michael

6: (to list) It brings a tear to my eye to hear that 3 asked Dad if the money he spent on her lessons was worth it! Oh how lovely a moment it must have been for dad and 3. Dad just schooled me in canasta. He literally was trying to teach me.... but luck was on his side. I'm so lucky to be here making memories with my loving poppa bear. Thank you 5, 3 and Dad for making this happen. Especially 5. Magic street. My heart goes out to 2 and families. I love you all and wish I had a magic wand to make all things better. Please send my love to Mom. See you all soon.

Publisher: I will give you an option now. When I checked your manuscript I found out that other paragraphs were not indented. We can try plotting your correction like going through each paragraph and it would take us like a month to do it because it's quiet lengthy. I have another suggestion for you, if you will allow us to just indent all the paragraph then it would only take us 2-3 days. I need your response today so we can start the work.

M: Unless I misunderstand what you are saying, I don't think you understand the problem. The books are defective because someone at your end DID indent all the paragraphs (except the first one after a chapter) instead of leaving my author indentations as they are in the manuscripts I submitted to you.

The books consist of emails exchanged between the author and others and in between some of those emails are comments from the author/narrator. Without a line space between the end of an email and the beginning of a comment by "Michael" the author, the only way for a reader to discern when an email ends and narration begins is that in my manuscripts the narrator comments are NOT indented (while emails are.) So it's very important that my manuscripts be published the way the manuscripts were submitted. (With the exception that in my manuscripts I insert a hard break after each paragraph and that appears as a line space in the manuscript. It is acceptable that those spaces between paragraphs are removed or the books would be excessively long.) The solution from my point of view appears to be to publish my manuscripts exactly the way I submitted them except that hard breaks after paragraphs (line spaces) should be removed.

Will that work for you? Please ask questions if I did not make this clear, thanks. Enjoy the day.

M: (to myself) Yesterday I received my first three books in soft cover. However, they are the defective books (see above) so when I started reading Book 1 last night I soon put it down hoping that they'll make the corrections and send me corrected books.

A new thing has arisen though. As I opened pages in Book 1 I realized how massive a book it is at 800 pages. And how personal! I have little confidence today that it will be interesting enough to sell successfully. I think the entire exercise, the last 16 months, was most likely just for me. I don't know if even Suzanne and other major characters will read the series. *And with that I lost interest! I may not read the books myself...*

Jen has sent so few messages the last few days and with such brief and insignificant content that I am not even thinking much of her. Is she actively searching for another man? Will she too vanish from my life? I continue to favor the thought of not fighting this cancer, of just relaxing into whatever comes without trying to intervene. My great hope of course is for immortality, to actually *become* Adam with several beautiful sister wives and eventually to populate new planets with the race of man. My whole being yearns for those Eves to be with me. There is nothing I want greater regardless of whatever state of awareness I am in.

Yes of course, I no sooner write that than a message comes in from Jen.

Jen: I went to the dentist yesterday for my broken tooth. He is sending me to a dental surgeon today to have a root canal done. He said that particular tooth roots splits and goes up into the sinus. Anyway it is going to be a process. After it heals a bit I will go back to my dentist to have a crown built. Getting close to having my taxes ready for the accountant. Do you have any questions for me to ask him.

It sounds like you are having a grand time. I am so glade you are. Again with your girls alone. It probably has been years since you had 3 on your own. I wish I was there to hear her play that baby grand piano. My heart still hurts for the parents of 2's grandchild. Is the picture of her on the internet her and her mother. Love you.

M: Ouch, I feel for you re the tooth, not fun. I think re the accountant that you need to consider the possibility that you may inherit the business and the land. Then ask him whatever questions that brings to your mind as if you had already inherited the business within the current tax year.

I am completely aware that you need to look after your own best interests especially with me now having a shelf life. But I'm very curious to know if you are meeting with or in communication with any other man or men other than family and business? Will you be meeting anyone in Phoenix or elsewhere in the near future? You needn't answer that it's your business, but my active imagination won't leave that one rest for long so if you are willing to share openly and honestly that would be nice. It's difficult for me when we're so far apart and you seldom tell me anything about your personal life, I miss that. I do love you and hope we can yet have many good days together but I can also see things from your point of view, I think you will want to marry after I'm gone. Perhaps looking around right now is too early for you but I'm wanting to share your life and happenings and to rejoice when good prospects come into it. You will always be important to me.

2: (to siblings list) By way of further update my son and his wife have asked that the funeral be upbeat rather than somber and as such have asked that we not wear black but bright colours instead.

M: I understand their sentiments exactly, nobody wants to be the cause of grief or sorrow in another. Death from the point of view of the deceased is a graduation to be *celebrated* not something to be mourned. Death is a natural part of living. Think of the joy that comes when we step through the veil of forgetting into the arms of loved ones waiting to show us the loveliness that is our inheritance as children of God. Turn and go with them when you arrive, they have much to show you that is glorious and beautiful, I may be among them by then.

If I had a choice to live or die I would think of those here in mortality who quite naturally want to keep me for themselves and future shared experiences. But I would also think of those bright ones who want me with *them* even more. And I think I would go to them, I already feel them near. I know you will eventually come to us too when it is your time. In those moments *it will be party time in heaven!!*

I'll paraphrase some of the last words I said to my mother as she lay on the bed she would die in a few days later. *"Mom you have done well. It's ok to go now. There are many in heaven who are waiting for you."*

Please consider doing brightness and celebration when it comes time for me to go where so many others have gone before. They beckon now, they are calling me to heaven. I never did meet the little one in this lifetime so when I saw her in my mind yesterday she was already grown up. She is well dear ones, she is well. *Rejoice* for her and for yourselves that you got to know her. She did not die a moment sooner than she had planned when she came here. Think only of the lovely memories how enriched you are because of her, and let your tears be tears not of sorrow but the waters of rejoicing for a life complete, a life well done. I love you all, I'm so proud of you. Dad

1+: Thank you for that Dad. Your words have touched my soul and brought me peace.

Oresha: So nice to hear that your Doting Daughters are spending time with Dear Dad! :) Please keep me posted.... it will be great to spend some time with you when you're available ...:) Much Love & Healing Thoughts...

Jen: First. Of course I have not been in communication with any other man. I do not desire to be with any one else than you. Please don't let your mind go there. I am secure in my relationship with you for as long as you want me. If we are together or apart I will not be looking for another man. Second. I will ask the accountant about the business. Third. I think when you can fly you should come down and we could do a power of attorney and or make and notarize deeds for all current customers.

I just got back from the Endodontic. As soon as I got out to my car I called my dentist and told them the root canal is done. I made the earliest appointment for Monday with him. Accountant appointment on Tuse. then leave for Phonex the 25 to pick up the Van. I don't remember when your appointments are so I don't know if this is possible. If you could fly down we could travel from there or I could pick you in Las Vegas. We could take care of business before we start our travels. I sent you a picture of the flowers. Look you can see the steam sprouting small leaves. Love you Sweetie

M: Thank-you for reassuring me. The problem is that when someone I care about goes virtually silent or writes only occasional brief messages that say nothing personal I think because of past experiences that there is a problem with or a non-existent relationship or they are keeping secrets and hiding something/someone from me. That's the way you have been the last couple of weeks or so and I got anxious and insecure regarding you. My kids are hoping we will get together.

Technically my six weeks from the last time my chest was opened (when they took out the tube) is the end of this week. However as you know, it leaked even after I was at home so there was possibly air getting in and I don't want to take a chance flying right away, including to the funeral on Saturday this week.

Although I haven't yet heard back about the x-ray I'm pretty sure my lungs are doing ok, though the last two days I've been coughing and feeling some of the old symptoms again. It's possible for me to meet you in Phoenix on the 25th if you already have a ticket and we could go west from there. But I'm thinking that is pushing it and maybe I should wait until I see the doctor to see if it's prudent to consider such a long drive?? Maybe it's best that you come here until after that appointment then if I can we both fly to Vegas and go from there with a stop in Phoenix. What do you think? I love you.

Jen: What did you and 6 do today. She leaves tomorrow night I though you said. Gives you one more day of fun with her. Have you heard any more from old friends. Been out shopping buying little things to fix around the house. My washer and dryer are about shot. Been cleaning and planting in the back yard. Had to buy more ink for the printer to finish taxes. Cleaning Closets. Bought some water softener salt. Talked to a real estate management company about renting the house. Might list it online and see what type of responses I get. They told me I won't get more rent with it being furnished. So I don't know what to do. This is a few of the things I have been doing.

Love you and miss you sweetie, It is nice not putting so much pressure on each other. That makes it easer for me to get things done. I have much to do before flying to Phoenix and picking up the SUV. I picked up a cashiers check today to pay for the truck. I will know more on Monday on how long it will be before I get a crown put on my tooth. I still need to touch up paint in Basement. Make covers for the pillows on the swing out side. This is way down on my to do list.

M: So what you're saying is that you really don't have anything to do? :-) It's nice to get a longer message from you, I am interested in what you are doing and how your days go. It was a rainy day and 6 is quite content to stay in the house so all we did during the day is drive to the breakwater and walk a few yards. When the wind destroyed my umbrella we turned around and went home, the umbrella going in the trash along the way.

Last night we went to a poetry "slam" where 6 read one of her poems. The contestants were judged and she didn't get high marks. I thought her presentation was really good but it was hard to relate to the content of her poem. From my point of view there was only one poet among the twelve. We came home at half time.

I get the occasional email from friends but not many. I may walk with Oresha a time or two when 6 is gone, she keeps in touch though I haven't seen her for many weeks.

I've been drinking teas etc. that friends have recommended as cancer cures and I'm feeling pretty much normal - as long as I keep taking that particular brand of pain pill that is, that's the miracle drug for me at this point in time. Enjoy the day, I'm looking forward to being with you. I love you.

Jen: Earlier I went today when I opened the back door once again it was warmer out side then in. I stood on the back patio concrete and warmed my feet. It felt so good. The flowers are blooming and three of the fruit trees are in beautiful blooms. It is so refreshing to go outside and feel the perfect temperature. So of course gardening called me to work for about an hour. I don't like it when it is cold. It is suppose to cool down a bit this weekend. Love you

M: Wish I was there with you. When I look over photos of family events some I never even heard of I sure wish I was closer to my family. If I am granted enough good days I will try to visit them more often, I've been too long a loner. I hope you'll be at my side but I understand your need for "no pressure". I love you lots.

M: (to myself) I dropped my daughter off at the airport a few hours ago and in the inevitable post-visit loneliness called Jen thinking to have a pleasant conversation with her. But she had been reading some of our older emails and the conversation quickly got into a rehash of things like how I betrayed her by "falling in love" with other women after she filed for divorce. Anyway, I do need to back away and just accept whatever comes. It was still my hope before that phone call that she would come and live with me whether or not we formally marry. I visualized us traveling together for weeks maybe even months. But she is very far from wanting that. Tonight she said she would not visit my kids with me because she thinks they being Mormon will criticize us for not being married. She said she does not want to marry but a few minutes later talked about us getting secretly married in California. To me what is important is us living together full-time and that has not changed, her attitude remains the same as it was when I visited her last year and attempted to reconcile. She says she loves me and is not looking for another man but seems content with only visits now and then I suppose to "care" for me a dying man. And of course I got several lectures about not being an active Mormon.

How can this be Eve the woman with the exact same dream as mine? How can this be a perfect love gone right? Oh well, let's see what comes, I am accepting of anything except pain. I think it best that I die if I am not to be made immortal because now that I am dying and unavailable to other women, only in one of those two states do I stand a chance of gathering my fantasy family of equal spouses and having children. That is my dream, that is my great desire, that would be my greatest happiness.

Jen: I am sorry if I was not up beat on the phone. It really really meant so much to me that you called. That shows me you care. I am so sorry I was talking about your past. I guess if something like old emails bring sad and hurt feelings out in a person they should be deleted. *Its not the past I should think today. It is today I should think about. If I make today the best I can Then tomorrow will be the best yet. The best yet will always follow. When I made it the best today!* If I only knew how to write poetry. This would be my lesson for today.

How can I help you to be the best man you can be? Do you want to move toward the Mormon belief in God and what is promised to those that are sealed. Is it the hope of one or many women you search for in the next life that appeals to you most. What apples to me most is me and my husband and our children together in the next life. I don't think I could stand not having a man to love me most. Maybe that is a selfish thought but don't you want a woman to love you the most. I want total dedication toward each other until it is time to move forward and bring in other elements. Could you see us this way for a time in Heaven. If so please do your part and I will do my part to make it happen. I love you the most! We don't have much time left in this life so let think more about helping each other be the best we can. What would that be for you my love?

I am drying the roses you sent me. I want to keep them always near to look at. I guess I really do like flowers from my man. We may not always be together as much as we would like, we should be thankful for the time we can cherish. You give me propose to move forward. I love being with you. My heart cries out for us. Knowing my stumbling block took forward place today as we talk. I hope it does not keep you from calling me again. Yum, Yum kisses to you, Love you Sweetie

M: Please do not try to change me to "become the best man I can be". That's my job. Just work on changing *yourself* if you are not content where you are at present. I do not think in black and white, there is color in my points of view. It is contrary to Mormon teachings to think that the LDS Church is the possessor of all truth, it is not. I find truth in Mormon doctrine and I find truth elsewhere as well. Jesus summed up all the laws in one word "Love". There is much love among the Latter-day Saints, and there is much love everywhere else as well. There are many paths to get to the top of the same mountain peak. That vaunted "iron rod" beheld in a dream by a man writing in The Book of Mormon could represent *love* as much as specific doctrines popular (or unpopular) in his day. That dream was dreamt 600 years before the coming of Christ who fulfilled the law and the commandments and replaced them with the principle of love. Contrary to popular contemporary Sunday School teachings, those who strayed in the dream may be those who cease to *love* rather than those who cease to be members of a 2600 year old church.

There are many passages in the New Testament testifying that God is love and those who dwell in love dwell in God and God in them. Who are you to so harshly judge and put down your former husband and his friends and others who believe differently than you do but whose hearts may be filled with love as much or more than yours is? There is much arrogance in religions that teach God is only accessible and the highest heaven reached only by strictly obeying the dictates of that particular church or institution. There is great safety in loving all, God dwells in those who do. God does not command that His children love one or other of His children "the most". He commands simply that we love one another and cease to judge and criticize, for a bitter fountain cannot bring forth good water.

Then there is the 'romantic' kind of love or 'in love' as females speak of it, the concept of monogamy that most women desire, that their man be exclusive to themselves and none other, that he love them "the most" and bestow sexual favors on them alone. In some ways perhaps women are 'hard wired' to that desire. It helps them nest and raise children and have status amongst themselves. And perhaps men are 'hard wired' to plant their seed in any woman they find sexually attractive who will receive that seed whether or not the man is "in love" as women understand those words. Perhaps, as the title of a popular book reads, "*Men are from Mars, Women are from Venus.*" Why should a woman try to make a man female or a man try to make a woman male? Why not just delight in being who we are and rejoice that we are different, that God made male *and* female and gave each powerful sexual desires so the species would continue?

But yes for sure, I understand the tender feelings that can come with intimacy and romantic love. I understand the powerful feelings that come with courting and 'honeymoons' when everyone is at their best behavior and appearance. I understand loyalty. And I understand staleness and boredom too. I am seeking "a perfect love gone right". Whether it can be found in this world or not I do not know. It would have to be an unconditional fully accepting kind of love, a love that does not judge, or at least a love that forgives instantly should something distasteful be perceived and judged as so.

You write: "*I want total dedication toward each other until it is time to move forward and bring in other elements. Could you see us this way for a time in Heaven. If so please do your part and I will do my part to make it happen. I love you the most!*"

I treasure the love you express for me, I value it highly. But I am daily confronted with the question of how sincere that love is when you refuse to live with me or even to visit my family with me. It seems logical that a woman who loves one man "the most" would want to be with him more than with anyone else, that nobody and no thing would be important enough to keep them apart. In truth you have not changed, we are living apart when for many months I have held my door open for you, invited you in, and you have not come other than for visits, knowing that you would soon leave. You continue to say one thing and do another. That's a reality I have to deal with. It leaves me lonely, confused, unfulfilled as if you are just playing a game with me, a game that invariably results in you blaming me for your discontent and your frequent pity parties, saying that I "betrayed" you by "falling in love" with other women after you filed to divorce me. Is it your desire to have a heart that has been "broken" by a man? Is that what you are seeking instead of dwelling on love and joy and going forward?

I have told you many times that if we live together I will be sexually faithful to you. What more could you ask of a husband you love? Why do you feel a need to control his thoughts and fantasies as well?

I have told you many times that my fantasy, my dream, my great desire (unless after I die I find that there is something even more desirable) is to be the sole male in a family of equal spouses who love and get along with each other perfectly and whose task it is to populate new planets with the race of man.

I was always spiritual. As a child growing up in a Catholic family I was expected and was asked to become a priest. I would have done so willingly but I had a deep inner knowing that my greater desire was to marry and have children, and Catholic priests were forbidden that. Now as I live out the days of my dying there is within me a great desire to marry several wives and be the loving father of their children. (However that works out in the heavens. There are some who will say there is no marrying in heaven. Those same cannot say where Adams and Eves come from to populate new planets.) I will not change my dream, it is my greatest desire, I am becoming Adam.

Whether or not you can fit yourself into my fantasy I continue to hope that we can live together peaceably and love each other until one of us dies. It's all up to *you* as it has been for many months. My door remains open to you, I invite you to live with me, to walk the walk as well as talk the talk. Can you do that? Do you want to? *Will* you?

I was up at 3:30 a.m. writing the above then went to bed. Sometime between then and now I felt a strong connection with everyone and everything and a great love and acceptance for all. I think that is how God loves. I don't think He requires that His children not drink coffee or tea and that they pay money to a church to buy their way into heaven. If He does, then I believe that I have already in my 50 years of doing so paid the admission fee many times over.

I understand your beliefs, I have felt the peak experiences that sometimes come with being Mormon or not and I am ok with that. Believe as you will, go to church as you will, just please if you truly want me, don't make your love conditional on changing me into the image and likeness of your present beliefs and ideals. Be content with me as I am, or stop dragging out this divorce that you once wanted and move on if you must to a man who pleases you more, and live with *him*. Or, come and "care" for a dying man until he is gone and then get on with the business of living your life the way *you* want to live it. I believe that you can but keep in mind that at your age your active Mormon man is going to already be 'sealed' to at least one other who in the Mormon way will be 'First Wife' in heaven. Can you handle the thought of that? Or would you sooner take a chance on me?

I love you Jen, God bless you. I wish for you love and peace and a sure knowing of which way to go with your life. You have many choices. If you are not content with what I have and am then new doors will open for you as you once and for all walk away from me and search for a brighter painted door. Should you decide to come and live with me, I think I will love you sufficient for your needs and we can work out the rest with time and the intent to live together peaceably. *What is it that you want?*

Jen: (sent before she received the above) You know Sweetie, I hope we do spend more time together. Hope you and possibly me can visit your family more often. We will see. I just want the Church in our life. I need the sweet spirit I feel when I listen and hear words of really good spiritual men. All I ask is for you to personally repent. Between you and God. Please understand I need to do the same. Then we live the gospel of Jesus Christ to the fullest we can. Miracles will happen. I know we will be together for ever. I feel once you go I will follow soon. I two look forward to a new chapter.

M: (to Jen) 6 made a huge apple crisp just before she left so that's pretty much all I've been eating, with cheese melted on top. Not bad but she put too much oats on the top. She said that was to make it not taste too sweet. And speaking of sweet, 5 with probably the other two helping made an absolutely delicious cherry cheese cake, the best I've tasted. Unfortunately I got only one piece of it (big though) as the four of us played canasta. It was perfect in terms of sweetness to my taste, highly unusual. I have the recipe if you want it. I just had a glance in my freezer and there's even a frozen carrot cake in there, and a huge bag of chocolate peanut butter balls. I love my kids! I'm missing you sweetheart. I hope you come as soon as you can, and stay long content. Your M

M: (to 5) Tell me about today when you have time. Maybe a report to the long list when tomorrow's done? I discovered the carrot cake etc. in my freezer, thanks so much, I love my kids!

Jen: Hi sweet heart, I just got home. I have been helping my daughter decorate for a party. She hired a band and there was a pot luck dinner. I meet some nice people. She works with them on committee's. I quickly read your email and will reread when not so tired. I did not go to bed until 4:00 this morning and didn't get more than a couple hours so I am very tired. I was working on finalizing and rechecking accounting. I should know after my dental appointment what time frame they need to do my teeth. Then I can book a flight to come see you. Love

M: (to myself) Nice, but *"come see you"* is far from come *live* with you! Maybe it's best that way, she does not have the same dream as I do and wants mine to be the Mormon dream except with her exclusive even in the heavens. If that's what she really wants I wish it upon her, but it might have to be with another man. I'm secretly hoping that she is tending to her overweight problem while we are apart and will surprise me with a visible weight loss when next I see her. I'd really delight in that, it's very important to me. (Yes ladies, Michael gives the appearance of shallowness. But then you haven't walked in his footsteps the last several decades. I continue to think that spouses should take care of their bodies so they remain physically attractive to each other.)

Oresha: Evening Michael :) Here's something you might like to read about... It's amazing how Mother nature has her "medicine" hiding in "plain sight" sometimes... :) I hope you're having a good weekend

& getting out to enjoy some of this incredible Victoria weather... :)
Cheers..

M: I'll check around for the tea you mention to add to others that
I'm trying after getting tips from friends, thanks Oresha. I may never get
to die with all these caring friends I have. :-) You are welcome to come
over tomorrow or Monday if you want to. Maybe we'll walk to the Bay
Mall and get a kale smoothie on me?

Oresha: YES...You are SO Loved! :) Everyone near & dear to you
wants you to be around for @ least another 20-30 years!... ;) I have
a "meet-me" date tomorrow.. I'm picking him up @ the ferry from
Vancouver.. lol So we'll see how that goes... lol Monday might be a
plan... thanx for the offer... Let's connect tomorrow and decide... if you
don't hear from me by tomorrow night please email me & remind me :)
It would be wonderful to spend some time together and perhaps walk a
bit :) Cheers... ttys..... night. :)

M: (to Jen) Not that it matters, I had nowhere to go anyway, but I
lost the entire morning today. I was up for a short while to check emails
(nothing) then went back to bed for a nap and it was 11:45 when I woke
up! I'm feeling groggy and hoping that kind of thing does not become a
habit, it's disorienting.

My toilet stopped flushing yesterday, the chain that lifts the flapper
valve broke. So rather than staying dressed maybe for several days while
I waited for a knock from a repairman I drove to a hardware store and
got a new chain and valve. It was disconcerting to realize when I got
there that there were so many different shapes and sizes. But I bought a
"universal" fit and managed to install it. The toilet flushes now without
my having to plunge my hand into the cold water but I have to hold the
handle down until it flushes. Maybe you can figure out how to fix that
when you get here, I was never good at mechanical things.

I might make it a sluff day and not even get showered or dressed
today though I might have to go for a walk to clear this groggy head.
I researched a bit and found that the park with the giant trees near
Visalia, California is open year 'round. It's just that the road elevations
are as high as 14,000 feet so some of the park is only in the summer. My
guess is that we could see the tree you drive through earlier in the year

though. I'd like to stay nearby and explore the park for several days if we can manage that.

I hope you can hold off giving the SUV to your daughter until we complete our trip, maybe after the family reunion?? I sure hope you'll be there with me but I'll understand if it's not something you want to do. It's still very strange for me not to be with you. I continue to think of us as if we are married, I don't completely understand why we are not. None of your excuses seem valid to me so I always conclude that there's something you are not telling me that keeps us apart. But no pressure, I will cherish the moments you allow us to be physically together. Enjoy today.

Jen: I am also having a slow day. I slept in and missed 9:00 am church. My chest has been hurting today so I am resting. I have a big day tomorrow. I was told the SUV only gets about 12 miles a gallant of gasoline. We will be staying in hotels anyway so maybe we should drive your car. I think it is in better shape then mine but I am willing to drive it. After the doctor appointment we could leave in this direction. Just a thought..

M: It would sure be a lot less expensive to use my car for the trip because we'll be doing a lot of miles. That could work if we plan on driving no more than say 200 miles a day?? (I'll feel like going further but do need to rest often lying down.) And you could give your daughter the SUV right away, it would take the time pressure off you.

If my doc clears me for two months or so on the road we could leave soon after and head south. We could ferry from here to Port Angeles then catch the I-5 or ocean highway and take our time. North of San Francisco we could go to Visalia, California and see the big trees then back to I-5 and south to visit your family. San Diego, Yuma, Phoenix, Laughlin, Vegas, and stay as long as you need in Utah if my health permits. (If not, I could fly back to Victoria from anywhere and get the car later.) Then Great Falls, visit my kids in Alberta, through the Rockies back to Victoria and plan it from there, maybe tour Vancouver Island like I wanted to do last summer? You could schedule a visit with your kids then hopefully be back for the family reunion?? For economy we could stay in the same hotel chain when possible so we earn free nights.

Anyway, just some thoughts but I honestly don't know how committed you are to being with me for that long a period of time. I wouldn't want to drive myself from Utah to Alberta and back to Victoria so I'm hoping you'll hang with me and that we'll get along well, and that my health permits. What do you think?

I recommend my favorite pain killers for the hurting chest. Why the "big day" tomorrow? Will you be delivering the vehicle to your daughter in Salt Lake City and fly here from there? But whatever, please come as soon as you can and we'll work out the details, thanks.

Jen: That sounds like a good plan. After tomorrow I can plan how soon I can come to Victoria. Love you.

M: I love you too sweetheart, can't wait for you to be here. I'm committed to you if you'll have me. (And we can get along well. :-)

Oresha: Meet-me-date lasted from 10:30 this morning til tonight when I dropped him off @ the ferry @ 8:30PM!... lol Nice guy... very spiritual/intelligent...a real thinker.. perhaps a bit "intense"...lol One day @ a time... we'll see...lol I've learned not to "put all my eggs in one basket"!...;) As for Monday (tomorrow)...are you up for a visit in the afternoon? Kathy might be able to come along ... she's been wondering how you're doing :) She's been working really hard and could probably use a break... & would love to see you. Please just drop me a line when you can and we'll go from there :) Hugz..

M: Tell me what time tomorrow. Kathy is welcome to come too of course. I have three of your fav beers in the fridge but no lime so byol if you need it. I'm glad you are keeping 'busy' with the guys, intense or not. :-)

Oresha: Thanx... I'll chat with Kathy when I can get a hold of her tomorrow & get back to you asap. :) As soon as I hear from her I'll write and run a time by you :) I'm guessing maybe mid-to later in the afternoon... Sweet Dreams...ttyl... :) & I will BYOL.

Oresha: I just spoke with Kathy and she thinks she'll be back home just after 2:00... so if we walk over to your place it would be around 2:30-ish.... maybe... lol Does that work for you? Cheers... looking forward to catchin up with you :) Hugz..

M: I'll be home.

M: (to Jen) I'm looking forward to our road trip and trying to get some extra cash to pay my part. How do you like the changes I made today to my business website? Comments and suggestions are welcome.

A few of my kids are saying they're interested in inheriting some of my Arkansas land. I'll let them know the reality of property taxes and difficult sales etc. There's no point in giving it to them if it just goes to the government for failure to pay taxes. In any event, I'll make sure that you get first pick of the properties remaining at my death, I'm sure you would not let them go to waste.

Jen: Your website looks great. I just got back from dentist and my next earliest appointment is several weeks later. They said it would take that long to get the new tooth made and back. I will book a ticket for the 10th or 11th. This tooth is going to cost about $1800 I think. We have snow on the grown. Not really cold. But sure was a surprise this morning. Hope it does not last long. Is it cold in Victoria. It seem to be cold everywhere. Phoenix was 50 degrees. Love you.

M: I was hoping you could come sooner but you are doing your best I'm sure. You'll be here for my ct scan and doctor appointment, you may as well come with me. I still haven't heard about the x-ray so that should be good news. That's an expensive tooth, hope I don't have any. It's 46 degrees today and sunny, a nice day actually, almost as good as Phoenix. Energy remains good as long as I take Ibuprofen every day. What a miracle that is, though it's possible that there are other brands that would work just as well. I love you too sweetheart.

M: (to myself) A message came in from Elaine and I was only half way through reading it when Oresha and Kathy buzzed to be let in. Then during their visit, my phone rang twice. I didn't answer it but knew it was Jen calling. Life continues...

Elaine: Hi Michael, I've been thinking about you and wondering how you are doing... are you feeling OK?.... I imagine the warmer, Spring like days are making you healthier.... they are more healing.

I couldn't quite wrap my head around the picture you offered for me to paint with your faces... not that I'm any good at faces really, but

I can sometimes do a reasonable likeness. I just couldn't find the right scene in my head... and that's where all the planning begins. But I am really "gung ho" if Jen would want to take some lessons... I am good at that and Jen would love what she alone produced. I have all the brushes. Pigments go a long way, Opus is right downtown, and some good art paper is there and available. Just thought I'd offer that, because, work has settled down a bit, I've stood my ground as per shifts I can do, and have proven myself diligent and worthy as an employee. It's a bit like playing poker (with the joker). And nobody wants to do on call work after they've worked the day, so I have an advantage.

I still remain freinds with one of the ladies I started with, it seems like a happy union and I have so few girlfreinds. She got another job, as she is super stacked with credentials, so she is working elsewhere now. The third person who started has kind of dropped by the wayside and I don't see her much. I phone, but she will probably move from Victoria, feeling stuck and undervalued.

And so, let me know how you are.... I do hope that things are stable and you are out and about. Is your family still coming up for visits and company? Best regards and loving kindness,

M: Please take the pressure off yourself re the art, I'm fine with you not feeling up to it.

Two of my friends visited for a while today, they just left. And my three daughters visited for ten days, the last one leaving on Saturday. I'm about worn out right now with opera, oratorio, high tea and carousel etc. all on them, a treat for dad, it was fun. I'm now on my own until Jen comes. She'll be with me at least until my next oncologist appointment and we may take a road trip from here with my car soon after that. If that happens I'll most likely be gone for six or so weeks. The way I see it, if I need medical care along the way I can always fly back from wherever I happen to be.

I'm glad you still have one of the two new friends you told me about and that you have your shifts under control.

Although I'm not at all into S&M I did read the "Fifty Shades of Grey" books and thought they were quite well done. I noticed that the movie of that name is currently playing in Victoria and am planning to go. Would you be interested in going to the movies with me or coming over for chat and white tea perhaps? If so, name the day and time, I'm very flexible.

Jen sends her flight itinerary. I'm getting excited about being with her and giving us another go. This time I think we are both committed to a lifetime together. I hope!

M: (to Jen) Great price on the flight. Thanks for letting me know, it will be very nice to see you.

Jen: I have been cleaning and emptying out drawers this evening. Including your office. I came a cross the paper sent to us to be sealed in the temple. These are some of the qualities and characteristics you were looking for.

You must of filled this out for a LDS single sight before we meet. You said, "I believe that I have a lot to offer a choice LDS lady who has her eye on eternity. I would like my companion and I to list our individual goals/desires/dreams/talents, then work out plans to fulfill and realize everything we possibly can as individuals and as a couple – each helping the other to get the most out of life, to have joy, and to earn our exaltation together. Physical appearance is important to me but I'm not looking for perfection. Here are some of the ideal qualities and characteristics that I'd appreciate in a companion:

She's warm, loving, thoughtful, romantic frequently shows affection for me physically and verbally, intelligent, spiritual, knowledgeable, dedicated to the Church and Gospel, shares common interests, likes to cuddle, hold hands, touch and be touched often, can be passionate, physically active, likes to travel, wants to serve missions; allows me to write and to use my talents, preferably has independent means or is willing to work together to generate an income. Physically she's attractive, tall, slim to average, looks good in jeans. I want us to be best friends as well as spouses. I am very open and sharing and want to spend a lot of time with my companion. I'm easy going, few things make me want to have my own way, I give a lot but don't want to be taken advantage of. My ideal companion would sooner be with me than with anyone else in the world - home is where we are together!

Do you still want much of what you wanted almost 20 years ago. Love you sweetie.

M: Much of that is still important to me but obviously not all of it. (e.g. go on a mission etc.) I continue to believe that "home is where we are TOGETHER."

Elaine: Hi there again Tea and a visit sounds good. I'm out of the boots now so this means I won't be trundelling around in army gear any more! How about next Monday or Tuesday early afternoon...? I'm going to pass on the movie as it got such bad reviews, but thanks anyway!

(She's putting a visit off for a whole week so it's obvious that Elaine is not interested in being with me. If she was, it shouldn't matter what movie or event we go to, and it would be sooner than a week away. I'm ok with that, but it sure is nice to touch her and be touched by her. Had Jen been with me all these months there would have been nobody else. *And perhaps no books!*)

M: (to Elaine) I haven't read the reviews so maybe I'll pass on that movie too. I kinda liked your boots but hey, the short skirt was great, sexy you. :-)

Once again I want to be sure that if you visit it is because you really want to and not out of any feeling of obligation. We can continue to just swap occasional emails if that would work better for you, I do have excellent family and friend support so I'm not needy. Whether or not you visit, when she is here I will ask Jen if she'd like to take art lessons from you. I just wanted to make that clear. Enjoy the day Elaine.

Jen: I just found out one of my rentals has a sewage back up. Not good news. Had to contact my insurance. They sure are going to cancel me and I wonder with all my claims if someone else will insure me. Miss you

M: Expect the best. *Sometimes* it happens that way. :-)

Jen: I am leaving tomorrow won't have my computer. Will come back Sunday or Monday. My youngest is taking the shuttle down from

Salt Lake to pick up the suburban and spend a couple days packing food to take back with her.

M: I'll miss you even more with no communication at all, take care sweetheart.

Jen: It is warming up today. I am so glade. I don't function well when cold.

M: We're so alike, it's uncanny. :-)

Jen: The other day you made it sound like you are not as interested in your books as you were a month ago. Why? What is going to happen? I liked much of what you wrote. Don't think my input was good. But you are a magnificent writer.

M: I'm not interested in reading the books after having written and written and written and rewritten the manuscripts. And after the failure of the first e-books (since hugely revised) I am lacking in confidence that they will be commercially successful. I just don't have the funds to promote them above the other 8,000 new books a day that are published worldwide. It's an unfamiliar format and subject, it may not be popular. And even though it's fiction it's all intensely personal, maybe best published after I am dead?

But by the time you get here I will have the first three books in soft cover available for you to hold in your hands and read. Book 1 alone is 805 pages, very thick and heavy. If I had had the time I would have cut much more but it's done now and I'm glad of that. Your input was perfect, exactly what I needed after Suzanne went silent, you were really good.

Enjoy your trip. Take your laptop if you can, it's tiny and light if you don't take anything else except the plug, it will easily slip into a carry on. I think you'll really miss it if you don't take it with you. Or are you needing a break from me?

Elaine: Of course I want to visit.... we have such nice talks... I rarely do things out of obligation these days... only driving teenager and barn chores. Smiles

M: Just me over-analyzing as usual. Walked to the movies this afternoon and watched 50 Shades. You were right, not worth going to. But the Big Mac on the way home was worth it. :-)

Jen: I leave soon to catch the shuttle to Las Vegas. I love you and will miss you. I going to put the trash out in the street to be picked up. Love you sweetie

M: (to Jen) Thanks for writing, that helps. I wrote the following in my journal earlier this a.m. before receiving your two emails.

"I awoke this morning with a vague uneasiness about Jen's lack of communication last night when she is planning to be away with no computer for six days, has probably already left. She didn't even respond to my question asking if she needed a break from me and that is why she isn't taking her laptop with her, it would be so easy to do. The biggest part of me remains committed to her but there's also a part that remains uneasy about her, she could be leading me along, she once confessed to doing that. But then, she has a flight booked to come see me two weeks from now. I ask myself: *"So why should today be any different?""*

Relationships from a distance like ours has been are fraught with frustration and breed distrust. Much as you can't seem to accept it, your refusal to live with me and to live peaceably when you visit is the cause of the often recurring distrust we have for each other. None of the female friends I have would have manifested had we been physically together. But then, there would be no books either...

M: (to Jen) Thanks for your long second message this morning titled *"What caused the roll of distrust? What good can be regained from it or can it?"* It reveals where you are. I am undecided to respond or not but may do so. You'll probably get it a week from now since you don't want to slip that little laptop into your carry on and put the plug in your checked bag. That's hard for me to understand because it denies us communication. With the distrust we are both feeling this morning it makes me wonder if that's what you want, to get away from me entirely? I love you, I'm waiting for you to come back to me.

(I've decided to respond between the lines of Jen's lengthy message. She reads my mind from a distance every bit as well as Suzanne did. Must be a woman thing. :-)

M: Thank-you for sending your long message this morning. With my response it may get messy but now we're communicating, me learning from *you* where you are about certain things, and you learning from *me* where I am about those same things rather than either of us imagining we know the other better than the other knows him/herself so that our own viewpoint must be right even though the other denies it. That's the way it must be if we are to arrive at truth and understanding even though our points of view will seldom be the same. After all we are male and female, one from 'Mars' one from 'Venus'.

Here we go then, honest communication. We need to each deal with the emotions, it is not my intent to hurt you, just to help us both understand each other better and to face up to our own personal issues that have yet to be resolved. As usual, I will be open and honest while revealing where I am with issues that impact our relationship. I do not intend to hurt you sweetheart, I do want us to live together peaceably, I do love you.

Jen: If you don't want to read this it is ok. I know you sometimes write things that are hard for me to read. Just know I love you and will be seeing you in a couple of weeks. Will you be faithful till then. I think so! This was my thoughts as I laded in bed this morning. What causes a couple to loss trust in each other and can it be ever fully regained?

M: At what point in time after you divorced me did we become "a couple"? Divorce and subsequent property settlement does tend to cause intense distrust, especially the secret hostile way you went about it! I think we can regain our trust in each other if we live together long enough. But it's true neither of us fully trusts the other, especially when we're not together physically. You think I will have sex with another woman when we're not together and I think you might become so interested in another man or use whatever excuse you can come up with so that you won't ever live with me again. Those are both realistic fears, either or both of us can simply *choose* to make it so.

Jen: In general or with us as a couple. Is it still your belief that if a couple are not together it is ok to have another relationship or sex with someone else. As you told me in the past "if I was not with you then you were free to have other relationships and you only promise to be faithful is if I am with you full time." Is this still your belief.

M: Again there is the matter of your assumption that we are "a couple" when we are not married or living together and when you dissolved our engagement to be married by refusing to marry me. (I did not have sex with anyone except you when I thought we were engaged to be married. Still haven't.) The fact remains that we are both single and as such have the right to make friends with whoever we want to and to do with our bodies whatever we want to do with them. But to comfort you, know that it is highly unlikely that I will choose to have sex with another woman. If we were married or living together permanently then of course I would be sexually faithful to you, I have never cheated on my wife.

Jen: The following are the reasons you or some other men may justify their actions.

1. Being lonely is more powerful than being faithful.
2. Since your girlfriend is out of town may-as-well check the scene out for something better or more exciting.
3. It is a man's nature to cheat when the woman is gone.
4. Are most men like you and blame the woman for not being around to take care of a mans needs. he uses this as an excuse.

Chapter 10

———⟨❧⟩———

M: You seem deathly frightened that the man you are most interested in might have sex with another woman. You want his body exclusively for yourself, it is an overwhelming *obsession* for you. Your 'love' for him is entirely conditional upon him not having sex with another woman. My love for you is not that way, I have told you several times that even if you had sex with Al or some other man I *would* have you back if you chose to return to me. I do understand your desire but exclusivity is usually an expectation of married or engaged people who plan to marry soon. And even that expectation has faded away in general. Few people other than the very religious put such great heaven or hell importance on sexual relations. I think that sexual exclusivity is just an *ideal* for most women, they don't really expect it of their lovers or of themselves. Exclusivity did not exist in Old Testament times, or with Joseph Smith and Brigham Young, early Mormon prophets.

But neither marriage or engagement applies in our case because of *your* free choices - we are not married, we are not engaged, we are not living together. So I can only conclude that you want to control me and mold me into your personal ideal of what a male should be. Or perhaps it is your desire to lay blame and guilt trips on me to cover your own guilt and insecurity?

It's unlikely but what if I did have sex with another woman? What would be the worst thing that could come from that? Could you handle it? Would you be less discontent if you dumped that obsession to keep a single man exclusively to yourself? Would you walk away from me forever if I had sex with another woman? Would you expect me to do the same if you had sex with another man? We see these things very differently. Think about it?

Jen: I feel you once had these attitudes. It has been really hard knowing you put such little integrity into our relationship or it was just simply "you were that lonely and weak". Or you did not want to give up looking for something better than me. Is this true or how do you explain it? Was this how you felt these last couple years?

M: You divorced me and were not with me. I was a single man doing what single men do, in addition to researching and writing a book. It was you who turned a separation into a divorce. Regardless of how you saw things at the time and may have been misadvised, that's a fact you have yet to deal with. Your not having dealt with it is the reason why you continue to attempt to blame me and lay guilt trips on me. *("It has been really hard knowing you put such little integrity into our relationship.")* From my point of view it was really hard knowing that you loved me so little after 18 years that you could suddenly and secretly divorce me and persuade a judge with untruths to give you control of everything I had so I could not even live had the judge's order with zero input from me been enforceable.

Jen: My belief is if we love each then I will be faithful to each other no matter what. One of the main reasons it was hard to fully commit to you was your attitude toward this. You figured you were a single man and would only commit to a relationship that was in your presence. I could not except that or would I ever except a man that does not promise to be faithful when I am gone. Of course we are all lonely when the person we love is gone but we remain faithful. Why was I never worthy of a promise of faithfulness at all times? These feeling run very deep within me.

M: I've addressed this in my earlier comments. Again it seems that you are trying to manipulate me and make me feel guilty so you needn't take any responsibility for what took place over the last 15 months. I don't know what period of that time you are referring to above but you may recall your lack of "faithfulness" with your own presence on singles sites, communications with other men, and more particularly your relationship with Al which was largely sexual. Is it not about time to forgive and forget rather than try to poke away at and find fault with the other? Do you honestly think you are so much better than I am that you are justified in laying all the guilt for what took place between us at *my* feet?

Jen: If you had never left me I would not be experiencing the pains of this situation. I will always believe you were wrong to leave me in search of Lola. It has put much fear of our out come in the next life that will be out of our control. But what ever it is we will fully except it and totally agree.

M: Who's Lola? I'm back, ripe fruit for your picking if you chose to. Is it not a time to *rejoice* instead of indulging in pity parties and guilt trips and "pain"? As for what happens after we die, I understand that you are steeped in the Mormon way and want to take me back to that. It is my wish for their sake that the Mormons are right, but for me I do not want to pass into the world of spirits and there get a home teaching assignment. I see much greater potential for joy and progress elsewhere. You cling to something that you don't even understand. If the Mormon dream is real and you qualify after your death what is it that you are planning to do in that highest heaven? Why is it better there than any other level of 'heaven' where you are perfectly happy and content?

Jen: Even in the nest life I fear your love for me would not hold for me until I was ready to except the next step. (I think I am very insecure and rightly so) I believe if it is possible for you, you would go ahead and find other women to surround yourself with and then have me if I choose to come along as a side dish. You know we women are all side dishes when there are more than one. Remember the old say. When a man saw a beautiful sexy woman they would say. "What a dish"

M: There is no point in speculating how it will be after we die, we simply don't know for sure until we're there, and that includes the Mormons. It is my belief that a belief is simply something we keep repeating, and Mormons do that daily. I was astonished at how quickly, mere moments actually, I was able to stand back and let go 50 years of belief. That doesn't mean the Mormon way is not a good way to live one's life. It means that there are many paths to reach the same mountain peak, and many ways to have happiness in this life. The bottom line as I see it is to love unconditionally and to create a happy accepting non-judgmental attitude within oneself. Such will endure into the eternities.

Regarding the "dishes", it is you yourself who create the separation. You know my dream, my fantasy, and that my door will always be open to you whether or not you choose to remain on the outside. If you adhere to Mormon doctrine you know that it is unlikely that you will have a man exclusive to yourself. Perhaps it won't matter so much after the death of these physical bodies, perhaps it's unconditional love and joy that matter most.

My understanding of your proposal after we die is that if I do not do as you want me to then you will go off with another man. (You threaten me.) My proposal is that my door will always be open for you should you choose to walk through it, or even if you remain on the outside and beckon me to play with you for a while. I will do that then get back to the business of being Adam, having fullness of love and joy and purpose, populating planets. I give you a *choice,* you give me none. I set you free of me if that is your choice, you attempt to bind me. You demand that I accept your notion of exclusivity even beyond the grave but that is not part of my dream, nor part of the Mormon dream for a male. You might find that you love your sister wives and have *fullness* of joy in them and your husband and children. But *whatever* your choice I wish you joy forever.

Jen: I know the next life will be wonderful. I wish at this time you would want to wait for me. It would make it so much easier to know someone loves you above all others is waiting for you. Very romantic isn't it but not when your man can't wait to get on the other side and search for his Eves. This is not something i can ask or require of you or anyone. The reality is you and I don't know if this is even possible for us. We may be assigned to something else when we first get to heaven. One thing I do believe is our progression will not stop here or on the other side of the veil. I know what ever it will be it will be right for each of us.

One other thing. I know I am no different than the other billion's of spirits that have moved forward. So what makes us feel so special or important. It is the people we are sealed to and want to keep connected to. We are speical and important to them. I think it is our temple sealing. Our you going to honor that. Is it important enough to you. You will be speical to all those family members you had sealed to your family. That will be our circle in the next life.

(This is just my opinion) Not all those women you feel connected to in some spiritual way that took priority over me and your family obligations. I am part of your family not Cleo, not Suzann or any of the others. They were distractions from your real path or destination. They were never meant or were ever really real. This resulted in distrust that may never be regained. I know you cherish and feel they were a God given gift to you. I don't see it that way. We did need a wake up call in our marriage but not that one. The results could have been one that you would have been very proud of if we just got help to save the marriage. If your love for me was not lost and replaced with distain toward me. At last, One good thing we saw the light and returned to each other and found we still love each other the most. Love you sweetie.

M: Thanks for expressing that. But know this, I never did "distain" you, I could always find love for you, always will I expect. I think we should cease to look beyond the mark, rejoice in what we have, and build upon it. Now will you get that pretty butt of yours back to Victoria so I can do more than just admire it as it walks *away* from me?

M: (to myself) Of course, now that Jen has put down Suzanne, after a long silence I get two messages from Suzanne reassuring me that it was not just a dream, that Suzanne was and is much more than a mere "distraction" as Jen in her turmoil and insecurity would have her be.

Suzanne: Yesterday I had a moment (probably better said moments) that was breath I will describe as pure life. I have a new patient, now in her 80's who has severe lung disease. She is a famous ballerina who has been on the cover of famous publications. I shall say no more for fear of Big Brother. Yesterday on my visit she was in respiratory crisis. I have come to understand when you can't breathe you PANIC!! (I had an episode of choking once and some gracious person saved my life with Heimlich maneuver.. I experienced Panic for those few moments.)

My sweet patient was very angry and tore into me yesterday as I walked into her home on all I was lacking in her care. I was a failure in her eyes and she has a most skillful use of the English language, from first hand experience! She was blaming me for this crisis! Wow the animation senecio from Brene (love our book club is on first name basis with our mentor and author) came alive. So, I was able to administer meds, make phone calls for equipment, and most preciously for both of us, stay with her and hold her hand and be present until her breathing eased after several hours. As I departed she hugged and kissed me. Best ever.

I drove home late but somehow knowing deeply God had prepared me after many years to be present at those minutes for that precious woman. I experience life in those brief moments of absolute wonder. I have found Brene's work gives me a new courage. And grateful for the blame animation video. Perfect timing for my life. I'm not rich or famous or powerful I'm quietly ordinary and I'm learning that is enough. I'm worthy to be loved just as each of us.

I hope to hear your stories. Our stories are the small flickers of light in the dark that guide us to joyful living. Blessings for us all today. Thanks for reading.

M: Thank-you for sharing that touching story Suzanne. Surely they were precious moments when a lovely accomplished lady who no doubt brought much joy to others was dependent upon you for the very breath of life. I noted long ago from the stories you shared with me that with you it is not only skill and training and experience that you apply as you go about your professional life. It's the very essence of LOVE that walks into the homes of the dying as you pass through their doorway. There could not be a sweeter angel to have at one's side in the final moments of life than you Dear One. I'm sure that most of your charges go to heaven with a smile upon their face, an angel having attended their passing.

I watched a three minute animated clip in which Brene Brown teaches the difference between sympathy and empathy. You of course are all about empathy, actually *doing* beneficial things for those who come into your care. That's real life *you* sweet one, I love you. And I also really really liked the wild one in you, our dear Suzanne. :-)

I will soon point you to where you can get my first three books in e-book or soft cover format. I must warn you that they are massive though, some 2,000 pages in the three books, and written in an unfamiliar style. I just didn't think I had the time to cut and polish more before publishing. They are already out but there was a publisher mistake that they are now working on rectifying, I'll let you know when it is the modified version on the shelves.

Suzanne: Dear one, I think of you often and send a prayer. How are you???

M: 800 mgs of Ibuprofen each morning and sometimes a repeat in the late afternoon keep me feeling like a fraud. I write much of the day, breathe normal, even walked a mile each way last night at a goodly clip to see the movie "Fifty Shades of Grey". So I don't know if things have advanced from stage three or not. But I must admit if I don't take the pain pills I soon know that something is not right with this bod of mine, especially when I lie on my back. I get pains on the right side of my chest and my heart seems to go into a gentle but persuasive complaint. Without that validation I might be tempted to think the docs got it all wrong, biopsy or not.

I think I told you that my four sons visited me in Victoria a few weeks ago. There were no spouses or children along so it was the first time since adult ever that I had the four of them together by themselves. Being Mormons they laid hands on their (apparently) dying dad's head and gave him a priesthood blessing, the stated purpose for the visit. We had some fun but it was mainly business, getting my temporal affairs in better order. (One son's a lawyer.) The timing was perfect for my psychiatrist son to be with me for the first visit with the oncologist.

Not to be outdone, my three daughters showed up two weeks ago and between the three of them stretched out the visit to ten days. Now *they* are fun! They never told me where we were going until the last moment but outings with them included a tour of Butchart Gardens, ride on a carousel (I got the lion), high tea, beaches, parks, seaside walks, Italian opera (Lucia Di Lammermoor), an oratorio (a tragedy, well done), and Death by Chocolate in the Bengal Room of the Empress Hotel. I think they figured, *"so what's it going to do, kill him?"*

It was a bit of a crash when the last one left on Friday, but who am I to speak to you of loneliness? But they left my fridge and freezer and cupboards filled with goodies, they take care of their dad. Unfortunately the last one had to hurry off to the funeral of my only great grandchild in another province. (I still am not allowed to fly because my chest was opened so I didn't go.) She was two and a half, was wearing a hoodie that got caught on a nail. She slipped down unobserved and was hung. Care was administered and she was helicoptered to hospital but after three days in ICU she decided to stop breathing and move on. There was no negligence but I'm sure the mother will feel guilty for a long time, whereas the rest of us will gradually move on with our lives, the wee one becoming a lovely but distant memory, you know about such things.

Two of my female friends visited on Monday but I'm on my own until my ex Jen will flies in from Las Vegas and most likely stays a few weeks. If the doc clears me for it I may do a road trip with her now that Spring is getting serious. Our fruit trees are long in glorious white and pink blossom, daffodils standing yellow tall in fields that remain green all the year long. We'll drive south to San Diego, Phoenix etc. then maybe a few weeks in Utah and north from there to visit the rest of my kids. Then west through the Rockies back to my seaside city in good time for an explore and a family reunion. In addition to my seven kids and their families, my four siblings will join us for the last three of a seven day event. That's the plan anyway. We'll see how this unpredictable beast inside me behaves, and how well Jen and I get along this time, it's not always smooth sailing for us. :-)

Take care Suzanne, you are precious to me. Send more stories if you want to, Book 4 is open and growing daily. It will be published even should I die before the manuscript is submitted, I've seen to that. It's nice to have held three of my soft-cover books in my hands even though they are being revised. I'm grateful for health and energy. Enjoy the day sweetie, thanks for the prayer, you're a lovely one. Hello to your ballerina for me, tell her I'm dying too, maybe we can get together. But let her know I don't own a tutu and never shave my legs so she doesn't hang around too long. :-)

Oresha: It was SO nice spending some time with You! :) Thanx for your hospitality... Beer/Nuts/CHOCOLATE!...;) Night... Hugz... :)

M: Thanks for visiting and for friendship.

Suzanne: So sweet to hear from you. I have missed you. Your life sounds incredible, wonderful, so good. You are doing all the right things to live longer. Laughter and joy bring healing. Isn't sad that dying is what brings such love and connection. We should live that way every day. Be sure and go to Dr. if heart gets too out of rhythm, it could be you have collected fluid on your lung. I enjoy all your loving compliments, you may think I'm more angelic than I am! I'll try to share more stories. Do you ever hear from our Florida heavenly Goddess? Does she know of your cancer? Love you.

M: It's true that I may think you are more angelic than you do. But I'm also aware of that other delightful creature, you know, the one we named "Suzanne". Oh la la, *that* one oui oui! :-)

I went for a scheduled chest x-ray more than a week ago and they haven't called me so I think I passed. In fact I'm sure that I passed because my lungs feel clear and fully functional. It's possible that I was going along with just one lung for many months. I think you sensed something wrong when we were in Las Vegas. I noticed a change in stamina as far back as when I was living in Yuma.

I'm not sure that I *want* to live longer sweetie, there is much that is calling wondrously from the heavens though I have enjoyed this lifetime immensely and continue to do so in many ways, except for the loneliness part, yes, that one. I am on the brink of my greatest adventure and my friends are offering cures: laughter and joy, distance healing, alkaline water, goji berries, parsley root, dandelion root, "shoot a root toot" as our once goddess used to say.

Yes, she knows. She wanted to fly here when she first heard but didn't have the means. And I wouldn't encourage that because I have much family and friend support, including a knowledgeable and caring hospice nurse, one born in the great state of Texas. She has had many downs Cleo DeLeon but seems to be on an up right now, still living in Florida, taking addiction counseling referrals from a doctor and apparently doing well by them. She continues to talk about her projects but I don't think has made much progress towards manifesting them.

It was you Suzanne who encouraged and moved that along after Cleo suddenly dumped me a day or so after her heart operation. I thought you were in love with virtual her like I was, and of course you had me wrapped around your finger at the time so I flew 2,000 miles each way to visit her a second time. It was a fun adventure though and made a great story for the books, that woman was willing to play in my fantasy sandbox and my but she could write! I recently suggested to Jen that she and I fly to Costa Rica to dip in the Arenal hot pools but she immediately thought it was to bring back memories of my time there with Cleo. It wasn't, but ok, that proposed road trip is promising, a side trip to the giant sequoias before reaching San Francisco perhaps...

Be well, please stay in touch, your messages light up my life, always did, except when they didn't. Lovely frustrating Suzanne, there would not have been books without her. Send me your postal address and I'll have the three softcover books delivered to you when the revised ones are ready for print on demand. Maybe you'll be the only one to read them all the way through, I can't find enough interest to do it myself after having written and revised the stuff over and over. Who else would lose themselves in 2,000 pages unless they could find themselves in them?

Suzanne: I've become quite untrusting of the online dating. So many lies, deceptions. I hired a matchmaker a few months ago. I had some pleasant dates but no sparks! Am I silly to want sparks at my age??? I do have a date tomorrow. I drive into Austin for dinner at very nice Tuscany Restaurant that serves all the incredible courses in true tradition. Yes I'm lonely but learning about myself. I'm in a book club in Austin, we are reading a book called Daring Greatly by Brene' Brown. We meet once a month, have potluck dinner and very stimulating discussion for 3-4 hours. It great to be so stimulated. My heart reaches out to you.

M: Personally I think male/female/sparks are the greatest invention of all. And I think that long-term boredom is the greatest of all pains. How could we possibly be bored with eternity when we have love/romance/consensual sex? You are not at all silly for wanting sex at any age. It would be silly not to, I wish it upon you.

Vancouver Island is Canada's retirement haven, to here come the retired, the single, the widow, the divorced. There is only one eligible male for every nine eligible females on the island. I removed all my singles site profiles quite some time ago but before I did I had hundreds, yes literally hundreds of expressions of interest. I met quite a few, some of them very nice women, some famous, some wealthy, some ordinary, some frauds with twenty year old photos. I made some friends, some good ones, some not so. But you know the drill. I'm pleased that you have not given up and that you are getting out and meeting people. You have a whole lot to offer a companion lovely sexy intelligent you. And you do belong in a book club having stimulating discussions with others, you fit right in there. It seems to me that you are serving up life very well Suzanne. I only wish the loneliness would be addressed long-term for you, perhaps that will come when you let go and least expect it.

Your heart does not have to travel far to reach me dear one, it never did since that first hug in Loa. Perhaps in another state of awareness there will yet be a time for us. Sleep well, enjoy your date.

Oresha: Good Mornin' Michael... :) Yes... Friendships are so Wonderful ...I appreciate You as well! :) Here's another "natural" food that may help you feel better... if you can stand even one more of these... ha! ha!... ;)

This last guy I met on Sun. turned out to be a "piece of work"!... He questioned/challenged my integrity!... amongst other things... When I told him that I know who I AM and that I don't feel the need to have to "prove" myself to anybody... he got really rude & obnoxious!... DELETE!... lol This guy "said" he was on his spiritual path... well he certainly isn't "walking his talk" ...lol It never ceases to amaze me on how many screwed up people there are out there!... is it something in the water they drink ???? ...lol I'm pretty well over the "contrast" thing!...lol I have a "meet-me-date" for lunch in Duncan with a man from Nanaimo on Sat. ...we'll see how that goes.... lol Yet another lap or 3 around The Pond I guess... lol

Have a great day!.... Please let me know if/when you feel up for a walk or chat... Hugsssssss....

M: Ok, thanks for watching out for me, celery is on my shopping list. Maybe if I add peanut butter it'll taste tasty when dunked in my parsley and dandelion root goji berry alkaline organic raw tea. I mean, what's the worst it can do, kill me? :-) Enjoy your quest for a proper male.

Oresha: Now don't forget to wash it all down with a Corona & some Chocolate!... lol... We've got to enjoy the little things in life....:) A positive attitude & great sense of humour also goes a long way :) Thanks for the Smile... :) Cheers... Enjoy your day....

Oresha: I had to make a WalMart run today to pick up a few things.... and... guess what!.. I have been thinking about your Beautiful Candy/Nut Dish that we found last summer... (and kickin' myself for not buying one). Something told me to go over to the area where we found it.... and... Lo & Behold... They had one! Yay!..... lol So I now have a Twin on my coffee-table!... teehee...;) They must have brought more in... cause I didn't see it there before.. lol Ttyl..... Cheers....

M: Shoot, now I have to change my will.

Oresha: Now THAT'S Hilarious! I was going to say that... but I decided to keep it in good taste!.. Ha! Ha! ...so ya musta been reading my mind!... lol :)

M: It was a good read Oresha, I like fiction.

Oresha: LOL.... :)

Jen: I for got my phone. It was impossible to find a pay phone. I was to call my cousin when I got there. My daughter is sending it to me through over night mail. But have not received it. I took possession of the suburban and put my other daughter's name on the title. Looking forward to seeing you. I miss you lots. Any what I realized today I could email you through my sister's computer. We are going to the Rodeo Saturday. Anyway, what have you been up to. Hopefully the next time i send a email i will be on my phone. I will make sure my email is not open to this computer. Have you heard anything about your chest X-ray. I want to know how you are feeling and what is happening to your body and your mind. I just care. Love you

M: It's good to hear from you, I think about you a lot and wish you were here. It's 11:30 a.m. and I just now took the first pain pills today while doing only one dose yesterday. I wanted to find out how I am faring but my mind begins to fog and my body to feel ill at ease and worthless when it's too long between pills. But with them I am doing well. I walked downtown a couple of days ago to see a movie and walked briskly both ways without feeling any discomfort. I realize from the frequent hunger that my body needs to eat more often and got a Big Mac on the way home.

Friends keep sending emails with cancer "cures" and I'm indulging a bit even though the next life continues to call mightily. I drink parsley root tea, dandelion root tea, alkaline water, gofji berry tea, and since Oresha wrote about celery yesterday have been chewing on celery stalks. We're having a cold spell but I walked breakwater yesterday, my lungs holding out and serving me very well with never a sign of breathlessness like I used to have all the time. I haven't heard anything about the x-ray so my guess is that I passed with flying colors, it sure feels like I did. Now with all that, plus never mentally dwelling on the thought of having cancer, if I get a cure I'll never know what caused it. :-)

I really really miss you and hope we get along well when you come, and that you will stay a long while. It's hard for me being on my own when I've walked with a woman (wife) at my side for 50 years. Something's dreadfully wrong about being alone, cancer or not even though I handle it. I sleep much longer and more often now but part of that may simply be because of boredom now that I'm not anxiously engaged in getting books ready for publication. I'm hoping we'll make that road trip a reality, or at least do a cruise or resort, the winter here has been long and cold, I need to get away from it asap.

Is your sister still trying to be a match maker for you? My guess is that a lot of people who know your situation will try to help you that way. Selfish me hopes to get a few months with you first before you find and settle down with a steady male friend, which shouldn't be hard for you to attract, you're a pretty woman. Enjoy the rodeo. There's one every year where I used to live but I never got into that scene, it doesn't make sense that a grown man would risk life and limb to ride a bull or bucking bronco, but each to their own.

Be well sweetie, the thought of you coming to me lights up my life but the days until you come are dragging. There is no other I'd sooner be with than you but I am also aware that my shelf life is near complete and you need to be looking to your future and preparing for it. So I'll understand if your visits are short. Hopefully from now on they will always be *quality* time for us. P.S. for comic relief I'll copy below an exchange of emails between me and Oresha yesterday.

Jen: What type of fiction do u like? No my sister is not trying to fix me up with anyone. I only have eyes for u. Does Oresha brig out the worst in these men? Love u sweetie. (Yes, she used question marks, what's happening???)

M: Re the "fiction" that was of course a play on my "reading" her mind, supposed to be funny, she thought it was.

Oresha nevers seems to find the man she's looking for. I don't know if she has other (platonic) male friends in Victoria like me. We don't need to have Oresha and Kathy over when you are here but they do want to meet you so it will be up to you.

I doubt that you will make friends with either of them, maybe you'll find someone at church, or just put up with me and get out by yourself now and then if you need to get away. In addition to walking we could try to get to events outside of my little world. Victoria is a city of culture though I've had enough of ballet and opera. If you had a (hopefully female) friend in Victoria I'd encourage you going to such productions if you enjoy them. My fav will always be musical theater, we could maybe do some Vancouver and Seattle events, take the ferry. It's getting to the time where we can explore up island too, maybe spend a few nights at the west side of the island and walk the rain forests and beaches.

I get occasional emails from friends, Suzanne seems genuinely interested in how I'm doing, she certainly understands the process of dying. Elaine hasn't come over but writes occasionally. She says she taught art in school and is good at it. She'd like to give you lessons if you're interested. I almost never hear from Cleo and haven't heard from Carrie for quite a long time. And there you have it, there are no more secrets in Victoria....

Jen: Thought you might be interested in knowing that celery is a cooling food to the body so if you want to cool your body down eat lots of celery. Of course putting peanut butter on it might warm you back up.

Anyway enjoy experimenting with these unusual foods. Who knows something might help you feel better. My cousin told me my uncle died of lung cancer and only took Tylenol and he died without pain. Let's keep that in mind you don't have to be in a lot of pain when it is lung cancer. It might just be different that way.

Sounds like you're are still editing and entering emails into your journal. Are you creating this to leave to your children it would be nice for them to have a journal of your thoughts toward the end of your last days. OR Do you feel you need the vague remembrance of these other women to keep you going until you expire. Sometimes I feel they are more important than your own children. Or you honor their wishes before your children. Anyway it is your strange life and choices. No disrespect but it sounds like you're not much different than Oreshas bowes. You are probably much sweeter and. u know how to hold your tongue. It makes you a very wise man. I like that about you. Love you and will see you soon.

M: If I was the same as Oresha's "bowes" I'd have been deleted from her life a long time ago. I also don't think having and communicating with friends is "strange" even though you seem to think it is if it's me having friends and staying in touch with them. Maybe it's you who is strange?

I gave you instructions how to publish Book 4 which is the one I am working on right now. Do you not have them or the motivation to have that book published after I die? Please let me know so I can make other arrangements if you aren't going to do it, I was counting on you. No, I am not writing my journal for my children, some of them have said they don't want to read my books because I told them there is sex in them. Personally I find that (and your) attitude about sex strange. Don't you think eternity would be boring without sex?

M: (to myself) I just don't know if things will ever work out well for me and Jen, she seems to have so much hostility towards me, too often putting me down for things I see as ridiculous. Why are the "vaguely" remembered friends whose wishes I "honor" in my "strange life" now more important to me than my children? I don't want the last days of my life to be filled with contention and jealousies. Perhaps Jen understands that, is unsure of herself, and that's why she won't commit to live with me and doesn't want to marry? Would it have been better to not drag out this divorce, to have put an end to it many months ago regardless of how much we seem to love each other? Perhaps we each would have had proper companions by now. And now does she feel an *obligation* to care for me while I die and that's why more than anything else she will visit me in the coming months? I do believe she loves me, but why the put downs in her last message? Or does she not know that her comments are nasty from my point of view? We seemed to have been getting along well until she wrote about my "strange life and choices" and that I was no different than the men Oresha rejects.

She was severely abused by two former husbands. I wonder if the hostility she so readily expresses towards me is linked to that abuse and buttons are being pushed that impact me and our relationship unfairly? Anyway, regardless of how negative she is I will do my best to live peaceably with her when she visits and should we travel together. I have my dreams, my fantasy life, but as far as *this* world is concerned Jen remains number one. I hope we can get it together and enjoy each other for the duration. It doesn't make a whole lot of sense to stress over the next life when *this* one obviously needs repairing...

Jen mentioning a painless death from lung cancer makes me think of the *ideal* way I'd like my death to be. She would come when I am wide awake and aware, a lovely angel telling me the time she will return so I can close off this book before then. I will do so, submit the manuscript to the publisher, and a few minutes before that time (so nobody can interfere) I will send a message to family friends and loved ones that is already prepared and addressed, telling them I am gone and that I love them. My beautiful angel in white and glory will return at the appointed time, stretch out her hand and gently lift me painlessly and effortlessly and joyfully from this ailing body. We will hug and she will be my guide for the next while as I renew acquaintances and get oriented to a new life. She may turn out to be one of my Eves and us inseparable, that would be so nice. But how it will *really* be? I do not know, she hasn't come yet.

As for being serious about becoming Adam I continue to cling ever so tightly to the opening statement in each of my books: *"As my soul roams the universe it will always be with the utmost thought and fixed determination that I am becoming or that I AM Adam!"* As I drift within layers of sleep and while awake I often silently repeat such words as: *"I am Adam. I love my beautiful wives and children."* I try to see myself with them more clearly. I live for them. And because I have not allowed myself to become aware of how to make this physical body immortal, I DIE for them! Whether it is with this present physical body or with another, we will regroup and do *whatever* needs to be done, get new bodies if we must. I WILL be the sole male in a family of loving spouses. With my wives my Eves I WILL become Adam and populate new planets.

So if I die dear reader, know this that somewhere sometime on some planet my dream has become my reality. It cannot be any other way, that is impossible to conceive of. I will have a perfect love. I will know fullness of joy. In dreams and imagination I am already there, I *am* Adam. As you read these words does your whole being cry out that WE ARE ONE? Perhaps there are some of us from my own family here in mortality right now. Perhaps there are many other Adam and Eve families here, each in their own way, dreaming their own dream, attracting the like-minded. Do my words prompt you to make this exact same dream, or one more familiar your reality?

I have been steeped in western religion but exposed to many forms of thought all my life. I have been curious and bold to quietly explore where many so devoted to religion and tradition would not dare venture out of fear of losing that goal of making it to heaven after they die. I think now that God is my Higher Self. I think that I came from God who spun off a tiny portion of Him and Her a spirit me to animate a physical body, experience mortality, and make choices. I think when something inexorable rises from deep within me and expresses itself to the universe with the words "I LOVE YOU" that I am in those moments praying to MYSELF! I think that I am going home to ME but with chosen adventures along the way. *Are you like that too?*

I break then with western religious thought. I break with the notion that I am dependent on some invisible all powerful creature in some invisible realm to fulfill every whim of mine, or to blame if my stuff doesn't arrive on time or some seeming innocent is maimed or dies. I move closer to but avoid the completeness of the Greek Pantheon on Mount Olympus. Zeus does not rule over me for I too am LOVE, we all are, we create our own reality. I break with the notion that we come to planets like this one to do battle and experience pain and tragedy. I believe that we create our own lives by the thoughts we dwell upon, the desires we choose. I believe that our emotions are our unfailing guide, that as we choose only thoughts that come with happy feelings we create only happy lives for ourselves even as others loved ones at our side perhaps may choose differently and thus live lives that are quite unlike ours. It is not "luck" that makes one prosper and another not, it is conscious willing CHOICE in the midst of an ever flowing wealth of diversity that makes the difference. We need but to observe and the universe is ours to explore fearlessly for after all, we ARE the universe, our own unique portion of it.

Too much of philosophy, not enough of application? Ok, figure it out for yourself if you must, pay attention to what your emotions are telling you and dwell only on love and joy, we exist for that. With your choices manipulate where you find yourself in the universe. Are you contained in a tiny canoe paddling furiously upstream because you chain yourself to tradition, the beliefs of others and refuse to think for yourself? Or are you free to roam a beautiful cruise ship with all the creature comforts imaginable, moving with the flow you have created for yourself for there is only *awareness*? Try too imagining your body and everything as only vibration. Then with that imagination see yourself vibrating faster or higher. You will find in that exercise chronic happiness, for God is love and Love and Joy dwell at the highest levels of vibration. Or, be like me for almost my entire life and choose religion and tradition. Then *maybe* when you die you will reach some vague notion of heaven that others tell you is where you'll go if you are obedient to them and give them money all your life. The choice is yours...

I know, I am but an ordinary man who gets carried away and rambles trying to convey things in words that perhaps can only be conveyed by the sharing of similar experiences. Does the above make any sense to you? I am not trying to convert anyone to anything, just passing along things that have recently worked for me even before I was told that I am dying. Now, I expect to experience even more. I may continue to share while I can but already this manuscript is 130,000 words and I know my books are too large, I might close at 200,000 or a bit less. Maybe I'll need a fifth book to record how I became Adam? I do enjoy this rambling, I like writing, it's a happy thought to think of doing more. Watch then for Book 5? Are you up to it? Talk to me at <u>www.becomingadam.com</u> if it's set up for feedback. I and those real people behind the major characters in my books would like to interact with you if we can.

I am preparing a message to send to some of those who have actively participated in the making of the Becoming Adam series of books. There were hundreds I interacted with from a distance mainly from online singles site contacts whose stories were unwritten or were deleted from my manuscripts in the interests of making the books shorter. One woman in particular whose input at the very beginning was *vital* is unknown because she refused to allow me to include her emails in the books and went silent. Her input would have made a book of its own and she would have remained throughout the story like Suzanne did. She is highly intelligent, a better writer than I am, and has documented near death experiences that taught her much. Because of her and her trail of beckoning emails, I drove my brand new motor home Loa some 2,000 miles from San Francisco, California to Texas where I met Suzanne and the rest as they say is history. All of those others were instrumental in the creation of me as writer and my manuscripts as books. Here's how that email might read when I send it to the few whose email addresses I still have.

My Dear Friend, Due to my having inoperable lung cancer and the uncertainty and tiredness that come with that I decided to self-publish my books and rush them into production even though I know I could have done a better job as author. I wanted to hold them in my hand while I can, I have now done so. The first three books are available in e-book and soft cover format at many retailers, including at the links posted on my website http://www.becomingadam.com Book 4 is a living manuscript soon to be published, perhaps posthumorously. (Smile with me?) My pen name for the "Becoming Adam" series of books is "Michael Demers". You may have known me by a different name, or may have completely forgotten that our paths ever crossed, they did or your address would not be in my files.

I did not know what I was getting into when I left the woman who was then my wife, my comfortable lifestyle, and my beautiful retirement home. I only knew that burning inexorably within me was a desperate NEED to write a book. I was a man on a mission, except I didn't know what that mission was. It unfolded line upon line and is still being revealed as I am now eight months away from living in the motor home called "Loa" and unexpectedly now living out my dying. (I'm good with the dying, it's a fascinating experience, you should try it sometime. :-)

You may not be aware of it but you helped me write the series of four (maybe more) "Becoming Adam" series of books. I needed at the time what you provided whether or not the experience could be perceived as negative or positive, major or miniscule, I had to have it. Who knows, perhaps we travel in the same 'soul group' or eternal 'family' and came to this planet to help prepare its people for the leap to the coming Golden Age, I feel it a mission to do so. I experienced a constant flow of 'coincidences' and spiritual experiences as I wrote the journal that would become the books. Thank-you for being you. Thank-you for being there for me when I most needed you whether or not you were aware. In some ways you too are author of these Becoming Adam books even if your story was deleted because there was no space remaining for it. You influenced me, gave me hope perhaps in a lonely moment that I could have drowned in, or helped me learn by exposure how to handle deep emotion without falling apart. There must be an opposition in all things so we can learn how to discern what we really want, and make choices. Your opposition if such it was was needful for this young writer to become what he had to be to get it all out, the story that was percolating inside him.

Once I got into it and dealt better with the loneliness of living on my own after decades of marriage, it became my intention to teach New Thought truths in my books. But I knew I'd only be preaching to the already converted if I wrote a conventional book on the subject. To potentially reach a larger audience I melded the teachings into stories that will hopefully be entertaining enough to sell the books. It is known that sex sells (think 50 Shades of Grey that sold 100 million books and is a movie) so there is sex in my books. You may find yourself in those stories anonymously, only you would know that the story was inspired by yourself, and what *really* happened. In my real life male loneliness it was the thought of sex that drove me to and from where I needed to be not only physically but mentally so these books could manifest. Forgive me if I have not represented you accurately or rewrote your messages too severely, I took fiction writer's license liberally.

Although my books are based on events that actually happened and there are real people behind most of the characters, the books are essentially works of fiction that only incidentally (it seems) teach metaphysical/spiritual principles that I believe to be true, everything is embellished. I use an experimental format (peeking into private emails rather than traditional conversation.) It is my hope that readers will get used to that style but it may be a difficult sell, that remains to be seen, I'm asking for your help in promoting the books. It may be that the style I have used is the only way to reach and teach readers who would otherwise shun a conventional New Thought or New Age metaphysical or spiritual book. I think these books contain truths that are important for people to know as this planet draws close to a new state of awareness and makes the leap into a new "Millennium".

I hope you enjoy reading the books (huge as they are – I did my best to edit with the time allotted me) and will refer the Becoming Adam series of books to others. I am asking you one thing, my dying wish, that you positively mention these books in social media that you currently engage in. But please do not reveal my real identity or location or contact information or that of anyone else you think may be represented by any of the characters, we'll trust each other with that.

Wish me and all of us well and godspeed. I now embark (happily) on the greatest adventure we will ever know, that of dying. I am sending this message to people I am or was in contact with whose email addresses I have in my files. Feel free to forward this message to friends and media, but please delete all email addresses except your own. I hope you are well. I'm delighted that our lives touched, you have enriched mine. And because of that you have also enriched the lives of many others, perhaps it was meant to be that way.

Enjoy the day.

Michael Demers

www.becomingadam.com

Jen: I thought that might spark some conversation. I see nothing wong with u having friends. I will follow what yuo want with book 4. What made u think I woulden't. I do not think there will be free sex as you see it. It would be nice if we can but not all will be able. love u

M: What a glorious day today! It's still cold for me, I wore my winter jacket over a summer t-shirt, but clear skies on a weekend means everybody in Victoria heads for the sea. I sat at the end of breakwater this afternoon taking it all in: ships, sail boats, snow-capped peaks across the strait. I'd heard of people watching sunsets over the ocean for many weeks to catch a glimpse of a green flash that sometimes happens as the sun touches the sea. I saw that today in daylight and it wasn't just a flash. There must have been a wave or disturbance on the water and the sun was at just the right angle to turn that into a glorious sparkling emerald green that lasted several minutes. It was about the length of a canoe in the distance then grew longer before disappearing.

Re your provocative last message I wrote in my journal: "She seems to have so much hostility towards me, too often putting me down for things I see as ridiculous. Why are the "vaguely" remembered friends whose wishes I "honor" in my "strange life" now more important to me than my children? Does she feel an obligation to care for me while I die and that's why more than anything else she will visit me in the coming months? I do believe she loves me, but why the put downs in her last message? Or does she not know that her comments were nasty from my point of view? I wonder if the hostility she so readily expresses towards me is linked to abuse from former husbands and buttons are being pushed that impact me and our relationship unfairly?"

She writes again with a similar message, I'll respond between the lines.

Jen: Number one question I have for you. Why do you make sex so important in your books when most successful books do not involve sexual exploitation. Why would a man with so much talent like yours think stooping so below to have a successful book. It is a shame you would write something you feel you could not read to your children and grandchildren. Is that the legacy you want to leave because it is. Of course I will honor your wishes. Why because I love you.

M: Your point of view is exceedingly strange, why is sex such an obsession for you? Or is it that you want to put me down so you can pretend that you are better than me in some way? Who is "exploiting" who in my books? Do you think that sex between consenting adults is "exploitation"? Why is it "stooping" to write books that contain sexual scenes? Do you not enjoy movies that contain such scenes and rejoice when it all works out in the end? I kept comprehensive journals and books of remembrance for decades and printed and gave them to all of my children. Those are what can be read to my children and grandchildren, and they can view the video and audio recordings my children made of me when they were here. Have you done the same for your children and grandchildren? My "Becoming Adam" books are not written for my family, I told you that.

And by the way the recent "Fifty Shades of Grey" trilogy sold 100 million books, one every second at its peak and is now a movie. Those books are all about sex and not just sex but kinky sex. Sex sells! I knew that and decided to give it a try so the important teachings in my books that I feel it a mission to convey would reach an audience that would otherwise shun spiritual/metaphysical media. Who are you to put me down for that? Do you not think it important to *help* and encourage rather than criticize and discourage the man in your life from manifesting his desires and doing it the way *he* feels it best to do? You act more like a man than a woman sometimes, well ok, *often!* I guess that's ok in today's day and age, I'm ok with a woman any woman having her own fantasies and desires. Just not ok with her thinking *her* way should prevail over that of the significant adult males in her life. Equality would be good but there IS a difference (a delightful difference in my view) between male and female, there are good reasons for that.

Jen: Regarding my comments about Oresha. I thought that might spark some conversation. Your family probably think we both are strange. I see nothing wong with u having friends. Oresha seems to delete most men before she has a chance to get to know them. I will say this if she knew what I knew she would have deleted you also. Thats all.

M: You judge your former husband harshly and put him down quickly and often. Is that the Mormon way? Would it please you if my friends "deleted" me from their lives? Do you feel yourself in some kind of a competition with them? Are you jealous of them?

Jen: I will follow what you want with book 4. What made u think I woulden't. You told me you were not interested in dealing with the other books anymore and not writing but now you are telling me now you are working on a fourth book. Thats fine its just that you confuse me with the comments you make in contradicton.

M: It is not me who is contradictory. It is you who misinterprets what I write, judges negatively, and creates a false story. Your fight is always with yourself. When you feel good about yourself you feel good about others and where needed give them the benefit of the doubt. I am the one you feel safe to pick on because you know I forgive easily and move on. Don't pretend that you don't know I am writing book 4, you know that clearly.

What I said about losing interest is that I have now held my first three books in my hands but am not interested in reading them. Maybe most people who write books feel the same, they've already read the manuscript over and over again, they've done their part, they just want to let it go now for all it may be worth, and move on to the next book. You write: *"Are you creating this to leave to your children."* You should have known that I was not writing book 4 for my children so I assumed that you were not planning to have book 4 published if I didn't get to it before I die, that you somehow thought it was only meant for my children.

Jen: I do not think there will be sex as you wish it to be in heaven. It would be nice. I never heard of a near death experience where they talked about people heaving sex. I did read where a man observed some people who had sexual addictions and could not complete or satisfyingly that urge. My understanding is not everybody will be worthy or called to be in families that are having children. You were once on that path and are on a lesser path. Now you write your own fantasy.

M: You acknowledge that it would be "nice" to have sex in heaven but turn it into an undesirable "addiction" because organized religion turns something natural and beautiful and needed for the propagation of the species ("multiply and replenish the earth") into a heaven or hell guilt trip so they can better control their members and keep them engaged in the "repentance" process, you just can't do it between you and God alone they teach. Politicians do likewise, always ensuring that there is a crisis of some kind somewhere to justify their existence. I do not believe that I am on a "lesser" path as you judge me to be. That is your own fantasy. As a matter of fact, where I am now began many years ago when I pondered how eternity could be managed without boredom. I asked that question of God and a powerful chain of circumstances unfolded that resulted in my knowing clearly that I for one would not be bored with eternity because I would always be with wives having sex and children. I like my fantasy, I believe that I am becoming Adam.

Jen: I love you and just want to be with you. I hope somewhere down the line (in heaven) you and I will become worthy to have a family through are eternal ceiling. That's the only way I know that it will be possible. Even Joseph (Smith) Brigham Young had to follow and live the rules that were put in place by God. In hopes it was make them would worthy of a like pure women. Not lesbian women. Lesbian women are not pure vessels. Of course Satan would call them that. I am sure he has surrounded himself with such activity. But since he is spirit I doubt if he can have sex.

M: There you go as usual, judging everyone and everything by your meager understanding of the doctrines and teachings of the church you choose to affiliate with. Does not the atoning blood of Jesus Christ in your belief also apply to women who prefer to have sex with other women than with men? Do you not think that God loves all of His children? Do you honestly think that He would throw any of them into fire and torture them with painful burning torment for eternity with no possibility of escape? Would you do that if you were God and any of your children were disobedient to priests and popes on earth and didn't confess their 'sins' to them? Is it not taught that God is love and love is the opposite of fear? Doesn't it seem more logical that such a thing as hell is an invention of religionists who want to control people by fear so they are perceived essential and the people will give them a living and more to keep their institution going?

Do you consider yourself to be a "pure vessel" and "worthy" to have children beyond the grave? Does the Mormon church teach you such a thing? Do you understand the Mormon concept of "exaltation" other than it being the highest heaven you can aspire to? If you make it there (by your actions on earth that made you "worthy"??) what will you do there? Why do you think you will have children in heaven other than those you already gave birth to on earth, at least those who are judged "worthy" enough to be with you in the highest heaven?

Jen: Just some thoughts that I've had go through my head on the subject. I miss you can't wait to see you we will have a great time and we will get along well. love you

M: I am looking forward to your visit and possibly traveling together in my car if I am cleared by the medical people and we're getting along.

Jen: Went to the rodeo and now home and relaxing also head Mexican food while out. I will be leaving in the morning and wish I was leaving to meet with you but that I have to be put off for a while.

M: I understand that you have to get that tooth fixed, the two weeks will pass. Some things we see very differently and may never be able to reconcile. But I love you sweetsie, let's do our best to get along and enjoy each other. That way maybe we'll be judged "worthy" of something better in the heavens. Should be worth the try. :-)

M: (to myself) While I was writing the message above Jen sends a series of emails that are very far from encouraging. Am I wrong in writing to her so openly, or is it not what I write that provokes her? I think I will not respond to any of the messages that follow, to me they are cutting and nasty. I could easily conclude that she has no real love for me, just a need to control and dominate. (I know, my female readers will most likely think differently. But your writer is *male* dear ones, we *are* different.)

Jen: I sent you a very long email hope you got it but not sure if it went out on my phone The print is so small it makes it hard for me to see. I'm just guessing. Love you and miss you so very very very very very very much we will have a great time and will get a long wonderful. Just don't get upset when a woman is feeling emotional. With your condition that might happen from time to time I will try to make myself aware of it and control it but it's hard when you're losing the love of your life. Do you understand you are the love of my life. Of course you can trust me with 4 to get it published if you wish. Is there somebody else you would prefer other than me I hope not. See you soon sweetie.

I think you were telling me its very important to have friends and I am the strange one for not having friends I guess I should be looking for some male friends. as you have told me its very important for you to have female friends meaning then I must have male friends to be normal just like you. I certainly want to be normal. Thanks for the good advice I'll work on it right away.

Jen: I found my glasses I hope this makes more sense. What are you talking about I don't have hostility toward you. You read too much into comments. I don't like what you wrote below. You are right friends are very important female or male they are very important. I understand unique female friends and I understand from what you shared. I need male friends. Absolutely nothing wrong with that. I understand the loneliness and the need for friends. I see I should search for male friends. I am so glad Oresha is such a good friend and is there for you anytime you call her back to soothe lonely days. I see the situation clearly. Glad it was such a beautiful day and that you were able to get out.

What I am going to say is not hostility it is a request must ask of you to honor. I would feel better if you just left me out of your book and talk about your other woman. Just leave me as the woman you left in the backyard and never mention me again. Then I don't have to be concerned about the fact that what you have written will leave me with great shame. It bothers me you don't care. Maybe in some way you are trying to get even with and just keep me around for material in your books. You are the love of my life I love you the most but there is much in the new michael that I don't respect. It has been painful to observe those desires you have installed. It has been painful to listen to some of your newfound beliefs and your discarding qualities of a good man that you once valued. I miss that man. I hope tomorrow is as glorious a day as today was for you.

Jen: Tell me what is it about you or your characteristics or gifts that would cause me to want to come and spend the rest of my life with you. You say I should not come to be a caretaker. I agree. Now what do you offer sacrifice me. I never felt caring for your or your illness was a sacrifice. So that's off the board. Now tell me what is it about you that would be so desirable for me to give up so much here to be with you there.

One thing that bothers me is. Your overwhelming need to have women. I'm just not enough for you and I can't be with you all the time. You left and you blame me for not being there. it should be you coming to me. Until now. I understand your illness and you can't come full time. Tell me what am i worth and what are you willing to sacrifice to be with me. if you're not you're not and should I have the same attitude.

You have reminded me many times that if I am not there then there is no promise of faithfulness. Do you realize how low of a blow that is. When two people are supposed to be in love and one expresses that type of an attitude. Well I'm going to tell you what it does to the other person he causes him to lose a lot of trust in the person they love they love the most. Yet I do not give up my hope. But this proved wrong over and over. Your needs are more important then me. This has nothing to do with the word friends this has to do with what you mean by the word it may take on a whole different meaning. Holding hands with a woman and walking is more than being a friend. Not Saying you did that but I know if opportunity arose and you like the woman you would. You see I know you are that type of man once you were not that man I like that much better.

Jen: Yes I have the information to publish your books you sent me I put it in a special folder.

Chapter 11

———— ·❦· ————

M: (to myself) She drops the 'atom bomb' telling me to leave her out of my books. Jen, *the books are already published and on the market!!!!* Does she think she will endear herself to me by going out and finding males to be friends with at this point in time? Surely she knows that what I want is for her to be physically with me for the rest of my life and when she is, SHE is my exclusive friend? And that when she has to be away for a while I will not have sex with another? But I am at peace, I know where I stand with this relationship. If she chooses to be unfriendly or to stay away that is her choice and I will deal with the emotion of losing her, yet again. No, I will not respond to those messages. Let her chase me for a while if I am important enough to her to chase, that seems to always work best. If I lose her I lose her, I did my best to be open and honest. I presented her side faithfully, published everything exactly as she wrote, though admittedly she did not get into my journals to comment on my comments about her comments, I suppose that is unfair, but I wanted you to know *me* too.

Jen seems to be ashamed of how she comes across in my books. But most of my readers will be women and maybe to that fairer sex Michael is the villain and Jen the heroine? That however is not the way I had hoped it would be. I had hoped that Jen and I would put past grievances behind and find in each other a perfect love. Is it too late now for that, especially when she seems determined to find other men, maybe go back to Al when she gets home tomorrow to 'get even' with me for having female friends? I wonder. I do wish her well. It will hurt if she goes to other men now that she knows my days are so short. But she is single (by her choice) and I must accept whatever she chooses for herself. I say to myself *"I am Adam, I love my wives and children"* and I am calmed, all is well in the heavens where I shall soon take up abode. It is peaceful there, heavenly really...

Jen: (responding to my earlier updates about Elaine, Suzanne, Oresha, and Carrie) Thanks for the update I really appreciate the information you gave me. It definitely reassures me. You could make it sound like if Oresha would be going to be a lover he would take her. Or am I reading into something that is not there you seem to be drawn to her what is it about her that you like so much. Do you really want to see me or have me with you. I guess you must because you talk about the associate I can be doing together separate. I am like you I need reassurance sometimes. Maybe we suffer from the same condition. Give me both still have trust issues.

M: We do have trust issues, it's easy to have when we live a thousand miles and more from each other. I do not encourage Oresha to visit, it's just that she is a faithful friend, she even came over to get the manager to let her in my apartment when she lost contact, not knowing I was in hospital. And she continues to express what I think is genuine concern about me, she knows there is no possibility of romance for us, she just wants to be a friend. I have *zero* interest in having sex with her! I thought I'd told you that several times already.

Yes I DO want you to visit. *After all, this is the guy who has been trying to get you to move in with him for the last nine months!!!* Sure we disagree about our fantasy worlds, but that's not the reality we find ourselves in at present. You live alone only because you CHOOSE it to be that way. You are single only because you CHOOSE to be single. You have a man who wants to live the rest of his life with you, you say you love him but you CHOOSE to not be with him. You could change all that, you are single, you are free, you can do what you want, it's entirely up to you. And meanwhile as you make up your mind about this particular man, why not come and visit him and stay a while so you know the real him better and he you?

You seem to be ashamed of how you come across as a character in my books. But most of my readers will be women and maybe to that fairer sex Michael is the villain and Jen the heroine. That however is not the way I had hoped it would be. I had hoped that Jen and Michael would put past grievances behind and find in each other a perfect love. Is it too late for that to happen now?

Jen: It is really weird the words how statements turn out when you reread what you talked into a cell phone. When I re-read I'm not even sure what I was trying to say or the point I was trying to make. Anywho have fun kind to figuring it out or just delete it I seem to be feeling emotions, NOT sure why have them. One thing I do know I need you and I love you.

M: I love you too sweetheart, come and let's give it a good try to live together in peace for a few weeks at least and take it from there wherever if anywhere it leads.

Jen: We are supposed to have a winter storm with lots of snow and then going to be prepared with blankets and supplies if you're travelin. The suburban has extra wide tires and 4 wheel drive. I should be ok. The only thing is I wish it was going to see you.

M: Perhaps you should leave immediately and beat the storm? 4 wheel drive does not help you see the road any clearer or stop sooner, that's a heavy vehicle to bring to a halt if you suddenly see something in the way in a storm. If I was you I'd get out of there right now. But keep me informed and for sure send a message as soon as you get home. Drive safe sweetheart, you are precious to me.

M: I don't know the forecast but if you do leave tonight, plan on going only as far as Las Vegas and stay the night there if you get too sleepy or tired. You should be fine getting home from there tomorrow?

Jen: Talking about the book. Michael may find he went too far. The perfect love can not exist in 50 shades of grey. It can only exist in two pure virtuous human beings. Self indulgence exist in 50 shades of grey that is not love. 50 shades of grey are the shades Satan uses to sucker us in. You have to admit he knows how to entice. Is Michael lost in the last 50 shades of grey. until he moves into the light he will never find the perfect love. Jen believes Michael can return to the light and give up 50 shades of grey that bind him. It is in the light but the perfect love exist and waits. Take Jens hand so that both can reach up and fill their heart with that perfect love that is pure sanctify of God.

M: Have you read 50 shades? You don't even make sense, you just want to make me into the image of the man you think I *should* be. For you it's never enough to be just me the way I am is it? You must have control, me putting my hand in yours so you can lift us up kind of thing. What on earth is "pure sanctify of God" supposed to mean anyway?

You talk so silly sometimes, you certainly did not have this religious fervor when I lived with you for 18 years, you were much more relaxed and tolerant of others it seemed to me. You didn't even go to the temple sometimes for years, and now you're gung ho on it all. Why?

It seems to me that the choice you have if you really do love me is to be with me while I live and *then* look for a Mormon man who agrees to live with you for the rest of his or your lifetime and then as one of his wives in heaven *if* that turns out to be the way it really is after death and *if* you both qualify for that highest heaven and *if* you can stand to be other than his "First Wife" forever. Or, to look for that Mormon man *now* and walk away from me permanently to complete the divorce you began. It's your choice of course. Or take a chance on me and let go of your fantasy that there is a better man than me for you waiting to find you? After all, if I fail you you've always got your spirit man who says *he's* your Adam but you have to die to be with him. You're being silly sweetie.

It is not likely that I will ever enter a Mormon temple again in this lifetime. So if you are going to continue striving to be "a good Mormon" and "a pure virtuous human being" (which I am not you say) you have a choice to make don't you? At least I'm honest about it. What do you want that you *can* have?

Jen: Would you please fix my spelling ceiling to sealing. Also I noticed I had some uddering words just before Joseph Smith and Brigham Young could you give it a clear meaning or delete it. Below are some thoughts to think about.

I don't believe I am judging or putting myself above anybody elses lifestyle I just want the highest and the best for me and my partner. We must come to a mutual understanding if we are going to be happy together I am being honest in what I am searching for. Tell me do you believe in sin? Do you accept all men's standards as being equal to yours ? And they should act to their own level of fairness. In which somewhere along the line develops into justifying their actions. Do you believe in God the Father and Jesus Christ? Do you not believe sexual sin's? As long as you don't think your hurting anyone.

When you had sex and were marrisd you hurt me. When you had sex with a woman one day and left her to come to my bed the next night in hopes I would take you back. HURT ME. You also hurt her by not being the right man and still took her to bed. She kept herself full of alcohol to get through the week knowing it was another deep disappointment. As a man you should not of taken her to bed. You should have let her keep her dignity and backed off and remain friends. I am glad she is a woman that forgives and I'm sure the memories not sweet. Unless you lied to me. Does that mean sexual activity is justifiable? If a man believes by killing a another man that he believes is a very bad make it justifiable ? A man that robs a bank because he knows people who are in need is that justifiable? We were given the 10 commandments to follow because we all tend to justifying differently. Look at the great harm some societies have brought up amongst their people I just justifying their action.

M: When you secretly divorced me and lied to a judge to take everything away from me. HURT ME. I did not have sex until after I found out from one of my business customers that you were divorcing me and had taken everything away from me on false pretenses with no opportunity for me to tell the judge my side of the story. You DIVORCED me! I was a single man from the day you filed, the rest was just bureaucrats and lawyers doing their thing, mere paperwork, you had already walked away from me, dropped the deadliest weapon possible upon a married couple, the atom bomb, divorce.

But it seems your intent tonight to be as miserable and contentious and blaming and guilt tripping as you can be. So be it, you've done it many times before. I can only conclude during times like these that you have no genuine love for me, *you would divorce me again if you could!* You ask me the kind of religious questions a Mormon bishop would ask during a temple recommend interview. It seems that you are trying to gather written evidence to present against me in a church court and try to get me excommunicated. If so *why*? What would it matter to you? (Though it might to my kids.) You have a contentious spirit Jen, you cannot be the Eve Mother of Nations I seek for my fantasy world, she is not like that. So walk away and end this divorce once and for all will you? That always seems to be what you really want even though you pretend that you love me. If you did you would be pleasant and do your best to please me instead of to drive me further and further away from you all the time.

And by the way your Suzanne story is just a fantasy you dreamt up, you do not know her, she was not "hurt". And it was several weeks after I was with her in Las Vegas before I was with you and you took me to your bed, not the next night. (You were visiting your son, I waited for you in Mesquite, and then your other son came.) I thought at the time that you were ready to reconcile like I was but it turned out all you wanted from me was sex. You astonished (and hurt) me months later when you told me you were not at all ready to reconcile at that time. I thought you were close, I would have moved back in and all these months of loneliness and mistrust and confusion and enmity would never have been. You don't want me Jen, face it, if you did you'd be here with me doing everything you can to court and win me back to marriage. I am always pleasant to you except when I feel I must defend myself and the truth, I don't refrain from doing so, you see that as a slam. I love you unconditionally, it's always YOU who starts and drags on the contention. Why? But why should it matter, you have again proven to me that you are not mine, maybe never were. Good-bye, enjoy your life if you can.

Or come and visit me long enough for us to try to reconcile properly, my door will always be open to you, this lifetime and the next because I DO love you - it's not me trying to keep us apart, it's always you. Make up your mind what you want and go for it without trying to force others to be what you demand they be. Sure, I could have ignored your rant tonight but I chose not to, it needs to be cleared up once and for all. *Clear it up will you?* Your fight is always with yourself. And don't pretend to be concerned about me, I have loving supportive family and friends, I will be well, you know that. You are still welcome to come and visit me, but you are not welcome to bring the spirit of contention and enmity into my home and my life, my last days are to be lived in peace, why should they not be?

Jen: Regarding old e-mails. Delete it don't put it on your journal. Every writer probably deleted more pages than what is in the book maybe several times as many pages. Nobody wants to hear same subject over and over delete it!. If the writing is bad on my part deleted it!

M: My books are already published and on the market. Jen does not come out perfect, neither does Michael. As it is with every novel, each reader judges each character for themselves, it's that way in real life too. You presented Jen well I thought, quite human, quite believable. It's you who judges yourself harshly because you want to think of yourself as someone you are not. You're still good enough for me to love and to want to be with though. I only wish you'd love me the way I am without trying to force me to be someone else. Or leave me once and for all if you can't stand who and what I am. There may be others (such as your neighbor) who you could learn to love properly just the way they are. (I'll bet you wouldn't try to change *him*, at least not until long association made you realize he wasn't everything you want.) Whatever your choice I will always wish you the very best. Take care, good night, good-bye if that is your choice, it's not mine.

M: (to Jen the next day) There, we have done it again, proven to each other that we *each* have much in our past that is undesirable and unlovely and could be valid cause to find grievous fault with the other. Are we more content this morning that it is so? Will you come for a visit and try harder to live peaceably with and enjoy this man even if he is not everything you want in a male companion? We needn't talk of marriage, I can accept you as you are except for the contention, that must be left behind. I must have peace as I prepare my exit from this place of choice and learning. *"Blessed are the peace makers for they shall be called the children of God."* :-)

You can escape from me anytime you want to, in fact if you buy a one-way flight here, I will buy your one-way home the instant you ask. Are we worth another try do you think?

I assume you are home now so let me know what email address to use to send messages to you. Was the storm bad? I can't really think of how it could be between Phoenix and your Utah home. I continue to love you. Your man in Canada.

M: (to myself) Jen phoned as she was leaving Phoenix and we talked a while, she unwittingly pulled off the road and parked in a *cemetery* of all places. Symbolic? She wanted to know if I still want her to come to Victoria. I assured her that I do but I can't live with contention, we need to see if we can get along. Perhaps visits of three or so weeks would be best for us, we'll have to see how it works. She asked if I would move to Alberta to be closer to my kids and I said I would if I was confined to being inside a building, that the cold would not trouble me then. But obviously in asking that she is confirming yet again that she does not see a permanent future with us living together. This lady will almost certainly not be my wife again because she freely chooses not to be. Divorce seems to have worked for her, I guess from her point of view it was a good thing she speedily filed for divorce when I left to write a book.

Was she so discontent that the thought of divorce was stewing inside her for years before she acted upon it I wonder? Can she accept me now for who I am? I don't think so, she will continue to try to make me a temple attending Mormon again. Not such a bad fate actually, but unlikely to ever be because my beliefs have changed since stepping back and looking at the entire picture of organized religion, not just the Mormons. There is better to be had than motivation through fear and guilt, happiness comes whether one professes membership in a church or not. The promised possible goal of getting to a higher heaven of course is attractive, church is not all negative. Others may see church very differently, especially if they crave the sociality, the singing, familiar ritual and sense of belonging.

Can Jen and I find peace and enjoyment in each other's company? I don't know yet, it sure would be frustrating if she sleeps in my bed but denies us sexual relations. Still, cuddles would be better than being alone, though she tends to be up all night anyway. Maybe we'll do better next time and she won't leave in a cold shoulder huff like she did the last time she was here. It's all up to us I guess for I am not searching for another in this lifetime as long as there is the realistic hope of us living peaceably and contentedly together for long periods of time. She did mention on the phone though the importance of having friends so I think she will be inclined from now on to look for male companionship other than mine. Knowing that my time is short could easily move her quickly into a deeper relationship than friendship with another man. I'd have no choice but to let her go to her man if it developed that way, her life must go on. Perhaps that's why she would favor me moving closer to my kids. I can't blame her, it's just that she says one thing and does another *and that's horribly confusing!*

M: (to Jen) You asked me on the phone if I would move to Alberta to be closer to my kids when I get to the point of needing care. I said if I was housebound that I might because then the cold would not trouble me. (Though I'd probably have to go out for medical tests etc. now and then so it would be unpleasant.)

I assumed from your question that you have no intention of us living together long-term and that you will soon follow up on your expressed desire to make friends with other men. I'd sooner you didn't but that is your business. I just want you to know that my preference for my last days is for the two of us to live together as if husband and wife as often as possible, at least until I am needing frequent physical care. Should that time come I will understand completely if you leave to take up the rest of your life with a man who can take care of all your needs, I do not wish to be a burden on you. And you may need to do that sooner should opportunity arise, such as your neighbor's wife dying and he proposing to you. Please keep me informed about things like that, I will never intentionally cage you or hold you back from a greater happiness.

I tell you this so there is no misunderstanding. I continue to feel as if we are still married but I have no right to impose on you because in fact we are not. I DO want us to live together as much as you will allow it. (Assuming that we can keep the peace when together, at least most of the time.) I may never understand the discrepancy between your frequent profusions of great love for me and your unwillingness for us to be together except for visits. But I expect that you have your reasons for what you do and I will always welcome your presence. Please comment.

M: (to 5 cc Jen) I still have the winter blahs (nothing else wrong with me swear :-) and would love to get to a warm destination fast. I'm feeling pretty good right now so I have high confidence that my health would permit such a trip. High on my used to be list was a cruise on either the Royal Caribbean Oasis or Allure or both (the largest cruise ships in the world.) Maybe a back to back East Carib and West Carib or how about a week or two or so in a nearby (Fort Lauderdale) timeshare in between and do both the ships?

I think Jen might go on this and it would be nice if you were with us. Someone else along would be helpful for Jen if I have to rest a lot. I think Jen will be visiting me, so check flights for both of us from and return Victoria. We might do a road trip with my car soon after we get back, it could include Alberta. Are you interested in checking this out for us and maybe going along?

S: (cc Jen) Always. Let me do some research.

M: (to myself) Tonight out of boredom and loneliness and a whole lot of newly renewed insecurity about Jen I went to the singles site we used to both frequent and looked at the selection of males about Jen's age within a few miles of her city. And wow, there are a whole lot of men who I think she would be interested in at least as much as me even if I was in good health. The competition is severe and I think she's aware of that. Is that why she asked me what I have to offer her that would be better than what she has going for her in Utah? Her comment about needing male friends combined with her hoping that today would be a glorious day for her makes me wonder if she is with Al or another male tonight or at least making contacts and plans for the next few days. How can I possibly compete? *I can't!* I know, we've been there before many times but this is real time for me and I thought I'd let you know. I think I'll let Jen know too.

M: (to Jen) I'm sure you've been home for quite some time now and I'm missing you, was hoping to hear from you soon after you got home.... (I'm copying this message into one I sent later, you'll read it soon.)

M: (to Jen's other email address) Just in case you are only checking for messages on your cell phone account, today I've been sending them to your regular email address. Please check there and respond tonight, I'm very insecure about you again, thanks.

Jen: I am home and safe. Just a bit tired.

Jen: (re the cruise) I think so. Need to think more tomorrow and check on flights. I have my companion ticket. Could we get there with Alaska airlines or close. PS: If we could get a bigger cabin 5 could stay in the cabin with us.

M: (I'm including in this message one I sent to Jen earlier, my hope being that she will write between the lines and respond to both messages.)

When you suggest that 5 stay in the same cabin as us are you suggesting that you and I sleep in separate beds? That's important to me, I doubt that I'd enjoy a cruise if I don't even get to cuddle you during the night. Please clarify that and respond fully to this and my other email where I confess my insecurity about you and ask some questions that I hope you'll give me honest answers to and comment freely. Your one line sentence last night saying nothing about what you did when you got home until late last night leaves me even more insecure. If I at least *knew* you were seeing or communicating with another man I'd know better where I stand with you and could put you on the periphery of my life going forward if need be, please grant me that. You have hardly shared anything personal since you last walked away from me. You continue to tell me you only have eyes for me but you don't tell me about your days, I crave knowing and sharing your life.

Please communicate honestly and openly with me, that's the only hope we have of becoming comfortable with each other again. As it is right now we're both strangers at a distance. The last time I laid eyes on you following a prolonged kiss that I initiated I saw only a cold shoulder, you didn't even look back as you walked away to airport security. Been there, done that, don't like it, especially when I still feel that we are married. Am I silly to feel that?

Should I move on preparing for my death with no thought of any significant woman in my life except my own children and siblings? What do you advise? I need to get my focus secured and my emotions in a proper place. I'm working on life-ending events and must get it right.

Am I just a burden on you now and your thoughts are with or hoping for another man?

Did you call or message or get together with Al or any other single man yesterday or in the past month? *I feel that you did!* Please clear that up one way or the other. I need to know so I can work on a lasting peace within my soul that is based on truth. You are exceedingly important to me. Are you currently registered on any singles sites?

I'm feeling hugely insecure after that exchange of quarreling messages in which you said you'd be looking for male friends and had a lot going for you in St. George. So what do I have to offer you better you ask. And then your phone call yesterday as if you were trying to assess the situation with me and decide to contact or see another man or not when you got home.

Yes, I'm a lot like you, very insecure, loving the other but not living together. We had a big tiff again. Tell it true. Reassure me. I won't be angry with you either way except for silence or deceit, and I'll always welcome your visits even if there are other men in your life. I just have a burning need to know if you are in touch with another male or not.

Please respond, I know you are capable of telling me the truth, and also of deceiving me. Which is it this time? Let's get this uncovered if you are keeping secrets, I think you owe me (and us) that. I love you intensely but I don't trust you. You can change that last part with open and honest and full non-evasive communication. Today would be an excellent time to make it your top priority to sit at your computer for a while and open up to me. I look forward to reading your responses to these two messages. Write between the lines if it's easier that way to respond to every question I ask.

Here's my earlier message:

I'm sure you've been home for quite some time now and I'm missing you, was hoping to hear from you soon after you got home, at least to let me know you'd arrived home safely when snow was threatening along the way. I think I must be in love with you or something. :-)

Can you tell me about how long you plan to visit this time? I'm curious to know too if you will actually be looking for one or more male friends like you said you would be? (You said that you have a whole lot going for you in St. George so why would you come to me? Does that mean a lot of male prospects?) Yes, there's still that part of me that is jealous, I'm selfish, wanting you to myself, especially when we both know my time on earth is short so any friendship you have with a male could quickly move into much more and you'd leave me. (Can't say as I'd blame you for that, you have a life to live, my candle's about burnt out, sorry I didn't do better by you but we had a lot of good years I'd say.)

Do you care to comment honestly about the above since we had that tiff last night and everything may be changed again and I'm horribly insecure about you? Do you still have a desire to see Al? Your neighbor? Someone else close enough to your home or in California to be friends with? About how much time together do you think you will allow us over the next six months? Will you need to get away now and then to see other men do you think?

Missing you lots, sure wish you were here, it will be such fun walking with you holding hands, I'll be proud of you pretty woman. We ran into my next door neighbor a few times when you last visited. I saw her look at your face curiously the first time and how she instantly bowed her head and slumped her shoulders, knowing there was no way she could compete with lovely you. I like it that way.

Talk to me about the above? Can we be close again and share our lives and thoughts for a while, maybe my duration however long or short it turns out to be? Just writing that made my heart do a few loud beats and I feel ill as though it may be notice that my time really is short even though I feel ok much of the time when I'm on the pain pills. Tomorrow I'll feel fine again I expect, it's most likely stress more than anything, you are very important to me, I don't want to lose you again. I love you, I want you near, write me please. If I didn't care for you I wouldn't write such impassioned messages would I? Please ponder that and write to me fully and honestly...

M: (to Suzanne) I have neglected daily meditation for so long now that when I made the attempt last night it was only with difficulty that

I was able to grasp enough focus to attain a vibratory state in which the mind is cleared of all concerns, the universe is right, the heart is alive with love and joy. In that state I realized yet again that we attract everything we think about whether it be something we want or something we do not want, it matters not to Law of Attraction. We are Creator, we must be obeyed where there is clarity. All we think of for more than a few moments is automatically created spiritually and in time will be fulfilled though possibly modified or even deleted from manifestation by conscious change of thought and expectation. WE GET WHAT WE THINK ABOUT WHETHER WE WANT IT OR NOT!

Too long now this suspicion and enmity between me and Jen has been manifest. For too long I have been writing books filled with the same story because for too long I have been thinking the same thoughts. I will make more attempts to enter and hold that state of vibration where I think of and expect only that which is positive. I will think of and expect from me and Jen only a perfect love, a love at last gone RIGHT. But being human she is free to choose for herself. Will she join me in such thoughts and expectations? If not there will be another or others attracted to me who have the same dream as mine. That's how the universe is built. I like it that way...

Now where's my angel to tell me the moment of my death so I can get this manuscript concluded and in the right hands? I feel that it may not be long now, there is much that is beckoning me to better places. I go wide awake and aware, accepting the *fullness* of LIFE.

Do you get anything from such expressions Suzanne? Do they make sense to you? Is that the kind of thing that might one day be discussed in reading circles such as yours in Austin? Should I live, should I or another extract such meanderings from the 2,000 pages and publish them as one small book? Are they important enough for such a thing as that?

5: Yes, I am in for a separate cabin. I would also do the ocean view.

M: (to 5 cc Jen) I'm ready to book an ocean view cabin today, waiting for Jen. Are you ready for this Jen? Should I book an ocean view for us today?

5: When Jen is in, I will book my own cabin. I have to figure out who would come. Probably 6, although 1 of us may end up "accidentally" going over board!!

M: I'll visit the one who drowns but may not be able to break into a jail. I'll let you know when I hear from Jen.

5: Ha! Ha! 6 is in most likely. Ya, just let me know what Jen thinks. If she is not interested, are you still wanting to go? I did the numbers and it would save us $280.33 each for 3 people in 1 ocean view cabin. Anyway, I thought I would give you a back up plan as well just in case you are interested in one.

M: Yes I would go without Jen, I'm never sure of her and really need that sunshine. The three of us in the cabin would work as long as I get quiet time to rest when I need to. Oh, yeah and first in the shower each morning, and fresh ear plugs as needed, and, and... :-)

Jen: I was not suggesting anything you read into. We don't have to go on a Cruse to cuddle. I like spooning. As far as getting home. I pick up a few things at the 99 cent store. I stopped for gasoline a couple of times. I made it safely to my door. Turned up the heat in the house. Then unloaded the van. Put everything away. Sister and cousin text me to see if I made it home safe. I went and pick up the mail. Put two loads of cloths in the washer and unpacked my bag. Went to bed and watched a boring movie and fell asleep and woke up and sent you a short message. Went back to bed.

You kept telling me I am strange for thinking anything unusual about your female friends. That is not true. Why would you be concern if I have male and female friends. I am not different than you. You get defensive when it comes to your friends and put me down. If you think I might be doing the same things you see fitting you get upset and insecure. I don't understand why you would feel so insecure about us. I am not the one that was looking for a lover when I told another woman at the same time I loved her and wanted her. If I found another man you would be the first to know. I don't go around searching for another love when I have one. You have become to much of a man of the world. I don't operate on that level. I am faithful even when my man is not with me. I went straight home last night and meet with no one. If a time comes that I feel we are only friends then I will let you know. Even then I don't think I would look for another man.

Interesting how you feel married now when a year ago you were married and you claim you were a single man. You live a lie to fit the image you tell yourself. You give the situation the twist you want. It leaves me insecure. I have always felt married and acted accordingly. That is a lie I live. I am not registered on any single site that I am aware of. I get messages but they are trying to get me to come back. Most of what you write is just in your head. As I have told you many times I am a one woman man. That does not mean I would not have female and male's as friends. You have expressed how rewarding it was to have Oresha contact management to make sure you were ok. I believe if you thought one of your neighbor's might be in trouble you would also contact management to check on them. That is a friend and a good neighbor..

As far as living together other than taking care of you full time most likely will not happen with out marriage. Many things would need to change for me to re-enter that walk. I would love for it to happen but to many obstacles are in the way. Mostly your new found beliefs and your dreams of the next life do not fit with the plan we have been given through a prophet of God. I could except if you just believed and became the best Latter day saint you could. I mean live it in everyway. I don't care what man thinks but I do care what the man I marry thinks. Of course I understand I can not or would I want to change something that is impossible. For that reason it is out of my hands. I can only let known what I want in a husband. You were a good temple going man when I married you the first time. I want him back.

I can't do anything about the first books you published but I can request you to remove me from book 4. Just say Jen died before the perfect love or just disappeared. I think much of our emails are rubbish. We quarrels back and forth over the same things and that is old an no one is interested in garbage between to people. Think about it. You do not want to know the garbage that went on between 5 and her husband to get to a place their marriage is solid and happy.

You ask can we be close again. Of course we can. Even when discontent we are on each others mind. We can have peace but what are you willing to do to have that. Is it you that needs to change. Is it me that needs to change. Do we just except and see what the other is capable of doing that brings peace. Is this honest enough. Love you.

M: Yes, that is honest enough, you have reassured me immensely.

Now, are you in to share the cost of the two of us in an ocean view cabin for that cruise? If so I will go ahead and book it. It's likely that 6 will share a cabin with 5. We'll have fun beating the two of them at canasta even though 5 cheats. I'm on to some of her tricks now because she was my partner against 6 and 3 when they visited. :-)

Let me know about the cruise right away. That will get some more warm days behind us before we do our road trip if that's still on, we can decide for sure when we get back and I recheck with the docs if need be. I love you honey.

M: (to myself) There is much that I could comment on in Jen's response. But in my desire to end the enmity and write a new story I will let it go. Hopefully this will be the last exchange of emails like that one, the beginning of a new era of trust and hope and love between us. If we each have friends of the opposite sex so be it, that's what we want, why should it not be? And hard as it is to take, if Jen does not want to marry or live with me then so be it, that is her choice, I cannot go back and be the man she married almost twenty years ago. I will do my best to enjoy the together time she gives us.

I have learned that once one yields oneself to Law of Attraction that life not only flows abundantly without effort, but that it comes line upon line precept on precept as we allow our higher self to do the planning. Today, with that unexpected email sent to Suzanne the thought entered my mind to write a small book called perhaps *"The Book of Musings"* by Michael Demers. It should be easy to make, a simple matter of copying some of the paragraphs from my books that I think are particularly interesting into a manuscript and writing subject headings. That would promote the series too, if the book sold. It's a brand new desire, I'm interested in what Suzanne will have to say about the matter.

M: (to Jen but not sent) Please forgive me for asking all those old questions yet again. I believe that will now put the matter to rest for all time and we can get on with a relationship based on love and enjoyment. It's disappointing that you have chosen not to marry and live with me but I understand what you are seeking. It's just that I can't go back twenty years and become again the man you married. But keep in mind that you divorced that man long before you knew that he had "new found beliefs" that you choose to judge a deal breaker to remarriage. I accept you as you are and look forward to being with you as much as you will allow us to be, I think we can have a lot of fun playing ourselves.

Please respond about the cruise, three weeks on the warm Caribbean is just what I need right now. Shall I go ahead and book ocean view for two and you'll reimburse your share when you get here? (And right there Jen called and said to go ahead and book it, so I won't send this message to her.)

M: (to 5) Jen just called and she's in. So I'll book an ocean view for the two of us right away. It shouldn't matter that much if we're located nearby but I'll let you know our room number unless there's the option of a free upgrade if I let them pick our room at the last minute. I'm loving it, three weeks at sea in a warm place, love it, love it, love it!

5: Awesome! I'm really excited. I will talk with my hubby and get 5 and myself booked as well.

5: Hotel is booked!

M: Now get booked on that ship.

5: Yes!!

M: (to Jen) I've got the cruise booked.

M: (to Jen) Good job getting the flights, looks great, this is coming together real well. I'm so looking forward to this, thanks so much for coming with me, what a treat! I'll let you know when I hear back from 5 but you and I are going for sure.

Oresha: Are you enjoying this B-U-Tiful weather? :) When did you say that Jen is coming back to town? If you'd like to get out for a

walk anytime, since the weather is getting better... please let me know...
:) I put a profile up on Spiritualsingles yesterday... today I got my 1st
"Hello"..... from a 57yr old guy from TEXAS!... too far away... sigh...
lol ...and an "interest" thing from a guy in Ontario.... @ least he's in
Canada!... but too far away... I'm going to "feel" it out for a bit before
I possibly consider upgrading... see if anybody from near by seems
interested... Meanwhile.. I'm still doin' laps around The Pond...lol
One day at a time.... :) I hope you're doin'well... enjoy the rest of your
evening! Ciao...

M: I walk most days. How be you come over tomorrow afternoon
(or whenever convenient) if it's not pouring rain and I'll buy you a kale
smoothie at the Bay Mall, walk both ways, or maybe from there to the
park?

Jen and I will be doing a 21 day Caribbean cruise with two of
my daughters. I don't care what the oncologist tells me at my next
appointment, the cruise and flights are booked, I'M GOING!!! :-)

I was on Spiritual Singles for quite a while. It's nowhere near as
prolific as POF but there are interesting people to at least message with
from a distance, they'd probably all be interested in The Orb Lady. I
was once in touch with a good looker who lives on an island near Spain.
She said she was a high priestess of some ancient cult and as such would
dance naked on the beach in the moonlight for me then take me to her
cave. Just before I bought my ticket :-) she told me she went on a cruise
with a man who paid for everything but was angry with her because
she wouldn't give him sex. I told her the man would have reasonably
assumed that was going to happen when she agreed to share a cabin
with him all expenses paid. She abruptly broke off the conversation. :-)

Oresha: Hey M...:) I just took a peek @ the weather ch. ..... it's
only going to be 7 tomorrow.... & maybe a bit of a windchill.... brrr...
lol It's supposed to get warmer as the week progresses... 11 on Fri. &
13 on Sunday! Woohoo!.. How about later in the week then? ...if that's
OK with you? I'd love to walk with you, where ever you'd like :) How
AWESOME that you're going on the cruise with Jen AND Your Girls!
You GO-Boy!!!!... Yay!... :)

Good thing "The High Priestess" shared the info with you... about the "look but don't touch" thing!... before you bought your "ticket-to-paradise"...ha! ha! ;) Can't understand why she got "Pissy" with you!... lol Sounds like there just might be some "interesting" types on there... lol Now a Handsome-Polynesian-God who's independently wealthy.... might get my attention!... and ...if he's into ORBS... even better!....HA! HA! ;) Take care.. Ttys... let me know if you're OK with waiting til it warms up a bit more? Night.... Hugz..

M: I walk anyway, winter jacket, but you call the when.

Oresha: Ok.... let's chat a bit later in the week & see if the weatherman is still behind this forecast... lol I just enjoy walking more when it's warmer.... Ttys...

Kris: Hope you are enjoying your time with family. Just thought I would send this airline deal... should you wish to do some travelling. It needs to be booked soon.

M: (to Kris) That's so sweet of you to think of me like that, thank-you so much. Ironically about four hours ago I booked a non-refundable return flight to Fort Lauderdale. Two of my daughters (and my ex) are doing a 21 day cruise with me. But I'll research the destinations available for this promo. I hope you are well.

M: (to Jen) As usual it never rains it pours. Less than two hours after you booked the flights to Florida I got a message from Kris. She gave me promo codes for 40% off flights including destinations such as Ireland and Hawaii. Look it over and let me know if anything interests you.

Kris: Great... hope you can get something that works. Much kindness

M: (to myself) I have a rain check from Kris for dinner at her home so I agonized a bit about not asking her if it was still valid before Jen gets here and I'll be tied up for weeks, maybe months. But I feel totally committed to Jen now as if we are married, so there's no point in moving anything along with Kris, it would only make Jen feel suspicious and jealous.

Yesterday as I walked along the sea I consciously tried to stop admiring women from a point of view that includes sexuality, thinking of myself as married and faithful to my wife. It *worked* - for a while! But no, don't get the idea that Michael Demers is not interested in sex anymore. Trust me, he *is*. Obedient Mormons don't have sexual relations outside of marriage so I'm hoping that Jen with her newly found religious fervor doesn't make touch a sinful thing to do. She won't marry me and she demands that I be "faithful" to her so I'm not sure what I'll do if I have to try to resign myself to not having sex for the rest of my life. My guess is that if I don't protest too much at the beginning it will evolve so that I can at least caress her most anywhere I want to, especially if she shares my bed and it's in the night.

Thus is the strangeness of organized religion and Mormons in particular who aren't even allowed to sleep naked with their spouse. (Though I expect that most do and live with the guilt and fear of not being "worthy" of the highest heaven when they die.) There is much that is good and uplifting in religion. And there is much that is controlling and silly to the rational mind should one dare to think about it. Is there a simmering pot of resentment beneath the piety and blind obedience of most religionists who struggle daily to deny their rebellious human selves? I think there was in me and it manifested as a form of hell: no need to wait, come get it, the promise of religion is true kind of thing. My teenage years in particular were a fierce battle as pious Catholic me tried to contain what nature was inexorably bursting forth. There was a period of several of my teenage years when I wouldn't go to a movie because it might be provocative and the beast in me could let loose. Yes, I was supposed to have been a priest and often acted the part. Friends would drop me off before heading to pleasure places, girls in another town who were looser than those in theirs they thought. The boys in those towns thought differently. My Catholic friends did not have such a struggle as I forced upon myself. After all, confession was easily had kneeling in dark places, and absolution white as snow instantly followed mea culpas and Hail Mary's. Everyone knew the priest wouldn't tell their parents so it was a good gig going there at the appointed times.

My dear sweet mother was trapped in religion from birth (not Mormon.) Her own mother was a saint, they sacrificed their lives for others, denying themselves the pleasures that come with physical bodies and life on earth. (At least I think they did.) Once after coming back from church in her old age, mom had a weak moment and asked me her son, a Mormon high priest, if there was a God. Of course I assured her that there was and the topic was closed for all time. Sure she died sweet, a well respected pillar of religious testimony example and encouragement to those who knew her. But did she get to the highest heaven her church proffered? Nobody knows for sure but her if the pious life of sacrifice and denial was worth it. Religion brings peak moments, moments found also in meditation, the reading of good books and poetry, the arts; none of which but religion demand denial and sacrifice for the hope of some nebulous distant reward. I think it's really all a matter of feeling good about *ourselves*, we exist to know joy. *Religion is a gamble.*

Jen: (to 5 cc me) It will be wonderful seeing you 5 and 6. It has been awhile. It will be lots of fun. Love Jen

5: I am excited too. And all the canasta is the icing on the cake!!!

M: (to 6) I am delighted that you and 5 will be on the cruise with me and Jen, it should be tons of fun. Just be prepared to lose often at canasta (we'll let you win a few times) because you'll be partnered with your sister instead of with me. :-) Oh well, c'est la vie, win some, lose some, smile, shrug, survive to do it again another day, it's the process and never knowing for sure what's ahead that's so fun.

I never did hear from anyone about the funeral or about the gathering at 1's, not a word. I'd appreciate a report (from someone) on how that all went down and if you handed out the papers I gave you to distribute. If so, how were they received? (It was a last minute decision to do that, it wasn't well thought out.) I wish I could have been there but as you know I wasn't allowed to fly yet and the thought of a road trip through the mountains in the winter was overwhelming. Jen is arriving here soon, we hope to see you and 5 in Florida the day before we sail away. And yes, it doesn't matter what the oncologist tells me at my next visit, I'M GOING!!

5: (forwarded to Jen) Jen, I can't wait to see you. I've really missed you. Especially during the holidays. You've always been in my thoughts and prayers and I welcome our reunion! I'm sure with 6 on board we'll have lots of fun things to do together.... not to mention more than a few rounds of Canasta. We'll have to convince 6 to switch the teams up sometimes! LOL. See you soon

Jen: I am clearing out some of my old cloths and paper books to give away. Is there anything I have of yours you want me to keep. Like some really nice suits.

M: I have only one suit with me and almost never wear it. But if I ever visit you in Utah it might be good to have a suit there so I don't need to bring one with me for church. Do as you will though, those kinds of things are easily replaced if need be.

I continue to marvel at the miracle that a couple of little red pills do for me. Sometimes I am feeling like I'm dying (literally), like this morning, and being the tough guy I am sometimes I keep on typing. Then in a while the pills I took start to kick in like the drug they are or a warm brandy and I'm fine for many hours. (Not sure if I've ever had a warm brandy, that just popped into mind, guess I must be a fiction writer. :-)

It's nice to get ordinary messages from you like this one. I just got out of bed again, haven't showered yet today at 2 p.m. but my dreams are pleasant, the stuff of fantasy books and movies. Me and bare-breasted others riding horses without saddles thundering carelessly across a green prairie *alive* with the motion and the moment, swiftly bridging a hill while the people on the other side exclaim: *"The gods are coming!"*

Yeah, in the fantasy that would be me, it's fun and we're harmless. Oh, and unicorns and centaurs are real too, just thought you'd want to know. :-) I suppose *whatever* we want we can create. I'm all for that, the universe is big and we are in it, I love that part...

Strange huh? Don't bring a bra, I'll take you riding without a saddle lovely you. That's more fun than religion, tastier than warm brandy in a glass, eyes fluttering as you flirt with me your king, knowing that what's yet to come is inexorable after a frolic like we had today. Oops, probably should wake up before I start to type. :-)

Jen: I just ironed a short sleeve white shirt of yours. Would you like me to bring it?

M: Naw, keep it there for my visit, where I come from the king wears no clothes. :-)

5: Sweet! ! Our return flight doesn't leave until late that night (the earlier ones were too early for getting off the ship). That gives 6 and myself some options (like the awesome mall in Fort Lauderdale! Poor 6!!).

M: Watch your language daughter! Don't you know it's rude to use four letter words? Now you've gone and done it, just *had* to copy Jen in didn't you? You guys are going to have to get me a day room in a hotel near the airport while you wander the awesome m...

Jen: I found a black belt with one of your suits. It looks like new. Glade your pills work so well. Make sure you get a big bottle for the cruse. Ask the doctor for a pill that will give you the energy you need to travel.

Are they both men and women in your dreams with you or just women. I guess if the Gods are coming then you and the others are their children playing. If we could create what we want why did we come down here. It has so much suffering. Why not just stay and create your fantasy world.

Who are you talking to..... nothing in the imagination is real. But the brain sure can create something much better than anything we create in real life. Could you get to a state that these dreams are all you need and a real woman can't measure up to what is in your head..... I am sure most of us could create that when to many disappointments of earthly reality stop our hoping. At least you don't get hurt or disappointed. Could you settle for a earthly disappointment like me that is old and not your ideal weight. Sounds like you enjoyed your dream.

(She sure knows how to take the fun out of fun nowadays, didn't used to be that way. Why would her response to such a frolic as that include the words "suffering" and "disappointment"? Will *anyone* like my writing? Maybe I *will* go and get a bottle of brandy, this woman's driving me to drink. :-)

M: I thought you'd get a kick out of my fantasy, guess not, too religious for fun now?

Jen: No I got a kick out of it. Its just a fantasy isn't it? They are fun. I also know from experience a man can not measure up to some of my dreams. I just don't prefer fantasy over the living but if I was dying i would want to visit the other side and remember the sweetness of it when I return. I would not like to ride a horse bareback with out a top or bra. It would hurt the breast to have them flopping even a young firm woman would find it painful. but not so in dreams. Nothing hurts.

I washed and ironed 8 really nice button up colored shirts and 4 white shirts. Several pairs of dress pants that look like new. I wiped and pressed and found them and about 6 belts. Two brand new pajamas still in the box. Three suits. You only need under clothing, socks and shoes when you visit.

M: I guess I could wear the pj's when I hike the desert with you, or I suppose bring some jeans. Thanks for doing that though, now hang them in your closet and it'll look like a man lives with you. Assuming my health holds it's realistic to think that I could spend a few weeks in Utah during the road trip. I think I'd like that but I don't know where we'd be staying if you are renting out the house? The bare breasts of course were just a man's fantasy, a woman would know better. Everything else is true. Er, maybe not the unicorns, centaurs maybe. :-)

I do love you sweetheart. Let's serve this up enjoyable for however long or short it lasts. I think we're perfectly capable of doing that if we don't talk negative or try to change each other too much. The way I see it, if we can come to enjoy each other and our differences in this lifetime we'll more likely do the same in the next.

My sister: Hi how are you doing.

M: (to sister cc list) Health wise I am about the same but very low on energy when the pain pills are about to wear off, it's a miracle drug for me at this point in time. Jen is flying in soon and in a flurry of messages over the last three days she and I and 5 and 6 are booked on a 21 day cruise. That will be two days after my next appointment with the oncologist but I am determined to go regardless of what I am told. The CT scan should be a reliable bench mark as to how fast this thing is progressing. Sometimes it seems to me it's very fast but much as I look forward to more pleasant days with family and friends I'm ok with moving on, I've experienced much of life and feel ready for what's to come.

I'll most likely drop in to pick up the letter you have for me when Jen is here so you two can visit a bit. So all in all life's good and there's a lot to look forward to. But yes, there is for sure something seriously wrong with my body, I feel it clearly before the pills kick in and it's not pleasant. I sleep and nap a lot, need to. I've had a great life though and seven wonderful children, can't complain. Maybe I should copy in everyone on the list, I communicate regularly with a few but seldom with some so this may be news for most. Oh, maybe I'll just send this to the whole list, you're on it, take care sis, see you soon.

Oh, if you want to get together sooner just let me know and I'll come get you, the sun is warm and pleasant now, good for walking. I was on the beach gathering sea glass this afternoon. I felt that I needed a winter jacket when I walked out of my building in the shade but had the jacket off and sleeves rolled up while in the sun. The tides have been far out each afternoon for a couple of weeks. It's very pleasant along Dallas Rd. a dream really for a Saskatchewan boy to live out his last days in this magnificent seaside city, I've been so blessed.

M: (to Jen) My complaint over these many months has been that you would not give us enough time, it was my desire as you know that we live together again and still is. Although I acknowledge that we may never marry or live together by your choice because among apparently a number of reasons you keep, I cannot go back twenty years and become again the man you married.

But I want you to know that I am very pleased with the several commitments to us that you have made lately: giving up looking for another man, coming to visit me next week, going on a cruise, and possibly taking a long road trip together. For the first time in more than a year I am feeling that maybe there *is* a future for us greater than just an occasional visit as friends. I like that thought, it gives me the stability and hope that I need to keep my thoughts on you exclusively, thank-you for that. I hope we can get along and make it worthwhile, life's short.

Jen: I checked on my membership site with Alaska Airlines and we both are listed to go. This is our conformation.

M: I'm ready! I went to bed later last night, about midnight instead of the usual 10:30ish and awoke this morning feeling real good as if a gift had been given me. Maybe the gift of a bit more time. I don't know that for sure but it would be nice to get to know you again so I'm better prepared to meet you at your coming and show you around your new worlds. After all, Adam came before Eve. :-) Keep in touch, little messages through the day cheer me, they make me think you are thinking of me. I love you.

Jen: What a sweet message. I like what you right my prince charming. I to had a good nights sleep.

Elaine: Hi Michael, Elaine here. Sorry I haven't been more diligent with communications! I took on some extra shifts, covering somebody wanting time off at work, but I do want to get together. Can we set up a time... say Friday at 1? Carve it in stone.

Yes, and I've been busy trying to edit my apartment in preparation for moving out to my mobile. I gave notice here, as my tenant is leaving. So, in any case, I do hope that you are enjoying the sunshine, and your family is supportive and keeping up with the visits or calls. Can we do Friday? Even though I get off work at 8:30, I am quite all right nowadays with the reduced workload! Cheers

M: It seems that the lost is found. Sure it would be fun to get together with you and Friday at 1 is fine. Will you be coming to my place?

M: (to myself) With the exception of the past few months I've been a married man almost my entire life. I was always faithful to my wives and never had another female friend when I was married. So by so readily allowing Elaine back into my life am I being "unfaithful" to Jen? My guess is that she would think so and be jealous. But I'm single, I'm living alone, and I like being with Elaine. I consider her a platonic friend similar to Oresha, though Elaine and I touch whereas that is now a rare commodity with Oresha except for a hug at greeting and departure. I'm not conflicted or torn by my acceptance of Elaine's offer to get together, I'm pleased, it will be nice to be with her again. Maybe we'll walk for a kale smoothie then to the park and see if I can go on to the sea from there, make it a pleasant afternoon. But I do think I'm going to get flack from Jen when she finds out that I was with Elaine.

Oh well, it's *my* life I'm living, Jen needs to deal with her own insecurities, she's in fact my number one, has been for a long time. If Jen was here she'd of course be at my side as I walked with Elaine. (Though frankly I can't imagine that ever happening, Jen's too jealous.) Unless of course some miracle happened and Jen agreed to take art lessons from Elaine and they became friends. Gosh it would be fun walking with those two like a thorn between two roses, each of us getting along swell with the other. Jen of course would be the one in bed with me each night, this is reality. I don't indulge in such thoughts much anymore though, it's as if Jen and I are already married and living together, *and you know how she is.* :-)

Jen: We were a bit younger in the attached photo. You even had color to your hair.

M: Those were happy days, I loved my home in the woods and you and 'our' kids. It took me back to the wonderful time it was when my own children were littleuns. I hope to get to see the girls again, I miss them. Will your children ever accept me back the way it was do you think? Gosh, I'm talking as if I'll be living a while, guess this morning's dose of pills has kicked in.

1: (to list) Thank God for modern medicine. Dad I'm proud of you for taking attention to your needs. Don't forget that pain loves to sap energy. What did the CXR (chest x-ray) show?

M: (to list) I haven't heard anything about the chest x-ray. It was to see if fluid is building up again but was ordered by the oncologist at the cancer clinic and he knows I have an appointment with him coming up. So my guess is that the x-ray didn't show any problem or I would have heard about it. My body confirms that, I have not been breathless for a long time. It's wonderful, I think I've been wandering around with only one lung fully functioning for many months, maybe even a whole year or more. I noticed lack of stamina when I was in Yuma last year. Even though I was walking a couple of miles every day (it's always warm and sunny there) when I tried to jog I couldn't go more than a few steps.

I'm feeling good about living longer, as long as the Ibuprofen continues to work as it now does that is. It's a useless feeling to not have enough energy to do the things you need and want to do, I guess you know all about that 1 and a few others in the family. My reaction at this point at my age is to want to go to bed and sleep with the hope of awaking in a world where bodies function perfectly. Though I suppose one could adapt here from a normal lifestyle to lying in bed watching the soaps all day (heaven forbid.)

Am I likely to have to increase the dose and frequency of the pain pills as time goes on? If so, if I stretch it now and put up with some discomfort and low energy (e.g. take only one dose a day instead of two) will that increase the time before I need to take more pills each day, or does it matter? It's great to have professionals in the family, I like to tell people that my psychiatrist, lawyer, and chiropractor sons keep their dad well adjusted...

I'm so proud of each of my children, what a great blessing as you are, my heart overflows with love for you. I'm sometimes overwhelmed with the joy of being a father. I hope such joys will be forever and increase. Enjoy today dear ones, life's short but the heart goes on and on...

1: Dad 1+ and I will be away but with internet contact 17th - 29th. Have you reconsidered phone contact? What about video chatting? When are you coming to visit? 1+ and I are planning to come for a weekend. We hope that's okay Love

M: You are always welcome to visit me, I'd like that very much. Jen and I are doing a cruise won't get back to Victoria for three weeks. I will probably have internet but please don't send photos, it's 75 cents a minute on the ship and very slow downloads. When we get back if she doesn't need to get back to her family Jen and I may explore Vancouver

Island and then possibly leave on a lengthy road trip in my car that may eventually get us to Alberta. Either way I'll see everyone for the family reunion. I'm hugely pleased with that, we owe much to 5 for her initiative in so many good things. If you can work around that tentative schedule, let me know when you'll be visiting. I still much prefer email instead of phone calls. 5 left a video camera here for anyone who visits to use to record interactions with their dad. You could someday show that to your kids and of course use the camera yourself when you are here.

Elaine: Yes! See you at 1! Kind regards as always!

M: Lovely. Unless you have other plans bring walking shoes and if it's a nice day we'll saunter to the Bay Mall, pick up a guess what and meander to Beacon Hill Park. If I'm good from there we can continue to seaside and along Dallas back to my place. Dinner somewhere on me if you have the time and the inclination? Or whatever, make it up as we go along perhaps, I'm completely flexible. But let's do what you have in mind and stick to your schedule if it's already planned.

Jen: That is my hope is you will live as long as you desire. The cancer has been on hold for 5 years. Why not another 5 years. Love ya

M: It is documented that 5 years are likely for 14% of those with my ailment as it is. But why do you say it has been "on hold" for 5 years? Have you suspected something in me? Or is it just a figurative way of saying it is possible that I could have become aware that I had cancer 5 years ago? It's likely that when I went for that CT scan for pleurisy about five years ago and they spotted something that it was beginning then. That doesn't mean it could have been cured at that point and besides we did not have the money to explore it further. But yes, I'd enjoy some additional quality years with you, especially if my books or land sell and we have the means to travel when we want at the standard we want. (E.g. balcony or suite on cruises, first class on long flights.)

Jen: A local mortuary sent me a phone message today and will do cremations any where in the US and Canada. I don't know how they compare to Canada. Do you want to check it out when here.

M: Nope, not my job, don't know when and where I will die, let the living take care of that. Besides it's not an expensive thing, my kids can easily handle it, less than $2,000. Or were you thinking of a local hot place for yourself? :-)

5: Oh yeah, 6 and I are all booked! Flights, hotel, and cruise!!

5: Are you all up to book a cabana on the private island days? It gives us air conditioning and shade with drinks and snacks and priority tenders etc. Let me know ASAP so I can book before they are all booked up.

M: Tell more, how much per person and is it worth it when we could return to the ship instead after the beach and hammocks wear thin?

Jen: I wasn't thinking of a hot place for myself but maybe I should. Love you

M: My arms maybe?

Jen: Yea your arms could do it.

Chapter 12

5: It is a little pricey. Pricier than I've seen, but will subsidize so that each of you pays $50 for each of the 2 times. I've done it before on the island (at 2's suggestion) and it is well worth it. Because you have to tender to get there, I prefer to go once and stay. There is a table and 4 chairs along with at least 2 sun chair lounger thingies. You get fruit and veggie trays with dips and salsa guacamole and chips along with several drinks (that you would pay for at the buffet lunch). Also they provide towels, misting showers for your feet and body after being in the ocean, and snorkeling equipment. It is an open cabana that is covered for shade and air conditioned. Sounds weird but works well. 2 and I played cards and enjoyed the ocean. It is nice to have the shade and a place to rest when tired. Anyway, I think that it is well worth it.

M: I'm in for $50 each of the two stops. I'm sure I'll get restless if I return to the ship too soon and will want to go back for another dip. Jen will have to speak for herself. I loved the clear warm water there, it's a bit of heaven for sure.

5: Sounds good. That is the only excursion that I am really interested in doing. Like I said, I have done it before on this island and on another private island. It is well worth it!

M: Jen and I are likely to just wander around on foot too, we've been to all the stops I think except St. Kitts/Nevis and I've been wanting to go there. Out of curiosity we may look at real estate on those two islands. If you buy a house there they make you a citizen and give you a passport. Could be fun wandering the world as a citizen of St. Kitts, whoever heard of it! How be you and your man buy the house and Jen and I sit for you when you're not there? No, we wouldn't charge you much for doing that. :-) Anyway, we stop there twice, could be fun looking...

6: Should anyone buy a house in St. Kits, I am always available for house sitting duties as well.... giggle. AS IF..... would be cool though.

1: (to list) There's no need to withhold the doses of pain medicine. Holding back is not likely to preserve length of utility. Stick to standard doses and intervals between doses. Since you definitively notice wear off it's likely best to not wait until wear off but to take the medicine around the clock as a regular dose. Your body should do better with prophylactic dosing rather than trying to chase the symptoms. All of this should be reported to and reviewed with your oncologist. What are your usual doses and dosing intervals, and have you learned anything else about Ibuprofen, ASA, or anything else?

Not hearing about the CXR probably means there's nothing significant but as they say 'Trust but verify'. You can call and ask for the results. Often in medicine doctors function with a typical person like you Dad on the basis of if I don't hear from him everything must be okay. Obviously you're not someone to be excessively complaintive but you have to adjust to a new life of paying attention to the bodily experiences AND reporting them. Let your doctors have all the information and then with them sort out attribution. For example I've been feeling more tired for the last 3 days but my daughters were visiting and I was doing more things and sleeping less in the day because of my desires to maximize the time I had with my daughters.

M: (to list) I'm already exceeding the recommended maximum daily dose of three pills by taking 800 mg (2 pills) at the same time twice a day. That maximum dose is probably just a cover their own recommendation. It would be very helpful if you would tell me how many mg I can take without it causing detrimental side effects. (Or killing me softly.) I always take a dose soon after eating in the morning and usually by about 5 p.m. I am needing more. I sometimes skip that second dose and sometimes (like right now, I think it's related to stress and not resting enough) I'm feeling ready for more well before 5 p.m. But from now on I won't go past 5 p.m. without taking a second dose. I'm not taking anything else other than a multi-vitamin most days and a variety of herbal teas such as dandelion and parsley root and goji berries that the folk know are sure-fire cancer killers.

Re the reporting that you suggest, I know enough about the lifelong independent streak in me to know that it is simply not going to happen. At least not until I can no longer cut my own toenails. That's my personal standard of determining independence. If a man can cut his own toenails he's good to go on his own. :-) If they dump me into hospice even if home care then I will be sure to report everything medically related. But until then I'll consider the only person needing to hear about my ailments to be my barber. (You'll be pleased to know that I haven't had a haircut for months.)

Thanks for the good advice, keep it coming. I need that because I'm not likely to check things out myself. My attitude is that the medical people are not likely able to do anything about it anyway, so why kill another good tree to file another useless report. If I was on prescribed meds then ok, they need to know what's happening so they can adjust dosage and frequency accordingly, but I'm not there yet. Working on it…

S: (to list) His hair is starting to curl at the bottom and is awesome!

M: Shucks you ain't seen nuthin yet, I'm gettin me a curling iron when Jen gets here, she'll probably know how to operate it behind my back.

You guys continue to make me feel like a fraud. Some of you have lived with this lack of energy I'm complaining about for years. But hey, I enjoy writing and that's what I get to do when you write back. Keep it happening, you're making my day… Dad

S: oh, and I was looking at the ocean view info and we can have fresh fruit delivered to our rooms upon request. I am so doing that. And I also want to do tea while we are on the ship.

M: Request white tea and white gloves for me please.

Jen: Sounds like a good idea with the fresh fruit and tea.

S: oh yes! And I will bring ziplock bags cuz you always need them on a cruise ship!

M: And snacks, bring lots of snacks, the sea breeze always makes me hungry. :-)

S: of course little piggy!

M: We leave Fort Lauderdale for our return flight at 6:40 p.m. Might need that day room for me unless I can get them to allow me to stay on the ship and sit in a comfy lounge until later in the day because it's a long haul home that night, we don't get in until midnight.

S: Let me see what I can do about that. 6 and I don't leave until shortly after 9pm so it might be a good idea to see if we can get a room that would let us check in so early.

M: It's important to be close to the airport I think. You three can dump me there and do your thing, I'll be fine in a hotel room, may as well enjoy Fort Lauderdale while you're there. I'll pay for the day room if it's not full price for just the few hours. But Jen and I will need to be at the airport by 4:30 p.m. so maybe if we can stay on the ship until about noon I'll be ok? I do like the idea of a day room though, then we can leave the ship when we're expected to and you three will have several hours to shop er whatever.

S: I am looking into things. I agree that we should have a room, whether we get off the ship early or not, I think that we need a room. Let me see what I can do. But let's get you moved to your new apartment before we go, it's ready, they called yesterday. You won't be far from where you are now, I think it will grow on you and you have room for visitors.

M: I'm not doing any heavy lifting. My job is to walk over there when the movers have it taken care of. :-)

S: That's what we want. I'll come if I can but it's all set up, just go for a walk when the movers get there, you don't have much for them to move and it's close. It won't take them long and they'll set up at your new place, you won't even have to unpack.

Oresha: How's your day goin?... Do you have time for a walk tomorrow afternoon.. say around 2PM? Ciao...

M: Sure. I suggest that we meet at my place I'll still be there. From here we'll saunter to the Bay Mall, grab a smoothie then sit in the park for a while and go our separate ways from there. Or what did you have in mind?

S: I got us a room at the same hotel we are staying at before the cruise. I paid an extra $25 for guaranteed early check in for whenever we arrive at the hotel. We have the room for the night, so we don't have to worry about when we need to check out. And they have a shuttle to the airport so that is awesome!!

M: That sounds perfect and it takes care of our transfer from the ship to the airport too. We'll catch their ship to hotel shuttle after breakfast on board then hotel to airport and you three will have loads of time to wander about Fort Lauderdale while I rest, couldn't be better.

1: (to list) Actually many things can be done but not unless they are known. The pills you are taking are dosed every 4 - 6 hours, not twice a day. Your taking a 800 mg dose instead of say 400 mg is likely because you're not taking the drug often enough so a higher dose is required so there's still some in your system 8 or more hours later. FYI that brand of medication in some studies is as good as Morphine in certain circumstances.

Why not try 400 mg every 6 hours? If you need longer duration at night when you go to bed then try a higher dose then. If you're going to take the pills regularly then make sure you stay properly hydrated. At least 3 litres a day. Your issue is most likely inadequate frequency of dosing. Don't forget that reporting does not equal complaining.

M: That's hugely valuable information for me, thank-you so much for suggesting that. From now on I'll try one 400 mg pill every four hours and see how that works. Excellent, you may have greatly improved my quality of life and my outlook for the future. I was getting concerned because sometimes I needed more and didn't want to overdose and possibly create more problems, so I went to bed or sofa or failing that macho, don't have time to bleed right now. But it seems I may have been just serving up the drugs wrong.

Good stuff, real good. Maybe there is some merit in "reporting" after all. But I'd have no idea how to go about doing that anyway and wasn't asked to, maybe later in the game. Meanwhile, keep an eye on your dad as best you can from a distance. As you know, it's not quantity that I'm after, it's quality. If with this advice I have more energy throughout the day, that's a big WOW!!!

4+ (wife of my fourth child, writing to the list) I just want to add, make sure you inform your doctors about any herbal teas or remedies you are using. Some herbs can have adverse effects when mixed with certain medications.

M: Thanks 4+. I received instructions before I went to the oncologist to actually bring with me containers of everything I was taking, even vitamins I think. But I didn't and 1 who was there at that meeting can attest that I was not asked. So I think at that/this point it doesn't really matter. (I mean, what's it going to do, kill me? As I'm lately fond of saying. :-) But yes of course I'll tell the doc about the Ibuprofen and will knock off the folk remedies if he asks about anything more than daily victuals, that's easier than walking in with a bag over my shoulder as well as several under my eyes. And no, I am NOT giving up my daily doses of Puff Souffles, gotta have some good reason for living. Say hello to my son for me, he doesn't respond to emails, and love to those wonderful kids of yours.

Elaine: Okey donkey. (There's a common Canadian expression "okey dokey" meaning agreed/will do, but yes, that's how she spelled it. :-)

Oresha: Sounds good to me :) See ya @ Casa d'Michael @ 2-ish tomorrow.

Jen: I took the books out of the car and packed them in a box and covered it with a plastic bag. I had a realtor call and say he might have a retired couple to rent the basement. They are building a house here.

M: Thank-you, I will probably try to get them to 4 though he may be entirely into e-books if he ever gets the chance to read anymore. It's just that I've carted those books around since I did my Bachelor of Arts decades ago and loved them. Should I die, think nothing of giving them away if anyone wants them.

The word must be getting out that your place is for rent. If you don't have to pay the mortgage it would be nothing for you to get a hotel room for us should we want to stay in Utah for a while. Does that 40% flight discount interest you at all? We have only four more days to make a booking if it does.

I saw Lynne the clairvoyant on the beach today. I looked down for a while but she didn't turn to wave so there's no connection anymore and I just walked on as I usually do now. You and I seem destined for each other, let's do our very best to make it enjoyable for the other, we deserve that.

1's counsel today about taking Ibruprofen in smaller doses more frequently gives me great hope. If I can have energy all the time the balance of life can be very good indeed. Sleep well sweetie, it has been a great day for me today with that hope for energy, we'll see how it works out. I love you.

Jen: I did check on the flights but not right now. Maybe after we get back it would be best to fly back to Las Vegas and take my car and travel to the red woods. I only took the newer paper back books and packed them. The others are still in the book case. I think 1 gave good counsel today. Love you sweetie

M: (to myself) This is hugely disappointing to me. I keep thinking as if we are married and will be together for the rest of my life but she isn't even up to doing that long road trip with me or visiting my family. I think I need to be on my guard and not close every door and window irrevocably to the (very slim) possibility of another coming into my life if there is yet time for that. I completely fail to understand her great professions of love for me and me the only one and yet be so hostile about us living together. She knows that I still value sex and in her newly found religious fervor she may withdraw from any form of that at all while at the same time refusing to marry me so she can have sex within the bounds of her beliefs. What is her game really? *I was wanting to be married when I die...*

Suzanne: My thoughts are you should share now in words your journey. I will keep them as part of my hospice book. Others will find great comfort in sharing such precious moments. I know I will be blessed by them.

M: (to myself) For months I have been wondering if Suzanne really has hospice stories in mind because in all these many months she only shared three stories though alluded to a few more. We were even going to co-author a stand-alone book of hospice stories at one time but she never sent more to me. I understand quite clearly now that she is either writing her own book or has another writer to help her with it. And she's doing what I am doing with hers, using my emails in her own book. Or is she just telling the story of my dying in her own words perhaps, it being just one more story among many? Either way, she was invaluable in getting my books written so if you are reading this you have Suzanne to thank for its existence.

Is this stuff *really* of interest to others I wonder? Will my books be read and enjoyed? Suzanne did not say what I sent her was of interest, what she did say was to share my own story of dying. That's quite different. I'm thinking more often that this whole experience was just for my own learning. But if so I did my part, my words are 'out there' for all to find and read should there be an interest in them. I should be content with that. The thought passes through my mind just now that I could blog real time about my dying experience and draw attention to my books that way. But even Book 4 I hesitate to publish because it reveals where I am presently located and a whole lot about my family and others, there may be valid privacy concerns.

M: (to Suzanne) Shoot, now I have to live long enough to read your book. :-) You are welcome to use any of my messages you want to, I'm certainly using yours in mine sweetheart. If you hadn't kept it secret that you are writing your own book or have another co-author we could have worked some promos of mine into yours and of yours in mine. But now my first three books are already published. (We can still get your title and author name and website in my Book 4 if you let me know soon, I haven't submitted it yet.)

I always wondered why you never shared more than three stories with me, it seemed strange when at one time we were even discussing co-authoring a stand-alone book of hospice stories separate from mine. I waited and waited for your stories to come but they never did. But I'm pleased to know that your stories will be told, I think they are important. All the best with your project, please stay in touch, you are precious to me. And if you want to know more of my own personal experience with dying, you know what your questions do to me. :-) Sleep well sweetie...

M: (to Jen) So it looks like the long road trip I was imagining is off then. That's ok if you don't want to spend so much time with me, you do have other things to do and your own family to spend time with. But I'm trying to understand you better. Is it because you are fearful of visiting my children? I confess I'm still thinking as if we are a married couple and will always be together. I need to stop that once and for all and just enjoy your visits when you come. I should be content with you coming next week and a three week cruise together, that should be a memorable experience, thank-you for agreeing to that.

Jen: The following is a suggestion. What do you want to do? I was thinking it would be easier on you if we flew to Las Vegas go to Utah for a few days. Then on to the red woods, beach, LA sites I want to show you then on to Phoenix and the back to Utah for a few days or more then head North. If I don't go with you on up to Canada then you could fly to Great Falls and have 5 pick you up. I would visit my daughter and family in Salt Lake City. By then it would be time to go back to Victoria for your family reunion. I fell married to but we are not in the site of your kids. I know they are nice about it but that it is.

M: That could work but I would be doing it your way not to make it easier for me because if we did it my way and took my car from here we'd take our time and only go as far in a day as is comfortable for me anyway. I had in mind possibly being six weeks or more on the road including Alberta and back to Victoria through the mountains. But that is taking you away from your own family for a long time and I should not expect that of you. I don't quite understand the part where after visiting in Phoenix and going to Utah we then "head North." Are you suggesting you stay in Salt Lake City while I fly to Alberta, do my visit then fly back to you? If you won't be going to Alberta with me it would be better for me to fly to Great Falls from Las Vegas on the cheap airline, make my visits, then fly home to Victoria since I won't have a car to be concerned about. You could then visit me again anytime if you want to.

Are you planning to be at the family reunion or should I book a room for myself? I'm hoping you'll be there but I'll understand if not because you choose to be uncomfortable around some of my kids and their mother will attend for sure. And that may trouble you. But it's very clear to me that you will not be visiting my kids in their homes for whatever reasons you may have. I suppose you and my kids might think there would be competition for my USA assets after I die and that could cause some bad blood? Is that one of your reasons for not wanting to travel with me to Alberta? Do you sense such enmity lurking silently waiting for me to die? I always look for the best so I may become aware of such things but I quickly let them go. I do know you are welcome to visit my kids in their homes with me at this time. They'd be delighted because they know how important you are to me. But of course I can't speak for how it will be after my death, you may have realistic cause for discomfort though I know they all genuinely like you at this time.

But anyway, road trip or not you have cleared up something for me with your words today. I now understand that I need to accept that you and I will never marry again because you use that as your excuse not to visit my kids months from now when we *could* be married. It's simply not your choice to marry me, you can't see it happening, and as time goes on you strengthen in that position. The future you want for yourself becomes more consolidated and you are making plans accordingly. Your reasons for not marrying me may be completely valid and realistic too, you're a grown up girl and a smart one. It is quite right that you watch out for your own best interests.

I'm not angry at you for doing so, I'll always welcome your visits. You have an endless variety of options other than me available and always will. I can now settle that matter in my mind, it has been troubling me. I've often tried hard to visualize us married again and it never came easily. It was a matter of loyalty more than anything for both of us as much as we share a genuine love for each other. We'll just be good friends for life. (Unless it gets into a matter of me needing care in which case my guess is that you'll be there for me much of the time. And I'll be grateful that you are, knowing that you could be elsewhere whereas a spouse would be bound to the duty.) There is some beauty in that.

God bless you Jenny, we're very good friends, I do love you. I'll be watching for you after I die but don't come too speedily, there could be much that is pleasant left for you in this world and you have children who need their mom much more than mine need me. That's just the way it is...

M: (to myself) I had thought to end Book 4 right here but events today have made me change my mind, there is more that you need to know about me and Jen and what happened before I died. Here goes...

Jen: Watch the movie Elsa and Fred on Netflix.

M: Netflix is not working on my TV anymore, maybe you can fix it when you get here and we'll watch that movie together.

Jen: We are going to have many moments to connect and share our deepest thoughts. We have a marriage sealing that we both want intact. Is that not more important than a earthly paper. Death does not break that chain but of course you also have your first wife sealed to you because she never remarried. Do you want her also in the next life because of that sealing or will she want to go with an other man.

M: I have no idea what she wants nor do I care. We'll all face a new reality after death, at present it is just fantasy.

Jen: You spent 26 years of your life with your first wife. That's a long time. I was hoping our marriage would live longer than that. it makes me sad that it didn't. Was it worth leaving me for Lola. Do you have any regrets. Your strong belief it was the right thing to do will keep me from ever marrying you again. Those beliefs will keep me from ever being fully yours. Even as much as I love you I can not trust you enough to marry you when you cling to what you did was right. So we settle for being very good friends. As you said we have to except each others differences. I will be faithfully yours as long as you are faithful to me hear and the next life. Other wise there is no promise is there. It is in your hands.

M: I'll address some of those issues when I respond to your second message. But to have you as friend you demand that I be "faithful" to you here and even after I die! Please explain what you mean by "faithful". If it means me not having sex with any other woman then *you are demanding that I never have sex ever again in this lifetime!* I say that because you refuse to marry me and you want to be a "good Mormon". Good Mormons do not have sex outside of marriage. So where does that leave me? What would you think of me if I demanded that you never have sex again in your entire life in exchange for allowing you to visit me now and then? You make no sense at all Jenny. What you are asking smacks of revenge and punishment or at least of cruelty. Or perhaps it is a mind that is not thinking clearly. Which is it?

M: (to myself) Do you feel my devotion to Jen slip sliding away again? I do! After all this, will it prove to be true that Jen is just "my greatest temptation" and it's another (or none) who will be intimately with me when I die?
Or is this physical body destined to die?

Jen: Attached are a few more photos of good times.
M: Great photos lovely memories, we were so in love, thanks for sending them.
Jen: Thanks for that because we were. I thought we were in love. It broke my heart when you ran off the way you did. You say it was all worth it. I guess that's what you believe. That alone will keep me from ever marrying you again. We see the worth of the last two years so different. I am glade we salvaged at least what we now have. We can not change the past. I think the (loss) pain will always linger. We just move forward and enjoy what time we can manage to create.

M: You write: *"I will be upset but I expect you to be honest with me and say so."* So I will continue to be open and honest with you like I always am. I had hoped we were past the past but I guess my finally allowing myself last night to accept you once and for all for who and what you have become (just a really good friend, never again a spouse) and telling you that I have come to *accept* that status and not try to change you has opened the past again and it must be rehashed yet another time. I am not writing to hurt you, I am writing to reconfirm that you and I have very different points of view about the last year of our life and each of ours is valid. I find it sad though that you are not willing to let the past go and make a fresh beginning. But that's where you are, I accept that (and you) better now. I am less concerned and distressed about our relationship, it's squared away, I'm ok.

I do agree with you though that we should *"enjoy what time we can manage to create."* With my type of lung cancer the length and quality of life for me is never certain. My oncologist-given twelve months could stretch out to five years or more. And it could just as easily be five weeks or even five days. Nobody really knows that beast, I never even smoked, they don't know what causes it. People die from what I have all the time, some people with little or no pain, living life as if normal until they drop dead. Sometimes I feel as though it could come quickly. So, regardless of the present discussions and the subsequent emotion, please do come next week and visit me as planned and let's enjoy that three week cruise together. You can decide how much more time you want to allow us after that if any at all, the choice is yours, I will not cage you or make demands. Let's each do our best to forget the past and be in 'courting' mood when we're together even though we both know the result of the courtship will be negative, I will not wear your wedding band again.

You write: *"That alone will keep me from ever marrying you again."* Again and again you reconfirm that you will never marry me and that my feelings about you all along are correct. I love you, you love me, but we will never marry or live together again because you have chosen never to. You choose just to be friends as long as I will allow that. And should I not welcome your visits you will most likely quickly move on to another man and inevitably forget me like the other three men you married and divorced. You acknowledge that we *"can not change the past"* so it seems like a revenge thing for you what you are doing now, not allowing us to marry or live together. You like the "pain" the "broken hearts" and pity parties better than you do forgiveness and renewing. There is no Spring for you, only winters. You're presently stuck in the snows of your creating but may yet be able to be pushed or pulled out of the drift if you marry a fifth time, start fresh, and work at keeping your body and yourself always attractive to your new man. And maybe you won't ever come unstuck, chronic unforgiving is a very deep rut and you are getting older. But life's good, especially when we learn from it and strive always for greater happiness.

You *could* have kept this man Jenny! He proposed marriage, you accepted, and then you broke it off by refusing to marry or to live with him. He'd still like you to live with him full-time. What really is it that you want? The endless pity party? A different man to take you to the Mormon temple so you can be one of his wives in the eternities, and to bed so you can experience that after twenty years with just one man? (Al doesn't count, you didn't go all the way with him.) What what what? I cannot go back and be the man you married twenty years ago. What is it you want that you *can* have? You're lovely, you're financially independent, you're fun. Whatever it is when you've made your final decision, I am confident that is what you will attract. I had hoped it would be me but now I hope no longer, I accept you as the dearest of friends. Whatever it is you choose, it won't be me, you made that abundantly clear over the past nine months, I have finally accepted.

Ok, let's do the history yet again and get a final recording of our past the way I see it so we don't ever have to do this again to know where I am. Your firm statement yesterday that you will *never* marry me and my acceptance of that last night provokes it. You wrote: "That *alone* will keep me from ever marrying you again." You have other, possibly many other reasons to irrevocably reject my proposal of marriage. I didn't want to believe it because of your frequent profusions of great love for me but you told me in many ways that you wouldn't live with me again many times over the last nine months since I visited you and attempted reconciliation. All you wanted at that time was sex and of course I went along, I wanted you. You pretended we were still married because you hadn't heard from your lawyer that we weren't, it was a reasonable doubt I guess. But you really are a very different person than you let on you are, the facts reveal it but you try to hide it from yourself. You make excuses and throw guilt trips my way as you struggle with yourself. I like the wild side in you though, you needn't be ashamed to be a woman!! It's your newly found religious fervor and your attempts to try to force it on me that are not serving you or us well. I do love you darling.

I suppose I have as much excuse as you to walk away from you like you walk away from me. My guess is that a whole lot of people would think it acceptable for me to fulfill a lifelong dream, buy a motor home and write a book similar to "Travels with Charley" as was my original intent when I left home. It seemed an opportune time too because we were already separated by distance, me in Utah, you in California and it seemed that you would be there for months tending to your new grandson with no mother. I needed money to live and knew you would not allow me to buy a motorhome for this venture so I moved one of our streams of business income from your control where it had been for fifteen years, into my control. (*All I ever did was change a password!*)

Events proved me correct. You ran to a lawyer before I left home I think, filed for divorce, and got a judge to give you control of everything I thought I owned, leaving me with no income had it been enforced. I did not know that was happening let alone have a chance to tell the judge my side of the story, he was told there was no way to contact me. That was a lie, I was always on email and I think I was still home when he was told that. Two days after I left home your lawyer sent messages to my business customers to stop making payments on their real estate loans so the stream of income I was counting on would dry up. That was horribly nasty of you and you kept it all secret. I incidentally found out from a business customer that I was being divorced by the woman I'd been married to for eighteen years! When I left, you had a good business of your own and joint investment properties that gave you much more cash flow than I was counting on. I predicted your behavior well (except divorce, that still astonishes me.) As I saw it at the time what I did was the only way I could fulfill my dream to write what I hoped would be a great novel. Of course in retrospect we could have both acted differently and reached a workable compromise.

We didn't have to divorce, that was your choice not mine, I never planned that. And you did it so swiftly and secretly after 18 years of marriage, you really caught me by surprise. You still fail to accept responsibility for the divorce and continue to be unforgiving because as you put it I "ran off". That's how I see it Jen. I think you got yourself in a fix where psychologically you must cling to your own (twisted from my point of view) view of what actually happened so you can live with what you did to someone you once loved. Sure I can see it your way too, but for me it's mine that is closer to the truth of what happened, much closer.

Jen: Please watch a movie for me called Elsa and Fred. It has Shirley Maclaine in it. You will not believe how old she looks. It reminds me of the new love we refound. In some ways it is like a new love. If it reminds you of one of your new love with these other women, I will be upset but I expect you to be honest with me and say so.

M: We'll watch it together when you're here.

Jen: As far as the business goes. I don't expect you to give it to me. If your children want it please give it to them. I was coming to help *you* with the business in some small way. What it boil's down to is. What do you want to do with your business?

M: Leave it to someone who will benefit from it, can't take it with me.

Jen: As far as road travel goes. Its up for discussion. I was trying to make it easer for you but you feel the other way would be easy. I do need to keep in mind my budget.

M: Yes, the proper time to discuss the road trip is after we come back from the cruise.

Jen: The family reunion is for yours and your first wife's children and grandchildren. I just don't think I fit as I once did. It should not make much difference. You did not want me at the other family reunion. I became a outsider. You visited your sister alone and wanted nothing to do with my siblings. That's how I feel. Maybe you and your ex can reconnect as friends again. When we were married I went with you to be a support to you and enjoy the company of your children. There will be no time for you to be lonely with so many people. Let them honor you without my interruption. This reunion represents a living funeral in a very beautiful way. I would want nothing more from my children then something like this. I will have my beautiful moments with you.

M: Very well written Jen, I agree with you even though it would have been nice to have you at my side. If we were married everything would be quite different.

Jen: I am very much like you I am lonely with out you. There is no one else. The situation changed the outcome of our ending year. I Love you sweetie

M: Come visit me sweetheart, we have much to talk about as we hold each other tight. I haven't given up on YOU, just on the possibility of our living together. I can live with that.

M: (to myself) It's so strange, in the midst of writing the above I went to bed for a rest (as my cancer requires me to do often) fell asleep and when I awoke I discovered zero desire to send that long reply to Jen so I won't. It doesn't seem the least important to me now when it was all important before that nap. I think it best that I just take what comes when she visits next week and see what that leads to. At least the above will help clue you in as you begin to read this new book that Jen and I are presently living. I have no idea how long I will live, sometimes in the tiredness (and loneliness) it seems like I can slip effortlessly away anytime. If I do it is my hope that someone will submit this Book 5 manuscript to the publisher. I ended Book 4 abruptly last night, thinking to write at least another 50,000 words in it. It just seemed a proper place to start some fresh chapters. I think these books and my life lately are out of my conscious control and gone to a higher part of me. I've yielded to that, I accept it, it's working, there is greater purpose to my life than I am allowing my earthly self to remember.

Sometimes I think that Alzheimer's is settling in just in case the cancer doesn't take. I'm not living in the moment, at least not yet, but living in the week or so, events before that are needing some prompting or the details are hazy or forgotten, or don't matter. Priorities are shifting. Is that part of the preparation needed for a body that's about to die? Will I forget Jen? Will she forget me? I don't think so, we still have a great love for each other, though it's far from the perfect unconditional love I've been searching for.

And that's where it and I are at this bright sunny morning in Victoria, British Columbia Canada. I am expecting Oresha this afternoon to take a walk and share a kale smoothie with me. And Elaine's coming tomorrow, the first time in many weeks. Life's good when I've got the energy for it…

Ok, it's not noon yet but I've discovered why I suddenly lost my interest in sending the above to Jen. It's likely that she was composing the message below as I was sleeping, it just came in.

Jen: I read this section of a book. (She copies extracts into her message from a book called "True Beauty".) You told me you felt this way once. Is it important that I see myself different and will or do you see me different now. Tell me what you felt back in the days that you felt I was so unattractive that made it easy for you to leave. No judgment on you. I see it is my responsibility to see myself beautiful and attractive. It must start within. Thanks sweetie for being so understanding now and be patient with me. If the time comes and we both feel it is important we will marry again.

Jen: How are you today? I expected to have an email from you by now. Are you alright. If I don't hear from you soon I will call.

M: As humans, our fights are always with ourselves. Often others simply mirror what we think and feel about ourselves. When we feel good about ourselves we feel good about others and others want to be around us because we are making them feel good about *themselves*. Strive for joy by harboring only thoughts that *feel* happy. In that manner we can change ourselves, and enough of us can change the world. You and I darling can still find that perfect love I write often about, it begins by finding it within. Now get that pretty butt over here will you. :-) I love you. Michael

Jen: Do you see me different and how? I some times feel I am peaking through the pain but so easy to slip back into. I don't want to do that. It is getting closer and I will be with you.

M: I'm assuming you mean emotional pain and not physically induced pain like mine is? Or do you have a physical illness too and are keeping it secret from me?

Only when we are together for a couple of weeks or so will I know for myself if you are different. It hasn't come across in the writing yet but I have hope that you are on a really good path now. That seems to be a valuable book that you are reading, good for you for seeking out such materials. Like dying, your emotional healing process is something you must do alone. I'll try to remember when we are together that you are wounded too and give you the love and attention that you need to complete the healing. Tell me if I squeeze too tight. :-)

Isn't life grand though, I love it so...

Enjoy the day sweetie.

Jen: Don't forget sometimes we are at the mercy of others and we suffer the consequences they brought on. It is up to us to decide how we will handle it. Does not mean you have to go back to it. How we perceive our future is from our experiences. The past is our lessons. The future is to be looked at with what we learn.

M: Yes, I think you are right about that. But it is my belief based on experience that we attract to ourselves the people and circumstances we most need to get the learning we came here to receive. And yet, we exist to know fullness of joy so I think it is our duty to forget the past and go forward rejoicing in the celebration of this event called "life". Past experiences can only be negative if we of our own free will and choice *judge* them to be so. A beautiful attitude that can preserve us from the consequences of grave thoughts and feelings is to love unconditionally and accept that when another does something we think is harmful to us, they may simply be working out their own learning and we happened to be conveniently nearby to bounce off of. As we get in the habit of harboring only thoughts that feel happy and cease to blame others for our perceived misfortunes, we gradually attract only happy people and circumstances, a condition known by many names including fortune, blessedness, good luck, nirvana and cetera.

That's how I see it, it's all up to us to be happy or not, our choice, our attitude. I could choose to feel pain and broken hearted and blame you for our divorce the same as you blame me but instead I choose to forget the past and be happy moving *forward*. And look what it's getting me – YOU!!!

I recommend a little book called *"As a Man Thinketh"* by James Allen. It may be among the books of mine that you packed. That book has hugely influenced my life, I was exposed to it at a young age. I think the author thought it was worthless and never published it. Somebody else discovered it after his death and got the word out, it's now a classic. Maybe someday I too will a famous writer, but if so most likely not until I am long dead. :-)

1: (to list) Dad again just because the doctor doesn't ask does not mean something is unimportant. Doctors often take the lead from the patient. Remember appointment one with your oncologist was to assess you and establish your goals of care. The doctor had the results of the tests and most likely the hospital report, etc. Plus didn't you fill out forms? I don't recall. If so you were likely asked about what you take then. If not he likely had an indication of what if anything you take from your hospital discharge summary and/or your hospital admission history, etc. Everyone should always report the Rxs:OTCs/herbals/vits, and other treatments to all their doctors when seen. Dad please report on how ATC (around the clock) Ibuprofen works. Love 1

M: I recognize that many of my former priorities are shifting, things once important no longer are and a higher power than my conscious self sometimes takes over. For example, I spent a long time early this a.m. composing a response to a message someone sent to me. Then I ran out of energy (you know how that works) and went to bed for a nap. I fell asleep and when I next sat at my computer I had *zero* inclination to complete the message while before the nap it seemed very important. A few minutes ago I received another message from that person that explained why I no longer needed to send the long message I had been composing, the concern I'd had was resolved, perhaps while I was sleeping. Maybe such things are natural as complex organisms prepare to have a huge part of what they long identified as "themselves" peel off and become dust, some of it maybe drifting with the tides.

As I lay in bed or on my sofa I often watch the gulls flying. They are magnificent birds, equipped for land, sea, and air. And they PLAY! Sometimes I've caught glimpses of flashes high in the air and on closer inspection discovered that they were gulls out for fun, enjoying a soaring day. This morning it seemed that two gulls had collided midair but passed through each other effortlessly and kept going. I expect that I will soon notice that happen in skies that are much bluer than these, it's a grand adventure one's dying.

But one thing that hasn't changed is that independent streak that I've (sometimes secretly) harbored within me all my days. I hear what you are saying about the doctors and the importance of reporting to them. But it's not important to *me*. I'm dying, we all know that, that's why I'm seeing an oncologist. My priorities have shifted and I don't really care about vitamins and herbs and cures anymore. Should the oncologist ask what I am taking I'll tell him, but rather than take to the clinic containers of this or that or report on myself, I'll simply stop taking the herbs and folk remedies friends eager to help have recommended. It's just not worth it to me to engage in the physical process much except to alleviate pain and increase energy. Sure, there are things I'd like to do yet, many reasons to live, each of you included among them. But ultimately dying is something we do alone. I'm finding mine delightful, be happy for me...

I am now diligently taking one 400 mg tablet of Ibuprofen each 4 hours by the clock. I think it will be three or so days before I notice the change if anything. I still had to rest this a.m. the same as when I was taking two together only once or twice a day. Ask me again and I'll tell you how it's going then. I know you want to help me my son, I appreciate that, and you *are* helping in many ways, even your interest and caring means a lot. I love you, I'm so proud of your great accomplishments. The personal experience you've had with pain and loss of energy for so many years makes you perfectly qualified to keep an eye on me from a distance and provide sage advice, please continue and take the initiative even if it's ingrained in you not to do so. For example, it was my delightful experience with Ibuprofen several years ago when I had pleurisy that led me to try it again. It was only after I reported using it that you told me you had used it on yourself with similar results. Don't hold back, you can of course advise me by private email rather than to this list. But I think most people on the list are interested in our communications. It's not often that we get to share so intimately someone else's dying. Happily, I happen to be a writer and am wont to share.

Now back to my dandelion root tea and ginseng, parsley root to follow. :-) I love you all. Dad/Michael

Jen: It is just emotional pain. I do love you and want to be with you. I also feel I have family obligations and I want to be there for my family also. If we married what would be the benefits. Women are nesters and I see you not needing a nest. That leaves me feeling insecure. As loving friends I don't have to involve you with my insecurities. I am afraid of losing my children and grandchildren. Many of my family members are upset with the way you left me. Most men want to take care of a woman in more than sex and financial obligations. Although that comes with marriage. Maybe emotional security. But as your woman what can I do for you. Go to this link and watch the video. (It's about a woman who is going blind and her husband watches out for her without her knowing it.)

M: So in the video are you the wife or the husband? We don't have to marry. And we don't have to live together. What we have to do is get along, and enjoy each other when we're together. Deal?

Jen: I am going to get my hair cut now. Not to short just shaped to look nice.

M: You're probably doing that because you want to please some guy right?

Jen: That is good. "As a Man Thinketh" a man is. Well I think about what happened and I believe it was wrong the way you left and some of your actions. What I want is for you to make restitution by sincerely repenting and apologizing. This would move our relationship to a higher level. I would be the happiest woman in the world for us of both. By choosing to hang on to most of the mistakes you made these last few years brings sorrow to my heart. This is a choose only you can make. I believe it created repercussion's. It is one of the things that keeps me from wanting to marry you again. The choose is yours so be happy you are getting what I have to offer. It is still much. I have a few regrets in my life and I would easily remember them but I don't live in that moment. I wrote much more on the subject but you may not want to hear it. If you do let me know before I delete it. Love you.

M: Our lives could have been different but they were not. It is not me who is "choosing to hang on" to the past and who is indulging in pain and heartbreak and sorrow and pity parties and discontent. It is you who has not yet dealt with your past. Your fight remains with yourself. We do not have to marry, we do not have to live together, and we do not have to "move our relationship to a higher level." So why not let the past go and start enjoying your life and the man you say you love who is still here for a little while longer and wanting to be with you? Can you do that? Will you?

Jen: Yea, There is not much hope is there. You have always hung on to your mistakes. I don't understand a man that can not admit he made a few mistakes and own them. Don't you understand I can except you but I can not respect a person that can not admit he or she was at fault. This is not the character of a person I want to associate but be as you are. I am not on a pity party. I want a man that stands on principles and you seem to not know what that is.

Jen: Wish you wanted more of yourself and willing to learn from your mistakes but a man that has to much pride is blinded is he not. Your pride gets you into trouble.

Jen: To my sweet heart Michael, If I had a flower for ever time I thought of you, I could walk in my garden forever. I dried the roses you sent me. I smile each time I see them. For you are the man I thinketh.

M: Love me as I am, that's all I ask of you.

Jen: I want to respect the person I love. A man that does not hid from his mistakes.

Jen: This is what I was not sure about sending. I will now. I am disappointed in you. Yes I am glade we are not married and right now not sure I want to be your friend. You are to puffed up in your pride. I ask nothing of you. You do not deserve me.

I never was a person to hang around chronic negative people. I didn't have time for pity parties. Yet I have a listening ear to those that experience pain that needs to a listening ear. Moving on is the goal.

You have not forgotten I divorced you. You often throw it in my face as I throw it in your face. I just want you to realize your mistake. But not sure you are capable of that ever.

Many times I blamed you because you set the divorce in motion the day you ran off. Yes I could of sat with my head in the sand as you went on your journey to buy a motor home in secret and left behind a woman you said you were not attracted to any more. That's right any woman that has any self-esteem would divorce a man that justifies his mistakes. Nothing in the relationship has changed for us to remarry when you can not see what you did. Blame me all you want for the divorce as I said before I would do it again with the same situation. You left your first wife several times thinking she would take you back after your adventure at your families expense. She finally rebelled, got angry and said no more. Even this last time if she had not got mad you said you would of gone back. Du! What were you thinking? I almost think you are incapable of understanding for some reason and not capable of learning the consequences of this lesson. Even when a good man (Bishop) next door tried to wake you up to the unfairness you portrayed on your family you were shocked that he felt it would be unfair for you to come back to your family after deserting them. I am not saying this to make you feel bad just try to get you to understand consequences of our actions. If you do not learn from your mistakes you are destined to repeat them. I don't even think you realized you hit them on their cheek and if you did you expect them to turn their cheek for a repeat. You certainly expect me to.

Michael I like me. I have had a positive life and I do not believe I created pain in the marriage. You choose to be offended when I slept in another room. I know many married people in their latter years for various reasons sleep in different rooms. I never turned you away. You turned away from me. We both made mistakes. I agree. You were to proud to seek help and fix the marriage. You chose to run off. If you want me in your life then deal with this so we can move on.

M: (to myself) She judges my life to be a mistake but I do not. I feel hugely blessed and enriched because of the past few months, tough as they have been in many ways. I have fulfilled a lifelong dream to travel and write my experiences along the way and I am content. Perhaps I knew my time on earth was short and it had to be done then or never at all. If anyone other than me is reading this then whoever you are know this, that this series of books called "Becoming Adam" would not exist if I had not done what I did. So if you have been entertained and maybe learned something of value from these words, be grateful. And as for me personally, it is possible that many women will judge me harshly and side with Jen, I do not know. But if so, I am good with that, I love you anyway. So there, take that. :-)

Jen likes herself and I like me, I guess we'll survive without each other. I'll not respond, hopefully she just needs to get this stuff out and will show up next week anyway. But I'm never sure of her, to me what she writes is illogical and wrong, to her I am at grievous fault and she can't get over it she must have blood. I now enter the silent zone unless she breaks it first. I'll turn off my phone for a while too. I may be cruising without her even though I've (as usual) paid her fare, I'll eat the cost and go without her. It remains her choice to love me as I am, or to leave me. It has always seemed that she wanted to walk away forever but had to blame me for that leaving. Once again she has manipulated it into that from her point of view. Nothing has changed, except that she has *written*, and I'm grateful for that.

Oresha: It was Fun hangin out with you!.. Thanx again for lunch :) I just spoke with the guy I'm going to meet on sat. I mentioned that we had Fish & Chips for lunch @ The Bard & Banker... well.. have I got a SCOOP for You!.. .lol He said that he's tried many of the Fish places around town over the yrs.... & that his Fav is a place just off Bay & Cook st. He's been going there for 30 yrs.! ...lol So many F. & C. places.... so little time...sigh... lol... ;) Maybe you and Jen can check it out... & let me know whatcha think... :) Night..... Hugz...

M: Good night Oresha.

Jen: It would of meant so much to me to have you admit you took a wrong path that stooled the virtue of our marriage. I find it hard to move forward with you at times. I now retract this one request that meant so much to me. I have asked in so many ways to no avail. I do not judge you. You do just don't measure up to the man I married many years ago. The only thing I can figure is you would find it hard to live with yourself if you took a honest look at the past two years. I was that man and was willing to except him because we all make mistakes. But what do you do when a man can not even admit he was on a wrong path better yet he can not see his mistakes because his pride is in the way.

M: I love you darling. But I can live (or die) without you so it's entirely up to you to walk away forever or not, your choice. What I cannot live with though is the lack of peace, I *must* have that. So if you decide to show up next week, come prepared to wage peace with all your heart, that's the only war I will engage in with you.

Jen: Let it be your choose. I asked so little from a man of so much pride. Since winning is so important to you I will stay away. I hope this pleases you and your prideful heart. It will give you much comfort as you go to the grave.

M: This "pride" you dwell on is your invention and could just as logically apply to you as much as to me. And so is the battle that I apparently won today. I did not fight you, I wrote only kind words, your fight is with yourself. You're pretty good at that, you give yourself lots of practice.

But quite frankly it has seemed to me for many months that you constantly seek a way to walk away from me for all time but feel that you must have some way of blaming *me* for that walking away. You worked yourself into another blame game today, in fact it was so good that you feel justified tonight to write that you will "stay away." There is always very little that is valid about the excuses you use to push us apart. I fail to understand why you want to when you frequently profess such a great love for me and I encourage us being together. What are you waiting for? If you already had another man in your life I would understand completely, but you assure me that you don't. So I don't know what moves upon you to be so hostile.

But whatever, I do not cage you Jen, you are free to do as you will. It's just that I don't think you really know what you want, you seem confused and angry. I wish you were here right now so I could hold you and perhaps help you find some peace in what seems to be dark hours for you, I don't know what brought that on.

Just please understand that it is not my choice for us to be enemies as you seem to think we are. It is my hope that you will come next week as planned and will cruise with me. After the cruise we will better know what you want to do from then on, and that's what you will do. It's all set up, it should be a happy time for all of us involved. I don't know why you were so cranky today, just that you were.

As for the matter you demand that I confess to, I have told you many times that I do not regret my life, I am content with me. Of course we *both* made mistakes in the past. But why dwell on them when we could choose instead to go forward and be happy? I hurt you, you hurt me, that's life living together. We also had many happy times living together over the years, the photos you sent attest to that. It's all too easy for family and friends who know only one side of a story and have blood ties with only one of us to quickly forget those 18 years of love and closeness and blame one of us solely for the troubles we've had for a few months. What your family really wants is for you to be happy so of course in time they'll support your every choice for or against me, whatever makes you happy. I apologize for mine and forgive you for your mistakes. Do you apologize for yours and forgive me for mine? Can we look and move *forward* from now on even if it's only as friends?

I want you to come and fulfill what we have planned and paid for already. But you must choose for yourself. If you do come, I expect you to do your best to keep the peace. I continue to love you but if you stay away we will both soon become the same as the spouses we had before: insignificant, unloved, seldom thought of. Is that what you want?

Please forgive me for the real mistakes I made along the way, I forgive you yours. Please come, I love you sweetheart, you've had a bad day, and so have I. I did overdo my walk today and had some breathlessness but I also had a moment of dizziness when I was walking and had to stand still and balance myself to keep from falling, that was scary. I MUST have peace Jen, the stress and uncertainty you are causing is very difficult for me to handle. I feel emotionally dead inside today, no sign of life there, I have to deliberately work at some form of happiness. Please make up your mind what you want with me and let me know. I invite you into my life as much as you want it. I also accept if you don't want me anymore and choose to stay away, you are free to do so. The choice as always is YOURS!!!!

The Abraham Daily Thought just came in, I'll take the liberty of forwarding it to you. For me, it's almost always relevant, but maybe that's because I choose to look for relevance. Good night, I'm way past my bedtime. I hope tomorrow will be a better day for us but I'm still feeling dead emotionally and I think that's because our relationship is hanging in the balance right now, your choices could move us apart forever. Perhaps that's the best way for us to go, and maybe it's not...

M: (to Jen) At this point I don't even know if you are coming next week but just in case you decide to kiss and make up before then I was preparing for our road trip a few days ago and got a membership in the CAA auto club. It works in USA also for tows, flats, gas, etc. so you needn't think of that yourself, it's done.

Are you feeling better today? Still love me a bit? Coming?

Yes I know, you'll be tempted to not write or to stay away from your computer today so silence doesn't necessarily mean you're still mad at me. But please be kind and don't keep me in suspense longer than you feel you absolutely must. It's a huge stress never knowing where you are with us, knowing all too well that even though today may be swell, tomorrow you might threaten to tromp away again. It's an old game you play Jen and it's wearing and unpleasant. Do we *have* to fight?

Jen: I need reassurance. We all have pride to varying degrees but most often that is what causes man to fall. Understandings are a must.

Jen: I love you.

M: I love you too sweetheart, I want you in my life as much as you will allow it.

Jen: I will see you on the 12th.

M: Good. I'm wanting you, thanks for letting me know.

1: (to list) Dad my comments were most particularly about your Quality of life, although you should report anything you're doing so your oncologist and others can help you achieve YOUR goals of care.

M: (to Elaine) I enjoyed your company today Elaine, a most pleasant walk to the park and a chat at Starbucks. Thank-you so much for coming over, it meant a lot to me. And thanks for the art, I'm going to have it framed tomorrow, you're the greatest. I'm thrilled for you that you have a man of promise in your life, I wish the two of you the very best as your relationship unfolds. Take care and please stay in touch.

Elaine: It really was a sweet meet up... I really enjoyed seeing you too. I will stay in touch! Now, back to work! For me... Kind Regards on a sunny afternoon.

M: (to Jen) It's so strange how it is with me. Whereas my emotions were totally flat yesterday as if I didn't have any, now that I've heard that you are coming I'm overflowing with love for you again. And I'm *needing* you too, I think the next CT scan is going to show that this thing is advancing brutally fast, at least that's how it seems sometimes. I came back from a slow walk to the park this afternoon, responded to your messages, then felt that I needed not just to lie on the sofa but to go to bed which I did.

And wow, did it ever hit me that I am dying!! I'm still feeling it after the nap. There is much that is wrong with this body, it could slip from my grasp ever so quickly I think. It's not that I am not looking forward to that experience so long as it is painless, I am, it's the thought of how it will be for my children and you to awaken with the message that my shell has been found cold and alone. I'm so glad that you are coming, thank-you so much for that. I love you, you should be at my side from now on I think, I need to hold your hand as heaven moves upon me. It's a lovely feeling that I want to share with you as I go towards the light. I know you'll tell my children how it was. I'd like them to have that memory to cherish and tell their children, how it was when grandpa died with an angel at his side.

Please never feel pity for me for love's lost in that. Shower me with your best and tenderest love as I *"...slip the surly bonds of earth and dance the skies on laughter-filled wings"* as a Canadian fighter pilot wrote just before he was shot down and killed. Perhaps we needed to part for awhile you and I to polish our faded love and be better prepared for what's happening now, I'm sorry I hurt you. I love you sweetheart, you are so important to me. Yes I wronged you, we should have discussed my dream to travel and write and done it more orderly. I could have taken the fifth wheel though it won't really matter in the end, it will all work out. You could have traveled with me sometimes, it would have been good, I was so lonely. But we lived it a different way I felt the timing was just right. I love you and you love me in the end, that's what's most important. Come to me now and please plan to stay a while as I embrace fully that which I must. I'll try not to be a great burden on you or to prolong my duty unduly.

Elaine came over today and dropped off a small cave art painting of hers that she has been wanting to give me for weeks but never came. She says the man in the painting is me, the deer walking slowly towards me is you, and the horse running away from me is her. :-) She didn't stay long, we walked to the park then sat outside at Starbucks for a few minutes, we never held hands. She met a man she really likes, he has two acres and horses, he phones her all the time. I'm thrilled for her and wish them the very best. She was a friend to me when I needed a friend, we were never intimate, I've never kissed or touched her passionately. We're both glad it was that way because she knows you and I are destined for each other. Oresha walked with me yesterday. (It never rains it pours.) As usual her talk was laced with hints of restaurants she wants to eat at, that's important to her. I bought fish and chips for us at a Robert Service pub, a former bank she walked us into to show me around. That walk was very hard on me, it's when I got dizzy and almost fell. I really paid for the effort when I got home, she didn't come in. Don't be jealous, it's *you* I love, they both know that, even Suzanne discerned that many months ago and told me so, it's true.

See you soon my love. I think I must go back to bed now, this is the worst it has ever been, but maybe tomorrow I'll be all right again, perhaps very all right... Your M

Jen: Yea, That is interesting. As soon as you think I might be off the page you call in the troops. Does Oresha hold our hand or arm when you walk. I know they are not a threat but sometimes women try harder when they think they are losing and I am sure you would have been welcoming it.... Is this how you feel everyday or every so often. You always said you had mind over body. It is time to put it to work so you have a great curse.

What love's are you talking about. The women that did not work out this last two years. I don't have pity for you or them. They knew you were not right for them. Yet you hang onto that love you have for them.

Is that not true. I am proud of you and Elaine that it never went to sex. Interesting the women you are still friends with the most are the ones you never got to first base with. A wonderful lesson in that. If Al was not looking for sex we could have been good friends and done more things together.

M: Yes I was stupid again to be so open with you, it never serves me well. I thought I wrote you a nice love letter and you attack me for it and judge me "cursed". How awful you can be sometimes in your callous insensitive anger and jealousy, can you not see yourself for how hardened you have become? Why are you that way? What do you expect to gain by attacking me so severely other than to drive us ever further apart? Is that what you really want? I often think it must be or that there is another man in your life or a burning desire for one, there is no other logical explanation that I can accept as valid.

Oresha and I do not hold hands or link arms as we walk and she has no more interest in me romantically than I have in her, our friendship is purely platonic. I did not "call in the troops". It has been many weeks since I have walked with another woman other than my own children. Then after all those weeks those two write and ask if they can visit, maybe because they know I am dying and they care. It was not me who set the date of the visit in both cases it was them, one day after the other. I am still friends with Oresha and Elaine because they live in Victoria so it's possible for us to get together occasionally. Sometimes Kathy appears because she is Oresha's friend but she and I have never walked together. I have no current acquaintance with any woman you do not know about. If you'd read my letter properly you would see that the love I write about is for YOU and everybody (except you it seems) knows that I love you, I am not available.

With these words you have again seared my spirit and tainted yourself. But of course you know that I am forgiving and all will be well with me tomorrow. Enjoy yourself and your bitterness, you deserve it. Maybe tomorrow all will be well, it certainly is not today.

Jen: I was thinking after I read your email that friends are important especially when you are down. I think I will contact Al and ask him if he would like to be just friends with out physical contact.

Don't know if he can but worth the try. I did like riding in his sports car. Up to now I have turned him away.

M: Yes, I've been feeling that you still lust after Al. You know full well that if you two get together again some torrid or lonely night or even day (probably soon) you will abandon religious fervor and fulfill what your body craves from him even though you pretend that it is not so. You are a strange one indeed, hiding so much from yourself, or trying to. Or perhaps you are just trying to deceive me about what you *really* want, pretending that you are so much above me morally.

Is Al then what St. George has to offer you that is so promising that you are reluctant to come to me? (You won't answer my questions.) If you were a genuinely decent woman you'd at least wait until I am gone before you run back to him. You should not have to rush it, he'll still be there when I'm dead. A much more promising male friend for you if it's really just friendship you want would be your neighbor. He's Mormon safe, let him come in and chat with you, it seems that he wants to. As you unburden yourself to him and he to you you'll draw emotionally close, love will blossom, and that might lead to an interesting proposal when his wife dies. I give you permission should you become friends to talk to him about me, but only if you are certain that he will keep your confidence at least until I'm dead and not noise it as gossip around the neighborhood. (But then again, why should I care? I'll never live there again, it is not your choice to live with me.)

I get it though, your neighbor doesn't have a sports car! That's important to you after all those years with boring me. I don't blame you for craving what Al has to offer. You were great fun when we met, I took that from you, years of careless pleasure lost. I'm sorry I failed you so badly darling, I was too religious and uptight. Maybe Al can dance too. He'll do what he must to conquer beautiful sweetheart you. He has kissed you passionately, hugged, held hands, spent many hours with you, talked about personal things, had his hand down your pants with your consent, even had a touch of your shapely breast. And maybe there's more you've never told me, you want to pretend that you're better than me so you can attack me with seeming impunity. Al's got the taste of you alright, he's aggressive sexual horny male. And apparently has a big penis so you say. I'm not sure how you know about its size though even though you've felt it pressing into you with clothing on. Hmmm. Al will do what needs to be done to get your fullness and will keep you for a while until he gets bored with his new toy. *Is that what you want?* Are you running to him tonight? (You say you've turned him away *until now!*)

You know Al has not changed, he still wants to shove his massive manhood deep inside you and explode like he apparently does with so many women - *that's* his interest in you. I'm surprised that you think it a good thing to go back to him, you know what kind of man he is, it reveals what you really want. Take your pleasure as you will, you are single and free and I can't compete. I wish though that you'd wait if you really do love me as much as you profess. But whatever you choose to do I hope you don't get hurt because I genuinely love you, even the angry jealous unthinking woman you have become even as you pretend you're an angel.

Maybe tomorrow I'll feel better about you again, that seems to be the way I am. But also, maybe by tomorrow you'll have changed your mind about coming again. I never know for sure where you really are with me do I? You're so wishy washy honey.

I'm not angry about Al though, if he's who you want then grab him he'll be delighted. What I need is peace and stability so I can die properly. That's not fun is it? Make your choice Jen, and do it. Just let me know. You know my friends are no threat to you. You know Al is a threat to me if I value your 'virginity' and devotion to me, and I do. Is *he* the man you want to be with instead of me?

Jen: Well you have a good imagination don't you. I bet you wish it was you. Oh I forgot you ran off and went to Canada.

Jen: It was a nice love letter. I just don't like being made love to when you have these other women involved in my love letter. For that reason it takes the love out of the message. Makes me want to not come and It makes me want to go to Al. At least you are honest and let me know of your other loves, Oh excuse me friends.

M: They *are* just friends Jenny, you know that. You are not fair with me, you're so angry and bitter you can't contain it. Wish I could help but you won't let me, you want to push me far far away. It's working. But is that what you really want?

Jen: Thank you for admitting you left with out trying to work things out so you could of kept the marriage in tact and taken the 5th wheel. Your finances as you are well aware would have been in good shape if you had done that. But that is the past and we can not go back into the past.

Any body can write a love letter to some one. You wrote them to women you never meet. You feel in love with women you never meet. Saying that thank you again for the nice love letter. But once again you don't let go of women you had hopes for and would if they said yes. I am not stupid about your motives of the past. I hope to God they have changed for me.

You took each of those ladies on a date. One to dinner and the other for coffee. I can read between the lines. I hope Elaine is worth losing me over or you are so desperate you walk arm in arm with Oresha and wonder what is under those layers of clothing. You just can't come through for me. Well I will tell you about Al after the fact.

If I come it will to be a friend. I will sleep on the couch or air mattress in the living room. I will be a friend to you. I will take care of you. You can take me out to dinner like you do with them. We can sleep in two different beds on the ship. I will be a good Mormon girl and no longer feel as a wife........ I have no pity for you. You now have three friends.

M: I was just being open and honest with you as I always am. I have told you nicely many times that Oresha and I are just platonic friends and that I have no desire for it to be otherwise, we did not "date" we walked and talked as friends. I also told you that Elaine and I are just platonic friends and that she has a boyfriend she finds very promising and is pursuing, she has no time for me. It was just a quick visit today, I did not ask her to bring me art. Your comments are unthinking, uncaring, illogical, but impressive. You have revealed your true self to me and what you do not want. YOU DO NOT WANT ME IN YOUR LIFE!!!!!!!

I advise you to cease thinking of yourself as "a good Mormon girl" *you are not!* You are an angry deceitful woman that soon nobody will want to be around except those who just want sex or money from you. (And your family of course, they don't know who you have become, and they want you to be happy, they'll continue to blame me for everything, that will well work for you.) And there will be many who want you for sex, you look like a lovely desirable woman - you *could* be too, you once were. By tomorrow I will most likely continue to deceive myself into thinking that you haven't become such an unpleasant jealous angry being as you reveal you are, though it won't do me any good, you now say you hate me.

But I understand very clearly now that your choice is Al and other men over me. I do not want you as just a caregiver or another platonic friend while I do my dying. I was too attached to you, it would hurt terribly to have you around as such, not even cuddling. I have family and there will be hospice workers to care for me when I become dependent. It could have been a pleasant life for us but you deliberately choose for it to be otherwise, you stole the goodness away grinchy you. *I do pity you!*

Goodbye my darling, enjoy your life, you deserve everything you get, I hope it's all good and pleasant. I'm going to miss you. I guess I'm stuck with your half of the cruise then. If you had been honest with me earlier my daughters and I could have shared a cabin, that would have been much less expensive, but it's too late now. You could honorably reimburse the $1624 I spent on you but if not I'll eat it and go anyway. I'll probably miss you like crazy but tonight you have convinced me beyond doubt that you are insincere, reckless, and cruel. My daughters will miss you too, it will cast a dark pall on our enjoyment and on my life going forward. My children know how precious you were to me, it will be hard for them to understand why you ended it, especially at this time in my circumstances and them knowing I love and care for you. I wrote glowingly about you and our relationship in the group messages to all my children, their spouses, and my siblings. I was a fool. I should have known you better, you deceived me well.

As much as you will tell yourself and others a different story, it's YOU Jen who has broken us up forever, and for no valid reason that I am aware of. Anger and jealousy do not count you can control that and your attitude. Take care dear sweetheart, you could have been mine, I could have been yours. I'll try hard to forget you as quickly as possible, but it will be difficult. At least I know now what you really want. I've been asking you that question for months and you never came up with a clear answer until now.

If just being a platonic caregiver to a dying man is not your final decision, as I've been telling you for months, my door will *always* be open to you. I still feel great love for you as I write that but it's not bringing tears tonight, already I'm hardening to face the reality of life without you because you do not want me. It may be best for both of us that way, it seems that you will grasp at *anything* to walk away from me and blame me for it.

I DO NOT WANT YOU AS CAREGIVER AND PLATONIC FRIEND. After those 18 years, some of them beautiful, I could not handle that, *that's* not love…

Jen: You knew how I would respond and you went out with them anyway. Who are you kidding. Your self. I CAN NOT TRUST YOU!!!!!!!! After this please go far far away.

Jen: Well I was correcting my hurried email I sent. Since I wrote this one I got another from you. Now you are saying you do not want me to come at all or go on the cruise because we can not travel as friends or be together as friends. I don't know why?

You told me, you told Elaine not to bring a painting over to you. You told me you never cared if you saw her again. You were lying to me. You had plans to see her behind my back all along and in fact you did, you took her on her on a date. How cares if she went back up stairs to your apartment.

No…… telling me after the fact you had a date with her makes me so angry right now I hate you. You first sweet talk then have the gull to slip in your love letter you had two dates. All you were doing was trying to soften the blow. I can not trust you. You knew how I would react to this and you did it any way and then have the gull to add…. it…. to….. a…. love…. letter…… You really know how to keep the hurt coming don't you.

Then lash out how unfair I am. I guess your gift of pain toward me was not enough the first time. Why would I want to be with a man like that. Michael, I am not stupid. If you could of and if they would of, said they wanted to have sex with you, you would of jumped into bed with them. Even though you most likely can not preform you would of done what you could to please them and that's more than you were willing to do for me. Not that it matters anymore.

Ok I am not mad any more. You are just a jerk and I have to except these things from a jerk. I do feel some obligation toward you and will remain a good friend. Just take the love factor out of it and our fight is over. I will see you on the 12th. Dear friend. I think I can handle our relationship and not get jealous if I am just that. Keep your clothing on. Friends can still cuddle. My head has adjusted. Love between friends.

M: I explained all of this in my previous messages tonight, you judge and accuse me falsely. I do not lie to you, it is my openness that always causes the trouble, you can't handle it, you want secrets. All we were since you divorced us is friends. But it wasn't *platonic* friends, and that's why it worked. We loved each other and we acted (almost) as if we were married when you allowed us to be together. But now you want us to throw that love away and be platonic friends. I do not want that, I already have platonic friends who live much closer than you do. If you lived here I'd enjoy walking with you but not living under the same roof, you'd have become the same as my other friends. I cannot stand the thought of never being able to hold you with that tender love I used to feel for you and to cuddle you naked at night on those rare times you came to bed with me when I was still awake. It's *you* Jen who has destroyed us, you couldn't even be civil the few times you visited. You do not allow us to love each other properly, why are you so afraid of that?

It's better that we never see each other again. It could never work the way you want to go, you should know that, think about it a bit. You may have lost your love for me, think I'm a jerk, accuse me falsely and hate me. But that is not what I feel for you, I still want to think of us as married. But that thought is fleeing far far away tonight, you asked for that. No, we're done unless you come back the way we were. I simply cannot handle what you have become, there is no peace for me there. What you want to be is just a hateful farce, I won't go along with this 'new' unloving caretaker you. Tonight you have revealed your true colors and that you don't treasure or even want my love or to love me in return. Tonight I know why you won't live with me ever again. It's because you just pretend to love while all along you are after vengeance and punishment because you are unforgiving and dwell in the past much as you pretend that you are not.

I ask for peace and forgiveness you give me war and hatred. I cannot handle your jealousy, anger, false accusing, blaming and hatred anymore. Come back if you can come with love and peace and maintain it. I still love you and want the you I used to know. She was my darling, what remains of her is still my number one, or might be again by tomorrow. Silly silly foolish hopeless me... Can you offer some hope or is all lost then?

(I awake to the following four messages. All I can do is go into myself and forget her, finding happiness in other thoughts. I do not know this angry jealous irrational woman. I do not want to be with her.)

Jen: You knew already how I felt about you seeing Elaine and you knew how I would react. That is why you kept your date a secret from me until it was over. By then you got what you wanted. You did not care how I would react. You knew how I would be affected and would react. That did not matter because to you, your wants always come first when a lady is involved.

You are the one responsible for getting the this battle rolling. I am the foolish one for jumping on the ball. Ask yourself why do I get so upset when Jen mentions the name of another man. Why does Jen get so upset over me seeing other women. Why do I write nasty things when she mentions Al's name. Why does Jen write nasty things when I meet or see other women. Do you see a parallel? We are bring out the worst in each other because we know what buttons to push. You do it so well and I am so foolish to play into it. What do we do to stop this record from playing over and over? You really don't know how to get the Lady you claim to want.

Jen: In my emotional lowers I wrote this. My not be poetic but it helps me.

TO KNOW, TO PLAY, TO ACT, TO TELL A FOOLISH STORY

You knew what you were doing when you went out on a date with those ladies. You knew what you were doing when you sent me that love letter that included those ladies. You knew what it would do to my emotions when I read those words. You knew how I would react. You knew you would you would come up looking like roses. You knew the actor would play the part just as the writer wrote it. Its just a game with you. Its a game you play on me. You set me up and you take me down. You share cleverly that I am the blame. The problem is I fall for the game. No words speak louder than your actions. Your actions tell where the heart has acted. Your actions are not to reassure this lady. Your actions are for a story of a this lady. Are your words self serving. Are these words to tell a story. Are these words used to twisted and bring me down. You seem to be so efficient at it. The problem is I fall for those words every time. Oh! Here we go again. Who is the fool? I am the fool? I forgot your path of action. I forget the game you play I forget how you use words. Oh! here we go again. Who is the fool? I am the fool? Who is the fool? I really wonder?

Jen: To the man that ran off and left me in Utah. I am waiting for him to come back. want the you I once knew. A man that shared his love with only me and I shared my love with only him. My eyes never lust for another. Is it possible to have him back?

Jen: If you were honest you would of told me before hand. I do believe you did not kiss them. I do believe you held Oresha's arm and hand. You did take her out on a date when you took her to diner. You took Elaine on a date when you walked with her and took to have coffee. That's a fact. When I get away from your emails I want you back. When I read the double edge in your emails I want to run from them.

The options I see is this. Either you want me or you don't. You except me or you don't. You stop seeing and spending time with these women will end it with me for good. Oh what's the use. You have been seeing other women all along. What make me think you could love enough to give them up. I will not ask you to do something you do not want to do so I guess that means you give me up and keep them. A promise to be with only me is your choose and only yours.

M: (to myself) My response this early a.m. is to forward to Jen today's Abraham Daily Quote which comes in about midnight and is often uncannily relevant to where I am. It's about relationships and how to have a wonderful one by making a list of the *positive* things about someone you want to have a relationship with, and focusing on that which feels happy. That's exactly the message I am trying to get across to her, and exactly what she is avoiding. The point is that I am not trying to deceive or hurt her (she does that quite well by herself), I simply went for a walk with friends and casually mentioned it because I'm always open and honest. It wasn't a "date", there is no romance involved nor any expectation of romance. And anyway had there been, Jen is not here and I am a single man not engaged to be married to anyone. She accepted my proposal then broke it off by refusing to marry me. In fact what she wants now is to be platonic friends who visit each other now and then, hardly the type of relationship one would expect to be exclusive. She wants the things we had when we were married and living together after divorcing me and while refusing to marry or live with me. That's how I see it. Would I marry her now if she asked me to? No, yesterday and today I want nothing more to do with that angry jealous irrational woman. *But tomorrow I might.* :-)

I sent the above to Jen. I don't know if it will help resolve anything, she is in an extremely deep rut and far far away. I will focus only on good things and avoid any thought of her for a while because such thoughts are not pleasant and I need peace to have energy. But at least she's writing, I should encourage and welcome communication and not go silent to try to make a point she disagrees with.

I still love her much as she tries to change that. Maybe she'll come back when she has worked through whatever internal struggle it is that causes her to be so unpleasant. Can't she see what she is doing, what she has become? Who would want to live with someone as angry and contentious as that? Or does it not matter to her because she genuinely hates me and wants revenge for things of the past? In my fantasy I continue to search for a perfect love gone right. She is soft, loving, caring, tenderhearted, feminine, sexy, confident, happy, sincere, wise, dear dear heart, *Eve Mother of Nations.*

Is it because she has lost one former husband to death and is about to lose another that Jen is hastening her emotional severance from both by making herself unattractive to the one still living? Is that a winning strategy or would it be better to live in peace and love the dying one while there is yet time for that? Then part with wonderful memories to treasure for the rest of her life and beyond? She dwells in a dark place right now, I hope she will soon walk towards the light. I'll welcome her back to my arms if she does, I'd like nothing better. Jen could be my darling once more, she's not right now.

They say hatred lies close to love in the heart, deep emotion is one and the same. It takes but a click to make the switch from darkness into day. We see more clearly with the light on, it's a much happier place to be. Is she capable of changing her attitude about me today? Yes. Will she? Dunno, hope so, I want my woman back…

Jen: You lie to yourself even in this. You meet both of these ladies in hopes of taking them to your bed. You meet both of these ladies hoping for a long term relationship as a lover. Even when you were asking me to marry you. You still had hopes for Elaine as a eventual lover. They rejected the idea and you became a friend in hopes it would change. Now your realize there is no hope in getting them in your bed and settled for friendship. I see them as your friend now. But it was a date. When you take a woman to dinner or coffee and walking and share…. it is a date. You lost Jen because other women were important. Put that in your journal that's the more truth.

Ok. After straightening that out do you want me to come? I will do my part to get long as long as you meet my wishes and I meet yours to a comfortable level. Are you will to stop calling me names and putting down or in light. All that you write is to make you look good and me bad. Jen is gone don't put anything in your book 4 about Jen. Write she is gone. Write about your communication with your children. That is much more interesting and ours is depression.

M: You are wrong with everything you say, the "jerk" is your own creation forged in jealousy wrath and hatred, the liar is you. You have driven away a wonderful man who could have been yours again. I pity you.

We would not last a day with each other let alone six weeks. I do not know who you are only that you are filled with rage and contention and I don't like you. You have destroyed every tender feeling I ever had for you. I cannot even imagine giving you a sincere welcoming hug at the airport.

My greatest temptation is over and done with, she finally worked up enough power to blame me sufficient to get what she has wants. Sure I made mistakes but so did she, it didn't *have* to end this way. We lost each other and in that loss have found ourselves. Yes, I acted as if I was single when she was not with me, which was almost the entire time. I did that because I AM single!

But I am unafraid. I am content because I rise above contention and go forward with love and purpose. It's easy to be who I am, I am Becoming Adam, I walk always towards the greater light. It is there in the garden that a perfect love awaits my coming. I'll soon be there, *I'm going home...*

End of Book 4 of the Becoming Adam Series

Printed in the United States
By Bookmasters